SPEED DEMONS

"They'll call us humans out of politeness," Indira explained. "Or 'ummun,' which is close as they can come. But that's not how they think of us. We're demons."

"What?" said Julius.

"You heard me. Demons. Powerful and fearful creatures from beyond the known world."

"But — why demons? We haven't done anything wicked to them."

Indira smiled, and patted his cheek. "Poor Julius. In the monotheistic religions which shaped your cultural views, all powerful non-divine creatures are pure evil. But the original conception of demons doesn't necessarily carry the connotation of evil. Just tremendous, unbridled, fearful power."

"Why should they think we are powerful?"

"These beings are not stupid. They don't understand us, but they understand that we are very, very different. And then there's the frightening way we *move*. Other than size, what's the physical trait that all animals instinctively fear?"

Understanding came to him. "Speed."

ERIC FLINT

A Baen Books Original

Baen Publishing Enterprises
P.O. Box 1403
Riverdale, NY 10471

ISBN: 0-671-87800-X

Cover art by Larry Elmore

First printing, September 1997

Distributed by Simon & Schuster
1230 Avenue of the Americas
New York, NY 10020

Typeset by Windhaven Press, Auburn, NH
Printed in the United States of America

To my daughter Elizabeth

PART I:
The Threads

Chapter 1

As a young warrior, Nukurren had heard the demons come. She still remembered the enormous sound that ripped through the sky above Shakutulubac, capital of the Ansha Prevalate. She herself had seen nothing. The sound had awakened her from an exhausted sleep, and by the time she raced out of the barracks there was nothing to be seen but a huge red splotch on the eastern horizon. The strange mark on the sky was terrifying. The Mother-of-Pearl was always a featureless gray. What could turn it red with fear?

Others in the Warrior's Square claimed to have seen the Great Kraken itself racing east toward the ocean, spewing molten ink across the sky. So great had been its terror! They had pointed, with quivering palps, to the red blotch.

The capital had been gripped with fear. The Paramount Mother had summoned all her priests to the Divine Shell. For days the soothsayers had rolled snails, consulting the whorl patterns and the subtleties of the shellpile. Nukurren had watched them, surreptitiously, from her position guarding the entrance to the Chamber of Mothers. In the end, after much quarreling, the soothsayers announced that the great sound had been a cry of anger from Ypu. The Clam-That-Is-The-World was warning the Anshac to forego sin and corruption. They concluded by calling for eight eightdays of fasting. And, inevitably, for increasing the tithes to the temples.

Looking back on it many eightyweeks later, Nukurren thought it was from that time that she first began to develop her contempt for the priests. She did not particularly question their conclusions. But after watching them from the rare

1

vantage-point of a Motherguard, she had decided their motivations were far from holy. In truth, a venal and avaricious lot.

As she walked alongside the caravan, she remembered that day long past.

I haven't thought of that in years, she mused. *Why now? It must be all these rumors of demons.* Then, with a mental grimace: *Or maybe it's that the rapacity of these slavers brings those priests back to mind.*

For a moment, she pondered the question. For a number of eightweeks now, vague rumors had drifted across the meat of the Clam, telling of new demons. Not witches, which were feared but understood, but something else. The stories were vague in all details. But most of them placed the demons in the vicinity of the Chiton.

Which is probably why the caravan master is so edgy, she thought. *Not that Kjakukun doesn't have enough reason to be fearful, entering Kiktu territory in search of hunnakaku slaves.*

Nukurren looked to the north. The Chiton loomed on the horizon, dominating the landscape like a behemoth. It was not tall so much as it was massive. Great canyons carved the slopes. Its shape had given the great mountain its name.

She whistled derisively. *Half of the world's legends belong to the Chiton. These "demons" are just the latest.*

Although, the night before, Dhowifa hadn't shared her contempt for the stories.

"It's a fact that folk who've gone to the mountain haven't come back," he pointed out. "For many eightweeks, now."

"It's a big mountain," countered Nukurren. "Huge. Enough danger in that to kill off any number of small parties."

But Dhowifa had not been convinced.

"And what about this last party? That wasn't a small group of Pilgrims, who just vanished. It was a whole slave caravan. They were found dead at the foot of the Chiton. At the *foot*, Nukurren, not in the mountain itself. The slaves were gone without a trace. And the slavers and the guards were all dead. Great, horrible wounds they had. So people say. Strange, deep wounds—as if they'd been attacked by some kind of giant uglandine."

"Uglandine?" Nukurren had whistled derision. "You'd have to be asleep to be caught by a uglandine! Or crippled."

She stopped and surveyed the caravan.

Not that asleep or crippled doesn't describe this caravan pretty well, she thought contemptuously.

The caravan had stopped for the day, at midafternoon. The yurts had been erected in the middle of the trail, for no one had any desire to sleep amidst the akafa reeds which grew lushly on either side. Akafa was altogether noisome—smelly, and full of slugs.

Kjakukun herself had not wanted to stop before nightfall brought cover from sharp Kiktu eyes. But the helots who hauled the slave cages were exhausted. Not surprisingly—Kjakukun had driven them mercilessly for days. The caravan master had attempted to convince the slavers and the guards to haul the cages, but of course they had refused. It was beneath their status, and they had seen no Kiktu. They were convinced there were none in the area. It was Kiktu territory, true. But everyone knew that the Kiktu were far to the west, organizing themselves and their tribal allies to meet the Utuku menace.

Nukurren did not share their complacency. The Kiktu might be preoccupied, but she knew them well. The tribespeople guarded their territory closely, especially in the vicinity of the Chiton. The area around the mountain had become a refuge for the hunnakaku, whom the Kiktu revered. Slavers would not normally even think of coming here. The Kiktu were ferocious warriors, and they bore a total hatred for slavers.

Still, they were almost out of Kiktu lands. The expedition had been a great success—four slaves captured, when most expeditions nowadays considered a single hunnakaku worth the effort. Hunnakaku slaves were much in demand in the great prevalates of the south. Most labor was done by helots, or gukuy slaves, but it was still a mark of prestige to possess a hunnakaku. The most powerful rulers even ate the flesh of the creatures, on occasion, claiming it to be the world's greatest delicacy.

The world is full of evil, thought Nukurren. *Evil without end. I think it must have always been so, despite what the stinking priests say. And I am certain it will never change.*

Gazing upon the caravan, she emitted a soft whistle of contempt. She wasn't sure what she found more offensive—the slovenliness of the guards, or the brutality of the slavers.

She was a mercenary herself now, of course. Had been for many eightyweeks, ever since she and Dhowifa fled Shakutulubac. But she still had the training and the attitudes of an elite warrior, and she had nothing but scorn for the other mercenaries. She had made no pretense how she felt about them. They resented her deeply, but naturally they did nothing. Except—of this she had no doubt—whisper lurid and disgusting remarks to each other concerning Nukurren and Dhowifa.

A loud hooting from further down the caravan line drew her attention. A half-eight of mercenaries were clustered about one of the cages, whistling with laughter. She moved toward them.

As she drew near, she saw that one of the slavers was amusing herself by tormenting the hunnakaku in the cage with a blowpipe. The slaver was shooting practice darts at the mantle of the pitiful creature, who was cowering against the far side of the cage, hooting loudly, her mantle brown with misery. The four mercenaries apparently found the sight of the sub-gukuy's pathetic attempts to fend off the darts vastly amusing.

The darts were not deadly, of course. The blunted tips could do no more than lightly score the thick mantle of the hunnakaku, and the slaver was being careful not to shoot at the easily-damaged eyes. But the darts were painful; and the hunnakaku were by nature timid and easily frightened.

The gratuitous cruelty of the scene caused a sudden rage to swell within Nukurren. She shoved aside the mercenary before her. The mercenary began to protest angrily. Then, seeing who it was who had pushed her, she fell silent. Ochre uncertainty rippled along the mercenary's mantle, shadowed by pink undertones of anxiety.

Nukurren ignored the mercenary altogether and advanced upon the slaver. Feeling her presence, the slaver left off her amusement and glanced back. Back, and up, for Nukurren was a huge gukuy. At the sight of the warrior looming above her, the green pleasure tones in the slaver's mantle were instantly replaced by the same pink-within-ochre.

"What do you want?" demanded the slaver. She eyed Nukurren's mantle, trying to determine the warrior's mood. But Nukurren had long since learned to maintain the gray of placid indifference, no matter what she was feeling within. Partly that was due to her training as an elite guard, and partly to the male secrets of emotional control she had learned over the years from Dhowifa. It was very difficult to master *shoroku*, as the Anshac called the art of maintaining a gray mantle. As a rule, *shoroku* was a skill found only among high-clan gukuy. But Nukurren had persevered in the study for years. She found some spiritual solace in the discipline. And, as a warrior, it had the practical virtue that there is perhaps nothing so intimidating as a gukuy whose emotions can't be determined.

"What do you want?" demanded the slaver, once again.

Nukurren made the gesture of contemptuous dismissal.

"Go," she said. "Leave the hunnakaku be."

The slaver slid back two paces on rigid peds. Pink was now predominant on her mantle, and flashes of red fear were beginning to appear. Without moving her eyes from the slaver, Nukurren could detect the same colors on the four mercenaries standing nearby.

A surreptitious motion in the corner of her eye. Once of the mercenaries had touched her flail. Without looking at her, Nukurren said softly:

"If that flail comes out of its harness, I'll strip the mantle off your body and feed your guts to the slugs."

Casually, Nukurren drew her own flail. At the sight of it unharnessed, the mercenaries and the slaver fell back. Nukurren's flail was truly impressive. Twice the size of a normal warflail, it could only be wielded by a gukuy of her immense strength. And where most warflails were armed with flint or obsidian blades, hers gleamed with bronze. The weapon of an elite soldier. And the mercenaries were well aware that the warfork harnessed on the right side of her mantle was a twofork—the most difficult variety to master. The forks on their own mantles were mere sixforks, or even eightforks.

For a moment, all was frozen. Then the tableau was interrupted by the arrival of Kjakukun.

"What in the name of the Clam is going on?" demanded the caravan master.

Nukurren was silent. The slaver began loudly complaining of her conduct. The mercenaries said nothing, but began a slow withdrawal from the scene.

After listening to the slaver, Kjakukun stared at Nukurren.

"So? What's your explanation?" The caravan master's mantle showed only the dim azure-gray of annoyance.

"Pointless torture offends me. And the hunnakaku are miserable enough."

"What torture?" asked Kjakukun. The slaver's account of the events had not touched upon the darts. Nukurren gave a brief and dispassionate sketch of the scene when she arrived.

The caravan master's mantle flashed blue. But the anger was directed at the slaver.

"Fukoren, I've warned you about this before!"

The slaver cringed back on hunkered peds. Her mantle glowed scarlet.

"But—what's the harm?" she whined. "They're only hunnakaku—sub-gukuy!"

Kjakukun's blue did not diminish. If anything, it darkened.

"They're merchandise. Not to be damaged unnecessarily. If they're frightened too much, they get sick, even die. But that's all beside the point! I gave you an order, and you disobeyed me!"

The caravan master glared around. The four original mercenaries were now drawn far back into the small crowd of mercenaries and slavers who had gathered to watch the scene.

"This trip is dangerous enough," bellowed Kjakukun, "without indiscipline and sloppiness! We're still in Kiktu territory, you fools—and now there are these rumors of demons! I won't tolerate disobedience, do you understand?"

The caravan master was now addressing herself to the assembled crowd. She paused a moment.

"I've heard you grumble at the wages I'm paying Nukurren. Three times what you garbage earn. I'm as tight with copper as any, but for this trip it was worth it. I'll show you why."

The caravan master turned to Nukurren. Kjakakun's mantle flashed black. Implacable.

"Kill her," she said, waving a palp at the slaver.

Until it was seen, it was hard to believe that a gukuy as huge as Nukurren could move so fast. Before the crowd could even whistle with fear, Nukurren drew her fork and slammed it into the slaver's mantle. Driven by Nukurren's great strength, the two razor-sharp bronze prongs were driven completely through the ganahide armor and the tough cartilage of the mantle. With a twist of her palps on the crossbar of the hook, Nukurren flipped the slaver onto her side. The slaver's two tentacles clutched at the hook in a hopeless attempt to pry it loose. The six arms clustered about her beak were knotted in pain.

The killing stroke which followed struck the slaver like a lightning bolt. The blow drove the flail-blades deep into the unarmored soft tissue of the slaver's underbelly. With a great jerk, the slaver's bowels were ripped out and scattered about the ground in a spray of blood. Pieces of gut spattered the crowd. With another quick twist of her right tentacle Nukurren tossed the corpse of the slaver aside, freeing the prongs of her fork.

She squatted down on her peds and began cleaning the fork and the flail with a sponge. Around her she could hear the crowd whistling loudly. It was not the death of the slaver which shocked them, she knew. They were as callous a group of gukuy as you could find anywhere on the Meat of the Clam. It was the manner of it—the incredible display of ferocity, speed and strength. Many warriors boasted of being able to deal the *kutaku*, the single death-blow, but it was rarely accomplished in actual fact.

"And her gray never wavered," Nukurren heard one mercenary whisper with awe. She found some consolation in that comment, to counteract the great wave of revulsion which flowed through her. Not a trace of her feelings showed in her mantle, but she had to fight not to vomit. She concentrated on cleaning her weapons, slowly and meticulously.

I'm not even sickened by the killing, she thought wearily. *The stinking slaver deserved it. No, it's the sickness of my whole life. I think Dhowifa's right. But I just can't find any comfort in his* dukuna.

By the time she finished cleaning her weapons, the crowd had disappeared. The body of the slaver was still lying to one side. The pool of blood surrounding it had soaked into the soil. Scavengers were already approaching the corpse. Within a day, the body would be a festering mass of corruption, filled with slugs, snails, worms and larvae.

Typical slavers, thought Nukurren with disgust. *Well, if they're not going to bother giving her the rites, I'm certainly not.*

She rose and began walking toward her yurt. A soft hoot from the cage stopped her. Turning back, Nukurren saw that the hunnakaku was now standing at the front of the cage, staring at her through the bars. The hunnakaku hooted again.

Long ago, after their escape from Shakutulubac, Nukurren
and Dhowifa had spent many eightweeks living with the Kiktu.
Nukurren had gotten along well with the tribespeople, but
Dhowifa's pampered existence in the Palace had not prepared
him for the hardships of barbarian life. So when the old
Paramount Mother died, and the fury of the hunt for her
escaped consort died with her, Dhowifa had insisted on returning to civilization. Nukurren had not been unwilling, for
though she liked the Kiktu, she found their religious beliefs
bizarre. And their dietary fetishes and restrictions had been
annoying.

But while she was among them, Nukurren had been careful
to observe the proprieties. She had even learned some of the
strange language spoken by the hunnakaku. For the Kiktu
believed that the sub-gukuy were sacred. They called the
hunnakaku the Old Ones, and believed that they were the first
people created by their goddess Uk when she rained life upon
the Meat. They were favored still in her eyes, the Kiktu
believed, and their language was difficult to understand because
it was holy. All Kiktu learned to speak it—at least, as well as
was possible for gukuy.

So Nukurren listened. The hunnakaku hooted again.

MUST NOT DO

FEED

REEDS SNAILS BEAUTY

With difficulty, Nukurren translated. The speaking siphon
of the hunnakaku, she knew, was fairly similar to that possessed
by gukuy. But there were important differences. The hunnakaku
lacked the flexible lips and the hard ridges which enabled gukuy
to speak their complex languages. Instead, the hunnakaku
produced a hoot which contained a single thought couched
in various permutations. Dhowifa had once told her it reminded
him of a verbal version of the ideograms which the prevalates
in the far south used for writing.

The central concept was "feed." She understood that immediately. There was both the positive and the negative imperative
which was usually present in hunnakaku hoots. The negative
was at the center—a reflection, she thought, of the timid nature
of the sub-gukuy. "Not feed snails," then. The positive would

surround the center, as an alternative course of action. "Must feed beauty. Do feed reeds."

With sudden understanding, she stared at the body of the slaver.

"But why?" she demanded. "She was your tormentor."

Another hoot.

DEATH NOT END

GIVE

LIFE NOT LIFE

Strangely, it made sense. The hunnakaku were plant-eaters. They viewed carnivores, including scavengers, with horror. The horror was not the product of personal fear. Because of their size, the hunnakaku had few natural enemies. (*Except us*, thought Nukurren.) It was due to their belief that all meat-eaters were parasites, who stole life without returning it back to what they called the "Coil of Beauty." To be eaten as meat was to be denied re-entry into the Coil, to be doomed to eternal non-existence.

Or so, at least, the Kiktu had explained it to Nukurren. And it was certainly true that, within the limits available to their fundamentally carnivorous needs as gukuy, the Kiktu attempted to follow similar precepts. It was these attempts, of course, that produced the dietary rules and restrictions which Nukurren and Dhowifa had found so irksome.

Nukurren's tentacles twitched with irritation.

"You can't expect me to bury her!"

She whistled with derision at the idea, and began to march off.

Another hoot:

HORROR HORROR HORROR

IS

HORROR HORROR HORROR

She stopped, arrested by the tone of unmistakable anguish in the voice of the hunnakaku. After a moment, she made a decision and marched to the toolkeeper's yurt. The plaintive hoots of the hunnakaku followed her.

"Give me a hoe," she commanded. Without a word, the

toolkeeper disappeared inside and returned a moment later with the tool. Her mantle, Nukurren noticed with bleak amusement, glowed bright pink with apprehension.

Taking the hoe, Nukurren stalked back to the cage. She began digging a trench on one side of the trail, but as soon as she started the hooting began again.

MUST NOT WASTE

ROOT

WRONG THERE REEDS

She whistled sharply with anger. The hunnakaku withdrew fearfully from the bars, cowering in the interior of the cage. Her mantle flushed brick red. Fear, allayed by determination. She continued to hoot the same plea.

"You're as bad as the Kiktu and their damned fetishes," said Nukurren. But she abandoned the trench she had begun and waded off into the field of akafa. There, even though the reeds made the work far more difficult, she dug a new trench. Finished, she went over and grabbed the slaver's body. She was tempted to use her fork to drag the body, but she knew it would upset the hunnakaku. For some reason, the thought of causing further pain to the gentle giant was repulsive. So, ignoring her disgust at the snails which were by now crawling all over the corpse, she picked up the body of the slaver in her two great tentacles and carried it over to the trench. She lowered the body down. It was short work to hoe the soil back in.

When she was finished, she stared at the small mound in the reeds.

"You're still garbage," she said softly. "But for whatever it's worth, welcome to the Coil of Beauty. Personally, I hope you come back as a slug."

She left the reeds and went back to the cage. For a long moment, she and the hunnakaku stared at each other. She saw a creature whose basic shape was similar to her own. Bigger, of course, despite the fact that Nukurren was huge for a gukuy. The hunnakaku's peds were very short and bulky relative to its body. She lacked true tentacles. Instead, she had eight arms instead of six. The arms were bigger than a gukuy's, and clumsy-looking—they ended in a simple bifurcation, instead of the delicate triad which made gukuy arms such marvelous instruments for precise manipulation. The beak which Nukurren could see within the hunnakaku's arm-cluster was blunt and ridged, suited for chewing tough plants. Not at all like Nukurren's sharp-edged gukuy beak.

And what does she see? wondered Nukurren. *A monster, I imagine.*

There was no way to tell. Another wave of world-weariness rolled over her.

In truth, they are a better folk than we gukuy. But they are timid, despite their size and strength. And slow, and stupid. So we make them our slaves, when we do not butcher them outright. And now they are a dying race. The slavers catch fewer and fewer each year, and they won't breed in captivity. And if the Kiktu are destroyed by the Utuku, more slavers will come to this refuge. Kjakukun is just one of many.

She turned away.

And I am Kjakukun's flail. For three wires of copper an eightday.

On her way back to her yurt, she took some satisfaction in the fearful glances sent her way by those she encountered. As she passed Kjakukun's yurt, the caravan master stepped from between the hides which served as an entryway.

"Why did you bury her?" she asked. She seemed genuinely puzzled.

"The hunnakaku asked me to."

Orange astonishment rippled across Kjakakun's mantle.

"Why should you do its bidding? It's nothing but a slave— a sub-gukuy."

Anger boiled over, and this time Nukurren made no effort to control her mantle. Blue blazed. Despite her own impressive self-control, the caravan master could not prevent a pink flush from entering her own mantle.

And when Nukurren stepped suddenly near, the pink was replaced by scarlet terror.

"I work for you, slave-master," said Nukurren softly, "because I have to. I need the money, and—"

She did not complete the thought. Nor, even though she could have, did the caravan master.

Because only a filthy slaver would hire a pervert.

Nukurren waited, wondering if the caravan master was bold enough to sneer the words. But Kjakukun was silent.

Very wise, slave master. Very wise.

The blue faded from Nukurren's mantle.

"I work for you, Kjakukun. But I am much closer to the Kiktu in how I see the Old Ones."

The red faded from the caravan master.

"The Kiktu will kill you as quick as anyone!"

"True. Even quicker, for they would look upon me as a traitor."

Nukurren turned away, then back.

"Do not ever ask me questions, slave-master. I am your bodyguard, no more."

"I am your employer," protested Kjakukun.

Nukurren allowed a tinge of contempt to yellow her mantle, as she walked toward her yurt.

Dhowifa was in his usual place, perched on the cushions in a corner. After Nukurren entered, the two lovers stared at each other in silence.

"It's been a bad day," she said finally.

Dhowifa's mantle rippled with the chromatic complexity of which only truemales are capable. Sadness. Sympathy. Empathy. And, the undertone beneath and the sharpest accents, green love.

"I know. I watched from here."

After some silence, he spoke again.

"I have brought much misery into your life."

"Much happiness, also."

An intricate wave of pastel humor washed over him. "True. True. But still, I wish—"

"Wish what?" demanded Nurukken. "That we hadn't fallen in love?"

"No—never that! But—"

"The world is the way it is, Dhowifa. Why should you complain? Isn't that the heart of your *dukuna?*"

Dhowifa's arms coiled in a manner suggesting respectful disagreement leavened by good feeling. Not for the first time, Nukurren was struck by the truemale's incredible delicacy of expression.

"Not exactly," he demurred. "The concept of *dukuna* has a more impersonal philosophical thrust. It's not really—"

"Enough!" barked Nukurren. But the good humor was

obvious on her mantle. And, glowing ever brighter, the white of passion.

"You're insatiable," complained Dhowifa. But his own mantle rippled ivory, and there was no reluctance in the way the tiny truemale came toward her, his arms extended.

As he climbed into her mantle cavity, his tentacles gripping her head firmly while he extended his arms deep inside, Nurukken whistled her pleasure at his touch.

Yes, she thought, *you have brought me anguish, Dhowifa. But I wouldn't give you up for anything. Joy of my life. My love, who had none.*

His arms found what they were seeking. Pleasure turned into ecstasy, and forgetfulness of all pain.

Chapter 2

The demons attacked at dawn.

Nukurren was awakened by a shrill hoot of fear and alarm. With a veteran's instinct, she was instantly awake and scrambling for her weapons. She hesitated for a moment at the thought of donning her ganahide armor, but decided she didn't have time.

"Wait here!" she said to Dhowifa, who was stirring to life in his cushions.

She rushed through the hide flaps of the yurt and onto the ground beyond. There, she crouched for a moment in battle stance, fork and flail ready, to gain her bearings.

What she saw, in the faint light of the dawn, was at first more confusing that anything else.

What are those—things?

They were like nothing she had ever seen. Very tall and slender, like reeds. They moved with blinding speed, in a strange, jerky motion that she found hard to follow.

Before she could register anything else, she saw one of the demons spring toward a caravan guard. The guard was crouched, holding up her fork and flail in trembling palps, whistling with terror. In a movement faster than anything Nukurren had ever seen, the demon thrust forth some sort of huge stinger. As the stinger hurtled at the guard, Nukurren saw a brief gleam from its tip.

Metal! But what kind of metal shines gray?

The stinger plunged deeply into the camp guard's head, right between the eyes and into the brain. The guard died instantly, without a sound.

14

The demon planted a—*a ped?* wondered Nukurren; *was that long and skinny thing a ped?*—onto the dead guard's head and wrenched the stinger loose with its two tentacles.

Except they're not tentacles. They're like sticks tied together. And that stinger's a weapon of some kind.

That last thought restored her courage. They might be demons, but if they needed weapons they had to be vulnerable. Somehow.

She had no more time for thought. From the corner of her eye she caught a flickering motion. Then the gleam of a weapon coming straight toward her.

She was totally unprepared for a straight-thrusting weapon. No gukuy could deliver such a blow. But she instantly raised the shield protecting her palp on the crossbar of the fork, in the reflex of a fighter fending off blowpipe darts.

The weapon glanced off the shield and drove along her mantle, gashing a long but shallow wound. Nukurren ignored the pain. Her mantle was already criss-crossed with battle scars, and no mantle-wound was serious so long as the mantle itself wasn't penetrated. But she found time to regret the absence of her armor.

Nukurren whipped her flail around and struck a terrible blow on the lower portion of the demon's ped. The flail-tips did not penetrate. There was some sort of armor there. But she heard a strange cracking noise, and the demon collapsed to the ground, wailing horribly.

She drew back her flail for the death-stroke, but turned away. Her duty was elsewhere. The demon seemed incapacitated, and she was responsible for the safety of the caravan master.

She raced toward Kjakukun's yurt. On the way, she caught glimpses of the chaos around her. The guards and slavers were no longer attempting to fight. They were fleeing every which way in utter terror. But the demons which swarmed everywhere moved much faster than gukuy. Right before her, she watched as a fleeing slaver was overtaken by two demons. Pitilessly, the monsters drove their weapons into the slaver's peds, pinning it to the ground. A third demon flickered around to the front of the shrieking slaver, and drove its weapon straight into her brain.

How do they do that? wondered Nukurren. She recognized

the utterly deadly nature of the blow. No part of a gukuy's body was more vulnerable than the soft spot between the eyes, behind which the brain lay unprotected. But the very nature of a gukuy's tentacles made such a direct blow impossible. The dart from a blowpipe could strike there, but very few pipers could drive a dart hard enough to penetrate through the flesh into the brain. Eyes were a piper's target.

She heard a loud hooting from the cages holding the hunnakaku.

Are the demons slaughtering the pitiful things?

But when she risked a glance, she saw that the demons were smashing the locks of the cage. They were releasing the sub-gukuy! And now she recognized that the hoots carried no trace of fear.

Just ahead of her was Kjakukun's yurt. She was almost there. She saw the caravan master step out through the hides, carrying a flail.

Get back inside, you idiot! I can't protect you out here!

It was too late. From somewhere, a demon flickered into view. It drew back the stinger in one of its strange tentacles, and then jerked it forward in a blur. Astonished, Nukurren watched the stinger fly through the air, like a gigantic dart from a blowpipe. It struck Kjakukun right between the eyes. The caravan master was dead before her body could fall.

More than anything else she had seen, in that dawn of terror and chaos, the sight of the flying stinger shocked Nukurren. Except for blowpipes, gukuy almost never used missile weapons. Some of the primitive tribes to the far southwest used slings. The Anshac had experimented with the awkward devices, before concluding they were well-nigh useless. To be sure, the stones struck with considerable impact. But gukuy could withstand a great deal in the way of blunt impacts, and no gukuy had the tentacular dexterity to use the slings with accuracy. Even the southwestern primitives used them rarely.

Despair washed over her. *How can you fight such terrible creatures?*

But she had no time to dwell on it. A demon was racing toward her. Knowing what to expect, she twisted to one side to avoid the brain-thrust. The stinger drove into the front of her mantle. The wound was harmless; hardly even painful.

Nowhere on the mantle of a gukuy was the tissue tougher and thicker than on the edge of the cowl.

She lashed upward with her fork, striking the demon's tentacle. Again, that strange cracking sound. The demon ululated.

Full of fury and triumph, Nukurren whipped her flail around at the monster's upper torso. The blow was fast and powerful, but the demon's uncanny speed enabled it to interpose its other tentacle, which bore some kind of armor. The armor splintered. She heard another crack; the demon was hurled to the ground.

They can be broken! came the thought.

Another demon. Another. And another. Twisting like a slug, faster than she'd ever moved, Nukurren managed to avoid the death-blows. But this time the stingers penetrated through her mantle, into the flesh of her body cavity. The pain was intense. Even more intense was the knowledge of her certain doom. Such wounds invariably caused lingering death, by horrible diseases.

With no thought now but to wreak havoc, Nukurren hurled herself at her tormentors. Her fork and flail struck hard. One of the demons fell to the ground, clasping its side. Nukurren's flail had torn out a great swath of—flesh? A second demon, a huge one, was stripped of its weapon by a smashing blow of the flail on its tentacle. The third demon withdrew, moving with an odd gait, hopping on one of its bizarre peds.

A pause. She spun around, feeling agony as the stingers sticking out of her mantle flapped with her motion.

She was surrounded by demons. They were standing back, however, beyond reach of her weapons. Peculiar sounds were coming from them. Horrible sounds, full of spitting and gasping. A language, she realized, but like no language she'd ever heard. Through the haze of pain, she was finally able to discern some details of their shape, now that the demons weren't moving in a constant flicker.

Those are heads, she realized. *Those strange growths on the very top of their bodies. And the sounds are coming from those moving parts in front. Are they lips? Is that tiny thing a beak? It can't be—it only has one jaw.*

Then she saw the eyes. Those, at least, she had no difficulty in recognizing. They were almost like her own, except that they were so small.

Why aren't they attacking?

She moved toward one side. The demons there flickered
back.

They're afraid of me, she realized. *The slavers were butchered like uju. But I injured several. Some may even die.*

But the tiny hope faded. She heard a demon's voice, lower-
pitched than the others. Turning to face the voice, she saw
two demons in the circle surrounding her flicker aside. A new
demon appeared, stalking slowly through the ring.

The new demon was much bigger than the others. Taller,
and wider in its upper torso. It moved slowly, for a demon,
but she instantly recognized the total poise of its stance. As
bizarre as the demons were in their shape and their movement, she had no doubt of what she was seeing.

A great warrior. Demonlord.

The thing began circling her. Faster and faster. She spun
around. It reversed its circle. She spun again. She could feel
the stingers in her body tearing at the flesh. She realized the
thing was deliberately forcing her to wound herself further.

She had no chance in a prolonged battle. Suddenly, she
hurtled forward, whipping her fork around at the monster's
head. With triumph, she saw the demon block the blow with
its stinger. She had time to marvel at the strength and—*solid-
ity*—of the creature, before she brought her flail whipping
around at the demon's peds in the same blow which had
crippled the others.

But to her astonishment, the demon avoided the blow by—
flying? No, he *leapt.* Straight up, lifting his peds over the
whistling flails, and back down on the ground. Still perfectly
poised.

She knew, then, that these were truly demons. No natural creature on the Meat of the Clam could do that.

She saw the death-stroke coming. But now she was off-
balance from missing her own strike. She could not avoid the
blow. She could only make a last, futile attempt to twist aside.

The stinger plunged straight into her left eye. Deep, deep,
deep. Bringing an agony so great it left her paralyzed, as well
as half-blind.

Dimly, she realized her last twist had avoided the brain-
strike. But now she was doomed. She watched helplessly as
the demon champion took a new stinger from another demon.

Watched as it flickered slowly toward her, the stinger held in strike position. She was even, now, finally able to analyze the strange motion of its peds.

Like sticks, tied end to end. They don't really flicker, they jerk back and forth where the knots would be.

Suddenly her vision was occulted. A small body was swarming onto her maimed head, whistling with fear and anguish.

Dhowifa.

"Go away," she whispered. "Hide, my love. There's nothing you can do but save yourself."

But Dhowifa, normally more clever and shrewd than any truemale Nukurren had ever met, was now utterly lost in a truemale spasm of emotional frenzy. He clutched at her head, desperately trying to pull the terrible stinger from her eye.

It was a hopeless task for his puny strength. But, for some unknown reason, his arrival had caused the demonlord to pull back. The stinger in its stick-tentacle drooped. There was a rapid exchange of sounds between the demonlord and the others. Then, the demonlord advanced again, its stinger held at the ready.

It's going to kill us both, Nukurren realized with despair. *Oh, Dhowifa, you fool.*

"Go—please!"

A huge shape stepped between Nukurren and the demonlord.

One of the hunnakaku, she realized, even before she heard the hoot.

The concentration necessary to interpret the hunnakaku was beyond her. She was afloat in a sea of pain.

She heard hoots answered by other, strange hoots. The latter, she dimly realized, came from the demons. But she could only concentrate on one thought.

I will not die with these horrible stingers in my flesh.

Gently detaching Dwowifa, she gripped the stinger in her eye. She inhaled deeply. Then, drawing on every reserve of strength and courage, she drew the stinger forth. She whistled from the pain, but never hesitated.

She cast the stinger aside. It rolled toward a demon. The monster stared at the weapon, then at her. It did not move. None of the demons were moving, she realized. The hunnakaku was now standing to one side, silent.

She reached back and gripped the stinger protruding from the left side of her mantle. Again, she exerted her great strength. The pain this time was not as intense, but after she drew out the weapon she felt a great weakness wash over her.

She fought the weakness aside, barely. She reached back and grasped the last stinger. Again, a heave. But now her strength failed her. She could barely see out of the eye left to her. The weariness and the agony were overwhelming.

She felt a touch on her palp. Strange, eerie touch. She twisted slightly and looked back. The demonlord was next to her side, staring at her with its strange little eyes. Dawn was now fully upon them, and there was enough light to see clearly. Much of the demon's body was covered with armor, and most of the rest was cloaked in hides. And there was something very strange, she realized, about the armor on its head. But she could see uncovered stretches of the monster's skin. Black as night. Implacable.

The touch again. She realized that it was the demonlord. The monster pulled her palps from the stinger. There was something bizarre about the shape of its palps, but she was too dazed to make sense of it.

It's very strong, she thought vaguely. *But I think, if I were unwounded, not as strong as I.*

She was unable to resist. She let her tentacles fall. The demonlord seized the stinger and placed one of its peds on her mantle, next to the wound. A sudden jerk, the sharp pressure of its tiny ped on her body, and the stinger was out.

She lost all vision, then. And almost, but not quite, her consciousness. Around her, she could hear the mingled hoots of hunnakaku and demons. She could feel Dhowifa's warm, trembling little body clutching her head. Reason, always thinly rooted in truemales, had fled completely.

Poor Dhowifa, was her last thought before sliding into oblivion, *you were so proud of your mind. Now you see what terror can do.*

Chapter 3

Rottu waited in the shadows while the patrol passed. She was not especially worried. The warriors in the patrol were auxiliaries, not keen-eyed legionnaires. More concerned with ending their patrol in the warmth of an ashu-chamber than with finding suspicious persons lurking in dark alleys.

As they drew alongside the mouth of the alley, the warriors stopped and made a casual examination of its interior. But Rottu knew they would see nothing. There was only a single glowmoss pillar at the entrance of the alley. An old colony, moreover, whose light penetrated not more than a few steps into the gloom beyond.

Still, Rottu took no chances. Far back in the alley, she pressed herself more closely against the stones. Then, cursing silently, repressed a hoot of pain. She had forgotten. The walls of the tenements were crudely made, with many sharp edges and rough corners. Nothing like the polished, beautiful walls of the Divine Shell.

I'm getting old and sloppy. Too accustomed to the luxury of the Shell. I haven't been outside the clan quarters in—how many eightweeks?

One of the warriors began to make a perfunctory inspection of the alley. But she had no sooner taken a few steps forward than she suddenly recoiled.

Watching, in the darkness beyond, Rottu found it hard not to whistle derision.

She smells the stench of the corpse.

The corpse lay between Rottu and the mouth of the alley. When she had seen the warriors approach, she had deliberately

hidden herself beyond the body. If the squad of warriors chose
to investigate the alley closely, they would have to edge their
way past the thing. Several days dead, that corpse. Crawling
with scavengers. Putrid.

A nameless corpse, Rottu knew. Dead of hunger, or parasites; or the wounds inflicted by thieves, themselves desperate enough to rob a nameless one. A former helot, most likely,
escaped from the lands of her clan mistresses. Seeking, like
so many before her, a new life in Shakutulubac. And finding
nothing but death in the slums of the great city.

*There are more and more such, now. Driven by the increas-
ing tyranny in the land to seek refuge in a city which is itself
hooting louder and louder.*

*There will be another pogrom soon. The awosha have
already given the order. Many Pilgrims will die. We are too
many, now, to find safety in a few cellars.*

The patrol left quickly, as Rottu had known they would.
In eightyweeks gone by, in the time of Rottu's youth, the patrol
would have reported the corpse at the end of their night's work.
The following morning, a gang of slaves would have been sent
by the Mistresses of the City to remove it. But those days
were long gone. In the Shakutulubac of Rottu's old age, corpses
rotted in the streets. There were so many of them now. The
life of the poor and low-clanned had always been cheap. Today,
it was worth nothing.

Some time later, when she judged it was safe to do so,
Rottu edged past the corpse and left the alley. Allowing no
sign in her mantle of the repugnance she felt. There were none
to see her color, of course. But Rottu had been a mistress
of *shoroku* for too long to relax her discipline. A lifetime too
long.

Once back in the street, she hurried along. Hurried, but
took no chances. If she were spotted by a patrol, she would
certainly be recognized. The patrol, of course, would not accost
her. They would not dare. But they would talk, and the talk
would reach the Tympani of the Ansha. Then—disaster. Rottu
herself ranked high in the Tympani. But not high enough to
avoid the chambers in the cellars of the Shell. Not if it became
known that she was seen, late in the night, in that quarter
of the city which was known to be infested with Pilgrims.

Some of the Tympani are already a bit suspicious. I have

*been careful, but it is impossible to make no mistakes. I have
made very few, or my mantle would have been stripped long
ago. But it has been many eightyweeks since I entered
Ushulubang's service.*

She ducked into another alley-mouth and examined the
street behind her. Then, satisfied, continued on.

*I would not have taken this chance, except—there has
perhaps never been a parcel more precious than the one I carry
tonight. And I have not seen Ushulubang in so long. We must
speak together, for all the risk. I must make certain that she
understands the truth of the situation.*

This pogrom will be—terrible.

Rottu finally reached her destination, and gave the signal.
Moments later, she was following a pashoc through the laby-
rinth of cellars beneath the slums. Now that she was in the
relative safety of the underground, she admitted to herself that
there had been another reason she had taken the risk of
coming here personally.

*I must see Ushulubang myself. It has been so long, and my
soul needs replenishing.*

Ushulubang's quarters were, as always, spare and lean. A
simple pallet. A sturdy reading bench. A crudely-trimmed
glowmoss colony, which cast barely enough light for the sage
to read by. Barely, but enough. Nothing more. Even for a
former warrior like Ushulubang, the rigor of her life must
sometimes be trying.

But Rottu saw, with relief, that there were no signs of that
rigor upon Ushulubang. The sage was old, of course. But she
still seemed as vigorous as ever.

After they entwined their arms, Ushulubang stepped back
and whistled humorously.

"Why such an air of gloom, Rottu? Your mantle might as
well be pure brown."

"Stop making jokes, you old fool." From the corner of her
eye, Rottu saw the mantle of the pashoc glow orange and pink.
The young Pilgrim was shocked to hear someone speak to the
great opoloshuku in such an unseemly fashion.

*Let her be shocked. Someone has to speak the truth to this—
this saintly idiot.*

The green in Ushulubang's own mantle never wavered, of

course. Ushulubang enjoyed the rare occasions when someone flailed her. It reminded her, she would say, of the days
when she had wandered the world with Goloku. Days long
gone. The most precious of days. The days when Goloku had
flailed her with the truth, and shown her the road of the Way.

"Always so grim. Always so grim."

Ushulubang made the gesture of rueful acceptance.

"Very well, Rottu. I see I will not be able to avoid your
flail. But first—do you have the packet?"

Rottu withdrew the packet from where she had secreted
it within her mantle cavity. With considerable relief. The packet
was large and heavy. She extended it to the sage. Ushulubang's
arms made short work of unwrapping the cloth.

The sage moved closer to the light shed by the glowmoss.
Slowly, she examined the sheets.

"You have seen?"

"Yes, Ushulubang. I have made my own copies of the most
important sheets."

A tinge of pink came into Ushulubang's mantle.

"Isn't that a bit—"

Rottu interrupted with a rude whistle. The pashoc in the
corner of the chamber glowed azure and orange with indignation.

"Stick to philosophy, Ushulubang. Let me worry about
keeping things secret."

Again, Ushulubang made the gesture of rueful acceptance.

"I am well flailed. I had forgotten how uncouth you are!
But, as you say, you are the mistress of such things."

She gestured to the sheets.

"What do you think?"

"It is perfect. We will never be able to pronounce the
language exactly the way they do, of course. But the Pilgrims
on the mountain say that the demons themselves are changing their manner of speech to fit our needs."

Ushulubang issued a soft hoot of surprise.

"Truly?"

Rottu made the gesture of affirmation. "And in every other
respect, Enagulishuc is ideal. Clear and logical. And the written
form is very easy to learn, once one learns the strange method.
Even the barbarians at Fagoshau are learning it. More easily, in fact, than the Anshac."

Ushulubang looked back at the sheets. "That is not so surprising, Rottu. The *former* barbarians do not have their minds cluttered with the arcane complexities of Anshaku writing."

Rottu accepted the reproof without comment. In principle, she agreed with Ushulubang. All apashoc are equal on the Way. Still, it was difficult not to think of barbarians as semi-savage illiterates. Skilled in war, within their limits; and often surprisingly cunning in their statecraft. But—

"You agree, then?" she asked Ushulubang. "We will adopt Enagulishuc?"

Ushulubang made the gesture of hesitation.

"I think so, yes. From a practical point of view, it is ideal. Yet—there is still the deeper question to be resolved. We will be committing ourselves, Rottu. In a sense, at least. We will become identified with demons."

Rottu whistled derision. "And so what? All the better. Let those who oppress the Pilgrims find red in their mantles, for a change. There is no longer any doubt on *that* question, Ushulubang. No Pilgrim has yet been able to observe the demons in battle, of course. They move much too quickly for our warriors to accompany them. But they have seen the results. Entire slave caravans destroyed. With no casualties suffered by the demons, other than minor wounds."

Seeing the continued hesitation, Rottu pressed on.

"Ushulubang, facts are what they are. It is a world of evil and violence. We may wish it were not so, and speak against it, but the fact remains. And we have become too numerous to avoid attack by simply hiding."

Hesitation.

"Ushulubang, *there is a new pogrom coming*. It has already been ordered. It will take the Tympani some time to organize, but not much."

Ushulubang made the gesture of postponement.

"I know, Rottu. But we will speak of that in a moment." The sage laid the sheets down on the bench.

"You misunderstand my concern, Rottu. Goloku was a warrior herself, you should remember. She spoke against violence, true. But she was not reluctant to defend herself when necessary. As you say, if we can learn the skills of war from the demons, so much the better."

"Then why do you hesitate?"

"Battle is a small thing, Rottu. It is the soul which looms large on the Way. And these are, after all, demons."

"Demons who eat nothing but owoc ogoto."

"That is certain?"

Rottu made the gesture of affirmation. "Yes, Ushulubang. It is certain."

She pointed to the sheets on the bench. "You can read the report yourself. Many of the Pilgrims on the mountain have been living among the demons for eightweeks, now. They have watched carefully, as you instructed. Never—not once—have they seen a demon eat anything else. The demons themselves say they cannot."

"Do the demons say why?"

"Yes. They say any other food will kill them."

"Just so. It is fitting. Powerful demons, with the knowledge of great secrets. Yet—they cannot exist without the love of the world's simplest and most gentle beings."

Ushulubang made the gesture of certainty.

"In the end, that is what guides me. The minds of the owoc can be easily fooled. But their souls? Never, I think."

The sage turned to the pashoc in the corner.

"Spread the word, Shurren. Enagulishuc is now the language of the Way. All of the apashoc should begin its study. If they have already begun, they should intensify their efforts."

"Yes, opoloshuku. And the other matter?"

"That too is settled. Tell the Pilgrims to prepare for the journey."

The pashoc hurried from the chamber.

"What journey?" demanded Rottu. "What 'other matter'?"

Ushulubang whistled humorously.

"Excellent! Even the all-seeing Rottu remains in the dark. I am pleased. The secret has been kept. A difficult task, when it involved so many people."

"What are you talking about?"

"We are leaving Shakulutubac, Rottu. All of us, except for a few friars who will stay behind to continue the work of recruitment."

Rottu was dumbfounded. It took all of her mastery of shoroku to prevent her mantle being flooded with orange.

"Leaving? Where are you going?"

"To the Chiton, Rottu. To the mountain of demons."

"But—all of you? You too?"

She felt a sharp pain.

I will never see Ushulubang again. My soul will shrivel and die.

Then, drawing on a lifetime of harsh self-discipline, she repressed her emotions. She stood in silence for a moment, considering the question.

It is a brilliant stroke, actually. I would never have thought of it myself. The Chiton will provide safety from persecution. Long enough, at least, for Ushulubang to weave the Pilgrims into a thick cloth. The coming pogrom will strike at—nothing. I can easily provide enough places of safety in the city for a few friars.

Her cunning mind saw another possibility as well. But she pushed it aside. There would be time enough to deal with that later. For the moment—

Again, she repressed her emotions.

I will not live much longer, in any event. The steps I will need to take to enable so many Pilgrims to flee Shakutulubac will certainly come to the attention of the Tympani. I will be put in the torture cells.

In her mind, she whistled derision.

But they will learn nothing from my corpse. I have carried poison with me ever since I gave my soul to the Way.

And there is this, to bring comfort. Ushulubang will live. Ushulubang will live.

The sage interrupted her thoughts.

"Such an idiot."

Rottu stared at her, surprised.

"What does that mean?"

"Do you really think I would leave you behind? To receive the blue fury of the awosha? You are coming with us, Rottu."

"*What?* Impossible! I need to—"

Ushulubang's mantle flashed black. The sight of that implacable color on the sage's mantle stopped Rottu in mid-sentence. It was a color she had almost never seen on the opoloshuku of the Way.

"I command, Rottu. In this, I command. We will need your skills to assist us in fleeing the city. But only so much as you can do without throwing yourself into the torture cells."

"I can save—"

"You will save enough, Rottu. And you are not thinking clearly. You are only thinking of the escape. What of the arrival?"

"I don't understand."

"Just so. *Just so.* I am casting the fate of the Pilgrims into the coil of demons, Rottu. You may be a fool, but I am not. Do you think I would do so—without the assistance of my other eyes? Without your cunning at my side? *Fool.*"

Rottu considered the question in this new light. And concluded, as she had so many times in the past, that Ushulubang was truly a sage.

"You are correct, opoloshuku."

Ushulubang whistled. Rarely did Rottu allow that word of respect to issue from her siphon.

The two gukuy stared at each other in silence for a moment. They had known each other for many, many eightyweeks. Ever since a young Tympani had been assigned as one of Ushulubang's interrogators, following the first persecution of the Pilgrims. A very young Tympani. Old enough to be sickened at the cruelty she had seen in the torture cells. Young enough not to have absorbed the cruelty into her own soul. An interrogator who had found, looking for answers from Goloku's only surviving pashoc, a Question to which she had devoted her life.

Mistress of *shoroku*, Rottu's mantle remained gray. Ushulubang, though she was an even greater mistress of the art, allowed hers to glow green.

After a moment, Rottu turned away.

"I must be gone, or my absence will be missed."

"A moment, Rottu. I have a last question."

"Yes?"

Ushulubang gestured to the sheets on the bench.

"You have read them. Do the Pilgrims of the mountain continue to claim that the Answer is known? By the Mother of Demons?"

"Yes."

"Do you believe it?"

Rottu whistled. "I leave philosophy to you, old sage. I have enough secrets to keep me busy."

Ushulubang's whistle echoed the amusement.

"Just so. I myself do not believe. I believe the Pilgrims on the mountain have lapsed into the great error. I believe in the teachings of Goloku. There is no Answer. There is only the Question."

"As you say, Ushulubang. In this you are always my guide. We will know soon enough."

She turned and left the chamber.

Back on the streets, Rottu resumed her cautious movements. She thought of nothing, beyond the immediate needs of the moment, until she was quit of the slums. Then, however, she allowed her thoughts to flow freely. If she were seen now, she would be able to explain her whereabouts to the satisfaction of the Tympani. Awkwardly, and not without being the object of derision. An old gukuy, seeking pleasure in an unseemly manner.

Let them whistle. They will not whistle long.

Her thoughts raced down well-known corridors. Weaving her stratagems. It would be a cunning weave—the warp and the weft so utterly tangled that the thugs set loose on the streets would flail themselves. She would see to it that the names of true Pilgrims were lost. In their place, she would insert the names of informers. It would be those informers who would be forked during the pogrom. Their bodies dragged through the streets by the mob.

Let the Tympani of Ansha whistle.

Once only did Rottu's mind drift from her scheme. Dawn was approaching, and the sight of it creeping into the Mother-of-Pearl brought back an old memory.

The same sky, long ago, had once been marked by a strange and terrible sign. Rottu herself had seen it, and had trembled with fear. But, along with all other gukuy, the passing of many eightyweeks had faded the memory.

Until, not so very long ago, word had come to Shakutulubac from the mountain. The first small party of Pilgrims sent to the Chiton by Ushulubang, in search of a place of refuge, reported. Astonishing report. There were demons on the mountain. Demons who said they came from beyond the world.

Rottu had deciphered the strange numbers of the demons. She would never forget the thrill of terror which struck her soul like a lightning bolt, when she realized that the demons had left that mark in the sky, long ago. The world itself had turned red with fear at their coming.

And now, Ushulubang had decided to embrace this new and

mysterious power. To seek out the Mother of Demons, and her terrible children.

The Mother of Demons. The one being in the world, said the Pilgrims on the mountain, who knew the secrets of the future. But would not speak of them. Not even to her own children.

So be it. Let mighty Ansha flush scarlet with fear.

Eightdays later, however, when the truth became known, mighty Ansha did not glow red with fear. Blue fury was the color which flushed the mantles of the awosha, when they finally realized how thoroughly they had been duped.

The Pilgrims had evaded the pogrom. They were gone, all of them. Even the accursed traitor Ushulubang.

Gone where? None knew.

Executions were ordered.

Who then were the victims of the mob?

Informers. The mob had destroyed most of the Tympani informers.

Blue outrage. *Intolerable incompetence.*

The ranks of the Tympani were further thinned.

How was such a fiasco possible?

Investigations were ordered. Scarlet-tinged Tympani pursued the trail of evidence with great zeal. A tangled, twisted trail. But eventually, the culprit was found. Her name reported to the awosha.

Rottu? The awosha mantles glowed orange astonishment. *Rottu?*

Yes. It is certain.

Arrest her!

With Tympani officials in the lead, a squad of warriors raced through the halls of the Divine Shell. In the quarters of the highest-ranked members of the clan, they found the door to Rottu's quarters. The door was smashed open by the warriors. Flushed blue with fury and black with implacable purpose, the Tympani burst within.

And found nothing. No trace of Rottu, beyond a disgusting, scavenger-covered little pile on the floor.

Rottu's last shit.

Chapter 4

"The demons will protect the Old Ones," argued Kopporu. "And even if they do not, how can the Kiktu save the Old Ones if we ourselves are destroyed?"

Even before she heard the derisive whistling, Kopporu knew that she had lost the debate. She was universally recognized as the Kiktu's greatest battle leader, despite her relative youth. But she was not a clan leader, and this was not a battle. This was a full meeting of the tribal leaders, where clan status and venerable age weighed heavily in the balance.

And our ancient leaders have grown stiff in their minds, she thought bitterly. *They have come to believe in the myth of Kiktu invulnerability.*

Even as the thought came to her, one of the old clan leaders spoke.

"The Kiktu have never been defeated!" orated Taktoko. "Never!"

Not in living memory, no. But we too were once a small and unknown tribe, like the Utuku, until our conquests made us famed and feared. Like the Utuku.

"Does not even the Ansha Prevalate fear our flails?" demanded Taktoko. "Have not even their mighty legions whistled in fear at our onslaught?"

A chorus of loud hoots echoed her sentiments. Encouraged, Taktoko continued her peroration.

"The Ansha Prevalate only survives due to our benevolence! Should we choose, even they would fall before our flails!"

A few, faint hoots greeted this last claim. Most of the leaders present maintained a discreet silence.

At least they are not totally mad, thought Kopporu. *Taktoko is an idiot. She cannot see the difference between defeating a few invading Anshac legions and conquering Ansha itself. If the Kiktu ever tried to conquer Ansha, we would be destroyed. For that matter, if the Anshac ever seriously attempted to conquer our lands, we would be forced to give way. Just as we will before the Utuku. Except the Utuku will not be satisfied with our lands. They will devour us whole.*

She ignored the rest of Taktoko's speech. She had heard it all before—if not quite so mindlessly put—and there was no purpose to be served in further argument. She had lost the debate, as she knew she would. The clan leaders had scoffed at Kopporu's proposal to withdraw southward, with the aim of defeating the Utuku in the course of a long campaign. That was the traditional tactic used by weaker tribes faced with stronger enemies. Some of the battle leaders had been sympathetic, at the beginning, but the clan leaders had been outraged at the implication that the Kiktu were no longer the mightiest tribe on the plains. They had decided to meet the Utuku in the narrow throat in the Papti Plain between the Lolopopo Swamp and the great bend of the Adkapo. That was the traditional boundary of Kiktu territory. The clan leaders, full of pride, were determined to prevent the Utuku from desecrating the tribal lands.

It was the worst possible position, Kopporu knew, for the Kiktu to face the greater numbers and heavier forces of the Utuku. But the decision was now a foregone conclusion. She must look to the future.

Her course of action was clear to her—had been for days, since it became obvious that the Kiktu would attempt to confront the Utuku invaders directly. The tribe would be destroyed, broken into pieces. The clans and battle groups would be mangled beyond recognition. Her duty was now to salvage what she could.

A rush of emotions momentarily threatened to sweep over her. But she pushed it resolutely aside, maintaining iron control. Not a trace of her sentiments could show in her mantle, if she was to succeed in her plan.

Kopporu's attention was brought back to the discussion by the sound of the Great Mother's voice.

The Great Mother, she realized, had spoken her name.

"—that the demons will protect the Old Ones. Do these demons even exist? Has anyone seen them? They are nothing but a tale for new-borns!"

The Great Mother was glaring at Kopporu, her enormous mantle rippling with blue anger and yellow contempt.

They exist, Great Mother. I have not seen them, but I have seen their work. An entire slave caravan slaughtered to the last gukuy. Dead of horrible wounds, like none I have ever seen. And I have spoken to Pilgrims of the Way, seeking refuge in the Chiton.

But Kopporu maintained her silence. She had already lost much of the prestige with which she had entered the meeting. What little she retained would vanish if she engaged in a futile religious debate with the Great Mother. Most battle leaders believed in the existence of the demons, but it was a difficult thing to prove. Especially to old clan leaders, who did not look kindly upon new concepts.

Eventually, the discussion turned to battle stratagems. Kopporu knew that it would be a distressingly short discussion.

Amass our invincible warriors. Attack.

It was a method of battle which had served the Kiktu well in their various clashes with neighboring tribes. Not only did they outnumber any of the other tribes, but even when faced with combinations of tribes the Kiktu had always been able to rely on the justly famed individual prowess of their warriors and battlemothers.

It was difficult to argue with success. But Kopporu knew that the underlying reason for their victories against other tribes was simple:

Because the other tribes fight as we do.

The Kiktu methods had even served, in the past, to defeat invading Anshac legions. But Kopporu had participated in the last battle with an Anshac legion, as a young warrior. She had been stunned by the military effectiveness of the disciplined and organized tactics used by the legion. True, the Kiktu had won the battle. But they had greatly outnumbered the legionnaires, and, even so, had suffered three times the casualties.

In the years which followed, as she rose in status until she became a battle leader, Kopporu had attempted to adopt Anshac tactics to the extent possible. She had never been able to use the Anshac methods as much as she would have liked, of course. The inveterate individualism of the Kiktu warrior was a constant obstacle, as was their loosely organized tribal society.

Despite her efforts, the traditional tactics still prevailed. And those tactics would be disastrous against the Utuku.

They are the most brutal and vicious tribe which has ever existed on the Meat of the Clam. But they do not fight like savages. Their discipline is even harsher than that of the Anshac legions. The Utuku tactics are crude and simple. But what does that matter—when the Utuku warriors fight like mindless clams? And there are so many of them!

As she pondered these thoughts, Kopporu was waiting for the right moment to speak. It came unexpectedly—a gift handed her by the braggart Taktoko.

"And where does Kopporu wish to muster her warriors? In the rear—guarding the gana?"

Silence fell over the meeting. Only the faint sound of the wind—most of its force reduced by the ganahide walls which surrounded the leaders, isolating them from the curious tympani of the tribespeople—could be heard.

Kopporu rose slowly to her peds. She said nothing; simply stared at Taktoko for a long moment. With amusement, she noted the traces of pink which rippled through Taktoko's mantle.

Taktoko has just remembered that I am the best warrior as well as battle leader in this group. Not the best in the tribe—by a small margin. But more than good enough to peel her mantle.

Taktoko was nervously watching Kopporu's mantle, but Kopporu let not a trace of her emotions show.

Taktoko fears blue rage. Ironic—what I fear is a trace of green relief. The arrogant fool has given me exactly what I needed.

When she was certain that she had her emotions under control, Kopporu allowed black to darken her mantle. Her arms assumed the gesture of command. She spoke.

"I will lead the right flank. I demand the privilege, since my courage has been insulted."

As she expected, there was no argument. Several of the clan leaders spoke sharply on the subject of proper conduct

in debate, rebuking Taktoko. In soft voices—still loud enough
to be overheard—two of the battle leaders exchanged quips
as to the probable position of Taktoko. (The old leader's high
clan status was not accompanied by any comparable reputa-
tion on the battlefield.) The Great Mother even interjected
a remark concerning Kopporu's unquestioned valor.

By Kiktu battle standards, leadership of the flanks was
considered the most prestigious position. There were no tribes-
men to guard one's unprotected side. True, in this coming
battle, the small Opoktu tribe would marshall on the right—
but the Kiktu did not consider the Opoktu comparable to
themselves as warriors. Kopporu herself did not share that
general assessment. She had found the Opoktu as brave as any
gukuy, within the limits imposed upon them by their small
numbers. She even admired them for their cleverness, and was
on good personal terms with their battle leader Lukpudo.

In the coming battle, moreover, the right flank was considered the most dangerous position. The Kiktu on the right
would be against the Lolopopo Swamp, with little of the
maneuvering room that the warriors preferred.

*Uncertain allies, and a swamp at my side. They think me
brave because of that, when it is those two factors that I will
need in order to accomplish—*

She hesitated, grieved, completed the thought:
My treason.

That night, in the yurt she shared with Aktako, she finally
told her the truth. She was hesitant, but knew she had no
choice. Aktako was her most trusted lieutenant, as well as her
lover. Without her conscious assistance, the plan could not
succeed.

She had expected resistance, even vehement resistance. But
she had underestimated Aktako. After listening to the plot,
the old veteran simply whistled softly—not in fear, but in
admiration.

"I knew you were weaving some kind of scheme, but I didn't
realize how big it was. You always did have a better brain than
me."

Kopporu began stumbling through an apology, in which the
word "treason" featured prominently, but Aktado cut her off
with a rude hoot.

"That's nothing but shit! It's not your fault the clan leaders are idiots. You're just trying to save something out of the wreckage."

Ochre indecision mottled Kopporu's mantle.

"But how can you be so sure I'm right? What if we defeat the Utuku?"

"Then we defeat them, and life is simple. No one will ever know what you were planning except me." A whistle of amusement. "And maybe those swampsnails you've been collecting around you—for reasons which mystified me until tonight."

"They will say nothing. And I told the clan leaders—those few who asked—that I wanted the swamp-dwellers for scouts. To make sure the Utuku didn't surprise us by coming through the swamp."

Aktako's whistle combined amazement and humor.

"And they believed you?"

"I think so. They give almost no thought to the nature of the enemy, Aktako. The Utuku would never come through the swamp. Their tactics are designed for dry land—flat, open areas. In the swamp, they would be at a great disadvantage."

"That's what you're counting on, isn't it?"

"Yes. That and—" She paused, brown misery washing over her. "And the fact that the Utuku will be wallowing in their victory."

Brown rippled across Aktako's mantle as well. But within a short time, the brown deepened to black.

"Life is what it is, Kopporu. We do what we must. I have always taught you that—from the first day you joined my battle group."

The veteran stroked Kopporu's arms.

"So bright and fierce you were. And beautiful. I thought for sure you'd choose one of the younger and better looking veterans."

Kopporu whistled derision. "I may have been young, but I wasn't stupid. Much good it does you to have a pretty lover when the forks are shattering. I knew what I wanted—a scarred old warrior, wise in battle."

The two gukuy gazed at each other lovingly. Theirs was an unusual romance. Most Kiktu warriors went through a succession of lovers, but Kopporu and Aktako had been together for eightyweeks. At another time, under other circumstances, their mantles would already be turning white with passion. But on that night of sorrow, there was only the soft green of long affection.

They fell asleep sometime later, their arms intertwined. Aktako's last words were:

"You know what the biggest problem's going to be, don't you? How to keep Guo alive during the battle."

"I'm not worried about *that*. Guo's going to be a battlemother out of legend. The real problem will be to keep her from trying to rescue the Great Mother after the battle's lost."

"How will you do that?"

"I don't know, Aktako. I don't know."

Kopporu may not have been worried about Guo surviving the battle, but the infanta herself was sleepless that night.

Not worried about her survival, however, but about her conduct during the battle. She suspected, in the half-cocksure/ half-uncertain manner of youth, that she was probably the greatest battlemother produced by the Kiktu in generations. But what she *knew*, on that eve before the clash, was that she had never been in a real battle before. Her experience was limited to the practice field, and a few minor skirmishes with other tribes. But those skirmishes were meaningless—not least because the opponents had fled instantly upon seeing a battlemother.

The Utuku would not flee. It was not the least of their unspeakable savagery—the contempt in which they held all mothers. Guo knew that the Utuku did not even use the word "mother" in their own language. They simply called them "breeders." Utuku mothers were maimed at birth: the tendons in their peds slashed, so that the pitiful creatures could not even walk. Mothers captured from other tribes were treated likewise. And then condemned to a life of forced breeding.

I shall not be treated so, vowed Guo silently. *They will only take my dead body for meat.*

She picked up her mace and hefted it. A club, essentially, with six long blades protruding from all sides—edges out, not points out. It was a clumsy weapon, for a clumsy mother. But what it lacked in finesse, it made up for in size and weight. The weapon was huge. A gukuy warrior could barely lift the mace, much less wield it in combat. The mace was a weapon for battlemothers—designed to compensate for their awkwardness by using their enormous strength.

Staring at the mace, Guo's mantle turned suddenly yellow. Contempt—for the weapon and herself.

I wanted to use a flail—from the time I first began my training. Like a real warrior, instead of a giant slug.

She winced mentally, remembering the hard lesson Kopporu had given her. Guo had thought she could use a flail, at first. Was she not quicker and more nimble than any infanta in memory? She was, in fact. But all things are relative. A quick and nimble battlemother is still far too clumsy to properly wield a flail. Guo had not believed it until Kopporu matched her against Aktako with practice flails and forks. The experience had been utterly humiliating.

That same night Kopporu had come into Guo's yurt. The infanta had attempted to fade the brown misery in her mantle, with no success. Like all mothers—and she hated herself for it—she was all but incapable of controlling her color.

Kopporu no sooner saw the brown than she whistled derision.

"Do you wallow in misery because you can't float on the breeze like a puopoa? Or breathe water like a dikplo?"

Guo was silent.

"Foolish child! You are a *mother*, Guo."

"I want to be a *warrior!*" exclaimed the infanta.

"And what is that?"

Guo was silent.

"You think a warrior is grace—and speed?"

Another whistle of derision.

"I will tell you what a warrior is, stupid one. A warrior is not agility and reflexes. Mindless. A warrior is brain, and heart—at the service of the tribe. A warrior faces the truth unflinchingly. Do you understand?"

After a moment, miserably: "No."

"Still have the brains of a spawn! Listen to me, Guo. Learn to face the truth, peeled of its shell. The truth is that you are not and cannot be a warrior. If you still don't believe that, then tomorrow I'll put you back on the field and let Aktako make a fool out of you again."

Kopporu had let that sink in before continuing.

"If you can learn to face that truth, then perhaps you can learn to face another truth."

Unwillingly: "And what is that?"

"It is that if you abandon these foolish fantasies of becoming a warrior, and apply yourself, you can become the greatest battlemother in the history of the Kiktu since Dodotpi. Maybe even greater than she."

Orange astonishment flooded Guo's mantle.

"Really?"

A tinge of green entered Kopporu's mantle. The battle leader stretched out her palp and gently stroked the brow of the infanta.

"Yes, Guo. Really. You *are* very fast and nimble, for a mother. And you are incredibly strong. Aktako told me she could feel the earth shake every time you smote the ground with your flail."

A humorous whistle.

"Fortunately, she was far away by the time the blow landed."

"She would have been just as far away if I'd been using a mace!" protested Guo.

"True. But only a stupid infanta—or a stupid leader—thinks a battlemother can fight like a warrior. Your flankers will keep the foe from dodging your blows. Your task is to crush the enemy in front of you. And for crushing, the mace is a better weapon than a flail."

Kopporu fell silent. After a few moments, Guo had said softly:

"I will try to learn. With the mace."

"*And* the shield. *And* the visor."

Yellow contempt rippled across Guo's mantle, but she did not voice the protest. Again, Kopporu whistled amusement.

"You will learn to appreciate the lowly shield and visor, child. When you become a renowned battlemother, every piper in the enemy's army will be aiming at you. Would you rather be blind?"

Remembering that conversation, Guo's mantle was suddenly flooded a deep green. She, like the other two battlemothers and all of the warriors in the group, adored Kopporu. In part, that was because of Kopporu's brilliance as a battle leader. But her charisma had deeper roots. There was a—greatness in the battle leader's spirit. Even a young infanta like Guo could sense it.

Sadly, Guo reflected that Kopporu's potential would never be realized. Kopporu's clan was small, and Kopporu's own rank within it was insignificant. Her battle group, of course, was the biggest in the tribe. Warriors chose their own battle groups. Most chose the battle groups of their own clan. But many warriors sought acceptance into the groups of renowned battle leaders, regardless of clan affiliation. Almost three fourths of the warriors in Kopporu's group were from clans other than her own—an unprecedented figure in Kiktu history, so far as anyone knew. The clan leaders had complained, but the battle leaders had supported Kopporu. Many of the battle leaders were jealous of Kopporu's status among the warriors, but they were united in their determination to protect their traditional rights.

Guo herself was from a different clan—from the dominant clan in the tribe, in fact. It was unlikely, but not inconceivable, that she herself might someday become the Great Mother of the Kiktu.

She did not view that prospect with pleasure. She had no desire to become a mother. She wanted to remain a battlemother, surrounded by warriors.

Like all infanta, she had her moments of curiosity and interest on the subject of truemales. Strange, silly creatures. Flighty; given to emotional excess. But skilled, it was said, in the ways of pleasure.

But such moments were few and fleeting. Had life been as she would have wanted, Guo would have been born a warrior. A female. She would have taken a lover from the ranks of the veterans, who would bring her joy in the yurt and protection on the battlefield.

A sudden image came to her mind of the beautiful Kopporu reaching her arms into Guo's mantle—

She thrust the image away, horrified. *Perversion.*

She forced her thoughts to the future. She would probably not survive the morrow, in any event. The word had already spread throughout the tribe's warriors, in whispers— Kopporu was opposed to the plan of battle, although she had insisted on the command of the right flank. The deliberations of the tribe leaders were supposed to be held in confidence, but such news could not be contained. Kopporu herself had said nothing, but the word had spread regardless.

The warriors had greeted the news with mixed emotions. Anger at Kopporu's apparent disdain for the invincibility of the Kiktu warriors. Disquiet, because all knew of Kopporu's genius on the battlefield. Determination to prove Kopporu wrong. Fear that Kopporu was right. But, most of all, admiration for Kopporu's nobility of spirit.

Guo herself had no doubts of her own feelings. Her faith in the battle leader was absolute. And thus, she knew the tribe was doomed. But she would follow Kopporu's example.

She grasped the mace in a huge palp. So fiercely that even a kogoclam would have been crushed within.

The Utuku will never take me alive. I will die with the tribe. And I will slay the savages in numbers beyond counting.

She stared at the mace. It was a gift. Kopporu had given it to her on the day the battle leader announced to the tribe that Guo had completed her training and was accepted into the battle group as a battlemother. It was a gift worthy of a great clan leader. Guo had no idea how Kopporu had managed to obtain it. The haft of the club was made of uluwood, beautifully carved. But the treasure was in the blades—made of the finest bronze, honed to a keen edge. The blades of most maces were obsidian. Guo, as a young and untested battlemother, had expected a mace with flint blades.

That night, Guo made a solemn vow. If she and the Kiktu survived the battle, she would see to it that justice was done. Like many of the younger warriors—and even some of the older ones—she was tired of the stifling regime of the clan leaders. She had no wish to become a mother, but when the time came she would do so—without complaint. She would devote herself to rising within the complex, intrigue-filled world of the mothers until she became the Great Mother of the Kiktu.

When that day came, she would see that Kopporu was given her rightful place in the tribe. Traditions be shat upon.

Let the old clan leaders wail.

PART II:
The Warp

Chapter 5

Indira Toledo turned the page of the notebook. A passage caught her eye.

It's not as if I hadn't spent years thinking about it. I wanted to be an exobiologist from as far back as I can remember. Fought like hell to win a place on the Magellan. But all those years I was convinced the vertebrate Bauplan—or some variation on it—was the only suitable structure for large terrestrial life-forms. That's why I specialized in vertebrate paleontology.

Well, here I am. My dream come true. A planet full of large terrestrial life-forms. Including intelligent life forms—the first we've ever encountered. And the joke's on me!

Molluscs. Of all things—molluscs!

They're not really molluscs, of course. Hardcore cladists would lynch me for even thinking it. A totally separate evolutionary history. But the convergence is uncanny. It makes you wonder if old Arrhenius was right—all life came from spores drifting through interstellar space. That would make us distant relatives. Very, very, very distant. Even if Arrhenius was right, we'd be more closely related to algae and bacteria than we are to anything on Ishtar.

Indira smiled ruefully. She remembered criticizing Julius once for using the human name for the planet.

"Typical biologist," she'd said to him. "Arrogant beyond belief."

"But it's a great name!" he'd protested. "In most pantheons, the goddess of love and the god of war are separated not only in person but in sex. Ishtar was both. What could be more suited for this planet? A *goddess* of war and love. I should think you, of all people, would approve."

That had made her even angrier.

"I am *not* one of those feminists who thinks it's an advance for women to participate in slaughter. Anyway, that's beside the point—and you know it. Throughout history, the first act of aggression on the part of a more advanced society toward a less advanced one is to rename everything. Goes all the way back to your damned Bible. The first thing Adam did was name everything. That gave him the right to do what he pleased with *his* beasts. Columbus was just following the program. *Rhodesia*, for God's sake!"

Julius had grinned. "Egad, I'm exposed. Julius Cohen, slavering imperialist." He rubbed his hands, cackling with glee. "Wait till I get these natives into the gold mines! Copper mines, rather. Doesn't seem to be much gold on this planet, curse the luck. Pizarro'll never forgive me."

She chuckled, remembering the argument. Julius was the most good-hearted of men, in all truth. And, in the end, he had been proven right. For reasons which would have astonished all of the adult colonists at the time.

Her eyes watered. She and Julius were all that was left, now, of that small group of adults who had survived the first months after the disaster.

She raised her head and stared at the kolo-cluster down in the valley. They were all buried there. Vladimir Koresz. Janet Mbateng. Hector Quintero. Francis Adams. Following owoc customs, the humans had adopted the grove as their own cemetery. The owoc had a particular reverence for the kolo. Indira was not sure why, exactly. The owoc were not good at explaining things. But she thought it was because of the way the kolo always grew in dense clusters, the willowy shoots intertwining and curling about each other like vines. And they were pale green, color of tranquillity.

The Coil of Beauty. It was when she had finally grasped the meaning of that owoc concept that her gratitude toward them had crystallized into a profound love for the gentle creatures. Even Julius, once she had explained it to him, had been shaken out of his normally linear way of thinking. Thereafter, to her relief, he had stopped referring to the owoc as "dimbulbs."

She shook her head sharply, exorcising the sadness, and resumed reading.

I shouldn't be all that surprised. How long ago was it that Stephen Jay Gould pointed out how chancy the evolution of vertebrates had been? There was hardly a trace of chordates in the Burgess Shale, after all. Even on Earth, the phylum might have easily disappeared during the Permian extinction, if not sooner. And then what would have happened?

Still, I would have bet on some branch of the arthropods. But perhaps not. Maybe the very success of the arthropod Bauplan militates against them ever evolving into forms suitable of filling the ecological niche of large terrestrial life forms. And why should they? Popular mythology to the contrary, that niche has always been on the outer edge of existence. It's amazing, really, how the large size of humans prejudices our view of life. To this day, biologists talk of mammals dominating the earth. That's news to bacteria! Not to mention insects and worms. We, and all our bulky mammal relatives, are just rare clouds drifting over the teeming landscape of life. So were the dinosaurs.

It reminds me of J. B. S. Haldane's quip, when he was asked what his life's study of biology indicated about God. "He has an inordinate fondness for beetles."

No, not the arthropods. They've always been evolution's biggest winners. And winners don't evolve, in any major way. Losers do.

Still, it's odd that I haven't seen any signs of an arthropod equivalent on Ishtar. It's certainly not because of any lack of life! Ishtar's biomass is as big as Earth's. Bigger, probably, than today's Earth. About the same, I would guess, as the Earth during the Mesozoic. The climate's right—semi-tropical, no seasons worth talking about. Whereas the modern Earth is in an unusually frigid period of its existence. Has been for millions of years.

Indira smiled again. The words in the notebook brought back the first conversation she'd ever had with Julius. It had taken place shortly after the *Magellan* had left Earth orbit, on the start of the first leg of its voyage. It had taken three months to build up the ship's velocity to its maximum 13% of light-speed. During those months, the adults had remained conscious, getting to know each other in order to lay the basis for forging an effective team once they arrived at Tau Ceti. After the *Magellan* had reached its maximum velocity, and the crew was satisfied that the huge vessel was performing properly, all the adults had joined the children in coldsleep, there to spend the long years of the voyage in blissful unconsciousness. Weeks before that time came, she and Julius had become lovers.

But, she remembered fondly, *we began with an argument.*

Entering the large equatorial lounge, she had heard a man pontificating loudly on the stupidity of "ecofreaks" in general and their wails about global warming in particular. Mildly curious, and with nothing else to do, she had joined the small group listening to him.

"The idiots have no sense of the real history of life on earth," the man had been saying, as she took a seat on the armchair opposite him. "The average temperature on earth today is as low as it's ever been—at least since the Cambrian explosion. Probably lower. It's because of the modern configuration of the continents. It's not been unusual to have *one* ice-cap in our history. A continent often gets pushed over one of the poles by plate tectonics, just like Antarctica is today. But there's never been *two* ice-caps before. So far as we can tell, anyway."

Another man sitting around the circle of chairs (Vladimir Koresz, she later learned, one of the colony's doctors) had spoken up.

"But, Julius, there's no continent *today* under the north pole."

Julius had leaned forward, gesticulating with great animation (one of his characteristics, she learned over time).

"I know—that's the beauty of the whole thing! Instead, tectonics has encircled the north pole with most of the great continents. The flow of warm water which would normally keep the pole from freezing has been strangled. The result? The formation of a floating ice-cap. Do you have any idea of the odds against that happening?"

He drank from a cup of coffee sitting on the table before him.

"And that's my whole point. The Earth's climate today is a freak. It's not 'normal'—just the opposite. We live in a freezer. For almost the entire Phanerozoic Eon—"

"The *what?*" asked Koresz.

"Sorry. That's just jargon for the last 700 million years, since the evolution of multi-cellular life. Anyway, throughout that entire period—*700 million years*, folks—when life spread over the entire planet and evolved into all its wonderful permutations, the average temperature on Earth was *much* higher than it is today—ten or fifteen degrees, on the average. *That's* the normal temperature for the planet—*and* it's the optimum temperature for terrestrial life."

He set down his cup and spread his arms wide.

"You see? The real problem life has on earth today isn't global *warming*. It's just the opposite! The place is too damned cold. If we really cared about life, we'd go back to using fossil fuels. Crank up the greenhouse effect! It'd be great! It's not just that the temperature would be better, either. What's just as important is that the oceans would rise. That's another problem we have on Earth today. There aren't enough shallow seas and continental shelves, which are always the best environments for life to flourish. Raise the sea level a few hundred foot and we'd double or triple the area where life thrives the best."

She had interrupted at that point.

"I'd like to butt in, if you don't mind."

"Not at all!" said Julius, waving his hands.

She leaned over, extending her hand.

"I'm Indira Toledo. Historian."

"Julius Cohen. Paleontologist."

Her slender hand had been engulfed in Julius' vigorous handshake. He was a large man, fat in a healthy-looking sort of way. His complexion was ruddy, and his features were round and pudgy. Except for the kinky black hair, and the lack of a beard, he was the spitting image of Santa Claus.

Despite his harmless appearance, she was tense with anger. She tried to relax, because she knew that her thin, sharp features (normally quite attractive) were extremely intimidating when she was mad. But she couldn't help herself.

Arrogant bastard.

"Tell me, something, Mr. Cohen—"

"Please, please! Julius!"

"All right, then. Julius. I was born on the Altiplano. My father's Latin American. But I'm descended from Bengali immigrants, and I still have lots of relatives living in Calcutta. It's only been in the last generation or so that the Bengalis have finally been able to pull themselves out of some of the worst poverty the human race has ever experienced. They've even managed to limit the destruction during the monsoon season. But it's still a hard life, for most of them, and they're still packed together like sardines. What are those millions— *millions*, Mr. Cohen—of people supposed to do after you raise the sea level? Learn to swim? Or will you take them into all the extra space you've got in New York City?"

He shook his head ruefully. "Damn, my accent always gives me away." He stared at her thoughtfully, and she couldn't help but notice the intelligence in his eyes. Then, with a warmth that struck her like a great wave, his eyes had crinkled and a huge grin had spread across his face.

"Hey, lady, I really don't wanna drown a lot of cute little Bengali kids. Honest, I don't."

He made a self-deprecating gesture. "You've got to forgive my big mouth. I have a bad habit of fixing on a point and taking it to its logical conclusion. But I'm really not a stupid jackass, honest."

Then, more seriously: "I know we've got to maintain the earth's temperature where it is. The human race has only finally—barely—managed to carve out a decent enough life for everyone. The last thing we need to do is shatter all that hard work by upsetting the climatic apple-cart. It's just—oh hell, the thing that irritates me about these ecofreaks isn't what they call for, it's their goddammed self-righteousness. For all their claims to being the guardians of life, the truth is that they're at least as homocentric as anyone else. They just won't admit it. It's not 'life' they care about, it's the way life affects humans."

"I think you're being unfair."

He shrugged. "Maybe. But as a professional biologist I've always found that people have the screwiest ideas about life. Let me ask you something. Where would you rather spend a week's vacation—next to a beautiful clear blue lake in the mountains, or next to a swamp?"

She snorted. "What do you think?"

"Of course—at the lake. And while you were there, I'm sure you'd gaze out over that beautiful stretch of bright blue water and think serene philosophical thoughts about the glories of nature. *But are you aware that cold mountain lakes are one of the most inhospitable conditions for life?* It's true. That lake is a sterile desert. There are a few life-forms that have managed to adapt to those conditions—trout, for instance. But the biomass in that lake is a pittance compared to the life that thrives in a swamp."

He waved his arms about enthusiastically.

"Swamps are great! They're wonderful! Life adores a swamp! You don't believe me? Try walking around in a swamp sometime without stepping all over all kinds of juicy life-forms. *Really* juicy—soft, and slimy, and wriggly, and crawling all over the place."

She couldn't help but laugh. "Ugh! No thanks."

He grinned. "See? You're just another bigot. And that's my point. People will get all worked up over pollution in a mountain lake. Trout are pretty; tasty, too. But who cares about a swamp?"

He shrugged. "And that's fine with me, in and of itself. I'd much rather spend a week by a mountain lake, myself. Hate swamps. Don't know anybody who doesn't except herpetologists, and they're all a bunch of lunatics." One of the men nearby snorted. "But I don't go around preaching about the sanctity of all life, when what I really care about is life as it impacts on the human race. I'm opposed to destroying life where it's needless. But like any biologist—certainly any paleontologist—I have a keen sense that eventually all species become extinct. That's the way it is—and has been for eons, long before we humans popped onto the scene. So, to get back to your point, I care a hell of a lot more about what happens to people in Bengal than I do about the abstract fact that if we flooded the lowlands we'd enable millions of new species to come into existence. I'm just willing to be honest about it."

"That's all very sane and logical, Mr. Coh—Julius. But let me ask *you* a question. Would you rather have an ocean with whales or without them?"

He frowned. "What is this, some kind of trick question? With whales, of course."

"You are pleased, then, at the fact that the Earth's oceans are teeming with whales?"

"Sure!"

"Hmm. Yet it's a fact—I'm an historian, as I said—that the whales were only saved from extermination because of the actions of people who were not driven by logic but by an irrational passion. The type of people you call 'ecofreaks.' Had it not been for them, the great cetaceans would have disappeared. For it is also a fact that during the period of the great whale slaughtering, sane and logical men such as yourself stood to one side. Clucking their tongues at the barbarity of it all, of course, and shedding tears over the plight of the poor whales. But always quick to correct the scientific errors of the 'ecofreaks,' as if genocide and failing a biology quiz were of equal weight in the judgement of history."

She relaxed, slightly. "Mind you, I take some pride myself in my own rationality and logic. But I am an historian by profession. And if there is one thing that historians know, it's that nothing great was ever achieved except by those who were filled with passion. Their passion may have been illogical, even bizarre to modern people. Their understanding of the world and what they were doing may have been false. It usually was. But they were not afraid to act, guided by whatever ideas they had in their possession. Do not sneer at such people. You would not be here without them."

Silence followed for a moment. Indira was surprised to see that there was not a trace of irritation in the face of the man opposite her. Instead, Julius was gazing at her with a strange look. Interest, she suddenly realized.

Koresz spoke. "I fear I shall have to exercise my medical skills, lest Julius bleed to death from the many great wounds inflicted upon him."

Laughter erupted, with Julius joining in.

"If I'd known there was an historian in the vicinity," he chuckled, "I would have kept my mouth shut. 'Keep your fat lip buttoned around historians,' my mother alway told me. 'They're too smart for you.' "

Indira peered at him suspiciously. "That's a crude attempt at flattery."

He looked surprised. "What do you mean? It's the simple truth. There's no subject on earth as complex and intricate as human history. I get dizzy just thinking about the variables. Makes the double helix look like a tinker-toy! And there's no comparison to that mindless one-two-three the physicists putter around in."

"You're just jealous, Julius," laughed a woman sitting to his left.

Julius' rubbery face twisted into an exaggerated sneer.

"Jealous? Of what, Ruth? The money they shower you plumbers with? Sure. But I wouldn't be a physicist for all the money in the world." He shuddered. "God, think of it! Spend your whole life counting the elementary particles. How many are there, anyway? Bet I can count them all on my fingers."

He began imitating a toddler.

"Dis widdle piggy is da lepton. An' dis widdle piggy is da quark. Dere's *six* a dem! Or is it eight? Such a big number! An' dis widdle piggy—oh, boy, is this fun or what?"

Again, the circle erupted in laughter. When the laughter died down, Julius was watching Indira. For a long few seconds, they stared at each other in silence. Then the great warm smile spread across his face, and Indira felt her heart turn over.

I don't believe this, she thought to herself.

But it was true. Within three days, they were lovers. The weeks which followed, before they reluctantly entered the coldcells, were the happiest of her life.

Her reminiscence was interrupted by a commotion in the village below. No, she reminded herself, looking down into the valley, the "homeheart." She sub-vocalized the owoc hoot, trying, as always, to improve her pronunciation. The sounds produced by the owoc speaking tubes—evolved from ancestral water siphons, Julius had speculated—were very difficult for humans to reproduce. Children, with the plasticity of youth, managed fairly well. But she could only make herself passably understood. Julius never managed at all.

The difficulty was not due simply, nor even primarily, to the difference in sound-producing apparatus. The siphons of the gukuy were generically similar to those of their owoc cousins. But she had no trouble speaking any of the gukuy languages which she had encountered. Gukuy thought-processes, and the languages in which they were expressed, were much closer to the human norm than the strange gestalt-concepts of the owoc.

*That's because the gukuy approach life the way we do. As
a place to establish control, and mastery. A place to manipulate,
to change to our liking. A place to conquer. A place to kill.*

It was mealtime. The humans were gathering at the center of the homeheart, wearing their khaki-colored feeding
scarves. The owoc givers appeared, moving slowly into the
excited crowd of children. The boys and girls surrounded the
huge beings, hooting affection and stroking their mantles. Their
parents—themselves not much older than children—hung back
with greater dignity. Each human held a bowl, made from the
thick outer integument of awato-plants ("oh, hell," Julius had
said, "let's just call it 'bark'"; then he'd muttered something
to the effect that if he ran across Willi Hennig in the after-
life he was a dead duck). The owoc givers began regurtitating
into the great tureens located at the center of the homeheart.
When they were done, each human would scoop a bowlful of
the khaki-colored paste and retire to eat it.

Even after all these years, the sight made her queasy. She
herself ate the childfood, of course. She would die without it.
But she still refused to participate directly in the process. Julius
or one of the children would bring her a bowl, which she would
eat at a distance. Trying to pretend it was lukewarm porridge.
The children had no such compunctions at all. They had never
eaten anything else, and took it for granted. Even their parents
had only the dimmest memories of a life without childfood.

Julius had tried to find a substitute. His search had become
desperate, once it became clear that not all of the humans
could survive on the childfood. His daughter, among them.

But he had failed. Completely.

"Goddammit," he had exclaimed once, "if only Estelle had
survived the crash! She was the biochemist. I'm just a paleontologist. I can tell you why and how I think every form of
life I've seen on this planet evolved, and how they're related
to each other, and where they fit into the ecological zones and
niches. But I can't tell you why we can't eat anything. Except
the childfood."

He rubbed his face wearily. "I know it's a metabolic problem. It has to be. Most of the children seem to thrive on the
childfood, after an initial period of adaptation."

A long silence had followed. She hugged him, knowing he
was feeling the loss of his daughter. Ann had been a plump,

cheerful five-year-old girl, who, when she died in her father's arms only a few months after the crash, had looked like something out of a death camp.

"All the proteins, the amino acids—everything humans need to survive—are out there in that alien biosphere. If they weren't, none of us would still be alive. But there's something about the way they're put together that the human digestive system can't handle. Except that most of the children can survive—survive well, in fact—once the plants have been broken down in the owoc guts."

He rubbed his face again. "But I don't know why. After all this time, all I know is that meat is poisonous and we can only eat vegetation if the owoc process it." A dry, humorless laugh. "And we knew that within two months."

The first two months had been a nightmare, horror piled upon horror.

The confused awakening. Her muddled mind, still sluggish from the long years in coldsleep, had not been able to register much beyond the desperate urgency with which members of the crew had hustled her into one of the landing boats. All she had been able to grasp, as they strapped her into a seat, was that something had gone terribly wrong on the *Magellan*—ironically, at the very end of its immense voyage. An engineering malfunction of some sort, human error—she never knew. And never would. The only thought which had been clear was that Captain Knudsen had ordered all the children placed into the landing boats, along with a few adults. The adults, Indira realized later, had been ruthlessly selected by Knudsen. Those who had skills which the Captain thought would be most useful for survival (*and why me, an historian?* Indira often wondered; until the years brought the answer). The children could thus be saved—or, at least, given the best possible chance—while Captain Knudsen made the desperate attempt to land the *Magellan* itself.

Half-conscious as she was, the shock had registered.

"That's impossible!" she protested.

The face of the crew member strapping her down had been grim.

"It's a long shot," he admitted. "But Knudsen's a great pilot. If anyone can do it, he can."

The *Magellan* had never been designed to land directly on the planet. It was supposed to stay in permanent orbit, while the colonists were shuttled down on the two landing boats. Before he died, the pilot of her landing boat had told her of the *Magellan's* end.

"I swear to God," he hissed, "he almost did it!" He paused, coughed blood. Indira stared helplessly. She had not been hurt, beyond bruises, but she was pinned in the wreckage, her hands fluttering helplessly. There was nothing she could do—and, in any event, the pilot's body was a hopelessly shattered mass of bloody tissue.

"I watched it on the screen," he whispered. "He got through the jetstream—he almost made it! But then—" More coughing blood. "I don't know what happened. It blew up. There was nothing left—just a huge red cloud spread over the ocean."

Finally, in a whisper: "Like—like those old pictures of the *Challenger*." And he died.

Both of the landing boats had crashed. Although they had been designed for planetfall, they were carrying far too much weight—every cubic centimeter, it seemed, had been packed with wailing children. The first boat had landed in the center of a valley atop a huge low mountain, and in fairly good shape. No fatalities, at least. But in his over-riding concern to bring the second boat down near to the first one, its pilot had struck the mountainside, tearing the boat in half.

Indira had suffered little, physically. But the time she had spent—endless hours, it had seemed, although it had only been a few minutes—before she was pried loose were a nightmare.

What had happened to her children?

She had found Juan first. She would not even have known who the mangled little body was, if she hadn't recognized the shirt he was wearing.

But before the tears had barely started to flow, worse horror came. From somewhere outside the broken shell of the landing boat, she heard a piercing shriek.

Ursula!

She raced out of the ship, tripping and falling over pieces of wreckage. Outside, she cast her head wildly about, oblivious to her surroundings, trying to locate her daughter.

Again, the shriek.

"That way!" cried a man, whom she vaguely recognized as

Doctor Koresz, pointing down the slope. He raced off, Indira on his heels. They plunged into some kind of trees (trees? at the time she didn't care), floundering through the thick growth, desperately trying to pinpoint Ursula's location.

The child's shriek had become an unending scream of fear and agony.

Koresz found her first.

"*Oh God!*" he bellowed, lunging forward into a thick patch. A moment later he was hauling Ursula out.

There was a *thing* on her neck. Vaguely like a huge snail. With a cry of fear and rage, Indira grabbed the thing and yanked it off her daughter. The creature came loose, but she had a glimpse of a horrible sharp proboscis, covered with blood, and the terrifying wound on her daughter's neck.

She flung the thing to the ground and grabbed her daughter. Collapsing, cradling her four-year-old girl's body in her arms, weeping hysterically. She was only dimly aware of Koresz stamping the pseudo-snail into pieces.

She had hoped, at first. The wound looked bad, but the girl's carotid artery hadn't been ruptured. And after a minute or so, Ursula stopped screaming.

"Mommy," she'd whispered. And then she became rigid, and died within seconds.

In the time to come, Indira would learn that the creature which killed her child was a kakapoy. Like many of the snail-like predators on the planet, it was an ambusher, lurking high in the clusters of idu thickets. It would drop down on its prey and kill them with a venomous stinger. The venom was not designed to kill Terran life-forms, of course, but it was more than toxic enough to do the job.

The owoc had little fear of them. They simply avoided idu thickets, which were the only habitat of the small predators. But at Indira's insistence, the adults—and then the children, when they were old enough—scoured every idu thicket in the valley, year after year, killing every kapapoy they found.

She still maintained the patrols, even though no kakapoy had been found in the valley for years. Usually the most rational of people, Indira bore an implacable hatred toward the almost-mindless little killers.

She remembered little of what followed. Koresz had carried both her and her daughter's body back to the wreck of the landing boat. At first, she lay there dazed, unable to move, while all around her the few adults rounded up the surviving children. After a time, the sound of children crying roused her into motion. She did what she could, then, along with the others. She helped Koresz as the doctor organized the triage. Except for the unnatural paleness of his face, there was nothing in his demeanor to indicate the torment he must have been feeling. Professional relexes, she remembered thinking vaguely. It was only days later that she learned how Koresz had assigned one of his own sons to the group of dying children, those whose injuries were too severe to be healed. Somehow, the moral strength of that act brought her courage, if not comfort.

Of the rest of that day, she could remember nothing. Only that darkness came, oddly, in a gray and featureless sky.

The next morning, a party from the other landing boat arrived. Julius was with them, and his daughter Ann. The sight of them brought the first ember of restored life back to her soul.

Chapter 6

For Indira, at least, the terrible time which followed was but a pale shadow of the nightmare of the first day. For that reason, perhaps, she became more and more of the central figure in the human colony. Having been already deprived of her own children, she seemed better able than the others to withstand the despair which soon enveloped the colony, when it became obvious that they were doomed to die of starvation.

It had been she who forced the colonists to abandon the landing boats, which were far too cramped, and establish a camp on the hillside nearby. It had been she who organized the search for suitable materials with which to build shelter. It had been she who ordered a halt to all meat-eating, after the first three adults who attempted it died in convulsions. It was then she who organized the systematic experimentation with vegetable food. She used herself as a guinea pig more ruthlessly than anyone, suffering the vomiting and the cramps without complaint.

And while no one died from eating plant life, everyone got sick. Constant nausea became an accepted fact of colony life. Fortunately, only a few of the plants caused diarrhea, which can be so fatal for children, and the colony soon learned to avoid those.

For a while, hope was kindled. Nausea, after all, can be lived with. Only Koresz suspected the truth, from his examination of the colony's fecal waste. Diarrhea, no. But it was obvious to him that most of the "food" was being passed right through without use. Soon enough, it became obvious to everyone that the food was not sustaining them.

The children seemed somewhat more resilient than the adults. That fact, which Indira at first found reassuring, became another source of anxiety.

Who will take care of them when the adults are gone?

And the children were all very young. The oldest was only five. Most of them were three or four years old. That had been the Society's doing. The planning board had concluded, based on obscure psychological reasoning which Indira personally found suspect (but wasn't about to argue with, since she was a beneficiary), that the ideal colonists for the *Magellan*'s expedition would be professional single parents in their mid-thirties with young (but not crib-age) children.

When all seemed lost, the owoc had saved them. The owoc, and the quick mind of Julius Cohen.

The colonists had known the owoc were there, almost from the beginning. The large creatures were impossible to miss. At first the humans had been afraid of the things, because of their size. But, in truth, the creatures seemed very timid. Certainly they never made any threatening motions, and they soon enough began to avoid the humans, staying on the southern side of the valley.

Julius had studied them, for several days. He reported that the creatures seemed to be herbivores, and explained that herbivores are seldom dangerous, so long as they do not feel threatened. Thereafter, the colonists made it a point not to venture onto the southern portion of the valley.

Then a child wandered off, a small boy named Manuel. His absence was not noticed for some time, partly because it was hard to keep track of each individual in the swarm of children, and partly because the adults were now greatly weakened and listless.

Eventually, his absence was noticed. Indira and Julius went in search. The four other adults who were still alive were too weak to do more than watch the children in the camp.

After two hours of scouring the immediate vicinity, they began searching toward the south. After another hour, they heard the faint sounds of a crying child coming from a grove of tall, vaguely fern-like growths. As quickly as their weakened condition permitted, they plunged into the thick foliage. The cries grew louder.

They came to the edge of a small clearing. Through a screen of ferns, they could see one of the herbivores, staring down at the tiny figure of the four year old boy. Manuel was sprawled before the huge creature, crying.

He was wearing, Indira noted absently, a khaki jumpsuit.

She and Julius hesitated, frozen between their fear for the boy and their uncertainty of how to scare away such a formidable-looking beast.

The creature reached down with four of its arms and lifted the boy. It drew him toward its beak. The beak gaped open.

Indecision vanished. Indira and Julius began frantically pushing their way through the last screen of ferns.

Suddenly, a stream of thick paste gushed from the creature's beak. The paste splattered over the child's head and shoulders.

Manuel's wails were extinguished, as a large portion of the paste went into his open mouth. The boy coughed and spluttered.

Indira felt a hand on her shoulder. Then, to her astonishment, Julius forced her to the ground.

"*Stop!*" he hissed.

She stared back at him. Slowly, Julius lowered himself next to her.

"It's not trying to hurt the boy," he whispered urgently. "It's trying to *feed* him."

"*What?*"

"It's *true*. I've watched them—that's exactly how they feed their own young."

She looked back. In truth, the huge creature did not seem to be threatening the boy. It was simply holding him up, watching Manuel with its huge eyes (so uncannily like human eyes, except that they were four times larger).

The expression on the boy's face was almost comical. Utter bewilderment. His face, head and upper body were covered with paste. It was difficult to tell how much, for the color of the paste blended almost perfectly with his clothing.

Manuel's mouth gaped open again. To cry? No one would ever know, because another stream of paste gushed down his throat. He coughed, gagged. And swallowed. And then, while Indira watched in stunned silence, the bewilderment vanished from the child's face. He lifted his head, eyes closed, and opened his mouth once again.

There was no doubt now what emotion was being expressed by the child. *Feed me.*

Another stream of paste.

Indira tried to scramble to her feet.

"It's poison! Animal product!"

Again, Julius forced her down helplessly. (He had the great strength possessed by many large, fat men. Not all that strength had melted with the fat.)

"No! It's not milk, Indira. It's regurgitated vegetation."

"Are you certain?" she demanded.

He nodded. "Positive. This is actually quite a common method used by animals to feed their young. Especially when the food which the animals use is difficult—*oh, my God!*"

Julius was chewing on his upper lip, as he always did when he was pondering a problem. It was a slightly disgusting habit, in Indira's opinion, but she had not tried to break him of it. Her ex-husband had had no obnoxious personal habits; he'd just been a self-centered, unfeeling son-of-a-bitch.

She was still filled with anxiety.

"But—"

"But *what*, Indira? What's the worst thing that can happen to the boy? Die? He's going to die, anyway. Look at him—he seems okay."

And it was true enough. In fact, at that very moment Manuel began laughing, and playing with one of the creature's arms.

Julius frowned. "There's bound to be some of the critter's fluids mixed with it—saliva, digestive juices, that kind of thing. But—not enough, I think, to hurt the kid. It's worth the chance."

Suddenly, she understood the hope that was dawning in her lover's mind.

"You think—?"

He shrugged. "Who knows? It's a long shot, like filling an inside straight. But we're fresh out of full houses. And it's possible, just maybe. The plant life on this planet isn't deadly to us, the way meat is. But there's something in the way it's put together that makes it too tough for our digestive systems to break down. That's exactly the problem lots of young animals face. Evolution has found several solutions. The solution mammals use is mother's milk. This is another."

She made a face. "It's disgusting."

"Not as disgusting as dying."

She shook her head. "Julius, this is still no good. We can't use a helpless four-year-old boy as a guinea pig."

He nodded. "You're right."

And began slowly crawling toward the center of the clearing.

As soon as he broke through the ferns and came into the clearing, he was spotted. The creature pivoted quickly on its two rail-like fleshy "feet." Julius stopped moving. He opened his mouth.

Slowly, the creature lowered the child to the ground. And edged back.

Julius crept forward, his mouth open.

The creature edged back. Its mantle was now rippling with alternating bands of ochre and pinkish-red.

Julius stopped again. He started chewing his upper lip furiously.

The frozen tableau held for a minute, until Julius suddenly grunted.

"*Of course!*" Indira heard him say. Slowly, Julius turned his head back to her. His eyes, for some reason, were feverishly scanning her body.

His rubbery upper lip twisted into a grimace of self-deprecation.

"I am so *stupid*. It's so *obvious*."

Then: "Go back to the camp, Indira. Find something khaki-colored—as close a match as you get to the shade of Manuel's jumpsuit. A cloth of some kind. A *big* one—big enough to cover me, or as much of me as possible."

Her brows were knitted. "I don't un—"

"*Just do it!*"

Uncertainty vanished. As she raced back to the camp, Indira felt like she was floating on air. She had only a vague understanding of what Julius was trying to do, but she was suddenly filled with total confidence in her lover.

And hope. And hope. And hope.

Back at the camp, she ignored all the questions hurled at her. She just cried, over and again— "Manuel's okay, he's okay, he's okay!"—while she rummaged furiously in the broken shell of the lifeboat. Within a minute (which seemed like a hour), she found the khaki canvas she was looking for.

Like an antelope, back to the clearing. Then, at the last curtain of ferns, she screeched to a halt. Knelt, the canvas over her shoulder, and slowly crawled into the clearing.

Julius was still there, now holding Manuel. The boy was asleep. And, to her vast relief, the creature had not moved. It was no longer alone, however. Another had joined it. The two animals were standing side by side, staring. Their hides, she noticed, were still mottled with ochre. But the pinkish-reds had faded considerably.

She hoped she knew what that meant.

A look of relief washed over Julius' face when he saw her enter the clearing. He extended his hand.

"Toss it to me."

She shook her head, and kept crawling toward him. Once at his side, she unfolded the canvas and draped it over both of them.

They knelt there, clasping each other, facing the monsters, their mouths open.

After a time, they saw the pinkish-red fade from the hides, replaced by thin wavering stripes of green. After a time, they saw the green grow into solid bands—still against ochre—and the creatures approach. And the beaks slowly open.

Khaki life washed over them.

Remembering that day, Indira flipped back through the pages of the notebook, looking for the entry.

I should had gotten it immediately. I knew the creatures were chromatophoric. It must be the principal method by which they communicate (outside of the hoots), although I suspect that there's a lot expressed in the way they curl their tentacles. (No—the proper word is "arm." "Tentacles" are those specialized arms that squids develop, the long ones that end in palps. Tentacles are arms specialized for mobile hunters, and these critters ain't hunters of any kind.)

Nice, shy, friendly, giant octopi.

Octopus-heads, I should say.

Okay. Just in case this notebook should someday fall into the hands of an expedition come to our rescue—about a thousand years from now, I estimate—let's try to describe these beautiful nightmares. I don't want to draw down the curses of the historian, like those dopes in Roanoke who didn't keep any diaries. No, sirree. Worst cussers in the universe, historians. I know. I'm in love with one.

Here goes:

Imagine a body shaped like the thorax of a lobster. About the size of a buffalo. Except that a lobster's thorax is the carapace of an arthropod—hard and rigid. The carapace of these creatures is more like the mantle of a squid, without the flukes. That's it. Mantles. They must have evolved from something like squids.

But a squid's mantle is too soft to serve for a land creature. These mantles are much tougher. Cartilaginous inside, I suspect. Squids on earth still have a vestige of a shell inside their mantles. I suspect that on this planet the "molluscs" evolved something that serves the same purpose as a skeleton. Any large terrestrial animal has to have some kind of hard structure to support its weight. Probably pieces of shell-like material, linked together by a network of cartilage and muscle. Terrestrial analogies can be thought of. Some of the dinosaurs maintained rigid tails in a similar way. (Okay. Loosely similar. Give me a break.)

I can't be sure, of course, without dissecting one of them. (Oh boy. I mutter that in my sleep, Indira might cut my throat.)

(Come to think of it, I might cut my own throat.)

The body of the creature is enclosed by the mantle. A hard, but not totally inflexible, carapace. A thick integument covers the mantle. The integument becomes especially thick and hard (almost like soft horn), at the front of the mantle. What I've decided to call the "cowl."

I call it that because the front edge of the mantle looms over and protects the head below. Necessary, I suspect, because the head of this critter has no skull. But we'll get to the head later.

How does this thing get around? Well, here's where the molluscan Bauplan shows its possibilities. I'd love to know what the ancestor looked like. Just when you think it must have been a pseudo-cephalopod, you look at this thing's feet.

A two-legged gastropod. I kid you not. They're not "legs," of course. Not the slightest resemblance. Instead, the creature's peds are like fleshy—what can I call them? The closest analogy I can think of is pontoons. Except pontoons are rigid, and these peds are semi-segmented, like lumpy treads. Again, without cutting them open (down, boy, down) there's no way to be sure—but I'd bet that there's a complicated structure in there. Something like what must exist inside the mantle: a network of "shell"-slivers, cartilage, and muscle.

Lots of muscle. These beasties are strong. The entire body is held up, about fifty centimeters off the ground, by the two rail-feet. (Yeck. Let's stick with "peds.") It's a clumsy-looking method of locomotion, but—

But nothing. It is clumsy. And slow. It's a marvel that a "molluscan" Bauplan could provide enough flexibility for these things to evolve into land animals. Let's not ask for miracles on top of that. The simple fact is that the vertebrate structure is vastly superior to that of the—what do I call this phylum? Panzerpoda? God, no; ain't the slightest resemblance between these sweet creatures and the Wehrmacht!

I'll figure out what to call them later. To get back to the subject, measured by any standard of speed and mobility, vertebrates have it all over these creatures. That's not chauvinism, it's just a fact. From everything I can see—not just these creatures, but all the life-forms I've seen—humans are at least twice as fast as anything that moves on Ishtar. And we're slow, compared to most big warm-blooded vertebrates.

(Oh, yeah, before I forget. The critters are warm-blooded. The genuine article, too—homeothermic, endothermic, and tachymetabolic. I admit I can't prove the last, because I don't have the equipment to precisely analyze their metabolism. But I'm positive about the homeothermy and the endothermy.)

Back to the point. Compared to the dominant large-bodied terrestrial phylum on this planet (whatever we wind up calling it), vertebrates are:

a) Much faster.

b) More mobile, by a large margin.

Score one for the home team. (Visiting team, I should say.)

BUT—any football team that had one of these guys for a fullback would be invincible. Here's how the game goes:

Kickoff. Ball goes into the end zone. Start on the twenty. Hand off to Slow-But-Sure. Three minutes later—one play, mind you—Slow-But-Sure racks up six points. Guaran-teed. And introduces the world to a new culinary delight: linebacker pancake.

I kid you not. I can't imagine being able to knock one of these things down. I'm not sure a rhinoceros could do it.

And they're quicker than you might think. Their reflexes don't seem to be any slower than ours. It's just that their basic structure is so much more limiting than that of vertebrates.

Okay. Let's get to the best part. The head.

The head itself looks—

Oh God, Thy Name is Convergence.

—like an octopus. Almost to a T. Bulging "brow" (only here that's for real—more on that later), two gorgeous eyes (almost human looking, except they're the size of saucer-plates, and the iris takes up more of the eyeball), and a beak for a mouth surrounded by eight tentacles (OK—arms).

There are some differences from octopi, of course. (If there weren't, I'd give up my profession and start spinning prayer wheels.) The eyes are located on the front of the head rather than the sides, giving them binocular vision. And everything seems harder and tougher than on an octopus. The skin, the features, everything. Inevitable. The exact pathway and method was different, but no creature I can imagine could make the transition from marine life to terrestrial life without developing a watertight outer membrane. It's fine for octopi in the ocean deep to have soft, slimy skins. Try that on land and you'll dessicate.

Then, the arms are only generically octopoid. There are at least two obvious differences, one of which is major. First, the minor difference: No suckers. None. Not a trace. Instead—the major difference:

They've got fingers. Sort of. The arms brachiate, more than three-quarters of the way down their length (which, by the way, I estimate at an average of seventy centimeters). The tips of the arms consist of two mini-"tentacles," which have the following chief features:

1) They're flexible, like tentacles; not segmentedly rigid, like fingers.

2) They're flattened—unlike the arms above the branch, which are more or less tubular. (Think of thick fleshy spatulas, about fifteen centimeters long.)

3) The inner surface of the "fingers" consists of a roughened pad, useful for gripping, which makes perfect sense because—you guessed it; give the man a prize—

4) The "fingers" are opposed.

Yup. The critters can manipulate. (So to speak. We'll stretch the Latin.)

A faint glimmer of a possibility is coming to life somewhere deep in the recesses of your mind, is it not?

Yes.

Yesyesyesyesyesyesyesyesyesyesyesyesyesyes.

They're intelligent.

Not intelligent like in: "Isn't he just the smartest little dog?"

No. Intelligent.

Like in: Critter sapiens.

Chapter 7

Even Indira had been doubtful. The other adults were totally unconvinced.

"I tell you, they're *intelligent*," insisted Julius. It was five days after the discovery of what they would eventually know as "childfood." The adults of the colony were sitting around the campfire where they made a habit of gathering every night, after the children were asleep. This night, and for two nights past, the sound of hungry weeping was mercifully absent.

It wasn't much of a fire. They had found no substance on the planet which burned well. Dry wood, or its equivalent, did not seem to exist. On the lush, verdant world of Ishtar, everything seemed to be full of succulence. When vegetation died, it never had time to dry before it was consumed by "mosses" and what looked for all the world like toadstools. (The resemblance was not superficial—the colonists had discovered early on that the pseudo-mushrooms were highly toxic.)

The mosses, when "ripe," burned the best. But it was impossible to sit in the pungent fumes without gagging, so the colonists were forced to move constantly about the fire as the soft winds in the mountain valley shifted.

"That's nonsense, Julius!" expounded Dr. Francis Adams. (He insisted on the title. Indira thought it typical of the man, whom she considered a pompous ass. To her, "doctors" were people who healed people. Adams had a Ph.D. in physics.)

Privately, she thought Adams was right. But her dislike for the man drove her to speak.

"You can't say that. I'm not sure if Julius is right, but you have to admit that it's striking how these creatures have come to understand our needs."

Adams waved a dismissive hand. "Means nothing. Pure instinct. Julius already explained that these things are chromatophoric. They react to colors as indications of emotions and needs. Khaki just happens to be the color of hunger. That's what tipped Julius off—he saw that the child's clothing was almost the same color as the one which the creatures' young turn when they want to be fed."

He made it sound as if Julius had finally figured out that two plus two makes four. Indira clenched her teeth. She had no doubt that if Adams had been the one to have discovered Manuel, he would have been paralyzed both in mind and body.

"Pure instinct. Not uncommon, you know. Newly-hatched fowl will imprint on humans, if that's the first thing they see, and—"

Julius interrupted. "That's nonsense!"

He overrode Adams' splutter of protest.

"Look, folks, I know you've all heard stories about the marvelous power of blind instinct. And there's certainly a lot of truth to many of those stories. *But instinct is not magic.* It does not derive from some supernatural power. Every instinctive behavior on the part of an animal is the product of its evolutionary history.

"It's true, there are many examples in natural history of instincts being short-circuited. Adams mentioned one. I can give you a better example. Cuckoos lay their eggs in the nests of other birds. When the cuckoos hatch—they're big chicks—they expel the rightful hatchlings out of the nest. The parent birds instinctively feed whatever chick is in the nest, and ignore anything outside of it. So the cuckoos get to eat, while the legitimate heirs die of hunger.

"But the reason the cuckoo's stratagem works is because it fits so perfectly into the life cycle of the other birds. The parent birds are *expecting* a hungry chick to feed. *There*—in the nest. *At that time*. The cuckoo hatchling bears a reasonably close physical resemblance to their own chicks, and it's at the right place and at the right time, acting the right way. So it gets fed.

"None of those criteria apply to this situation. These—will somebody think up a name, for Chrissake?"

"Lobsterpusses," proposed Hector Quintero, the pilot of the first landing boat.

Julius glared at him.

"You will burn in the fires of eternal damnation," he predicted.

"How about 'land-squids'?" suggested Janet Mbateng, the chemist.

"Never mind!" Julius exclaimed, throwing up his hands in disgust. "I should know better. *I* will name the critters, drawing upon my vast store of professional learning."

He winced. "Even though, in so doing, I will bring down upon my head the most ancient and feared curse known to Man."

"What's that, Julius?" asked Hector.

" 'Hell hath no fury like an amateur scorned.' "

When the laughter died down, Julius sat erect in a magisterial pose, his index finger pointed to the sky.

"I pronounce these critters—*Maiatherium manuelii*. We can call them 'maia' for short."

"What does it mean?" asked Indira.

"Manuel's good mother beasts."

She had liked the name, as had the others. (Adams had snorted, but even he adopted the name within two days.)

Still, Julius was unable to convince them of his thesis. As much as the colonists had confidence in him, there just seemed too many facts about the maia which pointed in the opposite direction.

First and foremost, the maia used no tools. None. Even Julius was forced to admit, after carefully studying them for weeks, that he had not observed even a temporary use of casual tools, such as chimpazees exhibit when they dig for ants with a stick.

Second, there was the placidity of the creatures. No one for years had believed in the preposterous concept that humanity evolved from "killer apes." Dart's thesis—popularized by Ardrey—had been exploded two centuries earlier, when more careful study had shown that the australopithecenes were prey rather than predator. But still, it was difficult to imagine a species evolving into intelligence without *some* instinct for aggression. And, for all their size and strength, the maia exhibited not a trace of belligerence.

Adams had explained the phenomenon, in his inimitable style, as being due to the fact that they were herbivores.

Julius was no longer even pretending to hold Adams in anything but contempt.

"Is that so, *Doctor* Adams. Tell me something—are you a big game hunter?"

"Certainly not!"

"Didn't think so. Neither am I. But I know my natural history. Are you aware, *Doctor* Adams, which of the earth's great animals was most feared and respected by the old big game hunters?"

Adams sniffed. "The tiger, I suppose."

Julius sneered. "No, *Doctor* Adams. The Cape buffalo. A pure vegetarian."

"Is that a fact, Julius?" asked Hector with interest.

The sneer was replaced with a smile. Julius liked Hector. The pilot's skills were utterly useless now, but the young Mexican had proved to be an energetic and resourceful member of the colony.

"Absolutely. It's one of the great myths, this idea that you can directly derive a creature's temperament from its diet. Absolute nonsense! 'Carnivores are mean and nasty, herbivores are sweet and kind.'" He said the words in a childish singsong.

"You ever seen a bullfight, Hector?"

"Hey, c'mon, Julius. We don't have bullfights in Mexico anymore. Haven't had for almost a hundred years. Believe it or not, we've even given up human sacrifice."

Julius grinned. "I know, Hector. But don't lie to me. I'm sure you've seen videos. I have. One of the cruelest pastimes our species ever invented, but you can't deny it's fascinating."

Hector nodded.

"Okay. Does a bull eat meat? Nope. Would that make you feel any better, climbing into the *corrida* with just a cape and a sticker?"

"Hell, no!"

"Me neither."

Indira had interjected herself into the discussion.

"But those fighting bulls were *bred* that way, Julius."

The biologist shrugged. "True. So what? You can't make a silk purse out of a sow's ear. Evolution isn't magic. The potentiality has to be there in the first place. The fighting bulls of Spain were the product of a breeding program, true. But the program wouldn't have succeeded if bulls didn't have a capacity for violent aggression in the first place."

He poked the smoldering moss with a stiff reed, stirring it back into sluggish flame.

"What I wouldn't give for a cord of pine," he muttered. "Hell, I'd settle for a bagel. Burn better'n this crap."

Laying the reed down, he continued.

"It's true down the line, folks. Carnivores are aggressive in a particular way because they have to be to survive. But they have no monopoly on the trait."

"I agree," said Adams firmly. "It is well known that human beings are the most aggressive animals known, and we are omnivores."

Julius couldn't resist.

"We are, are we? Tell me something, *Doctor* Adams. You're close to forty years old, I estimate. When was the last time you got in a fist fight?"

"I have *never* been involved in a violent altercation."

"No kidding? Boy, what a sheltered life you must have had. I myself got into several fights when I was a teenager. How 'bout you, Hector? You come from the land of *machismo*. Bet you've been in more fights than you can remember."

Hector grinned. He enjoyed helping Julius bait the *Doctor*.

"You ain't gonna believe it, Julius, but I don't think I've been in a fight since I was fifteen. My brother."

Julius nodded. "I'm not surprised. It's probably the oldest myth of all, this idea that humans are filled with instinctive violence and aggression. Pure bullshit. We are probably the most *peaceful* species among the mammals."

He smiled, observing the looks of disbelief around the campfire.

"Sorry, folks. It's true. The fact is that the vast majority of human beings go through their entire lives without being involved in violence. Other than a mild experience as adolescents. Hell, most people nowadays don't even personally *witness* an act of violence. Whereas the vast majority of mammals— even *rabbits*, believe it or not—routinely commit acts of physical aggression against fellow members of their species. Human beings, on the other hand, are the most social of all animals. Cooperation, not conflict, has been the key behavioral pattern in our evolution."

"But Julius," protested Janet, "think of all the wars we've fought—all through history. Well, not for the last fifty years or so, I admit, but before then it seems like there was never a time when we weren't fighting a war. Someplace."

"Yeah, Julius," added Hector. "I hate to say it, man, but the old *barrios* were a rough place to live."

"I don't deny that human beings have a *capacity* for violence," he responded. "And when that capacity is triggered off—for social reasons, not biological ones—the violence which results is appalling because of our intelligence and our technological capability." A laugh. "I always got a kick out of those old horror movies. You know—Godzilla tramples Tokyo. What a lot of crap. If Godzilla had ever really wandered into Tokyo, there would have been a new item on restaurant menus the very next day. Godzilla soup."

He pointed a finger at Adams. "There's one thing I do agree with the *Doctor* about, however. It is, indeed, true that we are omnivores. But does *that* explain anything about our history? Human beings are omnivores, therefore—therefore what? Therefore the Inquisition? And the conquistadores? Therefore St. Francis of Assisi?"

He snorted. "Therefore *nada*. Zilch. When I say the name 'Inuit,' does that bring visions of slavering killers to your minds?"

People shook their heads.

"And yet they were an almost purely meat-eating people. The most carnivorous culture ever produced by the human race. Necessary, of course—not too many rice paddies in the Arctic. Now, let me turn the question around: who, in your estimation, was the most murderous single human being our species every produced?"

A brief, animated discussion followed. Various candidates were nominated, but within a short time agreement was reached.

Julius nodded. "Yeah. Adolf Hitler. A vegetarian."

Indira spoke up.

"I'm puzzled by something, Julius. If I understand you correctly, what you're saying is that the reason the maia are feeding us has nothing to do with instinct. Right?"

Julius nodded.

"Then why *are* they doing it? It's not as if there's anything in it for them. They give to us, without getting anything in return. How do you explain that?"

"I don't know, Indira. I'm just a biologist. I've reached the limit of my understanding. These creatures are not animals. You can't explain their behavior by pointing to their biology. I know the rest of you aren't convinced of that, but it's true. What that means is that they are feeding us because of something in their *culture*."

Years later, she could still remember the intensity of his stare.

"So *you* figure it out. You're the historian."

Eight months after that discussion, a maia died. And Julius finally won the argument.

The humans had begun mixing freely with the maia since they began eating the "childfood." (Which Julius persisted in calling upchucksalad, or pukewurst, or barfburger—to the vast irritation of Indira and the other adults.) The maia had seemed edgy around the adult humans, at first, even though they continued to feed them. Then Julius ordered everyone to start wearing as much green-colored clothing as they could find. From studying the creatures, he had concluded that green was the color of tranquillity—and love, he suspected. Thereafter, the maia seemed to relax around the adult humans.

Adams argued that their behavior stemmed from pure chromatophoric instinct. Julius insisted that the reason the color green calmed the maia was because the creatures realized that the humans *understood* what it meant.

"I don't think the maia are actually all *that* intelligent," he'd said to Indira in private later. "Sapient, yes; bright, no. Like austrolopithecenes. No, more than that—say, roughly equivalent to *Homo habilis*, or maybe even *Homo erectus*. But they're sure a lot smarter than *the Doctor*. At least they understand that *we're* intelligent."

The children, once they got over an initial hesitation, fell in love with the maia. Like giant, walking teddy bears. At first, the adult humans grew nervous at the sight of swarms of children romping around the maia—especially after crawling *under* a maia became a popular game. But it soon became obvious that the creatures were conscious of the childrens' actions. The maia never harmed a human child, not even inadvertantly. And they never seemed to become irritated at the children's antics—even after the children invented a new game, which they called "ride-the-maia."

The day came when Indira saw a maia pick up a child and gently place the girl on the cowl of its mantle. And she wondered.

Then the day came when Joseph Adekunle, the son of the *Magellan's* electronics officer, came running to her.

She watched him approach with fondness. She would never admit it to anyone (for she maintained a public stance of being an impartial mother who loved all her children equally), but the truth was that Joseph was one of her favorites. He was one of the oldest children in the colony (six, now), and big for his age. Big, and extraordinarily athletic. Only Jens Knudsen, among the boys, and Ludmilla Rozkowski, among the girls, came near to him in physical prowess. But Joseph never abused his strength, never acted the bully, never boasted or bragged. To the contrary. He was invariably helpful to the smaller children. And on two occasions that Indira knew of, when Joseph had witnessed a larger child abuse a smaller, the boy had taken the perpetrator aside and quietly informed him that if he thought he was such hot stuff Joseph would be glad to prove him wrong. He was a charismatic figure, even at the age of six, and he had become, almost as if it were a law of nature, the central figure in the children's generation.

He was also—it was obvious to Indira, even at his age—extraordinarily intelligent.

You would have been so proud of him, Susan, thought Indira, as she watched the boy race across the valley floor and begin climbing the hillside toward the camp. She remembered the electronics officer of the *Magellan*, with some sadness, but not much. It had been over a year since the disaster. She had even finally been able to stop grieving for her own children.

She had not known Susan Adekunle well, but on the few occasions when they had met she had taken an immediate liking to her. It was impossible not to. The Yoruba woman had been invariably witty and cheerful, in her inimitable big and booming style.

Big. Susan Adekunle had been at least six feet tall, and not at all slender.

And judging from the evidence, thought Susan, *Joseph's father must have been even bigger.*

The boy was now halfway up the hillside.

He certainly inherited his mother's color.

Joseph's skin color was something of a rarity in the modern age, after two centuries of unparalleled war and migration (and then, blessedly, a world at peace for the first time in millenia) had thoroughly mixed up the human gene pool. The majority of the human species had blended into various shades of brown, usually accompanied by dark hair and, more often than not, at least a trace of epicanthic fold to the eyes.

Joseph, on the other hand, is going to look like an ancient Ashanti king when he grows up.

Among the children in the colony, only Jens Knudsen and Karin Schmidt exhibited the same kind of extreme racial differentiation. They were by no means the only white children in the colony, but they were the only two who would grow up looking like Nordic stereotypes—yellow hair, bright blue eyes, skin as white as milk.

Indira's idle musings vanished as Joseph came near. Tears, she suddenly realized, were pouring from the boy's eyes.

She rose to her feet hastily.

"What's the matter?"

"There's something wrong with one of the maia!" cried Joseph. "With Wolugo!"

She had time, before she started hurrying down the hillside, to wonder at Joseph's use of the name "Wolugo." Since they began playing with the maia, the children had begun imitating the creatures' hoots. Over time, they became adept at producing the strange sounds. They even began mixing maia hoots into their own conversations.

The children began insisting that the hooting was a language. Excited, Julius had immediately experimented with his own attempts at hooting. But he had given up, after a few days, in total frustration.

"There's no way I can do it," he'd grumbled to Indira. "I had a hard enough time with Spanish, and if that hooting's a language it's totally unlike any language on Earth. Although I think it's tonal, like Chinese."

Then, snarling: "And if I have to listen to one more snotty little brat make fun of me, I'll commit mass infanticide."

Indira's interest had been aroused. She herself, unlike Julius, had an extraordinary aptitude for languages. She was fluent in seven, including all four of the global tongues (English, Spanish, Arabic and Chinese), and could make her way fairly well in a number of others.

But when she tried learning "hoot," she hit a brick wall. It did, in fact, remind her in a certain way of Chinese. (A very vague, generic, way.) But she couldn't wrap her mind around any *concepts*. More than once, she felt she was on the edge of grasping the inner logic of the hoots. But, always, the moment slipped away.

In the end, she gave up. Had she been certain that the hoots were really a conscious language, she would have persevered to her last breath. But she was still not convinced that Julius was right.

The children, on the other hand, for all that they had teased Julius' hopeless attempts at hooting, often expressed the opinion that—at least on the subject of the maia—Julius was the only adult in the colony who had any brains.

And for the past three months, the children had started referring to individual maia with proper names.

Even as she ran through the valley alongside Joseph, Indira could not help but smile at the memory of a conversation between the boy and Francis Adams the previous month.

Joseph had casually referred to one of the maia as "Yuloc." Adams had smiled, in his condescending way, and remarked:

"Is that what you've decided to call it?"

Joseph had given the man a look which belied his years. "Yuloc's not an 'it.' She's a *she*—like almost all of the maia are. And *I* didn't give her the name. It's her own."

Then:

"People don't decide what to call other people. You call them by their *own* names."

"Is that so?" mocked Adams.

The next words, coming from a six-year-old, had astonished her.

"Yes, *Francis*, it is."

Adams shot to his feet like a rocket.

"You will call me *Doctor Adams*, young man!"

Joseph had said nothing. He had simply stared back, and up, at the man looming over him. Without a trace of fear or cringing, his face filled with a dignity she would never have imagined possible in a boy that age.

Gasping for breath, she and Joseph reached the spot in the valley where the boy was leading her. As she drew near, she saw that a large number of maia, and what looked like every child in the colony, were clustered near a grove of tubular, fleshy plants. She recognized the plants. They were the favorite food of the maia. The humans had called it "sortasaguaro," until, beginning a few months earlier, the children had started calling it "oruc," insisting that that was the proper name for the plant according to the maia. Julius immediately adopted the name, with the other adults eventually following suit.

She edged her way through the throng. At the center, she came upon a pitiable tableau. One of the maia had collapsed. The creature was lying on its side, hooting softly. Indira immediately knew the position was unnatural. She had never seen a maia lying on its side before. When the creatures slept, they simply lowered themselves straight to the ground.

Brown tones rippled through the mantles of the maia observing the scene. If the children were to be believed—and the scene she was watching gave strong support to their opinion—brown was the color of misery. The stricken maia herself was also dappled with brown hues, although the predominant color was ochre. Then, as Indira watched, the ochre faded. A few brown stripes continued to move slowly across the maia's mantle, but now green rapidly appeared and spread.

The maia surrounding the scene began hooting. There seemed, somehow, a questioning tone to the hoots.

The stricken maia herself had stopped hooting. Suddenly, to Indira's astonishment, the color of her mantle deepened— first to dark green, and then to midnight black. She had never seen that color on a maia before.

As if it were a signal, three of the maia moved to the fallen one's side. Using their cowls like great shovels, they levered the creature upright. Two other maia moved forward, one on each side of the stricken one, and leaned into her. Then, most of her weight being carried by the two helpers—

No, realized Indira suddenly, *pall-bearers*.

—the trio began making their slow way north. Everyone followed, maia and human, the maia softly hooting and the children sobbing.

On the way, they met Julius and Korecz, who had come to see what the commotion was about. The biologist and the doctor fell in with Indira.

"What—" Julius started to say, but fell silent at the sight of Indira's sharply upthrust hand.

Slowly, the procession made its way north, until they arrived at a grove of striking green plants, twisting vine-like things that curled and wove into each other like an enormous free-standing ball of spaghetti. The color of the stricken maia's mantle, Indira noted, was now very close to that of the vine-plants.

The "bearers" gently set the stricken maia—

Wolugo, thought Indira fiercely. *Her name is Wolugo*.

—down to the ground. Then, they edged back. Silence followed, for minutes. Wolugo was motionless, except for a faint movement of the fleshy flaps deep within the recesses of her mantle cavity, back of the octopoid head. Julius had often speculated that these were the inhaling orifices for some kind of lungs (or their equivalent).

The rest of the colony's adults arrived at the scene during the course of that long wait. Adams was the last to appear. The metallurgist examined the scene for a moment, then said loudly:

"Yes, of course. The elephant's graveyard."

Indira was shocked at the expression which flooded Julius' face. For a brief moment, she thought the biologist was actually going to strike the man with his fist.

She was even more shocked when she discovered that she was hoping he would.

But the moment passed.

Not long after, Wolugo died. Indira had no doubt of the moment. Deep within the mantle cavity, she could see the maia's flaps stop moving. And, in the space of but a few seconds, all color fade from her mantle, until there was nothing but gray. It seemed, to Indira, the dullest gray she had ever seen.

She found herself fighting back tears. When she realized

what she was doing, she stopped fighting, and let the tears flow freely. All the humans, adult and children alike (except Adams), were doing likewise. And she saw that, across the mantles of the living maia, stately waves of brown and green were slowly moving.

A few minutes later, the maia began behaving strangely. Several of the maia left, heading back toward the oruc grove. One of those remaining began a peculiar movement on a patch of soil next to the vines—a kind of slow side-to-side two-step, dragging its peds.

After a minute or so, Indira saw that two mounds of earth were slowly piling up on either side of the patch.

Understanding struck her like a bolt of lightning. Her mouth agape, she turned to Julius.

But Julius was not there. He was already striding up the slope of the mountainside, heading toward the shell of the shattered landing boat. The place where the colony stored its tools.

Not long after, she saw him return. He was carrying a shovel in each of his hands. And over his shoulder were draped strips of various types of cloth and fabric. Green fabric. Brown fabric.

He smiled at her crookedly, but said nothing. He made a gesture to Koresz with one of the shovels. Koresz took the shovel without hesitation. And the doctor did not have to be told to drape strips of colored fabric over his shoulders.

That done, the two men advanced slowly onto the patch of cleared soil, facing the maia who was creating it.

The maia stopped, stared. Ochre bands were added to its coloration. Julius made shoo-ing motions with his hands, which, to a human, would have signaled: "Move back."

When he saw that the maia wasn't moving, Julius sighed heavily.

"Ever play football?" he asked Koresz.

"Please! I am not a barbarian."

"Well, rookie, lend me a shoulder anyway."

So saying, Julius stooped and lowered his upper body until his shoulder was butted gently against the cowl of the maia. Koresz, uncertainly, followed suit.

Then, slowly but with as much strength as he could muster, Julius attempted to push the creature back.

It might have moved an inch. Maybe. But the hoot which it emitted carried a clear tone of surprise.

Julius straightened up, grimacing, rubbing his lower back.

"As I feared," he muttered. "It's like trying to block Lawrence Taylor."

"Who?" asked Koresz.

"An ancient legend from the dawn of time, Vladimir, whose name is known only to barbarians like me who happen to be the few football fans left on Earth in these effete modern days. A hero, from the Golden Past. A demi-god. Think of Hercules, or Theseus. Or both rolled into one. Sorta like that."

He stared at the maia, chewing his upper lip.

"I guess we'll just have to try to dig around—"

Suddenly, the maia edged back until it was clear of the patch.

"Well. Thank you. Took you long enough, dimbulb."

He started digging. He and Koresz.

It took a long time to dig a grave big enough to accommodate the body of Wolugo, especially since Julius insisted on what he called "the regulation six feet." Indira, when she took her turn with the shovel (all the adult humans took a turn in the grave, even Adams—although he only lasted fifteen minutes), suggested to Julius that the maia were probably accustomed to shallow graves. But Julius had been unmoved.

"Yeah, probably so. But I finally found something that humans can do for them that they can't do very well for themselves, and I'm not about to do a slipshod job of it."

Despite her aching muscles, she found herself suddenly in agreement with his point of view.

By the time they were finished, it was late in the day. Indira was not surprised to see that, while the humans had dug the grave, the maia had been gathering clumps of oruc.

Food, to sustain the dead in their voyage.

Nor was she surprised to see that Joseph had organized the children to provide their own gifts. And so it was that when the body of the maia Wolugo was lowered into her grave, she was accompanied not only by clumps of oruc but by strips of cloth, small tools (whose use she would not have understood), toys, trinkets, and several of the small bowls that the colonists had made to eat the maia-food.

It was those last gifts, more than anything else, which brought tears to Indira's eyes.

Bowls. So that the gentle giant, if she encountered starving children in the afterworld, could once again give life to the dead.

The next day, Indira left the human camp and went to live with the maia. She remained there for months, refusing all contact with adult humans (even Julius; but he was not hurt, because he understood), and refusing to speak to the children if they used any Terran language.

When she returned, the adults gathered about the evening campfire. Her first words were simply:

"The name 'maia' is wrong. They are called *owoc*."

When she told Joseph, he nodded, and corrected her pronunciation.

Interlude: *Nukurren*

For Nukurren, the first two days after her capture were a blur. She recovered consciousness briefly, at several intervals. But beyond a vague awareness of Dhowifa, she recognized nothing before lapsing again into darkness.

Then, just after dawn on what she would learn was the third day since the massacre of the caravan, she awoke clear-headed. Very, very weak. But clear-headed.

The first thing she saw, out of her good eye, was Dhowifa. He was nestled under her cowl. From his closed eyes, and the way his beak and arms twitched, she thought he was dreaming.

"You're so cute when you're asleep," she whispered softly.

His eyes popped open, glaring at her balefully.

"I am *not* asleep. I'm *thinking*."

She began a retort to the effect that, the last time she remembered, he was as mindless as a snail. But the look of love in the curl of his arms, and the green hues which rippled across his mantle, stopped the words in her sac.

"Where are we?" she asked. Then, feeling a strange motion, she looked around.

She could only see to one side, but she saw that she and Dhowifa were being carried on a litter held by two of the hunnakaku. They seemed to be part of a caravan of demons and hunnakaku, climbing a trail on the side of a mountain. On the slopes above, she could see three demons stick-pedding alongside.

Those strange peds are very effective in rough terrain, she thought. Then, seeing the shades of brown in their skins: *But why are they so miserable?*

Her attention was drawn by another demon, who was stick-pedding alongside the litter. The demon was very large. Not as tall as the demonlord, but heavier. Nukurren was mostly struck by its color. The demon's skin was almost pure white, under the strange yellow armor which covered the top of its head and the rear of its upper torso.

That armor looks too soft to be much good. And this seems a strange time and place to be consumed by passion.

She voiced the last thought aloud. Hearing the sound, the demon looked down at her. The bright blue color of its eyes made her instinctively tighten her muscles. Only pure fury could turn a gukuy's eyes that color. But the creature did not seem enraged, and the tension brought pain to her ravaged body. She slowly relaxed.

"I don't think their emotions show on their mantles," said Dhowifa softly. "I have been watching them for days. They all looked the same to me, at first, except the big one. The terrible one who hurt you so badly. But now I can tell them apart, and their colors never change. Most of them are brown-colored, of one shade or another. But there is this big one"—he whistled amusement— "who looks like it's in perpetual heat. Some of the others are like that, although none is as white as this one. And there is the other big demon, who is always pure black. *Nobody* can be that implacable. Not even that monster."

"The demonlord."

Dhowifa glowed ochre.

"I am not sure they are demons, Nukurren."

Nukurren started to whistle amusement, but the rippling in her sac caused a wave of pain.

"And what do you know about demons?"

Exquisite turquoise—irritation, leavened by affection—rippled across Dhowifa.

"Would demons be friends with hunnakaku?" he demanded.

Nukurren pondered the question.

"It does seem unlikely," she admitted.

"And there's more, Nukurren. The—demons, whatever they are—you won't believe this, but I've seen it with my own eyes. *They eat the hunnakaku ogoto.* In fact, as far as I can tell, that's all they ever eat."

Nukurren was stunned into silence. "Ogoto" was the

Anshaku word. The Kiktu called it "putoru." The hunnakaku themselves, in their own language, called it "childfood."

Gukuy spawn only lived on ogoto when they were newly born. Within a few eightdays, they were able to feed on soft meat. But the tough plants which were the exclusive diet of hunnakaku were much too difficult for the young sub-gukuy to chew and digest. So they lived on childfood—the regurgitated contents of the adults' stomachs—for years. Until they were half-grown.

"Are you saying these monsters are *children?*"

"I'm not sure, Nukurren. It would seem so—but if there's one thing I've decided, these past two days, it's that there are too many peculiar things about these—demons—to jump to any conclusions. But I'm sure I'm right about the ogoto. For one thing, there are seven hunnakaku in this party. They freed the four who were in the cages, but where did the other three come from? They must have brought the hunnakaku with them. Why would they do that if not for the ogoto? Hunnakaku can't fight."

A sharp pain stabbed through Nukurren's ruined eye. She reached up an arm, felt a strange *thing* covering it.

To her surprise, Dhowifa pulled her arm away.

"Don't touch that!" he cried.

"What is it?"

"I don't know. Some kind of thing made of plants." He hesitated. "One of the demons put it there. On the first day. It put similar ones on your other wounds. I tried to pull the things off, of course, because I thought it was trying to poison you. But it wouldn't let me, and it's much stronger than I am. Then, it got this other one—" Dhowifa gestured toward the large white demon who was still stick-pedding alongside the litter "—to talk to me. It speaks Kiktu. I don't understand Kiktu as well as you do, and it's got a horrible accent, but as near as I can make out, it was telling me that the things will help you heal. And I noticed that it's wearing one too. I think it's one of the ones you injured."

Nukurren looked again at the white demon. On one of its upper—tentacles? no, they were jointed like its peds—its upper limbs, a large poultice was strapped.

"So I decided to leave them there," continued Dhowifa. "I think you should leave them alone."

He doesn't understand, Nukurren realized. *Oh, Dhowifa, now I must cause you more pain. But better that than to lie.*

"It doesn't matter, dear one," she said softly. "I am going to die, anyway."

She started to explain about the diseases which mantle-rupturing wounds always brought in their train. Dhowifa, the poor emotional little thing, tried to interrupt, but Nukurren plowed on. Better that he should face the truth now than to live in the fairy-tale world that truemales preferred.

Suddenly, to her astonishment, the truemale started slapping her with his arms.

"Will you shut up for a moment—you, you clamhead!"

Nukurren stared at him. The azure irritation which suffused Dhowifa's mantle was not, this time, mottled by any affectionate traces of green.

"I know about those diseases," said the truemale angrily. "Do you think I haven't been filled with anguish, worrying about it? Self-righteous fool. Snail!"

He took a deep breath.

"But this big white demon says—well, at least, I think that's what it's been trying to tell me—that you can be healed. When we get to where we're going."

"And where's that?"

Orange surprise. "Didn't you see it? We've already started up the slopes."

He stretched out a tentacle, pointing up and ahead.

"The Chiton."

Nukurren twisted, looked where he was pointing. The sight was awesome.

"We're going *there*? Why?"

"Because that's where the demons live. Or come from, I'm not quite sure. That's where the ones live who it says can heal you."

After a short silence, Dhowifa added:

"And, if I understand it, that's where the one lives who will decide what to do with us."

"And who is that?" She felt dread at the answer.

"The Mother of Demons."

Suddenly, a voice spoke in Kiktu: "How do you feel?"

Swiveling her remaining eye, Nukurren saw that it was the large white demon who had spoken. Its Kiktu was crude, and, as Dhowifa had said, the accent was horrible—harsh, and sibilant. But Nukurren had no difficulty understanding it.

"Better," she replied. "Very weak, but my brain is clear." She gestured at the demon's injured limb.

"And you?"

The demon flexed its limb—its right limb, Nukurren saw—and examined it.

"It will heal," replied the monster. "But it is painful. You almost tore it off."

For a moment, Nukurren and the demon stared at each other in silence. The bright blue color of its eyes was distracting. Despite Dhowifa's opinion, Nukurren automatically reacted to that color as if she were facing an enraged enemy. But, in truth, the whiteness of its hide never showed the slightest trace of blue fury. And, though the demon's shape and posture was like nothing Nukurren had ever seen, not even in her worst nightmares, there seemed something—

A memory came to her suddenly. Long ago, shortly after Dhowifa and she had sought refuge among the Kiktu, a young Kiktu warrior had challenged her to single combat. The cause, according to the warrior—Kokokda was her name—was her outrage at Nukurren's sexual perversity. But that had been a mere pretext, Nukurren knew. The truth was that the young warrior could not resist the challenge of fighting such a fearsome-looking gukuy, especially one who was reputed to have been a great Anshac warrior.

The combat had been swift and brutal. Kokokda had been quite good, very fast and strong, but much too full of bravado and incaution. It had not taken Nukurren long to leave the young Kiktu dazed and bleeding on the ground, even though she had been handicapped by the need not to kill or cripple her opponent. (It would have been tactless to slaughter Kokokda, given that Nukurren and Dhowifa were seeking sanctuary among her tribe.)

Days later, after recovering sufficiently from her wounds, Kokokda had entered the yurt occupied by Nukurren and Dhowifa. For a long moment, she had stood there, saying nothing. At first, Nukurren had thought Kokokda was seeking to renew the conflict, until, from the subtleties of color and posture, she realized that the young Kiktu was simply seeking to acknowledge a worthy foe and, in the confused way of youth, to gain her victor's respect.

Diplomacy had worked well then, and, Nukurren decided, would possibly work now also, even with a demon.

"You fought well," she said to the white demon.

"I fought like a fool," came the instant reply. "I'm lucky to be alive. I wouldn't be if you hadn't been outnumbered."

It was the simple truth, of course, but Nukurren tried again to flatter the demon with reassurances of its awesome prowess and skill. She had not gotten far into her peroration when the monster's—beak?—gaped wide and began emitting ghastly noises, like a swamp haktu barking in heat.

"I think that's the way the demons whistle when they think something's funny," whispered Dhowifa. Nukurren swiveled her eye back to examine her lover. Her arms made the gesture of skepticism. Ochre uncertainty rippled across Dhowifa's mantle.

"Well, I'm not *sure* of it, but I think so. As I told you, I've been watching them. They do it a lot."

Nukurren gazed back at the demon. The monster had ceased the hideous barking noises, but Nukurren saw that its— yes, she decided, it *is* a beak—was still gaping open. Within, on the top and bottom both, were a row of strange little white—stones?

"You are the biggest and ugliest gukuy I ever saw," announced the demon. Nukurren heard Dhowifa's hiss of displeasure at the insult to his beloved, but Nukurren shared none of it. Truth, after all, was the truth. Nukurren was the biggest and ugliest gukuy *she* had ever met.

"And you are also the biggest liar." A short, sudden burst of barking. "I fought like a stupid young fool, and that's the simple truth." More barking, very brief.

"Do not be offended. I'm the biggest and ugliest"—here came a word Nukurren couldn't quite grasp— "that I know. I'm not the quickest, but I'm the strongest. I rely too much on it." (A word, again, which Nukurren couldn't make out, but she thought it was a name) "is always warning me that my overconfidence is going to get me killed." The demon flexed its injured limb, and a strange *crunching* motion seemed to briefly flit across the features of its bizarre face. "And sure enough, it almost did."

A long silence followed. Nukurren tried to think of something to say, but she was feeling very weak and her mind was becoming foggy again.

"You were very brave," said the demon suddenly. Then, a moment later, its harsh accent somehow even harsher: "Why are you a slaver?"

"I am not," Nukurren replied.

"You were with them, and you fought for them."

"That is true. I was hired by the caravan master as her bodyguard. I did not like the work, but it was all I could find for Dhowifa and myself."

"Why?"

Nukurren hesitated, then, too tired and weak to think of a clever answer, responded with the blunt truth: "We are perverts." She heard Dhowifa hiss with displeasure, but ignored him. "We are despised and outcast because of it," she continued stolidly.

Again, the features on the monster's face *crunched*, although it seemed to Nukurren, in some way too subtle for her to grasp clearly, that it crunched differently. She heard Dhowifa whisper: "I think that weird thing it does with its face is the way demons gesture." Nukurren decided Dhowifa was probably correct. Other than the colors of their mantles, gukuy used their arms to express sentiments and attitudes. But the faces of the demons were armless.

The demon spoke. "I do not understand that word you used." Here the monster fumbled with the term, trying to reproduce it.

"Pervert," said Nukurren slowly and clearly. Dhowifa hissed again. "I am too tired to lie, dear one," said Nukurren softly.

"What does that word mean?" demanded the demon.

Nukurren explained, briefly and bluntly. Dhowifa was hissing like a kettle.

After hearing Nukurren's explanation, the monster fell silent. Nukurren examined it closely, but could see no indication of its attitude.

I think Dhowifa's right. Their—mantles?—never change color.

Suddenly, the monster moved away quickly, stick-pedding ahead toward the front of the caravan. Soon thereafter, a few loud and sharp commands were uttered in some utterly strange language and the caravan came to a halt. Moments later, Nukurren saw a number of demons approaching the litter. At the forefront was the white demon and—she felt Dhowifa flinch at her side—the demonlord. Black as night, implacable.

Seeing them side by side, Nukurren saw that the white demon was larger than the black one. Not quite as tall, but wider and more massive. The other demons—there were a total of eight in the approaching party—were considerably smaller. Four of them seemed to be flushed brown with misery. The remaining two were colored a very light brown, almost white, but not the same pale hue as the biggest demon. And as they came nearer, Nukurren suddenly realized that the strange attachments on top of their heads which she had thought to be soft armor were some kind of natural growths.

Parasites? she wondered. *Some kind of skinny worms? No, that doesn't make sense. They must be part of their bodies.*

The color of the growths varied, she saw. The growths on top of the big white demon were pale yellow, very bright. One of the other whitish demons also had yellow head growths, although the color was much darker, almost ochre. The growths on the remaining demons was dark brown, except for that on the heads of the demonlord and one other. Their growths were pure black. And there was something different about the shape of the demonlord's head growths—like thousands of tiny slender worms, also, but worms which were tightly coiled.

The eight demons drew alongside Nukurren's litter. Now that she could see them together, standing still in clear daylight, Nukurren saw that there were other subtle differences between the demons as well. The body shapes of three of them were somehow different, and the front of their mantles, under the light armor which covered them, seemed misshapen.

"Tell him what you told me," commanded the white demon, gesturing to the demonlord.

"Him?" thought Nukurren, astonished. *This monster was a* male?

Not possible. The white demon's Kiktu must be worse than I thought.

But then, again: "Tell him."

Could it be?

"Are you a *male?*" Nukurren blurted to the demonlord.

All the demons began that horrible barking noise. Nukurren

decided that Dhowifa was right—they were laughing. She was relieved to see that the demonlord was laughing also, and, when the barking ceased, that its—his—beak was gaping open, with those peculiar little stones exposed. The stones in his beak, she was interested to note, were every bit as white as the ones in the white demon's beak.

Yes, Dhowifa's right. And that must be their gesture of amusement.

The gesture seemed even more pronounced on the part of the white demon, and then, as if the creature could read her mind, the demon said:

"This"—it gaped its beak wider— "is our gesture of amusement. We call it a—" Here came a bizarre word.

"*Gurinu?*" asked Nukurren.

"Close enough," replied the white demon. "And I am also a male. These"—here the demon pointed to the three whose body shapes Nukurren had thought to be somehow different— "are female."

One of the three females stepped forward. She was light brown in color. Her eyes, like the black demon and one other, were very dark brown, almost black. Her head growths, like those of the demonlord, were also pure black, although hers were very straight and long. Now that she was close, Nukurren could see that her head growths were tied back behind her head by a cord. She was almost as tall as the black and white demons, although much less massive, especially in her upper mantle.

The female demon reached up with her tentacles—upper limbs, rather—and untied the cords which bound together the strips of lacquered yopo stems which made up her body armor. She drew the armor aside, and Nukurren could see that beneath, protruding from the light brown skin of her mantle, were two bizarre, soft-looking growths. Looking over at the male demons, Nukurren saw that no such growths protruded from their mantles.

"There are other differences," said the female demon, in a voice which, though harsh, was much lighter in tone than that of the male demons. Her Kiktu was better than that of the black and white demons, with a less pronounced accent.

The female demon retied her armor. "But we won't get into that now. Or else we'll waste half the day while" (here came a strange word, which Nukurren was sure was a name) "shows off."

All the demons except the big white one began barking loudly. The big white one, to Nukurren's amazement, suddenly changed color. It was a subtle change, but there was no mistaking it—the monster was turning pink!

Apprehension? wondered Nukurren. *That doesn't make sense.*

It made even less sense when the white demon's beak slowly began to gape wide open, in the gesture of amusement.

He's embarrassed, Nukurren suddenly realized. *But, I think, not displeased.*

The white demon spoke again: "Tell him what you told me."

To the demonlord, Nukurren repeated the explanation for her presence, and Dhowifa's, among the slavers.

For a moment, the demonlord was silent. Then he made a peculiar jerking motion with his head and turned away. He said something to the white demon in the strange-sounding demon language, and began rapidly stick-pedding away, barking out commands. Moments later the caravan was in motion again. All of the demons left the vicinity of the litter, except the big white one and the female one who had stripped away her armor.

"I think you just saved your life," said the white demon softly. (Here a strange word, but Nukurren was sure it was the name of the demonlord) "was beginning to have second thoughts about not killing you immediately when we captured you. Now he won't."

Dhowifa began to speak, but Nukurren cut him off.

"Why not?"

The white demon did something odd with its mantle, as if quickly raising and lowering its upper torso—where its cowl would be if it had one.

"You were not entirely with the slavers by choice. He hates slavers. We all do. And besides, he's curious."

"About us?"

"Yes."

Dhowifa now spoke, very softly, in his broken Kiktu. "You is—are, not by us, offended?"

"Offended?" asked the white demon. "Because you are"—he struggled with the unfamiliar word— "perverts?"

Dhowifa made the gesture of assent, and it was obvious to Nukurren that the demon understood the meaning of the arm-curls.

Again, the two demons gaped wide their beaks.

"It means nothing to us," said the female one. She moved closer to the white demon, and reached out one of her limbs. Then, with the odd little stick-tentacles at its tip, she began slowly caressing the back of the male demon's head, under the long, soft, bright yellow head-growths.

"My name is"—here she spoke slowly, carefully enunciating— "Ludumilaroshokavashiki, and this is Dzhenushkunutushen. We have often been lovers. More and more often, now, in preference to others." Her beak gaped. "Soon I think he will ask me to be his mate, if he can muster the courage."

The male demon's white hide was again suffused with pink.

"And what will you say?" asked Nukurren.

"I will say 'yes,'" replied the female demon, very softly.

Nukurren stared at the big white demon, Dzhenushkunutushen. The demon stared back at her.

And suddenly, uncertainly, deep within a monster's eyes, eyes the color of insensate blue fury, Nukurren caught a glimpse of something she had never thought to find in her bleak and lonely existence.

Chapter 8

Once the survival of the colony was assured, Indira had begun looking toward the future. Just a few days after the discovery of the maia-food, she had proposed, and the five other surviving adults had agreed, to begin a school for the children. They were faced with the fact that the technological base which they had always assumed would be the underpinning of the colony was almost gone. One of the landing boats was a wreck, not good for much beyond storage and scrap metal. The equipment on the other boat was still functioning (other than the engines, which were almost out of the complex synthetic chemical which they used for fuel). But Hector pointed out that the batteries which powered the equipment would soon be inoperative.

"They're nuclear batteries!" protested Adams.

Hector shook his head. "No they ain't, Doctor. Sorry. They're just little temporary units, designed to be recharged on a regular basis on the *Magellan*."

Adams began a vigorous denunciation of the incompetence of the expedition's planners, but Julius cut him off.

"Stow it, *Doctor* Adams! It's water under the bridge. Spilt milk. Let's get on with the business at hand."

Adams glared at the biologist, but he kept his mouth shut. Julius continued:

"The way I see it, we've got to completely put out of our minds any illusions that we can maintain an advanced technological culture. We've got to face the facts. Every single piece of advanced equipment on the boat—the computers, for instance—presupposes a whole technological support base that just doesn't exist anymore. The problem with the batteries is just the tip of the iceberg."

A sidelong glare at Adams.

"I happen to know how the temporary batteries in the lifeboats were chosen. Everybody on the planning board wanted nuclear batteries. But nuclear batteries are big, and there was nothing as valuable as space. So the decision was made to have nuclear batteries on the mother ship alone, and use small temporary batteries on the lifeboats. It's easy to sneer at that decision now. But it was the logical decision to make at the time.

"We're going to find the same thing is true over and over again. The minute any single component of any of the remaining equipment breaks down, that's it. There aren't any replacement parts, and we've got no way to make them. Even if we knew how, which we don't."

A shrug. "It's one of the prices we pay for having such a technologically advanced culture. We're all specialists, by and large. Take me, for example. I know how to *use* the equipment in a biological lab. But I don't know how to make it. I don't even fully understand how most of it works. The same's true for all of us."

He smiled. "Except Indira. The historian's profession hasn't changed much over the last five thousand years."

"So what do you propose, Julius?" asked Janet. "Specifically."

"I propose that we concentrate on teaching the children the essential tools of survival—physical and cultural. Reading and writing. Basic mathematics. Basic medicine. Shelter, and clothing. But most of all, we've got to teach them—which means that we've got to learn it ourselves, since none of us is a farmer—basic agriculture."

"That's nonsense!" expostulated Adams. "We can't eat the plants. And we don't need to, anyway—we've got the maia."

Julius stared at Adams in silence for over a minute. Indira started to speak, thought better of it. Everyone else apparently shared her reticence.

Finally, Julius spoke again.

"Do you believe in magic, *Doctor* Adams?"

"Of course not! And let me say that I find that remark highly—"

"Just shut up!" bellowed the biologist. It was the first time any of them had ever heard Julius raise his voice. All of them, including Adams, were shocked into silence.

Julius glared around the campfire.

"Let me explain something to you, people." He pointed to the south. "The maia are not your fairy godmothers. It doesn't matter whether you think they're animals or sapient beings. If they're animals, they're in ecological balance with their habitat. And if they're sapient, as I believe them to be, they're at the most primitive possible cultural level. *Do you understand what that means?"*

Silence.

"It means they don't have a surplus. They live on the edge of economic survival. Every ounce of regurgitated food which they provide us is an ounce which they don't have for themselves—or their own young. As it is, we're lucky that they don't have more than a handful of youngsters themselves. How many ounces—no, *tons*—of food are we going to be demanding from them? *Where's it supposed to come from?* The maia don't grow anything. They forage. There's only so much forage in this valley, and it's obvious to me that there's not enough when you add us into the equation.

"So—to get back to your point, *Doctor* Adams—while it's true that we don't need to learn how to cultivate plants for ourselves, we had damn well better learn how to do it for them. *Or we're going to die."*

He fell silent, still glaring. After a moment, Koresz spoke.

"I believe Julius' point is irrefutable." The doctor smiled crookedly. "If we are to survive, we shall have to adopt toward the maia the classic slogan of the Vulcans. 'Live long, and prosper.'"

Indira took charge, then, proposing a concrete division of labor.

Basic education in literacy and mathematics: Herself and Francis Adams.

Agriculture: Julius, with Hector as his assistant.

("What's this shit?" Hector demanded. "I fly almost twelve light years so I can become a *bracero?*" But he was grinning when he said it.)

Housing, clothing and dyeing: Janet Mbateng.

Medicine: Vladimir Koresz, with Janet as his assistant.

❖   ❖   ❖

Two weeks later, Julius added another basic skill to the list: weapons-maker.

"*What?*" demanded Indira. "Whatever for? We've seen nothing threatening to us in the valley except for a few small predators. We can handle those with shovels."

The expression on the biologist's face was somber.

"Indira, as part of my job I've been systematically studying the maia. I've gotten to know all of them. In fact, I've catalogued them in my notebook."

"So?"

"So two of them are *scarred*. Big scars, too. On their mantles."

Indira had noticed scars on one of the maia herself, but hadn't really thought much about it.

"An accident—"

"Not a chance." Julius was vigorously shaking his head. "They're not lacerations, such as might be caused by a fall. The maia never leave level ground, anyway. They're *puncture* wounds, Indira. Caused by some kind of tooth, or claw, or something."

Indira's face was pale. Julius smiled, in his lopsided way, and stroked her cheek.

"Sorry, sweetheart. There's trouble in paradise."

The other adults—except Hector—were skeptical. But Julius insisted, and Hector was released from his former duties in order to design and construct weapons. The pilot was not unpleased at the change.

"Hey, I've gone from field hand to head of the military-industrial complex at one fell swoop." He shrugged modestly. "It's a small step for a man, but it's a giant step for *La Raza*."

Then, more seriously:

"But, hey, Julius—it's a weetle bit hard to figure out what kind of weapons we need when I've got no idea what we're going to be using them against. What are we talking about here? Giant snakes? Super-snails? The creature from the black lagoon?"

Julius squatted and began chewing his upper lip.

"Let me try to apply my biological expertise, such as it is. As far as I've been able to tell, just about all the terrestrial animals on this planet fall into two basic phyla—pseudo-molluscs and pseudo-worms."

He waved his hand. "Yeah, yeah, sure, the worms are probably divided into umpteen different phyla, like they are on Earth. Who cares? A worm is a worm is a worm is a worm. Most boring critters ever made. A moving hose—food goes in one end, crap comes out the other."

He spit on the ground. "So fuck the worms."

More lip-chewing.

"As far as the molluscs go, based on what I've seen so far I've tentatively broken them down into six classes: the pseudo-snails, the pseudo—oh, screw the pseudo business!—there's snails, there's these things that are like land-clams, there's the whole chiton group, there's a pile of slugs, there's those bizarre little brachiating critters that have no equivalent on Earth except (so help me!) primitive primates, and there's the maia. The Ishtarian equivalent of cephalopods."

"There's also those weird floating things, like balloons. I've seen a few of them pass overhead."

"Yeah, I forgot about them. I'm dying for one of them to land in the valley so I can cut it open. At a guess, they're probably a whole separate phylum. Something roughly like what we used to call coelenterates. But they're all small. And they don't seem to have much capability for directed movement. From a distance, at least, it looks like they're just drifting with the breeze. I can't imagine them being dangerous—at least, not to something the size of a maia."

"So what's your conclusion?"

"It has to be something relatively similar to a maia. In the same general class, at least. Unless there's a phylum or a mollusc class I haven't seen—which is always possible, mind you; we've only seen a tiny portion of Ishtar's surface—it has to be a quasi-cephalopod of some type. Or types."

"You sure?"

Julius shrugged. "No, I'm not. But it's a hell of a good bet. If analogies to Earth mean anything, the cephalopods were the only large, fast-moving, advanced predators produce by the molluscs. By any of the invertebrate phyla, as a matter of fact. Well, there were the eurypterids, but I've never agreed with those people who think the eurypterids were—"

"Julius!"

"Huh? Oh. Sorry. Old habits die hard. All right, Hector,

to cut to the chase—yeah, I'm almost sure it has to be something like the maia. More or less, you understand."

The look Hector gave him was not filled with admiration.

"'More or less' doesn't cut it, Julius. We're talking *mano-a-mano* here, not horseshoes."

Julius threw up his hands with exasperation.

"So I'm not a genius!" He blew out a deep breath. "All right, Hector. Try to imagine a mean, bad-tempered maia. With some kind of long tentacles instead of short arms. The tentacles will have some kind of cutting or stabbing tip—something like a horn, maybe."

"Are they going to be bigger or smaller than the maia?"

Julius pondered the question.

"Hard to say. Among invertebrates, predators are usually bigger than their prey. The same's generally true for marine predators, including vertebrates. But the rule doesn't always hold up with advanced land forms. Quite a few mammalian predators are smaller than their prey."

"That'd be a break."

Julius gave him a sidelong glance. "Not necessarily, amigo. Predators who are smaller than their prey usually hunt in packs."

Hector rolled his eyes. "That's great. Just great."

Julius was chewing his lip fiercely.

"But whether they're bigger or smaller than the maia, the predators will almost certainly be faster. Course, that's not saying much. That'll be one of our big advantages, by the way. I can't be positive, but I'm almost certain that human beings will be able to run a lot faster than anything on Ishtar."

He pointed a finger at Hector. "*But*—don't assume that because we can run faster that our reflexes are any faster. These predators can probably move their tentacles as fast as we can move our arms. Hell, even the maia can move their arms pretty quickly when they want to."

"Yeah, I know. I saw one of the kids fall off a maia's cowl the other day. Damned if the maia didn't catch her before she hit the ground."

The pilot scratched his chin thoughtfully.

"Weelll. I'd kinda been thinking in terms of swords, but—"

"No! Swords would be almost useless. If you tried to use

it as a chopping weapon, you'd be trying to cut through that godawful tough mantle. Take hours. Unless you were *El Cid* or something, which we ain't. Same problem with axes. Look, Hector—there's one really vulnerable part on the body of a cephalopod: the head. Unless these critters are completely different from Terran cephalopods, which is possible but there's no way to tell for sure without cutting open—"

"Don't even think it, Julius."

"—I'm surrounded by saints! The point is, they don't have skulls. There's nothing protecting the brain except a mass of flesh. Which is probably thinnest right between the eyes."

"Well, you can use a sword to stab. Especially something like an epee."

Julius goggled. "You want to play *matador* with something that looks like a walking version of *It Came From Beneath the Sea?* Such a hero! Such *cojones!* Such a fucking moron!"

The pilot laughed. "All right, already!"

"*Spears*, Hector. We want *spears*. Something we can stab straight in with, while keeping a distance."

"Sounds good. What kind of spear, do you think?"

"You're asking me?" demanded Julius. "When we've got Indira? Who's spent a lifetime studying the wicked ways of times gone by, when men were men and didn't suffer fools gladly."

Indira proved a reluctant consultant, but Hector was finally able to get from her what he needed.

"It's basically an *assegai*," he explained to Julius four days later, showing him the spear he had made. "The blade's heavy, shaped like a narrow leaf, about forty centimeters long. It'll stab real good, and you can still chop with it if you have to. But instead of a short handle, like a real *assegai*, I put a long one on it. What do you think?"

The weapon was certainly ferocious-looking, thought Julius.

"I see you made the handle out of 'sortabamboo.' What's the blade made out of?"

"Steel. It's a piece of the battery shield."

"Why'd you use that? There can't be much of it. Why not use that stuff the boat's hull is made out of?"

"How many lifetimes you got? That's stuff's a weird alloy made out of titanium and God knows what else. Ask Adams, he could probably tell you. All I know is that they have to use special tooling in factories to work with it."

When asked, Adams confirmed that the metal of boat hulls was useless for anything except shelter and storage.

"Most refractory metal known to man. Titanium, basically, but—"

He began what would have been a long and arcane lecture on the process by which the metal was made, but Julius cut him short.

"Never mind, never mind. I'll take your word for it. That leaves us with a problem. We've only got enough of the shielding, and stuff like that, to make a few hundred steel spears."

"Then what's the problem? There are only a handful of us to begin with."

Julius restrained himself. "Some day, *Doctor* Adams, the children will grow up. And then they will have children. And then—do you get the drift?"

"I still don't see the problem. We'll simply have to find some iron ore and make our own metal."

A supercilious sniff. "You *do* know what iron ore looks like, don't you?"

Julius sighed heavily. "Of course I know what it looks like. Paleontologists are just specialized geologists, basically. But I have no idea how you make steel—or even iron—out of hematite. Do you?"

Needless to say, he didn't. Nor did Indira.

"But I'll tell you one thing," she said. "It's not easy. In fact, Julius, I wouldn't even think about it. Try to make bronze, if you can find copper and tin."

He frowned. "How do you know iron's hard to make?"

"Because it was invented so rarely in history. The only case that's certain is the Hittites. Many historians think that the Hittites were the *only* people who ever actually invented iron—everybody else got it through cultural diffusion. Personally, I think there's a strong case for an independent discovery in West Africa, and the Chinese—"

"For God's sake! Does everybody in this place have to play professor?"

She chuckled. "Sorry. The point is that bronze, unlike iron, was independently invented any number of times in human history. So it must be fairly easy to do."

Later, Hector commented: "Hey, Julius, you'd think all you

super-educated types would know how to do something as basic as make iron."

"Au contraire, mon ami. Our super-education's the problem. Did you ever read Jules Verne's *Mysterious Island*?"

Hector shook his head.

"Well, it's about a small group of men who wind up on a desert island in the middle of the 19th century. Without anything except a couple of matches and a pocket watch. But one of them's an engineer, and over the next few years he invents *everything*. From scratch."

Julius frowned. "Actually, I've always suspected that Verne was stretching the possibilities. But it's barely plausible. And you know why? Because the hero was a *19th century* engineer. A basic kind of guy, you might say. Whereas we——" He sighed. "As useless a bunch of over-educated specialists as you could ask for."

He glared at Hector. "That includes you, pal. Don't give me any of this simple-Sam-the-sailor-man routine. What do *you* know how to do? Besides fly spacecraft? Now, there's a useful skill in the stone age!"

Julius searched, but he found no hematite. Nor did he find any copper. Nor tin. Eventually, however, he found bronze. But he did not have to invent it, for it had already been invented on Ishtar. Any number of times.

Luckily, the discovery of bronze did not come for many years. Years in which the colony slowly settled into a stable and symbiotic existence with the owoc. Symbiotic, not parasitic. For although he was never able to invent metallurgy, the biologist was able to invent agriculture.

Julius had initially concentrated on domesticating the succulent oruc, whose leaves were the favorite food of the owoc. But he met with little success, for he soon discovered that it was a finicky plant. It would only grow in soil patches with just the right composition, and, try as he might, he was unable to reproduce the composition elsewhere in the valley.

Eventually, he concentrated on a bushy plant which looked vaguely like a soft-bodied manzanita (if such a thing can be imagined), which he had seen the owoc browse upon. Here, he met with almost immediate success. The plants were rare in the valley itself, although they were profuse on the hillsides. Since the owoc were poorly equipped by nature to climb hills, they only fed on those occasional bushes which grew at the fringes of the valley floor.

When he transplanted the upunu (as the owoc called it) to the valley floor, the plants flourished. For three weeks, before they began dying off rapidly.

The cause was obvious: each plant was infested with several softball-sized snails. They were a type of snail which was common enough in the valley, but was never seen on the hillsides.

The owoc called the snails "uduwo." But Julius put his linguistic foot down. He called them "cossacks," and that was the name they used when he led a horde of eager children, armed with spears, to wreak havoc upon the snails. They began by killing all the snails in the upunu field, and then scoured the rest of the valley. After two days, they came upon a swarming nest in the far north end of the valley. Julius pronounced the nest the root of all evil, whereupon the children gleefully committed mass gastropodicide.

Thenceforth, Julius would refer to the slaughter as The Day Kishinev Was Avenged, a phrase the children happily adopted without having the faintest idea what it meant. Indira knew, of course, but she chose not to enlighten them.

Within a year, large swathes of the valley floor were covered with upunu fields. The owoc took to the fields without hesitation, and upunu soon became the staple of their diet. It was noted, however, that they continued to browse on the oruc. Adams analyzed this behavior with sage remarks regarding trace elements and essential dietary supplements. Julius did not publicly disagree, for the possibility could not be discounted. Privately, however, he suspected the owoc had a sweet tooth.

Three years later, within a space of just weeks, the valley floor was suddenly covered with tiny little owoc, and Julius cursed himself for a fool.

It was not that he was concerned about overpopulation. It quickly became evident—to the distress of the human adults and the absolute horror of the children—that the initial flood of baby owoc would rapidly ebb. For the tiny creatures died in droves.

Died from disease, many of them; many more fell prey to snails and other small predators.

No, he was concerned about the emotional state of the human children. For they were utterly unable to comprehend the reaction of the owoc to the massacre of their babies.

The reaction was—nothing. In an offhand way, the owoc fed the swarm of tiny creatures. Not individually, as they did with the small number of owoc tots in the valley (if the word "tot" can be applied to a creature about the size of a black bear), but *en masse*. Adult owoc would periodically regurgitate great piles of food on the ground, which would rapidly be surrounded by owoc babies. (And then, within minutes, by predators.) But other than that, the owoc ignored their offspring as if they didn't even exist. Time and again, boys and girls would bring owoc babies, cupped in their hands, to the adults. Begging them to shelter the babies and protect them. The adult owoc would simply stare, apparently dumbfounded, and then amble away.

Joseph finally cornered an owoc, and spoke with her for an hour.

When the conversation was over, he came to Julius and said, fighting tears:

"She says—it's not very clear to me—but I thinks she's saying that the babies die because they have to. She says it's part of the Coil of Beauty."

"I know, Joseph," replied Julius sadly. He reached out an arm and hugged the boy. "She's right, you know. It's the way it has to be, with the owoc. It seems unnatural to humans, because we're K-strategists. But the owoc aren't. They're r-strategists."

Joseph demanded to know what that meant, and Julius explained it to him. The boy did not understand all of it, but he understood enough. That night, after asking the adults not to attend, Joseph called a meeting of all the children. (It was the first time the boy ever assumed that mantle of authority among the younger generation; it would not be the last.) He explained, in his own terms, what Julius had taught him. The children discussed the matter thoroughly, for hours, with a seriousness and gravity far beyond what one would expect of nine and ten year-olds. At the end, they were satisfied (if not happy). But Julius noted that each child took an owoc baby as a personal pet, and kept it free from harm.

He was upset at the situation himself, of course, as were all of the adult humans. But, for he alone, the emotion of unhappiness was offset by another.

Awe, and wonder.

I would have sworn (he wrote in his notebook) *that no intelligent species could evolve using the r-strategy. Prejudice, pure prejudice. We humans have always been Earth's quint-essential K-strategists, so naturally we assume that the repro-ductive strategy of producing a few (only one, usually, in our case) offspring—and then lavishing care upon them—is the inevitable method for the higher forms of life. It's not just* homo sapiens, *after all—most of the mammals follow the same strat-egy, even if they don't take it to the same extremes that we do.*

But the invertebrates have always been r-strategists. The hell with protecting a few kids. Just have a few thousand. Sure, most of them will get it in the neck. So what? A few will make it. Everything evens out in the end.

The owoc don't follow a pure r-strategy, of course. There's always been a handful of youngsters, ever since we arrived, and they take care of them well enough. That's one of the reasons I assumed, without thinking about it, that they were K-strategists. I'm willing to bet that as the babies get older— the few of them that survive—a critical point will be reached when different instincts kick in.

He was right. A year later, the surviving owoc babies be-gan to hoot, and it was as if the eyes of the adult owoc suddenly *focused* on them. They were very surprised, though— according to the human children, who were still the only ones who could readily understand the hoots—at how *many* young owoc there were. In fact, the adult owoc seemed utterly bewildered. The reason for the surplus, of course, was the human children. Julius estimated that 90% of the surviving babies were the ones the children had taken in as pets. But, bewildered or not, the adult owoc began taking care of their young. And there was no shortage of food, because of the upunu fields. There was even an unexpected side benefit, noted Julius with amusement. The human children, who had previ-ously complained bitterly about "field-work" and used every excuse to avoid it, were now the most assiduous of cultivators.

Of course, if I hadn't been so preoccupied with the immediate necessities of life in the colony, I would have been able to spend my time doing what I'd like to do, which is—hey, once a prof, always a prof—research. (Yum yum.) Which I've been doing, finally, this past few weeks. And made some discoveries.

The big news?

The owocs are social animals. Not social, as in: "Let's throw a party!" No, social, as in: bees; or ants.

I kid you not. All this time I thought the owoc were more or less like us. You know, boys and girls. Differences, of course. The sexual dimorphism among the owoc makes the miniscule differences between human males and females positively subatomic. The males are tiny, compared to the females. Tiny, and weak. At least, the bodies are. The heads are quite well developed. Much smaller, compared to those of the females. But I'm willing to bet that if you plotted the comparative brain sizes of the males and females against their relative body sizes, you'd find that they are just about identical on the EQ scale. So the two sexes are probably of equivalent intelligence. But other than that, the males are a shadow of the females, like super-runts. Hell, most of the time I see one of the few males (oh, yeah—note: males are only 6.25% of the population, by exact count) they're riding inside the females—nestled in the anterior mantle cavity, next to the head. Cozy as can be— even got a cowl over their heads to keep off the semi-constant drizzle.

(Time out for complaint: Is there ever any sunshine on this misbegotten planet? Day after day, the same solid light-gray sky. Makes Seattle look like Miami.)

Back to the ranch. The peculiar "riding" position of the males inside the females is so common that I'm even beginning to think it explains the (relatively) much longer arms of the males. Although that might be one of those "Just So Stories" kind of explanations. I can see where the males would enjoy it well enough—beats working—but I can't really see where there's any adaptive advantage to—Julius Cohen. Julius Cohen. Reproductive organs, dummy. That's why the male arms are so long. So they can reach way down deep inside the female's mantle, where the good stuff is. Talk about convergence! That's how male octopi transmit their sperm to the female—one of the arms is specially designed to carry sperm packets from the male sex organ to the female's. (If I remember right, that arm's called a hectocotylus.) More logical system than we have, when you think about it. Why waste valuable biotic energy growing a separate penis when you can do double duty with an arm?

OK. But why are all the arms long? If the owoc parallel the octopi, only one of the arms is adapted as a sexual organ. The others are just arms. So why are they all the same length?

Bingo. That's just the way the genetic switches work with the owoc. The regulatory DNA (or whatever equivalent exists on Ishtar—and would I love to know!—but I'm willing to bet that it's the same trusty old adenine, guanine, cytosine and thymine, or at least three out of four of them) has all eight arms linked. You want just one of them long? Sorry, ma'am. Only comes in the economy eight-pack.

Anyway. To get back to the point, I always knew there were males and females. What I didn't know is that there are also mothers.

I just thought Kupu, the female who hardly ever moves out of that one little oruc grove, was the owoc equivalent of the fat lady in the circus.

Turns out the reason she's four times as big as all the other females is because she isn't really a female at all, she's a "mother." This distinction seems bizarre to humans, because for us "female-ness" and "mother-ness" are almost identical. But among the owoc, they're practically a different sex.

No, that's not the best way to put it. Makes it seems like there's three sexes. And there aren't. There's only two—female and male. But the females come in variants. Female and mother.

Why not female (meaning mother) and "neuter." Because it slides around the question. What's a "neuter," after all? It's either a neutered something—male or female—or it's some kind of bizarre sex-that-isn't-a-sex.

Fie on it. Let's stick to the ABCs of biology. In all sexed species, the female is the fundamental sex. Gotta have females. Males—the thought grieves my chauvinist heart, but facts, as the man says, are stubborn things—are unnecessary. Oh, sure, lots of species use males to reproduce. (Including mine, praise the Lord.) But they can be done away with, if necessary. Parthenogenesis, for instance. So the basic body plan of any sexed species is female. Males are just a specialized adaptation.

Since the infertile females are far and away the most common type of owoc—and the dominant ones, insofar as that aggressive term can be used with these beings—it seems to me most logical to refer to them as the females, and to call the ones which are specialized to actually reproduce "mothers."

I'll stick with that for now. (Note: ask Joseph to talk to the owoc about it. Be interesting to see what they have to say.)

He did, and Joseph reported that the owoc term for female was, just as Julius suspected, used to refer to the infertile ones. Kupu was called a term which translated quite closely as "mother." Joseph also reported that, according to the owoc, males came in two variants as well—the fertile ones, which were by far the most common type; and a rare type of male, which was not fertile. According to the owoc, there was no representative of that quasi-sex currently living in the valley. There *had* been one, some (indefinite—the owoc were always vague regarding questions of time) period ago, but he had died.

Julius tentatively labeled the sterile males "eumaloo." And then drove himself crazy trying to figure out an adaptive reason for the evolution of infertile males. ("The most useless creatures imaginable!" he exploded once, in Indira's presence; to his everlasting regret, for she expanded on the theme, at length.)

So there you are—just like a colony of bees. A queen—the mother—who does all the actual breeding. A small number of males, to service her. And a host of infertile females, to do everything else.

Like all analogies, of course, you can't take it too far. For one thing, the owoc are intelligent (not very, but intelligent nonetheless) whereas the social insects are as dumb as—hey, what do you expect?—bugs. For another, owoc society has none of the "slavish" characteristics of insect hives.

But I'd be willing to bet that if the owoc were smarter their complicated sexual relations would produce all kinds of fascinating cultural variants. Including, probably, some variants that are savagely oppressive.

He proved to be right. On both counts.

Chapter 9

Doctor Koresz was the first adult to die, six years after their arrival on Ishtar.

It did not come as a surprise, for he had known for months he was dying.

"I do not know why, really," he had told them, lying on his pallet in the hut which the doctor shared with Janet and Hector. "I have only been able to scratch the surface, when it comes to understanding life and death on Ishtar. I *shouldn't* be dying, of course. I am only forty-two years old, and if I had not been in perfect health the Society would never have approved me for the *Magellan*. But—as Julius never tires of reminding us—facts are stubborn things. And the fact is that I am dying."

All of the adults were gathered around, except Adams, who had drawn more and more apart from the colony as time went on. He was the only one of the adults who still lived in the landing boat. All the others had long since moved into the huts which Janet had designed from native vegetation. The children were housed in four large barracks (no, "long houses," Indira had named them, after the Iroquois).

Except for Adams, the adults lived in two separate huts: Indira and Julius in one, the doctor and Janet and Hector in the other. The *ménage à trois* into which Hector, Koresz and Janet had happily settled, within a few months after the crash, was a logical enough arrangement under the circumstances. And sexual mores on Earth in the 22nd century were characterized by considerable latitude and tolerance.

Julius immediately named their hut "Sodom and Gomorrah."

And he demonstratively refused to come near it, fearing, or so he claimed, the wrath of God.

"You don't even believe in God!" Indira had once protested.

Julius chewed his lip. "No, I don't. But you never know. And if He does exist, He has two outstanding characteristics. Judging, at least, from the Old Testament."

"Which are?"

"He's the most hot-tempered, narrow-minded, mean-spirited, intolerant, anal-compulsive, bigoted redneck who ever lived. And, what's more to the point, he's a lousy shot."

"It's true!" he insisted, in the face of Indira's laughter. "Read the Book yourself. Somebody pisses Him off, does He nail 'em right between the eyes like Buffalo Bill? Hell, no! He drowns everything. Or He blasts whole cities, or drops seven lean years on entire nations. Indiscriminate, that's what He is. The Sawed-off Shotgun In The Sky. So I ain't getting anywhere *near* that den of iniquity."

And he hadn't, until he realized that Koresz was really dying.

"But *why?*" demanded Janet. She wiped away tears. "If it's a disease, maybe you can find a cure. You've done miracles, Vladimir! Not just with us, with the owoc too."

Koresz shook his head weakly.

"It is not a disease, Janet. At least, not in the sense that you are using the term. It is—call it massive systemic shock."

"Explain," said Julius softly.

"I cannot, Julius. Not clearly. There is still an enormous amount we do not understand about life. Organisms are adapted by evolution to a particular environment. Some are more finicky about it than others, but any organism only has a certain tolerance range. Humans do quite well, in that regard, compared to most animals. But we have long known that totally new environments place a tremendous stress on organisms. In unforeseen ways, often. Did you ever read any of those old science fiction classics, written before humanity actually got into space?"

Julius shook his head.

"It is fascinating, really. The writers all thought that weightlessness would improve human health. Seemed like a logical idea at the time, I suppose. Gravity does wear our bodies down. But we are *adapted* to gravity. And when we finally got into space, we discovered that we cannot survive weightlessness.

Not for really extended periods of time. Bone loss; muscle atrophy; eventually, Kabakov's syndrome and death."

He levered himself to a semi-erect position.

"But we *can* survive weightlessness for quite some time before we succumb. And that, I think, is a good analogy to what is happening to me. My body lasted for years, but it is finally just giving up."

Indira gasped. "Does that mean—?" She swallowed. "The kids—"

Koresz shook his head. "I believe the children will be fine. Young animals are more adaptable than adults. The ones who survive, that is to say. Typically, young animals either survive or they die quickly. But the ones who make it—"

He stopped, turned pink with embarrassment. "I'm sorry, Julius. Indira. My big mouth."

The biologist's face was pale, as was Indira's. But Julius smiled his lopsided smile, and said:

"S'okay, Vladimir. It was a long time ago. My daughter— oh, hell, if I'd left the poor kid on Earth she would have been all right. But here—" He sighed heavily. "Nobody ever said natural selection was kind."

He shook his head sharply, clearing away the memory.

"But what's important now is that I think you're right. A few of the kids who died in the first year, like Indira's, died of trauma. But most of them—just died. Nothing we could do to stop it, as hard as we tried. Lost almost twenty percent, the first year. A few the next year. But since then, they seem to be doing just fine. And you think they'll be okay from now on—and their kids, too, I assume?"

Koresz nodded. "Basically. Oh, I expect there will be a high child mortality rate. But the colony will survive that, especially if the children follow nature's age-old strategy. Be fecund."

He cleared his throat. "Which brings up something I have been meaning to raise. I have not said anything about it before, because it was a moot point. But the children are just about at the age where they discover a fascinating new game."

He gave them a hard stare. "I do not know what cultural prejudices may still be lurking deep within the recesses of your nasty little minds—"

"This—from you?" demanded Julius. "The pervert who's going to fry for eternity?"

When the laughter died down, Koresz continued.

"You *must* allow the children maximum sexual freedom. More than that. You must positively *encourage* promiscuity. This is not the time and place for the nuclear family and sexual fidelity. The gene pool is small enough as it is. I believe we have a large enough gene pool—barely—*if* the genes are mixed up constantly. Even then, genetic drift is going to loom large. I suspect we shall see the resurgence of all sorts of recessive traits. Hemophilia, that sort of thing."

His face grew harsh. "Natural selection will do its job, like always. But we want the genetic mayhem to be as small as possible. That means—"

"Swingers' paradise," snorted Julius. "Rome of the Caesars."

Koresz smiled. "Not so bad as all that, Julius. At least, I have not seen much of a sadistic streak among the children."

He looked at Indira. "Why the big frown, Indira? You never struck me as the sexually-repressive type." A chuckle. "Even though you and Julius have selfishly refused to share your treasures with us sinners."

Indira smiled, faintly. "It's not that, Vladimir. I have no moral problems with allowing the kids to develop a sexually permissive culture. I'm in favor of it, actually. It'll avoid a lot of social neuroses. No, it's just . . ."

She took a deep breath.

"It's just that up until now the boys and the girls have been on a equal footing. They understand that there's a difference between the sexes, of course. But they don't think much of it. Their games are completely integrated, and a number of the girls are emerging as leaders. But if they start having lots of kids, well . . ."

She fell silent. Koresz seemed puzzled.

"I still don't—"

"She's worried about the rise of the patriarchy, Vladimir," explained Julius. "She's mentioned it to me before, in private. Indira says that if the colony were to remain in the state of primitive hunters and gatherers that it wouldn't be a problem. Primitive cultures, she says, are generally characterized by sexual equality."

Indira interrupted. "There's always a division of labor between the sexes, but it rarely translates into a relationship of dominance and subjugation. But the point is that we're *not* primitive hunters and gatherers. We've already developed agriculture, of a sort—a kind of modified pastoralism, without the migration—and with everything else we've taught the kids they're well on their way toward civilization, of a basic sort. And throughout human history, the rise of civilization was always accompanied by a transformation in the relationship between the sexes. What's called the patriarchy."

She tightened her jaws. "Which was always *very* oppressive to women. Suttee. Purdah. *Kinder, Küche, Kirche.* You name it."

Janet interrupted. "But, Indira, that's all in the past. Really, it is. Oh, yeah, sure, you still run across a few guys with some Neanderthal notions, but it's never a real problem."

Indira was shaking her head.

"That's beside the point, Janet. You're right—*today*. But the modern equality between the sexes is only possible because of the vast wealth of twenty-second century civilization. Even then, it didn't come without long and bitter struggle. But our kids aren't going to be living in that kind of world. They'll be living in the Bronze Age—"

"If I can find any bronze," muttered Julius.

"—and abstract ideas have very little power in the face of social forces that emerge out of the material circumstances of real life."

She chewed her lip, unconsciously imitating Julius.

"I'll have to give it some thought. We won't have much maneuvering room, but there'll be some. Socioeconomic forces are the locomotives of history, but they're not impervious to cultural influence. And there was always a lot of variation in human history, within a range. I'd have much rather been a woman among the Iroquois, for instance, than a woman in ancient India.

"Or—" she frowned at Julius "—among the Hebrews."

"Bad enough I catch hell for what *I* do," complained the biologist. "Now I got to catch hell for what my ancestors did three thousand years ago?"

Unexpectedly, Hector intervened in the discussion.

"I think you might be worrying too much, Indira. There's something you're overlooking. I don't know much about history, but I know for sure that there's a factor in the equation here that never existed on Earth."

He jerked his head, toward the south.

"The owoc."

Indira was puzzled. "I don't get it, Hector. The owoc won't be able to stop—oh, hell, I wish Julius would stop calling them 'dimbulbs,' even in jest, but I can't deny that they aren't exactly mental giants."

Hector was shaking his head.

"You're missing the forest for the trees, Indira. It's not anything that the owoc would *do*. It's—just the fact that they *are*."

He gazed at the blank faces staring at him.

"Don't you see? The kids already think they're half-owoc. Hell, they're even starting to speak in their own dialect—English, basically, with a hefty dose of Spanish, Arabic and Chinese. *And* lots and lots of hoots. Sometimes, I can't understand what the kids are saying anymore."

He sighed. They still didn't understand.

"Look, folks. Just three days ago, I saw one of the littler boys—Kenny Wright—climb up onto Ludmilla's neck. For all the world like he was a tiny male owoc looking for his favorite spot. He didn't fit, of course, and at first I was afraid Ludmilla would beat him into a pulp. But she just seemed to take it for granted. Even carried Kenny around like that for half an hour.

"So maybe you're right, Indira. You know human history, I don't. But what I do know is that our kids aren't—they aren't just human, anymore. They're something a little different. Something new."

Indira was doubtful. But a small hope was born in her heart that day, at the deathbed of Vladimir Koresz. A small and faint glimmer, under the growing tidal wave of an historian's fear.

They buried Koresz three days later, near the kolocluster. All the humans in the colony attended, even Adams. And it seemed that every owoc in the valley was there also. Several of them owed their wellbeing to Koresz, who had over the years managed to find cures for a number of the illnesses which afflicted the creatures. The owoc, of course, did not understand the means by which Koresz worked his magic. Nor did they seem to care. They simply called him, in their hooting language, "the Stroke of Slow Beauty." (Humans, thought Indira, would have said: "the Touch of Long Life.")

Fortunately, not all of Koresz's skill went with him into the grave. Janet would never be his equal as a doctor, of course. Neither her own keen mind nor his careful tutorship could make up for the years which the doctor had spent learning his craft. But she was still very good. Much better—much, *much* better—than the medical practitioners which the human race had possessed for all but the last three centuries of its existence. And Janet had drawn around her four children who showed a deep interest in medicine. She believed that at least one of them, Maria De Los Reyes, had the potentiality for becoming a great doctor.

It was fortunate, and not a moment too soon. For, just as Koresz had foreseen, the children soon learned a new and vastly entertaining game. Less than a year later, the first babies began arriving.

They lost many of the babies, of course. But they lost none of the young mothers, although it was a close call with Keiko Watanabe. Janet performed her first Caesarean, and it was a success. Keiko and her child survived, although the girl would never bear another.

Indira was aghast at the child mortality rate, but Julius was (bleakly) satisfied.

"Twenty-five percent after one year," he said. "That's horrible, by modern Terran standards, I agree. But look, Indira—and please don't accuse me of being a cold-hearted biologist—it's better than what the human race put up with for most of its existence. In fact, a twenty-five percent child mortality rate is incredibly *good*, when you consider they're being born on an alien planet."

Indira knew he was right, but the knowledge didn't help much. Not when she had to help bury the pitiful little bodies. And then look at the hurt and bewildered faces of the children who had borne them.

But, over time, the children—teenagers, now—came to accept the facts of life. Here, of course, they were helped by the attitude of the owoc. Over time, Indira would be both appalled and fascinated by the way in which the inter-penetration of the two species' cultures would produce a unique hybrid. The humans would never share the owoc indifference toward new-born babes, of course. That was biologically precluded. They would care for them, and caress them, and nurse them, and pamper them. But they would withhold the core of their hearts, until the infants began to walk.

Eighteen months. That seemed to be the critical point. If a child could survive that long, and struggle to its uncertain little feet, he or she stood an excellent chance.

Janet Mbateng was the next to die. She knew it was coming months before it finally happened, just as Koresz had known.

"It's like something turned off, inside," she explained to them. "I'm just going through the motions, now."

She groped for words. "I can't explain it. It's not that I want to die, or anything like that. It's just—I don't know. Somehow I can just tell my body's given up."

The final weeks of her life, Janet spent every hour of the day surrounded by her pupils. (The nights, of course, were given to Hector; who held her wasted body in his arms, until he cried himself to sleep.) Hour after hour, passing on to them everything she had learned from Koresz. Hector tried to convince her to rest, but the little woman—no bigger than a child herself, now—adamantly refused.

In the end, she was satisfied she had done all she could. The day before her death, she administered the Hippocratic Oath to Maria De Los Reyes, and urged her other students to continue their efforts so that they too could become Doctors. (And they all did, over time.)

The last night, and day, she gave to Hector.

Hector followed her into the grave soon after. He claimed that he felt the same sensations that Janet and Koresz had described. Indira believed him, but Julius knew he was lying. The pilot's muscular physique never showed more than a trace of the horrible wasting symptoms which Janet and Koresz had exhibited. True, he grew very thin. But Julius knew that Hector hardly ate anything.

No, Julius knew the truth. Hector Quintero had become the closest friend he'd ever had. Over the years, working side by side, he had come to cherish the man's intelligence, cheerfulness, wit and courage. Inexhaustible courage, it had seemed.

But courage comes in different ways, to different people. Hector could face anything, except the empty vision of a future without Janet.

✦   ✦   ✦

Francis Adams, strangely, seemed indestructible. The physicist was a total recluse—had been since before Koresz's death. And for at least a year prior to that, he had stopped giving classes to the children. (Which Indira regretted not at all; Adams had been an unbelievably bad teacher, totally incapable of explaining things in a way which would be comprehensible to his students.) He dwelt by himself, as he had for years, alone in the landing boat. The last time Julius saw the portion of the boat where Adams lived, the place looked like a pigsty. Adams himself—formerly so fastidious—looked like a complete savage. He acted like one, too. He had screeched at Julius, his voice filled with fear and rage, ordering him to leave. The physicist had even seized a spear which he had secreted in his lair, brandishing it in a manner which would have been frightening if it hadn't been so pitifully awkward.

But Julius obeyed. There was no purpose to be served in doing otherwise.

For years, now, the only time the colonists saw Adams was at mealtimes. These had become the central institution of daily social life for the colony—a time of festivity and relief from the morning's labor in the upunu fields and the afternoon's labor in the large longhouse which served as a school. Twice a day, mid-morning and late afternoon, the entire colony would gather in the center of the valley. There, in a cleared space surrounded on three sides by the long houses and the adults' huts, and on the fourth side by an oruc grove, a line of owoc would slowly enter. Each in turn would regurgitate her childfood into six huge basket/tureens, made of ruporeeds coated with dried resin.

The baskets had been Indira's invention. She felt that receiving the childfood directly into little personal bowls was undignified and wasteful, since much of it slopped over the sides. (It also made her nauseous.) Once the childfood was in the tureens, each human would approach with a bowl and scoop out their own portion. Before retiring to eat in animated circles, the humans would stand before the watching owoc, bowing deeply. The gesture of respect had not been taught to the human young. They had invented it themselves, drawing on some deep pool of cultural inheritance.

Indira herself never scooped her own bowl. She insisted

on having a bowl brought to her, so that she could put out of her mind (more or less) the knowledge of where it came from. She was the only member of the human colony who felt that way, but the others had long since accepted her wishes.

Almost always, Julius was the one who brought her bowl. She wished it were otherwise, but she never said so, knowing it would hurt his feelings. Much as she loved Julius, she would have preferred another bowl-bringer, one who wouldn't smack his lips in anticipation of the meal, and make gross remarks such as: "Hey, the barf's good today!"

Adams would always make his appearance after the owoc left. The half-crazed physicist would emerge from his lair and scurry down the hillside. He would stop at the edge of the clearing, hunched, glaring at nothing in particular, saying not a word.

After a moment, Joseph would arise from whichever circle he was eating with and scoop out a bowl. He would approach Adams slowly and solemnly, and extend the bowl. After a moment, Adams would take the bowl and devour the contents like a wolf. Then, he would return the bowl and scuttle back to his lair.

The ritual was one of the many ways—unconsciously, thought Indira—that Joseph had established his position as the unquestioned leader of the younger generation. The children were afraid of Adams, she knew. The fear was not rational. Adams had never been a physically prepossessing man, even in his prime. Any number of the teenagers, of either sex, could have easily handled him. Jens Knudsen, who already had the size and musculature of a heavyweight wrestler, could have broken him with one hand. Ludmilla might have needed two hands.

No, it was not a physical fear. It was that the teenagers knew there was something deeply *wrong* about Adams, something that was utterly unlike anything else they had encountered. People fear the unknown.

But Joseph did not. He had not feared Adams as a boy. He did not fear him now.

His fearlessness, like the fear which the other teenagers felt, had little to do with physique. In that respect, of course, Adams posed no danger. The time when Adams could loom threateningly over Joseph Adekunle was long gone. Instead, Joseph towered over the physicist—and would have, even were Adams erect. At the age of seventeen, he was already almost two hundred centimeters tall. And while Indira thought that he would not grow much taller, she knew that his frame—already muscular—would fill out even further. By the time Joseph was twenty, he would be as magnificent a physical specimen as the human race had ever produced. Joseph would never have the sheer brute strength that Jens Knudsen possessed, but Indira had noted that he beat Jens as often as Jens beat him whenever they engaged in one of their frequent (and good-natured) wrestling matches. Joseph's speed, reflexes, and balanced poise were positively awesome.

But, as she watched the scene, Indira knew that the essence of it was not physical, but spiritual. The calm, confident serenity that exuded from Joseph's person as he watched the physicist take and gobble down his food did not stem from simple confidence in his muscles. They stemmed from the very soul of the boy.

Indira recognized what she was seeing. It was that vision the human race had always possessed of youth in its glory. Not arrogant, not callous, not vainglorious—simply the calm certainty of young strength and courage. Utter fearlessness in the face of danger; total willingness to stand against it.

The vision was found in all human cultures, expressed in a myriad ways. But Indira thought it had been completely captured only once, by the greatest artist the human race perhaps ever produced.

The superficial appearance was, of course, different. Joseph's skin was black; his hair was kinky; his features were African. But those were meaningless things. The soul of the boy was the same as that captured by the artist's genius.

The young shepherd, guarding his flock. Sling in hand. Poised, yet not tense; calmly gazing forward, secure in his youth, ready to deal with whatever horrors might come over the horizon. Lions; or bears; or perhaps even a giant. Whatever. It made no difference, for he would slay the monster without fail.

She had seen it once, that vision. In Florence.

The *David*, by Michelangelo.

David had not failed. Nor did Joseph, when the monsters came to his people, three months after Hector died.

The long years of the colony's peaceful existence ended, and gave way to the washing of the spears.

Chapter 10

The first slaver raid caught the colony by surprise.

It shouldn't have, in theory. The colonists had been preparing to defend themselves, and the owoc, for over ten years. Enough spears had been produced to arm every single human down to the new-born babies, with a number left over. The teenagers had been organized into five-person squads, which, in turn, had been organized into three platoons.

Hector, who was the only adult with any military training at all, had been selected as the commander of the defense force. The organizational structure was his idea, and it had been he who had drilled the young humans in basic tactics.

The other adults had participated in the training, in the first few years. But once the children became teenagers, all the adults except Julius stopped engaging in the exercises. And if Hector had had his way, Julius would have been barred as well.

"It's a young person's game, man."

"You're saying I'm too old and feeble and slow?" demanded Julius.

"Yes. Exactly. Precisely."

But Julius had refused to quit, to Indira's disgust. Indira had never been an avid supporter of the military exercises in the first place. And as the years went by without any signs of trouble, she came to the private conclusion that the training was a waste of time and energy. But she did not interfere, except in three ways.

First, she made clear to Julius that she considered his insistence on remaining in the defense guard to be a prime example of delayed adolescence, of which, to his discomfort, she pointed to numerous other symptoms.

Secondly, she insisted that if there was going to be a defense guard, the girls would participate on an equal basis. This had caused no difficulty, for Hector was quite favorable to the idea. In fact, he had appointed Ludmilla Rozkowski one of the three platoon leaders (the others were Joseph Adekunle and Takashi Mizoguchi). After the babies began arriving, Hector maintained the sexual egalitarianism by establishing a platoon rotation system. Each month one of the platoons was assigned the primary duty of rounding up and protecting the children in the event of a military crisis.

Finally, and most forcefully, Indira refused to accept Hector's proposed title for his own position.

"What's wrong with it?" he complained.

"Admiral of the Ocean Sea?" demanded Indira.

He pouted. "It's got a nice ring to it."

"Not a chance. You can be *Captain* Quintero."

The training had been maintained for several years, but it had slowly become more and more lackadaisical. After Hector died, the defense guard essentially disintegrated. Julius assumed the mantle of Captain, but he was too preoccupied with other matters to pay any real attention to the task.

In the last weeks prior to the raid, only a handful of the teenagers continued their training and exercises. They formed themselves into an informal squad, consisting of the three former platoon leaders, as well as Jens Knudsen and a few others.

The first sign of trouble was a sudden flurry of hoots coming from the southernmost end of the valley. When Julius first heard the hooting, while he was writing in his notebook, he shrugged it off. He was curious, for the owoc rarely hooted loudly, but he was not alarmed.

As the hoots continued, and seemed to grow nearer, he went to investigate. Still curious rather than concerned, he walked out of the hut carrying his notebook.

Seconds later he had dropped the notebook and was racing for the stand of spears next to the long houses. He still didn't know what was wrong, but he had no doubt that foul play was afoot.

An owoc stampede has a certain comical air to it, given their slow speed, but Julius was not in the slightest amused. He had never seen owoc stampede before, and at least one of the beings was bleeding from a large wound in its mantle.

Whether driven by fear, instinct, or a conscious understanding that the humans were protection, the owoc had done exactly the right thing. They ran (shuffled, it might be better to say) directly into the center of the human village. Thereby drawing their pursuers into what became an impromptu trap.

Julius spotted the first invader just before he reached the spears.

His first thought was: *Tentacles*.

Then, almost simultaneously: *Weapons. Armor. Intelligent.*

When he reached the stack of spears, Julius was so frantic that he knocked them over. Then, in his haste to pick up a spear, he tripped and fell flat on his face.

He observed the ensuing events from his belly.

Joseph was the first to grab a spear from the pile on the ground. The boy sprang into the center of the village. He was facing the invaders from a distance of five meters.

Did I call it right, or what? thought Julius. *The thing's the spitting image of an owoc, except that it's smaller and has tentacles. And that lean and hungry look. The peds are less massive, too. Must be faster—but why isn't it moving?*

Later, he realized that the creature must have been frozen with shock. It had never seen a human before, and humans looked like nothing else on Ishtar.

They moved like nothing else, too. Julius was amazed at the speed and ferocity of Joseph's attack. He was even more amazed that the boy never hesitated.

The spear sank two feet into the invader's head, right between the eyes. The creature dropped to the ground, instantly slain.

Three more invaders charged into the village. Joseph wrenched the spear loose from his first victim's head and immediately cast it at one of the new arrivals. The spear sailed through the air and struck perfectly.

By now, Ludmilla and Jens had arrived. They snatched up spears and took their position next to Joseph's side. Ludmilla handed him a new spear.

The three teenagers stood poised, facing the two remaining invaders from a distance of ten meters. Loud and rapid noises came from the invaders' speaking tubes. A moment later, seven more of the creatures surged into the center of the village.

Belatedly, Julius scrambled to his feet.

"Bring us more spears!" shouted Joseph.

Julius bent over and grabbed a half a dozen in his hands.

"Throw!" commanded Joseph. The three teenagers hurled their spears. Joseph and Ludmilla hit squarely, killing their targets. Jens' spear struck the cowl of his target.

In frustration, Jens raced forward and reached out for the spear sticking out from the cowl.

The monsters finally reacted. The one toward which Jens was running whipped its right tentacle around, wielding a weapon that looked something like a morning star: a wooden shaft about a meter long, from the end of which protruded eight spikes, each one about 20 centimeters long and tipped with some kind of sharp stone.

One of the spikes pierced completely through Jens' right calf. The boy cried out in pain and dropped to one knee. A moment later, another of the invaders lashed him with a peculiar weapon that looked something like a cat-o'-nine-tails. Jens threw up his left arm to ward off the blow. The weapon tore great pieces of flesh from his arm and shoulder. Anyone less massively built than Jens Knudsen would have been crippled. As it was, blood gushed all over the left side of the boy's body.

Joseph raced up and killed the one who had lashed Jens with one thrust of his spear. He timed his charge perfectly, stopping at just the right time and place to avoid the lash of the weapon.

Ludmilla killed another, using the same tactics. Race in; stop suddenly when the enemy whips the weapon around; lunge. If anything, the girl's strike was done even more gracefully than Joseph's. Julius was not surprised. The girl was not only big, she was possessed of uncanny speed and reflexes—as good as Joseph's, if not better.

As he watched, Julius was struck again by the discrepancy between Ludmilla's Russian name and her appearance.

She's the spitting image of a Manchu princess—no, warrior.

Jens Knudsen roared with rage and jerked his spear from his enemy's cowl. Still on one knee, the boy threw himself forward and drove the spear almost completely into the creature's body. He missed the brain—but three feet of spear driven through the eye, the head, and deep into the body beyond was more than enough.

God, that kid's strong! Got to work on his tactics, though.

A lifetime spent observing nature had left Julius with ineradicable habits. He wasn't much use in the actual fracas, but he never stopped observing and taking mental notes.

Julius himself squared off with another invader, but the "combat" which followed was almost comical. He skittered back and forth, well beyond range of the monster's weapons. Well beyond range of spear-thrust as well. For its part, the invader did likewise.

What a pair of wallflowers! Julius clenched his teeth, and prepared to lunge. It was not necessary—Joseph charged past him and killed his opponent.

Julius gasped for breath. Looking around wildly, he saw that the village was a scene of utter confusion. Incoherent human shouts and owoc hoots filled the air. Except for Joseph, Ludmilla and Jens—who was still in the fray, covered with blood—all the other humans were racing about in total panic.

No, not all. He saw Indira shepherding four little children toward one of the long houses. Her face was pale and strained, but she seemed otherwise calm and collected.

There were three invaders left alive. They spun around and began moving (quite rapidly, thought Julius—much faster than owoc) out of the village, back toward the south.

"Don't let them get away!" he shouted. Joseph and Ludmilla raced off in pursuit. Jens collapsed. From a distance, Julius saw Takashi Mizoguchi racing up from the upunu fields where he had been working. The boy was brandishing his only weapon—a useless hoe.

But the sight of him running toward them terrified the fleeing invaders. (The gukuy had not yet learned to distinguish between human tools and weapons.) Two of them veered farther to the right, still heading south. Julius watched with amazement as Joseph and Ludmilla slaughtered them like hardened veterans.

Joseph never even paused at the first one he caught. He

simply drove his spear through the creature's left ped, pinning it to the ground. The invader squawled and spun around in a half-circle, whipping its flail. Joseph avoided the blow by leaping high into the air. When he landed on the other side, he snatched the spear that Ludmilla tossed him (she was carrying two) and continued in pursuit of the last enemy while Ludmilla efficiently butchered the pinned one.

No—not the last one! Julius watched in horror as one of the invaders turned back and raced into the village. It was heading directly toward Indira and the children.

Everything seemed to happen in slow motion. Julius desperately tried to interpose himself, but he was too far away. He was a slow runner at the best of times, and the invader was moving much faster than he would have believed possible. He saw Indira spin around. Her jaw dropped open. She pushed the children behind her and faced the onrushing monster. The creature squawled and drew back its weapons.

Suddenly, from nowhere, Francis Adams appeared. The physicist was shrieking like a maniac, holding a spear in both hands. His strike was pitifully clumsy. The spear glanced off the leatherish-looking armor which covered the creature's mantle. Adams' opponent whipped its flail around; the weapon practically ripped the physicist's legs off at the knees. Still shrieking, Adams collapsed onto the monster, grappling it like a wrestler.

With horror, Julius saw the creature raise its head, clutch the physicist's body with its tentacles and six small arms, and bite his chest with its small but sharp beak. Blood spurted everywhere.

A moment later, Julius drove his spear into the monster's mantle. His own strike was poorly done. The spear didn't glance off. He managed to drive it through the armor and well into the tough tissue of the mantle. But it was neither a killing nor even a crippling blow.

He had no time for a second strike. The thing was *biting* Adams. He simply threw himself into the spear with the frenzy of desperation.

Luckily, Julius was a strong man. He managed to lever the monster onto its side, where it lay squirming and writhing.

God, the thing must weigh at least three hundred pounds. But it's let go of Adams.

At that moment, the rest of the defense guard finally arrived. Three boys and a girl, brandishing spears, surrounded the stricken monster. They drew back their weapons.

"No!" shouted Julius. "Don't kill it! I want to keep one of them alive!"

Hesitantly, they obeyed. For its part, the monster was now lying still. Its huge eyes seemed filled with terror; its body was colored bright scarlet.

Julius turned to Adams. He knelt and cradled the physicist. Adams' legs were a mangled ruin, and his chest was covered with blood. But his eyes were open and he was conscious.

"Take it easy, Francis, take it easy," crooned the biologist. "You're going to be all right. Your legs are a mess, but the wound on your chest isn't fatal. Looks terrible, but—" (He was about to say: "but I can see the white bone of your sternum, and it's intact," but decided against it.)

Thankfully, Maria De Los Reyes appeared. She took one look at the wounds and began bawling orders. Still blessed (cursed?) with his observer's instincts, Julius saw that a semblance of order and sanity was returning to the village. From the south, he could see Joseph and Ludmilla loping back. They were moving quickly, but it was obvious that all danger had passed. As soon as Ludmilla saw Jens' prostrate form, she raced over and knelt at his side, crying and crooning.

"Julius—" A whisper.

"Don't talk, Francis. You're going to be all right."

He glanced questioningly at Maria. She nodded.

But Adams seemed not to hear.

"Julius—I— I'm sorry, Julius."

"Sorry? For what?"

A faint shake of the head. "I just couldn't—I just couldn't be of much use."

Julius started to say something, but at that moment Adams went into convulsions. He died thrashing in Julius' arms, in less than two minutes.

Julius heard the children shouting. He looked over and saw that the surviving invader was also thrashing about. Within seconds, it too was dead.

I forgot, he thought vaguely. *On earth, octopi have poisonous bites. Must be true here also.*

He looked over at the dead body of Adams' killer.

Well, you bastards figured out one way to kill us. But you have to pay a hell of a price. It cuts both ways, asshole.

When they buried Adams the next day, Julius erected a marker over the grave, as had become customary. The marker, carved on a small block of stone, simply read:

> *Francis Adams*
> *Born Earth, AD 2126*
> *Died Ishtar, CY 12*

"CY" stood for "Colony Year." The colonists no longer knew what year it was by the Terran calendar, so they had established the day they crash-landed as the base for their own calendar. They still maintained, out of habit, the time measurement of years, months, and weeks. Ironically, the one advanced technological device which still worked was their well-nigh indestructable watches. So the colonists were able to keep precise track of time. But on Ishtar, these measurements were arbitrary and meaningless. The planet had neither seasons nor a moon. Constellations, which could have enabled them to calculate the year, couldn't be seen through the ever-present cloud cover. The Ishtarian day was the only objective criteria. It was slightly over 23 hours long, divided equally between daylight and darkness.

After a few minutes, as they stared at the grave, Indira heard Julius mutter something.

"What's the matter?"

Julius looked at her and sighed.

"I'm going to have to make another marker."

"What's wrong with this one?"

Julius shook his head. "He was a complete jackass the whole time I knew him, except for the last few minutes of his life. But that made up for everything."

The next day he erected a new marker. The only change was the name: *Doctor Francis Adams.*

The one positive development, thought Julius, was that he would finally be able to dissect a pseudo-cephalopod. But, again, he was frustrated.

"They want to *what?*" he demanded.

"They insist on burying them," said Indira. "And they're upset at the idea of harming them further."

"The things are already dead!"

Indira shrugged. "The owoc don't look at it the same way. They're quite insistent, Julius."

Inevitably, Julius lost the argument.

"I just don't get it," he grumbled, after the mass burial of the invaders. "Why should the owoc care what happens to the damn things? They're hereditary enemies. Carnivores, to boot."

Indira glared at him, fists planted on her hips.

"Is that so? The great biologist Julius Cohen has already analyzed the situation in every detail. The new creatures are carnivores, therefore—therefore *what?* I can remember you giving a different speech a few years ago."

Julius looked uncomfortable. "Well, I'm not claiming I understand everything about the watchamacallits. But I know a savage enemy when I see one!"

"Really? Such a brilliant mind. Let me ask you something, O great one. What was the relationship between the Amish and the Nazis?"

Julius frowned. "I don't understand the question."

"Really? How strange. A minute ago you had all the answers. I'll give you a hint—it's obvious."

Julius was still frowning. Indira snorted.

"They were both members of the human race. So, according to your logic, it would make sense to kill Amish because they belonged to the same species as the Nazis. Am I right?"

Julius hemmed and hawed, but Indira had him cold and he knew it.

She reinforced her point a few days later, after talking to the owoc.

"They're as unclear as they usually are, but there's no question that they don't think all of the—they're called gukuy, by the way—are the same. The owoc say that many of the gukuy—most of them, I get the impression—are dangerous and dreadful. But there are others whom the owoc seem to think rather highly of."

"Which others? And how can you tell the difference?"

Indira shrugged.

"That's great," muttered Julius. "That's just great."

❖   ❖   ❖

Within a few months, the issue was resolved. And it became clear that the difference between "good" and "bad" gukuy was not all that difficult to determine.

Before that time came, however, the colony went through a major social transformation.

The transformation occurred on two levels. On one level, the change was simple—the colony readopted Hector's military organization, with a vengeance. To Julius Cohen's great satisfaction.

The more significant change, however, he greeted with much less pleasure.

"Do you mean to tell me I'm *fired?*" he demanded, goggle-eyed.

Indira gazed at him patiently.

"I wouldn't put it that way, dear. I think of it as a necessary and beneficial transition in leadership."

"They're too young! Immature!"

"Really?" demanded Indira. "Then explain to me why they were the ones who—" She stopped abruptly.

Julius winced; looked away.

"Who saved the day. While yours truly, the great leader, tripped all over his feet and ran around like a chicken with its head cut off."

Indira's eyes softened. She reached out a hand and stroked his cheek.

"You were very brave, Julius. I was proud of you. And I saw no resemblance to a chicken whatsoever."

Julius puffed out his cheeks, exhaled noisily. His lopsided grin appeared.

"Nevertheless, it's true I didn't cut the most glorious martial figure."

He thought it over for a moment, then nodded his head.

"I suppose you're right. Joseph *would* make a better Captain. Or Ludmilla."

"Yes, they would. Much better, to be honest with you. But that's not even my main concern. The heart of the problem isn't military, it's social. And it doesn't just involve you, it involves me as well. All of us."

"What do you mean?"

"Julius, the children aren't children any longer. They have children of their own now, and they have for some time been assuming more and more responsibility for organizing the colony. As an historian, I can tell you that the way in which a society handles the transition of leadership from one generation to another is one of the key aspects of its health. There are few worse social cancers than an older generation that won't give way to new blood when the time is right."

"Yeah, I know. I've thought about it myself, now and then. I just figured—oh, I don't know. Later, I guess. I thought— I suppose I thought we still needed to lead things so that the kids would—what's the expression?—grow up in the path of righteousness."

She chuckled. "That's exactly why we have to step down now, Julius. Nothing gains greater respect for an older generation than initiating and leading a transition in authority. We won't be in the direct chain of command, any longer. But I strongly suspect that our moral authority will, if anything, increase."

The next day, Indira summoned the entire colony to a meeting. There, she explained that the time had come for the younger generation to assume the mantle of authority. She was a bit surprised at the matter of fact way in which the teenagers accepted the change.

I've lagged behind, she realized. *They've been ready for this for some time. What nice, polite kids.*

She was even more surprised at the outcome of the colony's deliberation. Both at the speed in which the decisions were made and the end result.

The teenagers adopted a five-person governing council, to be elected by direct vote. They ruled that the governing council would select one of its members to serve as the official leader of the colony whenever the council was not in session. The title of this post, proposed by Julius as a joke and immediately adopted, was "Admiral of the Ocean Sea."

Indira was the only one who voted against the title. But she was not too upset, for she knew it was a gesture of fondness and respect for Hector Quintero.

They also formally adopted Hector's military organization, and established the ranks of one Captain, three Lieutenants, and as many Sergeants as were needed to lead each squad.

Joseph then proposed that the Captain and the Lieutenants

should automatically become additional members of the governing council, with voice but no vote. He also proposed that, by law, no one elected to any of the four major military positions could also be elected as a voting member of the council.

His proposals were adopted, with almost no discussion. (More accurately, Indira realized, the discussions had already taken place informally over a considerable period of time.)

The elections also went quickly and smoothly. Indira and Julius were elected to the governing council. They both argued against the idea, but they were outvoted. Everybody else to two.

The other members elected were Maria De Los Reyes, Jack Turrennes, and Anna Cheng.

Joseph was elected Captain. Ludmilla, Takashi, and a boy named Andrew MacPherson were elected Lieutenants. There was a bit of awkwardness around the election of Lieutenants, for there were many who thought that Jens Knudsen deserved the position. Others felt that while Jens' strength and courage were unquestioned, he lacked other requirements for military leadership.

The discussion was frank and open, especially Jens' own comments. (The boy was recovering well from his wounds. The scars on his arm and shoulders were horrible, but Maria said he would eventually recover his full strength.)

"I haven't got the temperament," he announced cheerfully. "It's that simple."

He waved off the protests.

"I didn't say I was stupid or anything. But you've got to have people who can stay calm and think on their feet. Like Joseph or Ludmilla. Or Andrew. Me, I tend to forget everything else except what I'm doing with my own spear. It won't work."

Julius resolved the problem by proposing the title of Sergeant Major. His proposal was adopted by acclaim, and Jens was unanimously elected.

In private, after the meeting was over, Julius remarked:

"I don't really understand why Joseph made his proposal. About the Captain and the Lieutenants not being voting members of the council."

"He's very shrewd, Julius. I hadn't thought of the idea

myself, but it's a good one. It allows the colony to elect the people they feel most confident holding the military positions, without automatically imposing the military chain of command onto the colony as a whole."

"Still, I would have thought they'd want Joseph on the council, as a voting member. As the leader of the council, actually." He chuckled. "'Admiral of the Ocean Sea' Adekunle."

Indira shook her head. "I'm afraid the youngsters are seeing the picture more clearly than we are, Julius. They're expecting the military structure to be the dominant one."

Julius was surprised. "You mean they think we're going to be another Sparta?"

Indira shook her head again. "I doubt if they remember much of what I taught them about the ancient Greeks. And I mainly concentrated on Athens, anyway. Besides, the Spartan analogy's inaccurate. The military structure of Spartan society was shaped by the necessity of holding down the helot class that did all the actual work. It wasn't just militarist, it was class-ridden and highly oppressive. Our colony doesn't resemble that in the slightest. No, the structure's more like that of the Zulus, except it's democratic. Or the early Romans. That's probably a better analogy."

"Well, that's a relief." Then, after gazing at her for a few minutes:

"I notice that you don't seem too relieved. Why?"

"What? Oh, sorry. I'm—" She paused, heaved a sigh. "I am afraid, Julius."

"Of what? That we'll survive?"

"No, not that." A humorless chuckle. "Human beings have always been quite good at surviving. No, I'm worried about the future. What'll become of this little society we've built, after we're gone."

"We seem to be off to a good start. They're nice kids, Indira. Not a tyrant in the lot. And if there were, the rest of them wouldn't tolerate it. If I say so myself, we've raised them with good ideas."

Indira shook her head. "That means nothing, Julius. Or almost nothing. The forces that shape history have their roots in the most basic conditions of social and economic life. Good ideas are like the morning dew in the face of those forces."

"I don't understand."

She stared at him, grim-faced. "The Zulus were an impressive people, in many ways. But they were a disaster for their neighbors. So were the Romans, if you recall. It's easy to admire the culture of the early Roman republic. But the republic didn't last, Julius. It gave way to the empire, and all the rest of it. Not immediately, of course. It took centuries. But historians *think* in terms of centuries. Sure, *our* kids are filled with democratic and egalitarian ideas. How many generations will that last—in a Bronze Age society?"

She stared down the valley.

"What have we set loose upon this world?"

Chapter 11

Whatever the future might bring, the change in authority set loose an immediate whirlwind of activity.

The first thing Joseph did, after re-establishing the training program, was to institute a systematic policy of exploration and reconnaissance. Despite the fact that it had been twelve years since the humans arrived on Ishtar, they really knew very little about the planet except the immediate vicinity of the valley. Julius had often expressed a desire to explore further, but the press of immediate concerns had always led him to postpone the task.

The task would no longer be postponed. Nor was there any need to postpone it. Grudgingly, Julius admitted to himself that he had fallen into a pattern of inertia and routine. The truth was that the cultivation of the upunu fields did not require all that much of the colony's labor. In fact, the fields were producing a surplus well above what the owoc in the valley needed, even without the colonists engaging in constant toil. In the first years of upunu agriculture, the colonists had been kept very busy exterminating the uduwo-snails that proliferated every few months. But years of systematic slaughter had done their work. For the past three years, they had only found snails on rare occasions. And those were obviously recent immigrants from outside the valley—which only emphasized the importance of learning more about the region surrounding them.

The first exploring expedition was led by Joseph himself. The explorers were gone for only four days. (The limit was set by the length of time that childfood would last without

135

spoiling. Julius had once tried to find a way to prepare the childfood for longer storage— "puke jerky," he called it—but his experiments had not succeeded.)

When they returned, Joseph reported that the valley was nestled on a plateau atop the huge mountain, near to its southern crest. They had only been able to explore the southern and western crests of the mountain. According to Joseph, the western slope of the mountain was very steep and rocky. Humans could climb it, with difficulty, but the boy doubted that gukuy could manage to do so.

Nor was the steep slope the only obstacle to potential invaders. A river, coming somewhere from the north-west, curved around the western edge of the mountain, before disappearing to the southeast into a gigantic swampy jungle. The jungle stretched west and south-west almost to the distant horizon—many, many kilometers away.

The danger lay to the south. There, the mountain's slope was much shallower, and divided by many canyons which— from a distance; they had not gone down into them—seemed to provide relatively easy access to the plateau above. One of those canyons must have been the route followed by the invaders.

Joseph intended to explore those canyons, and soon. But his next project was to complete the circumnavigation of the plateau.

After resting for only a day, Joseph and his explorers set forth once again.

Four days later, they returned with exciting—and disturbing—news. The mountain plateau contained three more valleys like the one in which the colony was situated. Two of those valleys were of approximately the same size, but the third was much larger. It was located on the eastern side of the plateau. And there were owoc living in it. *And gukuy*.

"Gukuy?" demanded Julius. "Did you . . . Was there any fighting?"

Joseph shook his head firmly.

"No, Julius. We first saw them from a distance, while we were still coming down the slope into the valley. The gukuy were doing some kind of—dance, I guess you could call it. In front of a big hut of some kind, in a clearing on the floor of the valley. There were some owoc there, too. The owoc weren't participating in the activity, they were just browsing. But they didn't seem at all nervous. Their mantles were gray, with even a touch of green.

"We tried to sneak up and spy on the gukuy, but they spotted us once we got close."

Julius grunted. That was not surprising. If the gukuy were like owoc—and there seemed no reason not to suppose so; they were obviously cousin species—their vision would be better than that of humans. The beings' color sensitivity was especially acute, naturally enough. But they were also even better than humans at detecting movement.

"Then what happened?"

"It was the strangest thing, Julius. The gukuy started whistling, and they all turned red. But instead of fleeing, they—well, I know this sounds weird, but I'd swear they started trying to herd the owoc into the fern groves. As if they were trying to hide them, or something. And then some of the gukuy went into the hut and came back out carrying those whip-like weapons. But they weren't threatening the owoc with them. Instead, they started to come toward us. We left at that point. I didn't want to do anything further without discussing it with the council."

"It sounds like they were trying to protect the owoc," commented Indira. "That's a hopeful sign."

Hearing an odd noise coming from Julius, she eyed him quizzically.

"You don't agree?"

"Well, yes and no. Or maybe, yes or no. Oh, hell! The point is this: I agree that the gukuy were trying to protect the owoc. But I don't necessarily see that as a good sign."

"Why ever not?" demanded Indira.

Julius sighed. "Am I the only one around here with a dark and evil imagination? Indira, not everyone who protects someone else does so from good motives. Ranchers on Earth protect their calves against coyotes. So that they can eat the meat themselves."

Indira gasped. "You can't be serious!"

He shrugged. "I'm not saying that's what's happening here. I'm just suggesting we not jump to conclusions."

At the council meeting that night, it was decided that another expedition would be sent to the big valley. A larger expedition—a full platoon, in fact. But the size of the expedition was simply to protect Indira. Julius was unhappy at the idea of her going. But it was a fact, which he admitted, that she was still the best linguist in the colony. Her owoc accent would never be as good as that of the younger generation, but she was far better trained and equipped than they were to learn a new language.

It was also agreed that the colonists would attempt to convince one or two of the owoc to accompany them on their journey. The presence of owoc would, hopefully, reassure the inhabitants of the other valley. They would also make it possible to extend the length of the trip. One or even two owoc could not, of course, feed an entire platoon. (The colonists had found from experience that one owoc could feed three humans.) But they could enable the expedition to stay out for a few extra days.

To Indira's surprise, the owoc agreed readily to the trip. She had thought the timid beings would be fearful of undertaking such a journey. But it seemed that they had developed a mystical confidence in the ability of humans to protect them. It was, as always, difficult to understand the owoc. But she knew that the beings had, over the years, woven the existence of humans into their concept of the Coil of Beauty. The term which the giant creatures used for humans was "the Shell of Beauty." The term had not made much sense to her before. But now she understood.

For a mollusc, a shell is that which protects. So help me, we've become the guardian angels of their quasi-religion.

The real problem, in fact, turned out to be that *all* the owoc wanted to come. Oddly enough, Kupu was particularly adamant. She seemed quite upset (judging by the mottled blue and brown of her mantle) when Indira insisted that she could not accompany the expedition. It would be hard enough for any of the owoc to manage the trek through high country, much less the huge and bulky mother.

"Why in the world would she want to come?" Indira asked Julius later. "Kupu usually never leaves her oruc grove. *What's so funny?*"

Julius was howling.

"Don't you get it?" he gasped. "The other owoc want to come because they think it would be nice to pay a social call on their neighbors. But Kupu—"

He stopped speaking, choked with laughter. Indira waited impatiently.

"But Kupu wants to come because—" Wheeze, wheeze. "Because she's a *swinger*."

Indira was not amused, until the next morning, when Julius' little joke came to life. More than anything else, it was the dumbfounded expression on his face when she told Julius that the owoc were now *insisting* that Kupu had to come along.

"You mean—?" His rubbery face twisted into a befuddled scowl. "It's not possible! They're primitives. They can't possibly understand the dangers of inbreeding."

Indira was grinning from ear to ear. As much as she loved Julius, she often found him excessively opinionated.

"Don't ask me, O great biologist. But the owoc are quite clear on the matter—much clearer than usual, in fact. Kupu has to come along because, and I quote, 'the clan needs to twine itself further into the Coil.' Sounds like a clear argument for exogamy to me. But what do I know? I'm just a lowly historian."

Julius' glare was a joy to behold.

The trip was long and difficult. Not arduous, for the humans. Joseph had found that the mountain valleys were all interconnected by passes and gullies which posed no more than a mild challenge for humans in as good a physical condition as the colonists were. But it was hard for the four owoc who accompanied them, especially Kupu. Seeing how terribly the trip strained the ungainly mother, Indira was amazed at her stoic determination to continue.

I never fully realized just how ill-suited the owoc are to live in the mountains.

She turned and looked to the south. She could not see it, of course, but Joseph had described the vast, lush, flat plain which stretched south of the mountain to the distant horizon.

What horror must live on that plain, to drive these poor beings here?

The trip took so much longer than anticipated that Indira began to wonder if the humans could sustain their activity on the small amount of childfood they each received every day. When the expedition arrived at the first of the valleys which

Joseph had found, however, the owoc immediately began gorging themselves on the uroc which grew thickly there. At first, Indira thought they were just indulging themselves in their favorite treat. But when she saw the great quantities of childfood which they produced, she realized that the beings had understood the problem. Not for the first time, she had underestimated their intelligence. The owoc were perhaps not as smart as humans—they certainly did not think the same way—but they occasionally showed an uncanny grasp of things.

They stayed in the valley for an entire day. The owoc clearly needed the rest, and the humans were glad to eat more than rations. The next day, before they left, the owoc spent most of an hour tearing off succulent oruc leaves, until they each had as much as they could carry. When the humans realized what they were doing, they immediately made lashing material out of various vines which they found in the area. In the end, the owoc set off with their broad backs piled high with leaves.

Finally, on the seventh day of a trip which the humans alone could have easily managed in two, the expedition came over the crest of a pass and onto the slope leading down to the big valley.

God, it is big, thought Indira. *Three or four times the size of the one we live in. So much for my occasional worries about overpopulation.*

Then she remembered that this valley was already populated, and felt a sudden shame.

We are not conquerors, to do with this land and its people what we will. Let it never be so. Conquistadores are an evil of our past.

(It did not occur to her, then, that humans might not be the only conquistadores on Ishtar.)

As they descended into the valley, Indira gradually realized that this huge valley was much less thinly populated than their own. Even before the humans had arrived, the small valley to the south had been fairly thick with owoc. Twelve years of human agriculture had produced a bounty of food beyond the owoc's wildest dreams. That surplus, combined with the high numbers of surviving spawn, had resulted in a population density which sometimes reminded Indira of her visits to her mother's Bengali homeland.

Eventually—still at a distance of well over a kilometer away—she spotted the "big hut" Joseph had described. Joseph's description, she now understood, had been inaccurate.

He's never seen one before, of course. But if that's not a temple, I'm going to resign in disgrace from the World Historical Association.

The structure was quite large, given the limitations of the bamboo-like plant which the colonists had found to be the only suitable wood on the mountain for construction. On Earth it would have been labeled "three-stories." From what Indira could see at a distance, she doubted that the building actually had stories, as such. It was built along the lines of a simple A-frame. A shallow ramp led up to a terrace, which stretched across the entire width of the building. From a distance, she could not see into the building itself. The terrace was covered by the sloping roofs, but she could not tell how far back it ran.

Perhaps it runs all the way through. There might not be any interior walls at all. The building may just be a place for congregation. In this warm climate, the only real reason for shelter is to keep off the drizzle. And personal privacy. We humans have even adopted the dress of Polynesians. Sarongs.

She smiled wrily. Since Janet died, Indira was the only woman on the planet who covered her breasts. The young women simply wrapped the sarongs around their waists.

As they neared the building, Indira began to spot owoc and gukuy moving about. There were not many of them, and they were not engaged in the "dance" which Joseph had described. (Which, she now suspected, was some kind of religious ritual.) The handful of owoc she could see were scattered about, browsing on patches of oruc. The gukuy—she counted three of them—were all clustered in a field of upunu. Now that she was closer, she could see that the field had a cultivated look about it. Yet there was something odd about its appearance, which nagged at her memory until recognition came.

That field's absolutely infested with uduwo snails. Why don't they do something about them?

(It was not until later that she remembered what Julius had told her. The beaks of the gukuy were adapted for eating meat, not vegetation. The gukuy cultivated upunu fields not for the plants themselves but for the snails which fed on them.)

Indira now began rehearsing her speech of peace and well-wishes. Halfway through the rehearsal, the speech became a moot point.

The owoc, it turned out, had their own ideas on proper social behavior.

Suddenly, the four owoc with them began hooting loudly. Kupu's hoots were especially deafening.

Immediately, the owoc and the gukuy in the valley stopped what they were doing and looked up.

Within a few seconds, hoots were being exchanged back and forth between the owoc on the slope and the owoc in the valley. Indira understood the hoots of her owoc companions—poetic variations, basically, on the general theme of "howdy." She could *almost* understand the hoots which came in return.

It's a different dialect. But I don't think—a sigh of relief—*that it's a separate language.*

At first, the gukuy observing the scene showed no reaction but a mild mottling in their mantles. Green, Indira noted with relief. But then they spotted the humans; and their mantles turned, in an instant, scarlet and ochre.

Fear. Indecision. What frightening creatures we must appear to them. Nothing on this planet looks remotely like human beings.

The owoc in the valley seemed totally unconcerned about the humans (whom they had certainly spotted, at this distance). The beings were lumbering toward the interlopers, issuing hoots which Indira could generically recognize as happy greetings. And their mantles were now solid green, untouched by even a trace of any other color.

But the three gukuy in the upunu field suddenly broke and raced toward the "temple," whistling loudly. A moment later, four other gukuy emerged from the building. A rapid exchange of sounds and whistles.

Everything seemed to be happening at once. By now, the two groups of owoc had met and were beginning to intermingle. Formality, Indira noted, did not seem to be a prominent feature of owoc culture. But her attention, for the moment, was on the temple.

A moment later, as she had feared, the seven gukuy in the temple re-emerged and began hurrying toward them.

Bearing weapons. The same type which the raiders had

carried—those stone-tipped whips and long-spiked morning stars. (Flails and forks, the gukuy called them, as she would learn later.) And as they neared, she saw that blue was beginning to ripple in their mantles. Blue was a color rarely seen in the mantles of owoc.

Rage.

She saw the other humans in her party grow stiff and tense. Suddenly, at Joseph's command, the youngsters—

They're not youngsters anymore, you damn fool! They're warriors, and if you don't think fast they're going to react like warriors.

—reversed their grip on the spears.

Indira sighed with relief. Until she remembered that the grip which holds a spear in the point-down position of peace is the same one used to hurl it. And each of the—*warriors*—was carrying three spears.

She had not paid much attention to the military exercises, but she knew enough to know that Joseph had trained his people to start an attack with a cast of spears.

"Joooph!"

The youth did not look at her; his eyes remained fixed on the approaching gukuy. But he gestured with his hand, in a manner which simultaneously conveyed acknowledgement and surety. Then, when the gukuy were no more than thirty meters away, he hooted loudly:

> WE NOT GOOD
> PEACE
> IS BREAK ARE

The gukuy suddenly stopped. The ochre in their mantles strengthened. Red fear remained, but the blue began to fade.

Joseph hooted again.

> WE MUST OWOC
> FRIENDS
> US BE ARE

The owoc from both groups suddenly began hooting back and forth. The exchange was too rapid for Indira to follow, even if she had been able to understand the dialect of the new ones. But whatever they were saying, there was no mistaking the reaction of the gukuy. The blue disappeared entirely, as did the red. Ochre remained, but it grew slowly dimmer. And within minutes, faint traces of dappled green began to appear.

That's one of the great advantages chromatophoric beings have over we poor humans. Even if they can't speak another's language, they can still read their emotions. What must they make of us, I wonder?

Incongruously, she snickered.

A bunch of miserable monsters, whose leader is always implacable about everything and one of whom is always in heat.

She glanced at Jens, and had to suppress an outright laugh.

Not far from the truth, actually. It's amazing how the youngsters adapt to the owoc. Even though they know that human color means nothing, they can't help reacting unconsciously to Jens' white skin. I think every youngster in the colony has shared either Jens or Karin Schmidt's bed. Or both.

(She'd mentioned that to Julius, once. The biologist had laughed, and said: "Yeah, I know. On this planet, the myth is going to be that white people are hyper-sexual. Give it a few generations and I wouldn't be surprised to see pale skin make a genetic comeback. I doubt if the Nazis would be pleased, though, given the circumstances. Unless they decided the owoc were honorary Aryans.")

Eventually, expressing themselves in owoc hoots which Indira and Joseph were able to interpret, the gukuy invited the humans into the building which Indira thought to be a temple. Indira immediately accepted.

The minute she walked up the ramp, and saw the interior of the building (as she had suspected, it was open all the way through), all doubt vanished. There was no mistaking the meaning of the huge figurine which rested at the center of the temple.

It was not a carving, but a construct—a wicker-like framework of some kind, embellished and decorated with shells, precious stones, and carved—horn?

She was deeply impressed by the artistry of the piece. The style was in no sense naturalistic. It rather reminded her of the exaggerated style of ancient African carvings. Except for the intricacy of the detail, which had a vague resemblance to the ornate idols in Hindu temples.

But even more than the stylistic resonances, she was stunned by the essence of the figurine itself. It was the statue of a gukuy, in repose. Deep green, in color. She thought that the curl of the arms had meaning, as well.

But whatever the specific significance of any particular detail of the statue, the sense of the whole was unmistakable. Light years apart, and thousands of year later in time, an alien race had produced a being whose vision could not have been so different from one glimpsed on Earth.

Staring at the statue, she took a deep breath. Then, for the first time since entering the valley, felt the tension wash out of her completely.

Siddartha Gautama. The Buddha.

Chapter 12

"The similarity's only general, of course," she explained to Julius after she returned. "Until I learn the gukuy language, I won't be sure. Owoc is such a difficult language in which to convey precise meaning. Still, from what I could glean, their faith absolutely resonates with quasi-Buddhist conceptions."

"And just how did the teachings of the Buddha find their way to Ishtar—interstellar transcendentalism?" demanded Julius. "Have you become a mystic yourself now?"

Indira smiled. "No, Julius. I'm still the hard-boiled rationalist you know and love. But convergence operates on more than a biological level, my dear. It's not surprising at all, actually. Most of the great religions on Earth arose within a relatively short time, you know—in cultures scattered all over the planet. Beginning around a half millenium before the birth of Christ. In China, you had Confucius and Lao-Tse. In India, Buddha and the founders of Jainism, and the transformation of the Vedic traditions into Hinduism. In Greece, the rise of philosophy. For that matter, it was during the same general period that your Hebrew ancestors were hammering out their own faith. The last great world religion, Islam, arose not much more than a millenium later. A short time, really, in terms of the whole sweep of human history."

Julius was frowning. "I don't see the point."

"The point, Julius, is that this gukuy religion tells me a great deal about the general state of current gukuy society. Societies, I should say. The Earth's great religions and philosophies all arose in response to the development of civilization. Animism and tribal pantheons are inadequate to explain a varied and complex world. Intelligent beings inevitably begin to grope for universal truths. And a universal morality."

"That sounds like good news."

Indira shrugged. "Yes and no. All of the great religions created a basic code of ethics, which were actually quite similar in their principles. Variations on the Golden Rule, essentially. That represented a gigantic stride forward in human culture, no matter how often those principles were later violated in practice. But the great religions also quickly became a powerful tool for ruling classes to expand and strengthen their domination. Constantine's conversion to Christianity was accompanied by the Church's allegiance to the temporal authority of the Roman Empire, to give just one example."

"There are empires on this planet?"

She nodded. "At least one, that I know of. They call it 'Ansha.' Most of the gukuy in the valley are from there, in fact."

"Oh, great. Our next door neighbors are imperialist missionaries."

Indira hesitated, pursing her lips.

"I don't think so. I won't be certain until I learn their own language, but I'm pretty sure the gukuy in the big valley are refugees."

"Refugees? From what?"

"Religious persecution, I imagine. I don't think their religion is very old, Julius. A generation or two, at the most. The gukuy say the statue in the temple is a representation of someone named Goloku."

"Their god?"

She shook her head. "That's not the sense I get. More like a revered sage, or a prophet. The founder of their religion. But the point is that the gukuy talk about Goloku in a familiar sort of way."

Julius stared.

"Yes, Julius. If I'm right, we're not dealing with an old and well-established universal church."

She smiled. "We are there—with the apostles."

Later, Julius took her to the hut which had been formerly occupied by Hector. Once inside, she saw that the center of the hut's floor was dominated by a huge pile of clay, oddly shaped.

"What in the world is that for?"

Julius looked apologetic.

"Hey, I only got started. It's going to be a three-dimensional map of the mountain. I've already roughed out the western side."

Indira saw that the pile of clay was in the general shape of an oval. Julius pointed to one of the long sides of the pile.

"That's the southern slope," he explained. "I've just started there. That's going to be a lot of work, with all those canyons. But I've got the time, since it'll be a while before Ludmilla's expedition finishes exploring the east and north."

"It seems like a lot of work, Julius. It's very interesting, I admit, but why—"

She stopped suddenly, seeing the bleak look on her lover's face.

"It's a *military* map."

Julius nodded. "Yeah. Andrew suggested the idea, and Joseph immediately adopted it. Joseph asked me to start the map just before you left. He wants to have a good picture of possible invasion routes onto the mountain. And I think he's already thinking in terms of fortifications."

Indira sighed heavily. "Do you really think this is necessary, Julius?"

The biologist's voice was harsh. "Yes, I do. But it really doesn't matter what I think. Or what you think, Indira. *Captain* Adekunle wants it."

She stared at him. Julius shrugged. "You can't have it both ways, Indira. If the man's in charge, he's in charge."

She remembered the authority in Joseph's gesture when the gukuy were approaching, and nodded. And the fear in her heart suddenly flamed brighter.

Much to Julius' distress, Indira began making plans for an extended sojourn among the gukuy in the big valley. She would be gone for weeks, if not months, immersing herself in the gukuy culture and language.

But his unhappiness, and her plans, proved unnecessary. Four days after her return, a delegation of gukuy arrived from the big valley. Upon their arrival, they announced that *they* had come for an extended visit. So that they could learn from the humans.

"Except they don't call us 'humans,'" Indira explained. "Gukuy can't seem to handle hard aspirates at all, and sibilants are difficult for them. So I made it simple—we are now 'ummun.'"

Julius scowled. "Dirty, rotten linguistic imperialism, if you ask me."

Indira ignored the quip. She was frowning, deep in thought. "What's on your mind, fair lady?"

"Huh? Oh, nothing. It's just—I'm not sure yet. They seemed to agree to the term 'ummun' readily enough, but I don't think—"

She fell silent. Julius prodded her, but the historian refused to speculate until she felt she understood the gukuy language well enough.

Two months later, she understood.

"They'll call us 'ummun,' out of politeness. But that's not really how they think of us. We're demons."

"*What?*"

"You heard me. Demons. Powerful and fearful creatures from beyond the known world."

"But—why *demons?* We haven't done anything wicked to them. Or to the owoc, for that matter."

Indira smiled, and patted his cheek.

"Poor Julius. So stunted you are by that horrid Judeo-Christian outlook."

Julius scowled. "What's my ancestry got to do with this?" he demanded.

"In the rigidly monotheistic religions—which shaped your cultural views, regardless of whether you personally are still a believer—all powerful non-divine creatures are amalgated into devils. Pure evil. But the original conception of demons doesn't necessarily carry the connotation of evil. Although evil is always there, lurking below the surface. Not evil, actually. Power. Tremendous, unbridled, fearful power—which can, of course, often manifest itself in evil ways."

"Why should they think we are powerful? Our technological level's really no higher than theirs, when you get right down to it. Our theoretical knowledge is vastly greater, of course. That's even true for the kids, even though I often think the disrespectful little bastards think most of what we teach them are fairy tales."

Indira smiled. As much as he carped on the sins of the younger generation, she knew that the biologist adored them. Much more uncritically, in fact, than she did.

"It has nothing to do with technology, Julius. At a Bronze Age stage of historical development, there's really not that much difference between the technological level of civilized societies and barbarians. The difference is social."

"So?"

"So these beings are not stupid, dear. They don't understand us, but they understand that we are very, very different. And then there's the frightening way we *move*."

"Huh?"

She frowned. "Surely you, a biologist, can understand *that* fear. Other than size—and we're much taller than gukuy, even if they outweigh us—what's the other physical trait that all animals instinctively fear? Especially intelligent animals?"

Understanding came to him. "Speed."

"Yes. Especially uncanny speed, produced by unusual forms of motion. Didn't you tell me once that the reason humans have such an irrational fear of snakes is because of the way in which they strike?"

"Yeah. A coiled snake can strike like a lightning bolt, so most people think the reptiles are inhumanly fast. Truth is, a human can outrun any snake that ever lived."

"Have you ever thought of how the way humans move must look to gukuy? Like nothing they've ever seen. Almost magical, is the sense I get from them. Even with their excellent eyesight, their brains have a hard time processing our motion. To them, we—we flicker. Half-seen; half invisible. And so *quickly*. And we can move easily over terrain that they have to struggle through. You should have seen how their mantles were flooded with orange when they saw two of the children having a race up the mountainside."

"Orange? I've never seen that color on the owoc."

"No, neither have I. I'm certain that it's the color of astonishment. Owoc are never astonished. Puzzled, often. But then their mantles turn ochre with indecision and uncertainty. To be astonished—amazed—requires more of a rational sense of what is normal in the world. To the owoc the world simply is what it is. They may not understand it—they often don't— but they accept it."

Julius grunted. "True. They really aren't all that bright."

Indira's stare was stony.

"That's one way to put it. But there's another way to look

at it, you know. The capacity to be amazed presupposes that you believe in your ability to understand the world. When something then happens which doesn't fit your conception of reality, you are astonished and amazed."

"So?"

"So you see that as a sign of intelligence. To me, it's also a sign of arrogance."

"*Arrogance?*"

"Of course. Only an arrogant creature thinks it understands the universe. Like a cocky biologist from the streets of Noo Yawk."

She smiled sweetly. "That's why you're so often astonished and amazed, dear."

Julius' face twisted into a rueful grimace.

"Skewered again, damme. But what are you trying to say, Indira? You don't really think the owoc are as intelligent as we are, do you? Or as intelligent as the gukuy?"

She shrugged. "What's intelligence? To you, it means the capacity for rational, linear thought. Problem solving. In that sense, no—the owoc are like retarded children. But if you use the word 'intelligence' in a broader sense, who's to say? The only thing I do know, after years of living with them, is that the owoc view reality in a totally different manner than we do. We think in terms of truth and falsehood. Things are, or they are not. But with the owoc—"

She paused, then continued.

"Do you realize, Julius, that there is no equivalent in the owoc language for the concept of 'falsehood'—or 'lying.' "

"Hey, lady, give me a break. I never denied the sweet critters are as honest as the day is long. I'd trust 'em with my piggybank in a minute, if I still had one."

She shook her head. "You're missing my point. Perhaps I put it badly. In the owoc language, Julius, *there is no such idea as the truth.*"

"What? But how—"

She smiled. "You can't imagine that, can you? The concept of 'truth' is at the very bedrock of human consciousness. That's why"—the smile became a broad grin— "you are amazed at the idea that another species could even think at all without the idea of 'truth' at the center of their thoughts."

The expression on Julius' face caused her to laugh.

"Dear Julius! Did you ever read the poetry of Keats? 'Ode On a Grecian Urn'?"

He shook his head.

> *"Beauty is truth, truth beauty,—that is all*
> *Ye know on earth, and all ye need to know."*

She stared into the distance. "Perhaps that ancient poet understood the way of the owoc. We never will. But do not sneer at it, Julius. If I might quote from another great English poet:

> *"There are more things in heaven*
> *and earth, Horatio,*
> *Than are dreamt of in your philosophy."*

The next several months were a busy time in Julius' life, however, so he rarely had time to think about Indira's ideas. In truth, he saw very little of his lover. Indira, as she had years before with the owoc, insisted on living with the gukuy. Total immersion, she explained, was the only efficient way to learn a new language.

He missed her company, of course, but he was engrossed in his own work. Exploring expeditions were out constantly now, bringing back a steady stream of reports. The topographic model of the mountain steadily took shape and detail, until it was finally finished.

"I've decided to call the mountain *Mons Ishtar*," he announced to Indira proudly that night.

"That's nice, dear," she replied absently. "But the mountain already has a name. The gukuy were here first, and they call it the Chiton."

Julius was disgruntled, but he accepted the change in names. By way of obscure linguistic revenge, however, he began referring to the map hut as "the Pentagon."

The youngsters acquiesced in the name, although they didn't understand it. In truth, they thought the name was silly—the hut was obviously square, not five-sided. Indira understood the name, of course. She did not think it was silly; she thought it was grotesque.

But the next morning, when Julius examined the model, he admitted to himself that the name change was appropriate. Especially from the south, where all the gukuy seemed to come from, the canyons which were regularly spaced along the mountain's flank would give it the appearance of a ridged, flattish shell. Rising from the plain like a gigantic chiton, moving from east to west.

The view from the north would seem different, of course. There the long crest of the mountain broke sharply into a talus slope that, for the uppermost hundred meters, was almost a sheer cliff. From the north, the mountain would look like an enormous granite iceberg. (If there were such a thing as an iceberg on Ishtar, which Julius doubted.) But it was unlikely that many gukuy had ever seen the mountain from that angle. Beyond the base of the talus slope stretched a vast broken badlands, as far as the eye could see. By the verdant standards of Ishtar, the region to the north was a barren wasteland.

From a military point of view, that discovery was relieving. There would be nothing to fear from the north. The region was probably uninhabited. And not even humans could ascend the northern cliff, without specialized mountaineering equipment.

The danger lay south, and east. The eastern flank of the Chiton tapered down much more gently than did its western flank—like a flattened tail. True, the eastern slope contained the densest vegetation on the mountain—much of it a type of quasi-bramble which Julius suspected any gukuy would find well-nigh impenetrable. But there were still many open areas, providing relatively easy access to the entire plateau. When questioned by Indira, the gukuy confirmed that they themselves had reached the big valley through that route. (And still did. Over time, Indira realized that the gukuy in the valley maintained communication with their co-believers in the south.)

Joseph and his lieutenants, after discussing the question with Julius, decided to ignore the potential danger from the east, for the moment. The gukuy in the big valley would warn them of any invaders coming from that direction. It was decided that, after Indira established good enough communications with the gukuy, the colonists would request permission to station one of the platoons in the big valley. But until that time came, they would concentrate on the immediate problem. The southern slope, and its canyons.

There were six canyons along the southern flank of the mountain. Three of them veered off into cul-de-sacs, and could be safely ignored. But the other three led straight toward the summit—and one of them, the largest, reached almost to the crest.

Andrew MacPherson was assigned the task of planning fortifications. The task was daunting, given the small numbers of the colonists, but Joseph was determined to create a stone wall barring access through the canyon.

Andrew came to Julius for advice on how to design fortified walls. As he had years before with Hector, Julius steered him toward Indira. But Indira refused to discuss the matter. Later, she promised, when she was done with learning the gukuy language.

"Later" turned out to be much later. Indira had thought it would be easier to learn the gukuy language than it had been to learn owoc. True, she assumed the language would be more complex. But, on the positive side, she thought there would be two big advantages:

First, she suspected that the gukuy mentality was much closer to human than was the owoc. Second, the fact that both she and the gukuy could speak (at least to some extent) the hooting language of the owoc gave them a mutual verbal Rosetta stone.

Both of those assumptions turned out to be correct. But what she hadn't counted on was two other factors. One: there was no such thing as a "gukuy language." There were *five* languages represented among the gukuy pilgrims. Three of those languages obviously belonged to the same language group. They were among the languages spoken by the civilized societies which lived somewhere to the south. Two of them were quite closely related. (In her own mind, she thought of the relationship between the three languages as being similar to trying to learn French, Spanish and Russian at the same time.) Unfortunately, the dominant language of the three—and the language spoken by the majority of the pilgrims—was the "Russian" oddball. The language in question was called Anshaku, and she soon learned that it was the principal language of the largest and most powerful empire in that part of Ishtar known to the pilgrims.

The two other languages belonged to an entirely different language group—the language group spoken by most of the barbarian tribes which, she learned, inhabited the great plain south of the Chiton. One of the languages was Kiktu, the language of the largest and most powerful of those tribes. The other "language" was an argot, a Kiktu-based *lingua franca* which could apparently be understood by all of the barbarians.

After dithering a bit (as someone who was both adept at languages and enjoyed learning them), Indira decided that practical considerations required her to focus her efforts on Anshaku and Kiktu. All of the gukuy pilgrims from the south could speak Anshaku, at least to some extent. And while only two of the pilgrims who came from the barbarian tribes were Kiktu, the other barbarians could speak the language to some extent.

Even after narrowing it down, she was still faced with a linguistic task which would be equivalent to learning Russian and Arabic simultaneously.

And then another massive task was dropped upon her.

"They insist that I teach them to speak 'ummun,'" she complained to Julius.

The biologist shrugged. "So?"

Indira glared. "*So?* This—from a man who can barely speak one language?"

Julius shrugged again, grinning. "Hey, I'm bad at languages. But I don't need to be good at it. Most biological research is published in English. You don't really need any other language that much, except Spanish—which I can read well enough."

He chewed his upper lip. "Unless you want to be a dinosaur specialist. Then, of course, you have to know Chinese. Fluently." A shudder; another grin. "Not the least of the reasons I didn't specialize in dinosaurs."

Indira was still glaring. "But the whole thing doesn't make sense! There are only a handful of humans on this planet. Why should they take the time and trouble to learn our language when we're willing to learn theirs?"

Julius stared at her. "A question like that? Coming from an historian?"

He started counting off on thick fingers.

"I can think of three reasons, right off the top of my head.

One. They don't know how many of us there are." He held up a hand, forestalling her protest. "Oh, sure, they can see there's only a handful of us *here*. *Today*. But where did we come from? And how many more of us might follow?"

"I have every intention of explaining where we came from and why there won't be any more of us. Not for centuries, at the earliest."

"And how will you convince them? The beings on this planet can't have the faintest conception of astronomical reality. In all the time we've lived here, not *once* has the cloud cover broken. Not for even a minute. The earliest civilizations on Earth—even barbarians, for that matter—had a highly advanced empirical knowledge of astronomy. These people can't have any whatsoever. We came from beyond the sky—that's the most they'll understand."

"But—"

"But what, Indira? How can you possibly expect people at this stage of cultural development to understand the reality and the limits of an advanced technological culture like our own? You know and I know that the society was barely able to muster the resources to equip our expedition. You know and I know that it was a one-shot deal. You know and I know that humanity is still utterly preoccupied with the gigantic task of rebuilding our own planet. You know and I know that it'll be generations—centuries, more likely—before another inter-stellar expedition is sent out. You know and I know that faster-than-light travel has been proven to be a complete pipe dream, and that space travel is going to remain limited to slightly above 10% of the speed of light. You know and I know that means another expedition to Tau Ceti would take over a century to get here even *after* it left Earth orbit. You know and I know that even then the priority would probably be to try for a new solar system altogether."

He stopped and took a deep breath.

"When we signed up for this trip, love, the Society warned us that we couldn't expect a follow-up expedition for at least five hundred years. Minimum. More likely a millenium. But how are you going to even *explain* any of that to the gukuy—in any way that they could possibly understand?

"So how do you expect them to *believe* you?" He held up a second finger. "Which leads me to point two. If I were in their shoes (so to speak), I would damn well want to learn as much as possible about a bunch of strange *demons* who landed in our midst. Sure, right now the *demons* seem friendly, and there ain't many of them. But who knows? Best to learn what we can about them—and the best way to do that is to learn how to speak 'demon.'"

He stopped. Indira was scowling up at him.

"And?"

"And what?"

"What's the third reason, dammit? You said you could think of three, right off."

"Oh." He grinned, and made an annoying clucking sound with his tongue.

"Such a question—from an historian! Indira, what's the language that all bright young kids all over the world want to learn—as soon as they get to school?"

"English."

"Yes. But why? It's a completely foreign language—comes from a small little island half way around the world from most of them. Originally spread by rapacious imperialists, in fact."

Indira sighed. "Because it's one of the global languages. The dominant one, in fact. And because much of the world, especially Africa and large parts of Asia, are still so fragmented linguistically that knowing how to speak your own tongue doesn't get you very far in the big, wide world."

"Exactly. My best friend in college was from Pakistan. His English was better than mine. So was his accent, according to everybody except Noo Yawkers. But he barely spoke Urdu. I asked him why, once. He asked me if insanity ran in my family."

"But none of that's true here, Julius," protested Indira. "No human language occupies that position on Ishtar."

"True—and not true. I'm interested in something. You just called this planet 'Ishtar.' Why? You're always chiding me for being a linguistic chauvinist, Indira. But here you are using a name for this planet which was adopted on Earth over a century before we even got here. Why not use the native word?"

Indira took a deep breath. "Which one? Each language has a different name for 'the world.' Most of them mean 'the Meat of the Clam,' but—"

"But which one should you use? Without offending the others? So you took the practical course—you fell back on a name that's not offensive to any local foibles because it's so utterly alien."

Indira's eyes widened. "You think—"

"I think you're underestimating these people, Indira. I think you're dealing with some very intelligent people. Visionaries, in fact. Who are struggling to forge a universal faith which can be common to gukuy from all cultures."

He reached out and stroked her cheek. "So give them the universal language they need, love. The language brought by *demons* from beyond the sky, that all peoples and tribes can learn to speak without fearing their own culture will be subordinated."

She initially thought to teach the gukuy Spanish, but finally settled on English. True, English was a notoriously difficult language to learn. In many ways, Chinese would have been the best choice, since all of the gukuy languages tended to be tonal. But Chinese was a difficult language in too many other respects. The Chinese themselves had struggled for centuries to fit the precise rigidities of technological society into the amorphous grammar of their language. (The ideogrammatic writing style had been abandoned completely almost a century earlier, in favor of a modified version of the Latin alphabet.)

In the end, her decision was not determined by narrow linguistic factors. It was a simple fact of history that English was well on its way to becoming the universal language of the human race. At the historic Singapore Convention, where the world's language practices were finally agreed upon, English had been listed as simply one of the four accepted "global languages." The decision had been a compromise. Even then, English was obviously in a league of its own as an international language. But there had been no reason to ruffle the feathers of the Chinese, who were prone to complain that as many people spoke their language as did English (even though, in private, their representatives would admit that Chinese had never spread very far beyond the boundaries of those who were ethnically Han). And the French, outraged at their own demotion to a "regional language," had made clear that they would under no conditions agree to the elevation of English to the world's sole accepted global language. (For the first time in centuries, the phrase "perfidious Albion" had echoed in the corridors and chambers of diplomacy.) So, wisely, the representatives of English had cheerfully agreed to the polite fiction that English was only one of four "global languages," trusting to the logic of history and the common sense of the world's population to settle the question in practice.

Spanish would have been easier to teach to gukuy than English. But English was the language of the colonists, and many of the younger generation spoke no other tongue. And, in the back of her mind, Indira knew that someday contact with Earth would be reestablished. Centuries in the future, true, but it would happen eventually. Better then for the gukuy to be fluent in English.

Then, just as she thought she had settled the question, a new (and, to her, disturbing) twist arose. Joseph approached her, a few days after her conversation with Julius, and asked which of the four global human tongues would be the most *difficult* for gukuy to learn—even if they already knew English.

"Arabic," she replied instantly. "It's a Semitic language, totally unlike English. So's Chinese, of course. But gukuy could learn Chinese easily enough. I'm not sure they could ever really learn Arabic. Not to speak it, at least—the aspirates in Arabic are brutal. They could learn to read Arabic, I imagine. But Arabic script's totally different from the Latin alphabet."

Joseph nodded thoughtfully, and left. The next day he instituted classes in basic Arabic (oral and written), taught by six of the youngsters for whom it was their (still-remembered) native tongue. All members of the platoons were strongly encouraged to attend (which meant everyone except Indira and Julius). For officers and sergeants, attendance was mandatory.

Indira was upset, but she made no protest. 'If the man's in charge, he's in charge.'

She knew what Joseph was doing, of course. She didn't think she'd ever mentioned it in the history classes she'd given the children as they grew up. But it hardly mattered. Joseph was extraordinarily intelligent—certainly as intelligent as the officers of the United States Army during World War II who'd thought of using Navajo soldiers to send radio messages in a language which was incomprehensible to the Japanese Empire.

Battle language.

Chapter 13

The military training which Joseph and his lieutenants had reinstituted—indeed, taken far beyond the level achieved by Hector Quintero—was soon put to use.

A scouting patrol reported the appearance, on the lower southern slope of the Chiton, of a small party of gukuy slavers. The identity of this party as slavers was confirmed by the Pilgrims of the Way (as the gukuy from the big valley called themselves), when they heard the scouts' report. The gukuy on the slope were bearing large manacle-like devices, identical to ones discovered on the bodies of the earlier group of invaders. The Pilgrims informed Joseph that these devices were employed exclusively by slavers seeking owoc. The devices had no military use whatsoever.

Two platoons—Ludmilla's and Takashi's—set forth immediately to destroy the slaver party, with Joseph in overall command. Joseph chose those two platoons because Takashi's platoon had been experimenting with the use of shields, in addition to the light "sortabamboo" armor with which all the platoons were equipped. Joseph wanted to learn from practical experience whether the experiment would bear fruit. If so, he would arm all three platoons with shields. If not, Takashi's platoon would resume training with spears only.

The slaver party had moved. It took the human warriors almost another day to find them. The slavers had apparently chosen to approach the mountain-top through one of the smaller canyons. (Joseph took note of the problem; thereafter scouting patrols were instructed to continue shadowing the enemy, sending back only one individual to report.)

During the middle of that night, the humans surrounded the slaver camp on both sides of the canyon. Joseph thought that the slavers would not expect an attack directly down the slopes of the canyon, given the gukuy difficulty with steep terrain. (In this regard, he proved to be correct; and took note.) He also thought that by attacking in the middle of the night the humans would completely surprise the slavers. (In this regard, he proved to be wrong; and took note.)

The attack did not surprise the slavers. At least, not in the sense that Joseph had intended. As soon as the first human warrior began moving down the slope, the inhumanly perceptive eyes of the gukuy camp guard spotted her. The guard instantly raised the alarm. By the time the first human reached the base of the canyon (within seconds), all of the gukuy slavers were roused and armed.

Joseph was deeply impressed by the quick reactions of the gukuy; and took note. Later, in the course of discussions with the Pilgrims of the Way, he learned that the slavers' reactions had been unusually quick. The Pilgrims thought that these slavers had been exceptionally edgy—no doubt because they were fearful of Kiktu. He filed the information away; but ordered the platoons to increase their wind sprints and emphasized training in rapid movement over rough terrain.

Although Joseph failed to achieve the surprise he had intended, the net effect was hardly any different. The gukuy simply stared in shock and amazement at the bizarre shapes flickering down the mountain sides toward them, at a speed they could barely comprehend. Six of the ten slavers were butchered before any of them so much as moved. The remaining four did not survive more than fifteen seconds. Only one of them put up any kind of effective resistance at all. She managed to inflict a minor wound on a boy's upper arm before his spear went into her brain.

The boy was one of Ludmilla's warriors. A girl in Takashi's platoon was much more seriously injured. The injury resulted not so much from any skill on the part of her opponent, but from the fact that the large shield she was carrying had caused her to fall off balance when she reached the floor of the canyon. She was unable to move back quickly enough when the last surviving slaver almost accidentally flailed her leg. The slaver died immediately thereafter from three spear thrusts.

But the girl's leg was horribly mangled. So horribly, in fact, that she limped for the rest of her life and was unable to remain in the platoon.

(A fact which upset her deeply, until Joseph appointed her to replace Takashi as the head of the fortification project. The girl threw herself into the effort, as a result of which the mountain's fortifications took shape far more quickly than would have happened otherwise. Over the years, Adrian Harabi would become famed as the shrewdest designer of fortifications— and siege tactics—of any being in the known portion of Ishtar. But she would always take her deepest satisfaction from the first fortified wall she constructed, across the big canyon of the Chiton. The wall would ever after be called "Adrian's Wall," to Indira's amusement.)

Despite the casualties, Joseph considered the ambush a great success. An entire party of slavers had been exterminated. But more importantly, he and his warriors had learned much.

The shields were immediately discarded. Nine out of the ten slavers had been slain by members of Ludmilla's platoon— principally because they had arrived at the canyon floor several seconds before any of the shield-laden members of the other platoon. It was obvious that the protection provided by the shields was a poor exchange for lessened mobility.

Over the next two days, Joseph assessed the results of the battle with his platoon lieutenants and Jens Knudsen. In the end, they adopted what would become the central principle of the little human army's military doctrine. *Speed and mobility are the heart of victory. All else is subordinate.*

It was a simple idea, to them; even obvious. When they told Indira of their conclusion, she said nothing. She could have encouraged them, for she knew they were right. She could have reinforced their conclusion with a thousand illustrations from human history, had she so chosen. Indeed, Joseph waited patiently for long minutes before he walked away, the stiffness in his face the only indication of the deep hurt at her silence. Soon thereafter, his lieutenants followed him, their expressions equally stiff. Only Jens Knudsen remained behind; but he was silent, and would not look at her.

Some part of Indira wept, as she watched the tall figure of the boy she loved walk away from her. A breach had occurred, she knew. It would only widen in the years ahead; and might never be healed.

But she could not speak. Her love of Joseph had, in that moment, been overwhelmed by dread.

Of him. Barely eighteen, the boy was, with no experience or training to guide him. Yet, in one battle—not even a battle, a minor skirmish—he had grasped the secret which had eluded the vast majority of humanity's generals throughout the long and bloody history of the species.

The advent of mechanized warfare had made the secret obvious—but, even then, not in time to prevent the ghastly slaughter of the trenches in World War I. The Nazi blitzkrieg tactics had finally burned the lesson home, a generation later.

Of course, the secret had been known earlier. Much earlier, and by more than one general or people. But never, Indira knew, had the secret been taken closer to heart than by a people whose technology was barely Neolithic. A people who had created the greatest empire in the history of the human race.

As she watched Joseph Adekunle walk away, Indira did not see a tall boy whose ancestors had lived in the rain forest of West Africa. She saw the much shorter and lighter-skinned ghost of a different man, from a different continent.

The maneuvers of that man's armies had been measured in degrees of latitude and longitude, despite the fact that their only vehicles were horses and camels. His soldiers were reputed by his defeated foes to have been an innumerable "horde"; yet, in actual fact, he had been outnumbered in every battle he won. And he won almost all his battles. He had developed principles of discipline combined with lower-level initiative which, to his bewildered and hapless victims, had seemed like magic on the battlefield. He, and his fellow generals, had incorporated the systematic use of artillery into warfare, more than half a millenium before Napoleon. He had, centuries before the invention of electronic communication, discovered the centrality of what a word-besotted later culture would call CCCI— "communication, control, command and intelligence."

His armies, which continued his traditions after his death, shattered every realm which opposed them. China, the most powerful civilization of the epoch, had fallen to them. The cumbersome armies of Europe, moving like snails beneath iron shells, had been slaughtered like lambs. The vastnesses of the

Russian forest and people defeated every invader which came against them, throughout history. Except once. Except when they were conquered by armies trained and led by the greatest general the human race ever produced.

Subedei Bat'atur. Born into the Reindeer people, an extremely primitive and obscure tribe related to another obscure and only slightly less primitive tribe, called the Mongols.

Subedei Bat'atur. Commander of the *tumens*, the 10,000 strong divisions of Genghis Khan's armies.

By his lights, and those of his people, Subedei Bat'atur had been neither cruel nor sadistic. The Mongols simply approached warfare as a practical task, to be carried out as efficiently as possible. The nomads—derided as superstitious savages by the civilized peoples who surrounded them—had, in fact, studied warfare with the clear and unblinkered eyes of a child. They experimented with the tactics and methods of their enemies, and adopted those which they found useful. For all the breathtaking scope of their vision—which was nothing less than the conquest of the entire known world—they were neither haughty nor arrogant. Quite unlike the vastly more cultured Chinese mandarins and the (much less vastly) cultured knights of Europe, who thought there was nothing to be learned from others.

The Mongols taught them otherwise. Or, at least, taught them to fear what they could not understand or learn.

In truth, Indira had always had a certain genuine admiration for the Mongols. The commonly accepted verdict of later history, she thought, was quite unfair. The Europeans who, at the time, had been able to do nothing more than pray for deliverance (which they received, simply because the Mongols, having already conquered half of Europe, decided the other half wasn't worth it) had taken their scholarly revenge centuries later. The Mongols had become synonomous with pure and simple brutality.

How many people knew, Indira wondered, that the Mongols instituted and enforced a policy of religious toleration which was unheard of in the Middle Ages? (She even smiled, then, in that moment of heartbreak, remembering the time that the Great Khan Mongke invited representatives from all the great religions to come to the imperial capital at Qarakorum. They had come—representatives from Islam, Catholicism, Orthodox Christianity, Buddhism, Taoism—and had debated theology before the Great Khan and his court. Gritting their teeth, because the holy men were accustomed to other methods of settling accounts with heretics and nonbelievers. But the debate had not degenerated into violence. Not with the Mongol *tumens* prepared to enforce the law.)

How many people knew that the Mongols fostered the greatest explosion of trade and commerce that had ever taken place prior to that time between China and the western lands of Islam and Christendom? That they built, in China, twenty-seven observatories—and then invited the world's greatest astronomers to come from Persia to help the Chinese learn to use them? That the Mongols built hospitals and even a medical academy, institutions which would have mystified the Europeans of the time?

Almost no one, thought Indira, beyond a few professional historians. Whatever the glories of their later rule, the methods which the Mongols used to create that rule were all that remained in the common memory of the human race.

An admirable people, in many ways. But they had approached warfare with the clear eyes of a young and unfettered people. They had examined war, and grasped its secret.

Speed above all else. Mobility above all else.

Utter ruthlessness.

Their victims had numbered in the millions.

She watched Joseph walk away, paralyzed between the warm heart of a mother and the cold brain of an historian.

Julius soon noticed the quiet estrangement between Indira and Joseph, and was greatly distressed. In his clumsy way, he attempted to intervene. Indira, at first, denied that there was any such estrangement. Denied it hotly, in fact; and accused Julius of various unsavory psychological traits. She was lying, Julius knew—perhaps as much to herself as to him. He knew she was lying because the accusations had been grotesquely unfair (if not totally groundless): Indira's criticisms of Julius were normally rather mild—but excruciatingly accurate.

He then approached Joseph. At first, the boy also denied that any estrangement existed. But he did not throw up a cloud of anger. So Julius persevered, until he managed to crack, slightly, the shell of hurt which Joseph had erected.

"She is keeping secrets from me, Julius. Secrets I must learn."

Julius was dumbfounded. "Secrets? What secrets?"

Joseph groped for words. "Things she knows. She is wise, Julius. She is the wisest being that exists. Especially in those matters which are at the heart of things."

The boy gestured, in a way which encompassed both the village and the lands beyond.

"How people live, and grow. What roads they must take, and which they must avoid."

His face grew hard.

"And she also knows the secrets of war. And she will not tell me. My mother has abandoned me, when I need her most."

He refused to speak further. And Julius did not press him, for he understood the boy was right.

Yet, he also understood the fear possessing Indira. He did not feel that fear so deeply, himself. Perhaps it was because he was wiser; or, perhaps, more foolish. More likely, he thought, it was because he saw the world through the eyes of a biologist rather than an historian. A paleontologist, to boot—for whom all of life is a grand and glorious testament to the inevitability of extinction; and to the new life for which that extinction makes room.

As a human with a good heart, he regretted the suffering of the past. But he thought it had been a necessary evil, an inescapable part of the progress of humanity. Indira, ironically, had a considerably cooler personality than Julius. And she knew, even better than he, that the anguish of human history had been the inevitable accompaniment of human advancement. But she also knew—far, *far* better than Julius—just how truly horrible and protracted that anguish had been.

Historical suffering, to Julius—as to most people of the early 22nd century—was a pale shadow, an abstraction. He had heard of things, even read about them. He knew who the Mongols were. And Tamerlane.

But Indira had walked the barren vastnesses of Central Asia, where a great civilization had flourished while Europe was a land of fur-clad savages. Before the Mongols came, and Tamerlane. Julius had heard of those things, and read about them upon occasion. Indira had studied the chronicles, and looked at the ruins.

And the bones.

To the warm-hearted Julius, bones were the stuff of his

trade. To the cool and distant Indira, each bone had cried out with agony; and horror.

Common bones. Not buried in great sepulchres. The bones of illiterate peasants, lying where they had been kicked aside by conquerors. The bones of the ocean of humanity, the uncountable multitudes of unknown people whose little lives had been the real stuff of history. Without whose endless toil, suffering and perseverance, nothing else would have been possible.

It could be said that the end result of human history had been worth the cost. It was said often, in fact, in the 22nd century. By professional historians as well as laymen.

Indira did not disagree with that assessment. As an historian—certainly as a woman—she had not the slightest romantic illusions about the realities of human life during the long childhood of the species. That period, tens of thousands of years in duration, when a relative handful of hunters and gatherers had been simply a part of the biological landscape of the planet. Tiny cultures, which had been characterized by a degree of social egalitarianism which would not be recaptured until the last century of human history.

Thousands upon thousands upon thousands of years of relative peace and social tranquillity. And, she knew as well, lives of utter ignorance; ending at an age when modern humans were barely out of school.

No, modern civilization was worth the price it had cost. Indira had no doubt of it. Many times, back on Earth, she had closed the book she was reading; and heaved a sigh of relief that she was fortunate enough not to have been born in the past. Any part of that past—prehistorical or civilized. She had been blessed with the rare good fortune not to have been a hunter-gatherer; or a slave; or a peasant toiling in the fields of her lord; or the victim of a bombing raid.

Indira knew she had been blessed beyond belief. She had been born in the 22nd century. At the only time in the history of the human race when life was truly all it could be. A time when the daughter of Bengali peasants and Bolivian tin miners could aspire to anything.

And had. She had aspired to the stars, and reached them.

Until, caught in disaster, a courageous captain had chosen to include an historian among the handful of adults who would survive the catastrophe. Plunged, before she was knew what was happening, back into the Bronze Age.

Years ago, Indira had stopped wondering why Captain Knudsen had included her among the survivors. She knew. He had known that, if they survived, his children would need a guide through the terrors of history.

She tried to explain her dilemma to that Captain's son. For, of all the young leaders of the colony, Jens Knudsen was now the least distant. She tried to explain that history held no "secrets"; that there was no guide through its terrors; that anything she would try would inevitably fail of its purpose—not immediately, but over time, twisted into unforeseen pathways. Stumblingly, she tried to explain that the personal freedom, equality and social justice which 22nd century humanity took for granted was the end product of millenia of struggle and suffering. She tried to explain that, in the end, the precondition for that progress was the vast wealth of modern society, which was itself another end product of the long, tortuous, bitter road of history.

How then could she show them the way forward? In a new Bronze Age, a new Time of Troubles, on a new planet? All she could see in the future was an endless vista of pain. Every way forward led nowhere but down, twisting and winding back into the nightmare coils of ancient history.

Jens had listened patiently to her explanation. When she was done, he had simply shrugged.

"I don't doubt you," he said, "but I don't think you really understand. Joseph is absolutely right, and you are absolutely wrong."

"Why?" she cried.

Jens stood and looked down at her. His face, then, had been as cold as Joseph's.

"Because history is not something that used to happen. It is happening now, and we are in it. And things have to be understood, as best we can, and then things will have to be done, as best we can, and we will have to do them. Alone."

He began to walk away, and then turned back.

"I was too young when my father died to remember him. I know only that he tried to do the impossible—he tried to land a spaceship that was never designed for planetfall. He failed, but at least he tried."

✦   ✦   ✦

For months after that episode, Indira was plunged into a deep depression. She dealt with it by monomaniacally immersing herself in the language and culture of the gukuy pilgrims.

During that period, she learned much of their language and culture. Enough to develop a profound admiration for the gukuy of the big valley—coupled with an equally profound fear.

For Indira also, it was one thing to know a truth in the abstract. Another to grasp it in all its concrete permutations.

It was, indeed, a Time of Troubles.

She had intended, as her first act, to convene a meeting of the council, where she would explain the truth to the leaders of the human colony. But when Adrian Harabi approached her, and hesitantly asked for advice concerning the fortified wall she was building, Indira changed her plans.

First things first. She was ruefully amused to see how easily even she could make that decision. It was indeed true, as Samuel Johnson had once said, that the prospect of being hanged concentrates the mind wonderfully.

So she accompanied Adrian to the proposed site of the wall. Soon they were joined by Joseph and his lieutenants.

Joseph was stiff and distant, at first. But as Indira began explaining the historical experience of the human race—the hard-learned techniques of fortifications and siege tactics—she could see the old warmth returning to his face.

She was both happy and sad to see it. Happy, for she loved the boy, and was gladdened to see his love for her returning. And sad, for the means of its return was his eager apprenticeship in the science of slaughter.

When the meeting convened the next day, Indira began by saying that the language of the pilgrims should no longer be referred to as "gukuy." It would be like calling the languages of Earth "human." There were five languages represented among the gukuy on the mountain, she explained to the council.

"The main language is Anshaku. That's the dominant language of the Ansha Prevalate, the great empire to the south."

"How far south?" demanded Joseph immediately.

Indira understood his concern.

"I don't think we need to worry about the Anshac, Joseph. At least, not in the immediate future. Most of the gukuy in the big valley—there are about sixty of them, by the way, and they call themselves the Pilgrims of the Way—are from Ansha. From the helot class, mostly, although there are several former members of the lesser warrior clans—"

She paused, observing their confusion.

"Perhaps I'd better fill you in on the general picture."

A sharp look at Julius.

"If the crotchety member of the council will refrain from sarcastic remarks on the subject of professorialism."

"We are all ears, Indira," responded Anna Cheng immediately.

"I will silence the old crank, if necessary," added Ludmilla.

Indira repressed a smile, seeing the look of outrage on Julius' face.

"The social structure of the gukuy empires—let's call them that, for the moment—has basic parallels to the civilized societies of Earth's Bronze Age. Unstable empires. Independent principalities and city-states. Constant warfare and conquest. Dynastic revolts— except that the gukuy don't really have dynasties.

"That's the biggest difference between the gukuy empires and any human parallel. The reproductive methods of the gukuy don't allow for the development of dynasties—at least, not in the sense that humans use the term. The King begat a King, who begat a King, and so forth."

"They'd be queens," interjected Anna.

Indira shook her head. "No, not even that. I made the same mistake, at first. I assumed that gukuy society would be matriarchal, in the sense that human societies became patriarchal after the Neolothic revolution. But the differences between gukuy and humans run deeper than that. True, the females are dominant. In that sense, you could describe gukuy society as 'matriarchal.' But the gukuy females *are not mothers*. The gukuy don't have a simple two-sex system. Each sex is further divided. The big majority of gukuy are sterile females. They do most of the work, and the fighting. And they dominate gukuy society on every level.

"You have to understand what this complex sexual relationship means. The sterile females dominate gukuy society, but they are not the ones who produce offspring. So the simple hereditary transmission of power and wealth which characterized the patriarchal societies of Earth's early civilizations can't apply here. There's still a transmission of power and wealth. There has to be, for any ruling class to maintain its cohesiveness. But it works indirectly, through a sort of clan system. All gukuy in a given clan are born to a certain *generation* of mothers. No one knows which particular mother, because the gukuy—like the owoc—are largely indifferent to new-born spawn. Most of the spawn die off quickly, from disease and—"

She couldn't stop herself from grimacing.

"—from predating on each other. The ones who survive are adopted into the clan. The clans trace their lineage through a succession of generations of mothers, even though the offspring are not the direct descendants of the sterile females who actually rule.

"The end result is a social structure which has no close parallel on Earth. *Within* each clan, among the members of a particular generation, the relations between the sterile females seem to be relatively egalitarian. Even rather democratic, apparently, in the barbarian tribes. Power and prestige seem largely to accrue through personal achievement.

"But *between* the clans, and, to a lesser extent, between the generations, relations are based on strict hierarchic domination. That's why the proper term for these 'empires' is *prevalates*. Ansha, for instance, is that realm in which the Ansha clan prevails over all others."

"Where do the mothers fit into all this?" asked Maria De Los Reyes.

Indira shrugged. "They are highly venerated—especially the oldest mothers, who are called the Paramount Mothers. But they do not seem to have much in the way of real power. I'm reminded of the old Japanese imperial system. The Emperor was a revered figure—a god-like figure, actually. But his duties were essentially religious. Real power lay in the hands of the shoguns, the warlords.

"At least, that's the way it seems to be in the southern societies. But I want to emphasize a point here. Do not assume that all gukuy societies are the same. Among the barbarian tribes, the mothers seem to possess a great deal of actual authority—despite the fact that they are not venerated. In fact, the main tribe even has a class of young mothers whom they call 'battlemothers.' These battlemothers participate in warfare alongside the warriors until they become old enough to start producing offspring. The civilized societies seem to view this custom with disgust."

She took a deep breath.

"And there is a new and powerful tribe rising in the far west, called the Utuku, in which the pattern of sterile female warrior dominance is carried to the extreme. All eumales are slaughtered; as well as all truemales beyond the mininum necessary. The mothers are not venerated, they are simply slaves. Breeders. The Utuku even cripple them at birth."

Indira shuddered slightly. "And they eat the owoc."

A gasp swept the hut.

"It's true. Nor are the Utuku simply cannibalistic toward their owoc cousins. They also practice cannibalism on other gukuy."

"Are all of the barbarian tribes so cruel?" asked Ludmilla.

Indira shook her head. "No. Quite the opposite, in fact. There are a number of tribes living to the west. Pastoralists. There is apparently a type of animal on Ishtar which we've never seen. The gukuy call them 'gana,' and they seem to be the equivalent of cattle. Or sheep."

Julius leaned forward, his ears practically standing out.

"The dominant tribe is called the Kiktu. Barbarians, of course. But the Kiktu religion venerates the owoc. Some sort of animistic totemism, I imagine. The end result is that the Kiktu not only do not mistreat the owoc themselves, but they will not allow others to do so. There has been at least one tribe massacred by the Kiktu for mistreating owoc, according to the Pilgrims. And they tell me that the reason the owoc on the Chiton are so rarely molested is because the region south of the Chiton is Kiktu territory. The Pilgrims themselves fled to the Chiton partly because they thought they would be safe here from persecution. But they had to obtain permission from the Kiktu to pass through their territory. Slavers never come here, according to the Pilgrims, for fear of the Kiktu."

"Then why did that slaving party come here not so long ago?" asked Julius.

Indira's face grew grim. "It seems the Kiktu have been preoccupied, of late. They have been marshalling an alliance of other tribes for war against the invaders."

"What invaders?"

She looked to the southwest, as if she could see through the walls of the hut and the mountainside beyond.

"The Utuku. The cannibals are on the march."

Interlude: *Nukurren*

During the two days after regaining consciousness, Nukurren spent much of her time, while awake, observing the demons, and discussing her observations with Dhowifa. She was not awake for long, however, and less and less as time passed. Disease had seized her in its grip, and she felt herself growing weaker.

The white demon Dzhenushkunutushen was frequently to be found walking alongside Nukurren's litter. On occasion, he was joined by the female demon Ludumilaroshokavashiki—or Ludumila, as the male demon called her. Nukurren attempted to ask them about themselves, but the demons fended off all such inquiries. On the third day, to Nukurren's surprise, they began asking her about her own life.

At first, Nukurren tried to satisfy them with a few short sentences. But the demons insisted on a full account.

So, in the end, Nukurren obliged.

She had been born a helot in the Ansha Prevalate, clanless and outcast. Her earliest memories consisted of nothing but drudgery in the fields of the high clans, endless days waking at dawn and toiling till dusk. Even the simple pleasures of friendship with other young helots had been denied her, for she was ugly, and overlarge, and generally silent.

One day, driven beyond endurance by a particularly brutal overseer, she had turned upon her. The overseer had beaten Nukurren savagely with her flail, but Nukurren was already—though not yet fully grown—of unusual size and strength. She had wrested the flail from the overseer and had begun repaying her tormentor in kind, before she was overcome by many overseers drawn to the fracas.

Nukurren herself had almost been beaten to death, then. She still bore on her mantle the scars of that flailing. She pointed them out to the demons.

Ludumila ran her hand down the side of Nukurren's mantle. It was the first time a demon had touched her since the demonlord withdrew the demon weapons. Nukurren found the touch gentle and tender.

"There are so many scars here," said Ludumila softly.

"And I thought I was bad," said Dzhenushkunutushen. The demon grinned and took off his armor. His upper torso now exposed, Nukurren could see that the milky white flesh bore several ugly, puckered marks.

"That was my first wound," said Dzhenushkunutushen, pointing to an especially large scar on the upper portion of his left arm. "I got it in my first battle."

"How?" asked Nukurren. Dzhenushkunutushen began to explain, but was interrupted by Ludumila.

"Being stupid! Using his muscles instead of his brain."

Dzhenushkunutushen grinned again, and made the motion with his upper torso which Nukurren had learn to interpret as the gesture of bemused uncertainty. "I'm prone to that," admitted the demon.

"Yes, you are!" said the female demon forcefully. To Nukurren, her posture seemed stiff and rigid. After a moment, however, her posture relaxed. She extended a hand and took the hand of Dzhenushkunutushen.

"You have to stop doing that, Jens," she said softly. Nukurren observed as the two demons stick-pedded alongside her litter, hand holding hand. Had they been gukuy, she realized, their mantles would be glowing green, and it seemed to her the strangest thing she had ever encountered in a loveless world, that demons could love.

Some time later, Dzhenushkunutushen looked back at Nukurren.

"What happened then?" he asked.

"I was condemned to slavery, and sold to a slavemaster. I spent the next many eightyweeks chained and yoked, pulling a sledge filled with trade goods to the market in Shakutulubac. I finished my growth during that time, and by the end I was very strong."

Dhowifa interrupted. "Nukurren is the strongest gukuy who

ever lived," said the truemale proudly. "Except for a mother, of course." Nukurren noticed that her lover's Kiktu had improved considerably over the past few days, even though Dhowifa spoke rarely in the presence of the demons.

"Is that true?" asked Dzhenushkunutushen.

Nukurren made the gesture of bemused uncertainty.

"Who can know? I am the strongest gukuy that I have ever met."

"She is also the fastest gukuy who ever lived," added Dhowifa. The little truemale's mantle was rippling with that shade of green which signified pride and admiration.

"Is that true?" asked Dzhenushkunutushen.

Again, Nukurren made the gesture of bemused uncertainty. "Who can know? I am the fastest gukuy that I have ever met. Stop bragging, Dhowifa."

"Why?" demanded her lover. "It's all true! And that's all that saved you from the yoke."

"What happened?" asked Ludumilla.

"One day, in the market, I was seen by a captain of the Anshac legions. She was seeking recruits for a new legion, and she bought me from my owner. I was sent to the training camps to become a warrior."

"Were you freed?" asked Dzhenushkunutushen.

"Not then."

"Did you try to escape?"

"No. To what purpose? Where would I go?" Nukurren made the gesture of resignation. "I was not unhappy at the change. The work was much easier. It is true that I met with no friendship in the ranks of the legion. I was a slave, and despised even by the lowclan recruits. But I did not care."

Nukurren fell silent, mastering the lie. She *had* cared, and cared deeply, and had spent many nights in the camps filled with aching loneliness. But her shoroku, as always, allowed no trace of her emotions to show.

"You are lying," said the demon Dzhenushkunutushen.

Nukurren stared at him, wondering how a monster could see into her soul. Then she made the gesture of agreement.

"Yes, I am lying. I did care. But I became accustomed to it. Soon enough the other recruits ceased taunting me. After I was attacked by several of them, and I killed two."

"Were you punished?"

"For that?" Nukurren made the gesture of dismissal; yellow contempt rippled briefly in her mantle. "To the contrary. I was praised by my captain and promoted. And then I devoted myself to becoming a mistress of warfare. I was good at it."

Nukurren fell silent. She refused to speak again that day, for reasons which were not clear, even to her. But on the next day, when Dzhenushkunutushen pressed her, she resumed her story.

"There is not much to tell about the eightyweeks which followed. There were many campaigns, and many battles. I acquired many more scars, but I no longer remember which they were. I was given my freedom after one battle where I fought well, and promoted again. Had I been highclan, or midclan, or even lowclan, I would have been promoted very often. Even though I am ugly, and look stupid, I am not. I always observed things carefully, and learned from them."

"How did you meet Dhowifa?"

"After a time, I was promoted again, and assigned to the Motherguard."

"What is the Motherguard?"

"That is the elite legion which guards the Divine Shell."

"Nukurren was the only clanless helot ever assigned to the Motherguard," interjected Dhowifa. "*Ever*. She was famous."

"Stop bragging, Dhowifa."

"It's true! I remember the day you arrived. My bondbrothers and I snuck out of the Divine Shell to watch."

"And what did you think?" asked Ludumila.

Dhowifa hesitated. Nukurren made the gesture of amusement. "Don't lie, Dhowifa!"

The little truemale's mantle shimmered with a complex web of colors, which suddenly dissolved into green. "I thought Nukurren was the ugliest gukuy I had ever seen. I was terrified of her. Everyone was, I think."

"Not Ushulubang," said Nukurren.

"No," agreed Dhowifa. "Not her."

The demons stopped abruptly, and stared at the two gukuy riding on the litter. Ludumila hooted a sudden command, and the owoc carrying the litter stopped also.

"You know Ushulubang?" demanded Dzhenushkunutushen.

Ochre uncertainty and confusion rippled across Dhowifa's mantle. As always, Nukurren's remained gray.

"Yes," replied Dhowifa.

Instantly, Ludumila began shouting in the harsh demon language. The entire caravan came to a halt, and within moments the black demon came racing back to the litter. Watching him approach, Nukurren was struck again by the astonishing speed of which the demons were capable.

Once he arrived, a rapid exchange took place in the demons' language. The black demon turned and stared at the gukuy on the litter.

"Explain how you know Ushulubang," he commanded. "Are you Pilgrims of the Way?"

"No, I am not," replied Nukurren immediately. Dhowifa's response was slower in coming. The ochre hues in his mantle were now interlaced with pink apprehension.

"I am not either," said Dhowifa hesitantly. "Not really. But I talked with Ushulubang whenever I could, and she trained me in dukuna."

"What is 'dukuna'?" asked the demon Dzhenushkunutushen. But before Dhowifa could answer, the black demon interrupted with a sudden burst of incomprehensible language. Nukurren could not understand it, but she knew that it was a different language than the one which the demons had used heretofore. Even harsher, and full of sounds which no gukuy could ever hope to reproduce.

Within a short time, all the demons in the caravan were gathered about the litter. After a lengthy exchange in the new language, the black demon began hooting. At once the caravan resumed its progress, but now at a more rapid pace than before. Watching the owoc who were carrying her litter, Nukurren realized that the slow and ungainly creatures were moving at the fastest pace possible for them on such difficult terrain.

"Why are you interested in Ushulubang?" she asked the demon Dzhenushkunutushen.

"Because she is—"

He was interrupted by a few short and sharp words uttered in the new demon language by Ludumila. Dzhenushkunutushen fell silent. After a moment, he said curtly: "I am not to speak of it," and moved away.

Nukurren examined the female demon. She was able, from the experience of the past few days, to recognize some of the variations in the demons' features which distinguished one from the other. By now, the difference in body shape between female and male demons was clear to Nukurren. The demons also varied in size and color.

But there were other differences, as well, which were much less obvious. As with gukuy, these differences were mainly in the face. Gukuy recognized each other primarily from the different configurations of the arm-clusters and the subtle variations in the eye-orbits. Nukurren had already learned to distinguish one demon from another with regard to their eye-orbits. Despite their tiny size, demon eyes were much like gukuy eyes; and the orbits were generically similar, except that the demon orbits seemed made of some hard material beneath the flesh.

Some of the demons—about half of them, Nukurren estimated—had deep orbits. The orbits of the remainder were shallower, it seemed. The female demon Ludumila was one of these. Looking at her, Nukurren now realized that the flatness of her eye-orbits was due to an extension of the flesh coming from that strange feature in the middle of her face—the beak-above-the-true-beak.

"What is that called?" she suddenly asked Ludumila. "That feature which protrudes above your beak?"

It required a bit more of an explanation before the demon understood the question.

"A . . . *nosu?*" asked Nukurren. Ludumila made the peculiar bobbing motion of her head which Nukurren had come to recognize as the demon gesture of affirmation.

That was the key to discerning one human from another, Nukurren now realized. Ludumila's *nosu* was shallow and flat, spreading widely across her face. The black demon's *nosu* did likewise. Whereas—

"Dzhenushkunutushen's *nosu* is bigger than yours, and it protrudes much farther forward."

Ludumila began barking in the demon manner of laughter.

"We call it 'The Beak,'" she said, and barked again. Nukurren tried to understand the humor involved, but could make no sense of it. After a time, she felt herself growing weaker again and was less and less able to observe anything coherently. She felt very hot and feverish, and her mind began to wander. Disease now held her tightly in its arms.

At some point in the vague meanderings of her thoughts, she recalled Dhowifa's earlier remark. Half-unconsciously, her arms curled in the gesture of amusement.

I remember the first time I saw Dhowifa. I was not terrified of him. But I was apprehensive, and tense. He was very high-clan. Ansha royalty.

She had been standing guard at night, alone, by one of the side entrances to the Divine Shell. It was a shabby entrance, used only by servants. The stones of the arch were crudely cut and undecorated. The area was dim, lit only by a small, poorly-fed glowmoss colony.

It had been Nukurren's usual sentry duty. Not for her the prestigious post of standing guard by the main entrances, in daylight. Not for one as ugly as she, and helot-born.

She had heard a slight sound behind her, and turned. A small shape stood in the entryway. As soon as she had turned, the shape—a young truemale, she saw—scuttled back into the gloom of the hallway beyond.

"Who are you?" she had demanded, but her voice had been soft and, Dhowifa later told her, not unpleasant. After a moment, the truemale had come forward.

"I am Dhowifa," he said. Nukurren recognized him then, one of the Paramount Mother's recently wed husbands. It was very odd for such a one to be in that place, in the middle of the night, but Nukurren had not questioned him. After a moment, she had invited him to come forward, and had spent some time thereafter in casual conversation with Dhowifa.

On that night, the truemale had not explained his presence there. But he would reappear again, on many nights in the eightweeks that followed. After a time, as a strange friendship formed between the royal truemale and the lowborn warrior, Nukurren would learn of the cruelties of the Paramount Mother and the misery of Dhowifa.

By what manner, and by what route, the odd friendship turned into passion, Nukurren could never precisely recall. She could only remember that one night, with the rain thundering down, when the love and ecstasy she had only been able to dream of had finally entered her life. That it was a forbidden love and an unnatural ecstasy had mattered to her not at all.

Many nights of secret and illicit passion had followed, until the night when Dhowifa had crawled to her, only half-conscious, his little body a pulpy mass of bruises from the beating administered by the Paramount Mother. It seemed his love-making had displeased her.

They had left Shakutulubac that same night. Dhowifa had hesitated, in despair of leaving his malebond. But, in the end, he had not been able to bear the thought of returning to the Paramount Mother.

A pursuit had been organized, of course. But Nukurren had gained them a considerable lead by the simple expedient of slaughtering all the guards at the northwest gate of the city. Eight butchered guards could only be the work of a large raiding party from an enemy realm, or a massive conspiracy, or . . . Not for days did the Tympani realize the truth, and by then it was too late.

Remembering now, her mind a blur of fevered chaos, Nukurren finally fell asleep. But even in her sleep, her arms remained curled in the gesture of amusement. The captain of the guard at the northwest gate had often taunted Nukurren for her ugliness and her base birth. She had taunted Nukurren again that night, when Nukurren appeared out of the darkness, and the jibes had been echoed by her guards; until it occurred to them to demand an explanation for Nukurren's presence. Her drawn flail and unharnessed fork had provided the answer, though it was not to their liking.

The harsh sound of demon voices awakened Nukurren. Through her one remaining eye, she saw that night was falling. She was very, very weak; her whole body felt aflame. Still, she managed to look about.

They were high up on the Chiton, now, in a steep-walled canyon. Ahead of them loomed a large, partially-finished wall. A fortification, Nukurren realized, though it was oddly designed, with unusual projections and overhangs.

Those would be good for hurling stingers, she thought. *Any gukuy below, trying to force a way through, would find nowhere to hide.*

Atop the wall stood several demons, both female and male. A large door in the middle of the fortification, made of many interwoven and lacquered strips of yopo, suddenly swung aside. The litter was carried through the entrance, and the door was swung shut behind them.

That night the caravan rested within the shelter of the wall across the canyon. Fascinated by the demon methods of fortification, Nukurren tried to observe as much as she could.

But it was soon dark, and, in any event, she found it difficult to concentrate.

The next morning, she was awakened again by the harsh sound of demons speaking. She recognized the voices by their distinct tones and timber: Dzhenushkunutushen and the black demon. And, occasionally, the female demon Ludumila. The voices were very loud, especially that of Dzhenushkunutushen.

"Are you awake?" whispered Dhowifa. "I'm frightened. I think they're arguing."

Nukurren opened her eye—with some reluctance, for the effort caused much pain to her maimed eye. Before her she saw a fascinating tableau.

The two male demons, one of them as white as the other was black, were standing very close together, face to face. Despite their bizarre appearance, it was instantly obvious to Nukurren that Dhowifa was correct. They *were* arguing, and, she estimated, arguing very fiercely. The female demon Ludumila, Nukurren thought, was attempting to arbitrate—or, perhaps, simply to keep the argument from erupting too far.

Suddenly, the demon Dzhenushkunutushen gestured toward the litter, and Nukurren realized that they were arguing about her.

"The black one wants to kill us," whispered Dhowifa.

Nukurren made the gesture of tentative doubt. "I don't think so. He is implacable, that is true—"

"His color doesn't mean anything, I keep telling you," interrupted Dhowifa crossly.

"It does not matter. He would be implacable, whatever his color. It is in the nature of the monster. But—I do not believe he is cruel. And there is no reason, now, to kill us. They could have done it right after the battle, or at any time since."

"Then why—" Nukurren silenced her lover with a hiss. She was too engrossed by the interaction among the demons to be distracted.

Suddenly, she understood. The black demon, she had known for days, was the commander. The female demon Ludumila, she suspected, was his lieutenant. But she had been unable, before now, to determine the exact position of the white demon Dzhenushkunutushen.

Yet now, analyzing the exchange between the strangest

creatures she had ever encountered, she knew Dzhenush-kunutushen's position. And knew *him*, for all that he was a monster.

He was her. Just so, in times past, had Nukurren confronted an officer in the legions, when an issue had been of such importance as to require that a leader of warriors make a stand. Officers were to be respected and obeyed, of course. But, on occasion, it was also necessary to bring them to heel.

The demon shouting became very loud.

"They're going to start fighting!" hissed Dhowifa with alarm. His mantle rippled pink and red.

"No," said Nukurren firmly. "The black demon is a good officer, I think. And so he will yield."

The black demon made a sudden spreading motion with his limbs. He barked a sharp sound. Dzhenushkunutushen fell silent, though he remained stiff and erect. Very tense, Nukurren thought, interpreting the demon's posture as best she could. *Very tense, but, I think, satisfied.*

A moment later, the black demon began barking commands and pointing to various of the demons gathered about. Almost at once, the litter was picked up by four of the demons, including the black demon and Dzhenushkunutushen. Nukurren and Dhowifa suddenly found themselves being carried up the trail at a much more rapid pace than ever before. Soon the fortification was left far behind.

Nukurren was deeply impressed by the rapidity of their travel. She realized that the black demon had selected the four largest demons to carry the litter. All of them, she noted, were male. Still, Nukurren thought that she outweighed any one of the demons, even Dzhenushkunutushen, by a large margin. It would have been difficult for four large gukuy to carry her at a normal walking pace, much less at the astonishing speed with which the demons were climbing the trail.

Two other demons accompanied the party, stick-pedding alongside. One of them was Ludumila. She was the only female demon still present. Ludumila was large for a female demon, taller than most of the males, if not as tall as Dzhenush-kunutushen and the black one. But she was less massive, especially in her upper mantle. The female demons, Nukurren concluded, were capable of the same speed and agility as the males, but lacked the sheer strength.

Nukurren was surprised, therefore, some time later, when Ludumila replaced one of the male demons carrying the litter. The transfer took place with only a moment's interruption, and the litter was soon moving along as rapidly as before. As time went on, the demons carrying Nukurren and Dhowifa were regularly replaced by one of those who had been able to rest for a time, unburdened by the litter.

These are the most terrifying warriors who ever walked the Meat of the Clam, she thought. *If they are numerous, no army could stand against them. Not even the legions of mighty Ansha.*

Soon they reached a crest and entered a plateau. The demons began traveling faster still. Shortly thereafter, Nukurren lapsed into semi-consciousness. Dimly, vaguely, she heard Dhowifa conversing with the demon Ludumila.

Nukurren must rest! She is sick!

Soon. Soon.

She will die if she does not rest!

She will die if we do not get her to (strange human word— a name, Nukurren thought). *Soon! That is why we left the owoc behind and are carrying you ouroolvoo. Dzhenush* (the shortened name for Dzhenushkunutushen, Nukurren knew; odd; few gukuy used diminutive names) *insisted.* Short barks—laughter. *I thought* (again, a strange word—the name of the black demon, perhaps) *was going to burst a* (unknown phrase). *It's not often someone gets in his face like that!* Short barks. *It's good for him.*

A short silence. Then: *That's Dzhenush.* Even in her fevered state, Nukurren could not miss the affection in the bizarre demon voice.

Such strange creatures, with strange customs. Only among the barbarian tribes do officers mate with common warriors. But I do not think these are barbarians. I do not know what they are. Can demons be civilized? I hope not. No Kiktu barbarian was ever as cruel as Ansha.

But her ability to reason was vanishing, splintered by pain. One last, fleeting thought: *The demon Dzhenushkunutushen is a warrior, but not, I think, a common one. Nor was I. Nor was I.*

Everything faded into an incomprehensible blur. All that remained was the sense of Dhowifa's little body nestled in her mantle, blessedly cool against the scorching heat of the fever; and the tender stroking of his arms.

PART III:
The Weft

Chapter 14

Long before the battle ended, Kopporu knew the Kiktu were defeated. More than defeated. Crushed.

The outcome would have been certain even if the leader of the left flank, Ototpo, had not led an insane charge at the very beginning of the fray. The charge had shattered against the disciplined ranks of the Utuku. Ototpo herself had been slain, along with most of the main battle leaders of the left flank. A few of the survivors of the charge had attempted to make a stand, but they had not lasted long under the weight of the Utuku counterattack.

From that moment, the Utuku pressed their advantage remorselessly. They did not move quickly, true. Utuku tactics were designed to maximize their strengths—great numbers and rigid discipline. The Utuku warriors shuffled forward, mantle to mantle, grinding down everything before them. There was no room in that press for the clever fork-and-flail work in which the Kiktu excelled. Forks were useless, and in that style of combat the Kiktu were at a disadvantage against the heavily armored and shielded Utuku.

The Utuku ground forward, rolling up the Kiktu from right to left. Under their peds, the fern-like uyi which covered the entire central plain from the ocean to the Pokta Mountains was mashed to pulp. By routing the left wing of the Kiktu at the beginning of the battle, the Utuku insured that their enemy could not escape the trap created by the stupidity of its leaders. The route to possible escape led to the south, away from the Lolopopo swamp. There, in the flat vastness of the Papti Plain, the Kiktu might have eluded their slower-moving enemy. (The plan which Kopporu had tried, and failed, to get adopted by her tribe relied precisely on that vastness and Kiktu mobility for its eventual success.)

But that route was now closed off by the defeat of the left flank. Even had the war leader of the Kiktu been a quick-thinking realist, Giakta could not have marshalled her loosely organized army quickly enough to slip out of the trap that was closing in. The fleeing survivors of the left flank were spreading confusion and dismay among the warriors of the center. Even from a distance, Kopporu could see that the center of the Kiktu host was a swirling mass of chaos.

The Utuku did not fail to close the trap. Their greater numbers allowed their commanders to continually outflank the Kitku without easing up the relentless pressure of their front ranks. Slowly, but surely, the advance elements of the Utuku right curved northeast, until they reached the edge of the Lolopopo. The Kiktu were surrounded. The enemy on three sides; the swamp on the fourth.

The disaster was complete. Moved by a sudden impulse, Kopporu looked to the northeast and gazed at the Chiton. The long, flattish curve of the huge mountain was visible over the tall cycads of the swamp, even at that great distance. The mountain dominated the entire landscape of the northermost reaches of the plain. Mountain of myths and legends. And demons, it was now said.

She looked away. There would be time later, perhaps, to think of the Chiton. For the moment, she must bend every thought to the execution of her secret plan.

In that respect, Kopporu's position was better than she had feared. Better, even, than she had hoped. Through the course of the battle, she had badly bruised the Utuku opposing her. Ironically, in this last battle of the Kiktu, she had been able to impose her tactics to a far greater degree than hitherto. Partly that was because the forces under her command were disproportionately made up of battle groups with young leaders who had been gravitating toward her views for some time. But mostly, it was because the extreme desperation of the moment reined in the exuberant individualism of the Kiktu warriors. They were in a fight to the death, and they knew it. They placed their trust in Kopporu.

She had not failed them. Indeed, had the battlefield

consisted solely of her forces and those immediately facing her, the Kiktu would already be celebrating a great victory. Time and again, Kopporu's swift maneuvers—feint, retreat, counterattack—had utterly befuddled the Utuku. She had never made the mistake of crashing head-on into the massed ranks of the enemy. Instead, she had sliced off pieces of the enemy army and destroyed them.

Eventually, the Utuku had withdrawn into a purely defensive formation. Orders had come to the leader of the Utuku left, carried by a courier from the Beak of the Utuku herself: *Cease all attacks. Hold the Kiktu on the north against the swamp, until our entire army can be brought to bear.*

The flank leader had immediately obeyed, even though she knew that the orders were her death sentence. The Beak of the Utuku was cold and calculating, never hotheaded. But she was also utterly merciless toward failure. She would see to the destruction of the Kiktu, in the surest manner available. Later, in her great command yurt, she would dine on the disgraced leader of her left flank along with the captives.

So it was that Kopporu was given a desperately needed respite in the midst of the battle. She had time, now. Time to summon her remaining battle leaders and explain the necessary course of action. Time, hopefully, to sway them to her side. If not, time to impose her will.

And there was this added, totally unexpected, benefit: in the chaos at the center of the Kiktu forces, many of the young herders assigned to guard the gana had taken it upon themselves to drive the gana toward the right flank, away from the advancing juggernaut. Hundreds of gana were now clustered to the rear of Kopporu's warriors, almost into the swamp itself. From beyond the ganahide walls of her command circle, Kopporu could hear the terrified whistles of the beasts.

She had not expected to salvage any of the tribe's gana. Not many would survive the swamp, true. But perhaps enough.

Within the walls of her command circle, all of the remaining battle leaders were gathered. Aktako was there as well, along with six handpicked warriors. The battle leaders did not wonder at the presence of Aktako and the warriors. A battle leader of Kopporu's status was expected to maintain a personal guard. But they did wonder at the presence of the eight swamp-dwellers. What were disreputable clanless outcasts doing in the midst of Kiktu battle-leaders?

When Kopporu explained, the mantles of the seven battle leaders turned bright orange. Utter astonishment.

The orange she expected. Ochre was inevitable. Pink, even red, would be acceptable. Who would not hesitate or feel fear at her desperate plan?

But it was the blue of rage—say better, outrage—for which she watched vigilantly.

The color first appeared in the mantle of Yaua, as Kopporu had known it would. The old battle leader was fearless, but stupid; set in her ways like a clam.

Kopporu allowed Yaua to vent her indignation. As yet, the color of the remaining battle leaders showed not a trace of blue. But Kopporu was certain that the sentiments being expressed by Yaua were shared, to one extent or another, by all of them. The sentiments would have to be addressed, before further action could be taken.

"We cannot throw ourselves into the center," explained Kopporu patiently. "We would simply compound the chaos. No, worsen it—for the Utuku who are now licking the wounds we gave them would quickly follow. The trap would be complete."

"Your plan will produce the same result," pointed out Gortoku, one of the young battle leaders. "Even more quickly and completely."

"True," responded Kopporu immediately. "But we will not be in the trap."

She rose to her peds. "Understand. *Understand.* The Utuku victory is inevitable. We can do nothing to prevent it. One question remains, and one only—*will all the Kiktu perish in the trap?*"

"Treason!" bellowed Yaua. "Treason!"

Kopporu allowed blue rage to flood her own mantle.

"Yes, treason—by those fools who led our people to this disaster. *Fools like you.*"

She paused, quickly scanning the other battle leaders. Five, she thought. Five out of seven. Better than she had expected.

"The penalty for treason is death!" roared Yaua.

"So it is," replied Kopporu. Her mantle flashed black. Instantly, two of Aktako's warriors slammed the prongs of their forks into the mantle of Yaua. A moment later, the old battle leader was flopped onto her side. Aktako herself delivered the death stroke.

"That one also," commanded Kopporu, pointing at the battle leader Doroto. The murderous scene was repeated.

The five surviving battle leaders were shocked into immobility. Hardened warriors that they were, the utter ruthlessness of Kopporu's actions had stunned them scarlet with terror.

Kopporu noted with satisfaction that Gortoku was the first to bring her emotions under control. She had long thought the young gukuy was the best of the new battle leaders.

Her satisfaction deepened to pleasure at Gortoku's next words.

"Why not me?" asked Gortoku. Truly, a valiant youth.

"Have I ever punished a warrior for questioning me?" demanded Kopporu. "Even once?"

The red was rapidly fading from the mantles of all five battle leaders. Gortoku's was now pure gray.

The five young leaders looked at each other. Almost as one, their arms curled into the gesture of negation.

"No. Nor will I ever in the future. I am neither all-wise nor all-seeing. A battle leader who does not listen to the opinions of her subordinates is a fool."

The black in her mantle was still as hard as obsidian.

"But we do not have time for a long and leisurely discussion. There is only this much that remains to be said. I do not know what the future will bring us. It is a desperate course we take. But until we find our way to some place of safety, I will rule what remains of our tribe with a palp of bronze. You may always question my decisions. But once I have given a command, it must be instantly obeyed. To do otherwise is treason."

She did not feel it necessary to point to the gutted corpses of Yaua and Doroto.

"The penalty for which is known."

Again, she noted, it was Gortoku who took the initiative. "What are your commands?"

"Ropou will lead her group in a charge at the Utuku. But before reaching their ranks, she will call a retreat."

She looked at the battle leader.

"Do you understand?"

Ropou made the gesture of affirmation.

"The Utuku will think we are trying to trick them into another ambush." The young battle leaders whistled agreement. Three times that day, Kopporu had mangled overeager detachments of the Utuku by using that very tactic. Eventually, the Utuku had refused to be drawn into a charge.

"Under cover of Ropou's maneuver, the remaining battle groups will retreat into the swamp. Ufta's group will go first, taking the gana with them."

"The gana will panic," complained Ufta. "They will not enter the swamp."

Kopporu stared at her. She had almost ordered the execution of Ufta as well. Perhaps she should have.

Something of her thoughts must have shown, for Ufta suddenly announced that she would see to the task. At once.

Kopporu ordered one of the swamp-dwellers to accompany Ufta, to provide her with a guide once her group entered the swamp. The other battle leaders were likewise provided with guides. She then ordered the five battle leaders to their posts, after issuing one final command.

"In the event of my death, Gortoku will assume leadership of the tribe."

"What's left of the tribe," said Ufta softly.

"*No.*" The battle leaders stared at Aktako, surprised. Despite her personal relationship with Kopporu, the old veteran was always a stickler for protocol. She never spoke at the meetings of the battle leaders.

Aktako's own mantle was as black as Kopporu's.

"Ufta still does not understand," said Aktako harshly. "This *is* the tribe. From this moment forward, *there are no other Kiktu.*"

The old warrior waved a palp toward the south. In the distance, the clash of flails and forks could be heard. But above it, swelling, they could hear the shrieks of the doomed. The Utuku cutters had already started their work, in anticipation of the great victory feast.

Aktako made the gesture of negation.

"Those are no longer Kitku. They are meat for the conquerors."

As soon as the battle leaders left the command circle, Kopporu summoned the remaining swamp-dweller to her side.

The swamp-dweller was called O-doddo-ua, and she was what
passed for a leader among the swamp dwellers. Her name
seemed strange to Kopporu's ear, but she knew it was a common one among the helots in the Oukasho Prevalate. O-doddo-
ua, like most of the swamp-dwellers, was an escapee from the
southern prevalates. They had chosen the wretched and dangerous life of the swamp in preference to a life of ceaseless
toil and slavery. There were many Kiktu warriors—the great
majority, in truth—who despised the swamp-dwellers for that
choice. Kopporu admired them for it.

But whether they despised them or not, all the Kiktu would
now be dependent on the swamp-dwellers. The swamp was
a feared place, unclean; essentially unknown to the Kiktu. Their
survival would depend on the knowledge of the outcasts.

"Do you have any questions, O-doddo-ua?"

The swamp-dweller hesitated. There were traces of pink
in the ochre of her mantle, Kopporu noted. Not with surprise,
except, perhaps, at the absence of red. O-doddo-ua had known,
abstractly, that Kopporu was ruthless in her approach to reality.
But abstract knowledge is one thing, gutted bodies are another.

"You are afraid of what I will do to you, once you have
served us," stated Kopporu.

A sudden ripple of ochre washed over the swamp-dweller's
mantle, followed by the gesture of affirmation.

"I am not cruel, O-doddo-ua. Treacherous only when I need
to be. I promised that we would reward you if you guided
us through the swamp. The promise will be kept."

O-doddo-ua hesitated; then spoke softly, in the slurring
accent of the southerners.

"We have not agreed on the reward."

"True. I offered you five wires of bronze. I can now promise
you a few gana, as well. But that is all." Kopporu allowed a
brief ripple of brown into her mantle. "The Kiktu will have
nothing more to give. We are now a poor tribe ourselves."

"Not true, battle leader. You are rich in what the swamp-
dwellers treasure most. Richer now, I think, than ever."

"Indeed? What is that?"

"Knowledge of survival, and its needs." To Kopporu's surprise, the swamp-dweller's mantle turned black.

"Our reward will be adoption into your tribe. No, *more*.
Into your own clan, battle leader Kopporu."

Despite her iron self-control, Kopporu was unable to prevent her mantle from glowing bright orange. Not often, since she was a child, had Kopporu been so thoroughly astonished.

"*What?*"

"You heard. Those are our terms, battle leader. We have discussed it amongst ourselves, and decided."

"But—*why?*"

"We know the swamp, battle leader, but we do not love it. Not at all. We are tired of being outcasts. And we have long since abandoned the foolish notions of civilization. It would be good to have a place in the world. In the greatest clan of its greatest tribe."

Kopporu whistled bitter amusement. "Greatest tribe? Its greatest clan? Are you blind, O-doddo-ua? The Kiktu are no longer the world's greatest tribe, if we ever were. By tomorrow we will be not much more than outcasts and swamp dwellers ourselves."

O-doddo-ua said nothing; but the black mantle never lightened its shade.

After a moment, Kopporu made the gesture of acceptance.

"So be it, if that is your wish. But, understand this, O-doddo-ua: the decision is not mine to make. I am a battle leader only. You and your people cannot be adopted into the Kiktu without the consent of the entire tribe, in full tribal assembly. My clan is a small one, and the clan leaders are not—"

She stopped abruptly. O-doddo-ua whistled.

"Are not alive," she finished the thought. O-doddo-ua waved her palp to the south. "Or not much longer. All the clan leaders are gathered in the center, with the mothers. *You* will be the new clan leader, Kopporu. And your clan will now be the greatest of the Kiktu."

"Still . . ." She made the gesture of resignation. "I will do what I can, O-doddo-ua. The decision must still be made by the tribe as a whole. I will speak for you, that I can promise. But that may not be of any use. I myself will have to stand trial, at the next assembly. For treason and murder. My words may harm your cause more than they help it."

"We will take our chances. By then, much will have changed. The warriors will be shocked by your actions, once they understand what has happened here. Appalled, even. But by then, they will have spent time in the swamp."

"So?"

"So—the swamp has a way of teaching one to distinguish what is important from what is frivolous. And they will no longer despise we swamp-dwellers."

O-doddo-ua turned away.

"You will see, battle leader. You will see."

No sooner had O-doddo-ua left the command circle than Lukpudo entered. The battle leader of the Opoktu was bearing a new wound. But it was a slight wound, and would soon be lost in the welter of other scars which crisscrossed her mantle.

Kopporu watched Lukpudo approach with a mixture of fondness and deep regret. Fondness, for her trust in the Opoktu had not been mislaid—the small tribe had fought well and valiantly. Deep regret, for their loyalty was now to be repaid by treachery. Kopporu would attempt, at the last moment, to keep a way open for the Opoktu to follow her into the swamp, should they so choose. But she had not confided in them, and she knew that they would be too confused to act quickly enough.

She noticed that Lukpudo gave only the briefest glance at the bodies of the two murdered battle leaders as she approached. Lukpudo's indifference puzzled her. It was obvious the two battle leaders had been slain here, not on the battlefield.

The mystery was resolved at once, and Kopporu found herself astonished for the second time that day.

"When do we make our retreat into the swamp?" asked Lukpudo.

The Opoktu battle leader whistled amusement at Kopporu's orange.

"The Kiktu leaders may be stupid, Kopporu, but *our* clan leaders are most assuredly not. It's one of the advantages, you know, to being a small tribe. You have to be smarter."

"You *knew?*"

Another whistle.

"Not exactly. We have been planning the same maneuver ourselves. I almost raised the subject with you, once. But you're such an upright sort that I decided it best not to. I could not afford, you understand, to be denounced. But I began suspecting what you were up to when I saw the swamp-dwellers you were collecting around. There could only be one logical explanation for their presence."

Lukpudo made the gesture of derision, coupled with a swift yellow ripple across her mantle. The combination expressed exactly the same sentiments that a human would express with a snort.

"Leaving aside that ridiculous spawn's tale you were spreading about the danger of an Utuku sweep through the swamp. So I started watching you closely. You—and Aktako. I knew that if you were planning something, she would be in the thick of it. When I saw the hand-picked flails she assembled, I knew. You have never been one of those battle leaders who wants to be surrounded by a mob of personal guards. So why now? And why *those* guards?—all of whom I recognized as one of Aktako's old cronies? Who may no longer be the swiftest warriors on the field, but who are certainly the most deadly.

"From then on, I kept an eye on your command circle. Since the battle started I've had one of my warriors watching, to tell me the moment you summoned your battle leaders."

Lukpudo turned and gazed back at the corpses.

"Two only?" she asked. "I expected to see Ufta's body lying there as well."

"She almost was. But—I was not sure. And I have no taste for murder."

"You may regret the decision. Ufta is much smarter than Doroto was. Certainly than Yaua. But I do not think she has their courage." A quick flash of brown/green regret swept across Lukpudo's mantle. "They were valiant gukuy. But valor is no longer enough, in this new and terrible world."

She turned back to Kopporu. "Time presses, battle leader. For the duration of this struggle, the Opoktu will remain under your command."

"And after?"

Lukpudo whistled. "After? Why worry about that now, Kopporu? There may be no 'after.' The swamp, by all reports, is not much less terrible than the Utuku. If at all. But I would rather be eaten by snails than cannibals."

Another whistle.

"And besides, the future is not entirely grim for the Opoktu. There is this much to look forward to—we will no longer be the smallest tribe in the world."

"You have never been small in my eyes, Lukpudo."

For a brief moment, the battle leader of the Opoktu allowed deep green to suffuse her mantle.

"I know, Kopporu. We have always loved you for it."

The green vanished, replaced by black.

"What are your commands?"

Chapter 15

When Guo was informed by her battle leader Gortoku to prepare for a retreat into the swamp, she was too dazed to wonder at the order. Dazed, and exhausted.

There was no longer any doubt as to her conduct on the field of battle, although Guo herself had never once considered the question since the battle began. She did not consider it now. Did not even think of it, in fact. There was only room in her brain for the necessities of the retreat. Her place in that retreat would be critical, for it would be she (and her flankers) who would bear the brunt of the pursuit. Kopporu's tactics of drawing the enemy into a trap after feigning a retreat were based upon funneling the charging foe toward the battlemothers. There, unable to avoid the blows because they were penned in by the trap, the enemy would be crushed under the maces of the battlemothers.

The tactics had worked, brilliantly, until the Utuku had finally learned not to charge after fleeing Kiktu. They had learned, after three disasters, that the battle leader of the Kiktu right flank was a shrewd and deadly foe. And the Utuku warriors confronting Kopporu's forces no longer referred to the battlemother in their enemy's ranks as a breeder. They called her, simply, *the ghaxtak*.

"Ghaxtak" was an Utuku word. The Kiktu equivalent was "kuopto." Every barbarian language had an equivalent term, and all of them were based on a derivative of that language's word for fury.

But the word "fury" does not really capture the essence of the concept. The emotions experienced by gukuy are, fundamentally, the same as those experienced by humans. This is, of course, neither surprising nor coincidental. Human scientists, beginning with Darwin, had long understood that the emotions of animals and people are the inevitable by-product of evolution. An animal must know when to flee; when to fight; when to engage in sexual reproduction; when to hesitate; when to ignore. A biochemist can explain the exact chemical processes by which those patterns of behavior are transmitted through the nervous system. But an animal knows nothing of these formulas. It "knows" simply: fear; rage; passion; indecision; indifference. Those animals which evolve intelligence give these feelings names, and call them "emotions." And, as they evolve in a complex interaction with the evolution of their own intelligence, the emotions themselves become more variegated and subtle. But it is inevitable that animals evolving on two planets separated by light years in space would still arrive at the same basic emotions. There is no mystic truth here; simply the requirements of natural selection.

And yet, nothing is ever identical. In their broad range, the emotions of gukuy and humans are the same—certainly if the entire gamut of emotions, which vary considerably between the different cultures of both species, are taken into account. Still, they are different species; and, with regard to emotions, the biggest difference is that one is chromatophoric and the other is not.

There is an expression, among humans, that an individual "wears his heart on his sleeve." The cultural subtleties behind that expression, the product of a species for whom emotional dissemblance is physically easy, would puzzle a gukuy. All gukuy "wear their hearts on their sleeves"—on their entire bodies, in fact. Humans, of course, also express their emotions involuntarily. They burst into tears; they laugh; those with little melanin in their skins even turn pale; or red. But these involuntary reactions are a pale reflection of the rich pallette of a gukuy.

Hence, two significant differences. Gukuy are far more straightforward than humans in their recognition (including self-recognition) of their emotions. And they are far more sophisticated in their understanding of the subtle complexities of those emotions.

Combinations of emotions which, to a human, are a murky blur, are like crystal to a gukuy. A human warrior, in the midst of battle, experiences a confused combination of emotions (fear, rage, indecision) which he does not perceive clearly himself. Not at all at the time, and poorly in the aftermath.

But to the gukuy, these emotions are not a murky blur. A human observing a gukuy battle would see a vast and kaleidoscopic rippling of colors across the serried mantles of the warriors. Blue and red predominate, of course; for a battle is the epitome of rage and fear. But the ochre hues of uncertainty and indecision are often seen, as well. Gukuy battle leaders learn early to gauge the colors of their opponents. A sudden great surge of ochre across the mantles of the foe signals that the moment is perhaps right to press home the attack. And always, of course, the battle leader looks for the wave of scarlet which indicates that the foe has been beaten into pure terror. The time has come for rout and destruction.

Red; blue; ochre—those, the principal colors of a battlefield. But there are others as well, seen more rarely.

Gray is one. Gray is the "natural" color of a gukuy's mantle. A gukuy whose mantle remains gray in battle is one of those unusual gukuy who have learned to master their emotions even under extreme stress. It is an ability which is given a name in every gukuy language. It is always respected; never more than on the battlefield. Such a warrior is invariably a veteran, and a mistress of the art of war. On occasion, tinges of yellow will ripple across such a warrior's mantle. Contempt for the foe.

Black is another. Black is the color of implacability. Not the absence of color, as is the gray of self-discipline; but the sudden suffusion of all color in a ruthless determination to accomplish a task, regardless of cost.

The color is never seen in pure form on a battlefield. Pure black is the color of executioners, not warriors amidst the clash of arms. But it is not uncommonly seen in combination with blue. Never red, or ochre, or even pink. Such warriors are feared, for they have cast aside all fear and caution. They may not be skilled in battle, but they will sell their lives dearly.

And there is another color which is seen on a battlefield, on only the rarest occasion. It is the most feared of all colors.

Green. Color of love, and tranquillity.

It is never seen alone, nor as the predominant color; but rather as a gleam beneath the black and blue of implacable fury. The three colors combine into a hue which has no name in any human language. "Dark cobalt green" is the closest approximation in English.

It is the color of those rarest of all warriors, whom the Utuku call *ghaxtak* and the Kiktu *kuopto*. Centuries earlier, on Earth, a culture had flourished briefly which had a name which was strikingly similar. The victims of that culture had gathered in places of worship, crying out: *"From the fury of the Norseman, dear God deliver us!"*

They were called berserks, and they were the most famed and feared Vikings of all.

Since the first moments of the battle, that color, which the Kiktu called *kuoptu*, had suffused Guo's mantle. It had never wavered since. Even now, as she rested and waited for the signal to begin the retreat, the color on Guo's mantle did not even fade slightly.

To an opponent, kuoptu was a frightening enough color to see on the mantle of an enemy warrior. The sight of the enormous mantle of a battlemother suffused by the color was utterly terrifying.

Hours after the battle had begun, the Utuku were indeed terrified of her; and their terror was by no means unreasoning. They had seen countless warriors smashed into so much jelly beneath the blows of Guo's mace. The beautiful bronze blades of her mace were now dented and dulled, but it hardly mattered. The titanic strength of the young battlemother was such that she could have been using her palps alone—and had, on several occasions, with much the same effect as a human smashing a mouse.

Guo's flankers, and all the Kiktu warriors within sight, were in awe of her. Never, in the history of the tribe, was there a record of a *kuopto* battlemother. Mothers were, by their nature, not well suited to battle. Only infanta—young, still infertile mothers—could be trained as battlemothers; and few enough of those. And the training was so arduous and difficult, so opposed to the nature of mothers, that, among the western tribes, only the Kiktu used battlemothers as a regular practice. The custom was not the least of the reasons they were derided as uncouth barbarians by the civilized realms to the south. And hated by the Utuku, to whose culture of total female supremacy the very concept of battlemothers was a despised abomination.

It was still an abomination, in the eyes of the Utuku warriors. But it was no longer despised.

The legend of Guo had begun.

The signal came, in the form of sudden hoots. (The Kiktu, like most of the tribes, utilized a battle language; unlike the Utuku, who gave their signals through drums.) Guo and her flankers were the first to move to the rear, while the other warriors maintained a screen. It would take the slow battlemother longer to reach her position.

Following the scruffy-looking swamp dweller who had appeared as her guide, Guo entered the swamp. With disgust, for the swamp was a dank and noisome place. But she made no complaint. She did not understand the reason for the order, but she had complete confidence in Kopporu. Whatever the reason, she was sure it was a good one.

Within meters (a term which Guo, of course, did not use herself—she thought of it as several *goa*, a rather loose measure based on the length of a gukuy tentacle), Guo found that she had completely lost sight of the battlefield. The plains were behind her. All around, on every side except the pathway ahead, loomed the tall cycads.

Guo felt uncomfortable within the cycads. In part, that was repugnance at the strange growths which seemed to drip from every branch—not to mention the ubiquitous slugs and snails. But, for the most part, it was claustrophobia. She was accustomed to the open stretches of the plain, where the tallest plants (the relatively uncommon fuyu groves) were barely taller than a gukuy female—and much shorter than she.

Soon, to her relief, she entered a large clearing. The ground here seemed firmer than the soggy path she had just traversed. The clearing was roughly circular, approximately eighty goa in diameter. Her guide led her across the clearing and into the thick growth beyond.

"You are to wait here," commanded the guide, "with your flankers. Stay behind this screen of cycads, hidden from the clearing, until the signal is sounded."

Guo felt a slight resentment at taking orders from a clanless one, but she forebore comment. The orders, she knew, must have come down from Gortoku—perhaps even Kopporu. And, as she took the opportunity to examine the surroundings, she realized that Kopporu was laying another clever ambush.

The Utuku will think we are completely routed; stricken with terror. Why else would we flee into the swamp? They will follow us, into this horrid place—where their close ranks and armor will drag them down. By the time they reach this clearing, they will be confused and disoriented.

She watched as warriors continued to file into the clearing and were guided to take their places, hidden in the cycads beyond. Suddenly, the loud noises coming from somewhere behind her, further into the swamp, registered on her consciousness.

Gana! Kopporu has driven the tribe's gana into the swamp!

Guo was amazed—and awed—by the ruthlessness of her battle leader's actions. Very few of the stupid and ungainly gana would survive long in the swamp—especially since the warriors would be too preoccupied to guard over them. The young hordoro would not, without assistance, be able to prevent the terrified beasts from scattering in fatal confusion.

Guo knew, then, how desperate Kopporu must have been. The gana were the tribe's most precious possession—except the tribe itself. The battle leader had decided to sacrifice them, in the hopes of drawing the Utuku into a catastrophic trap. By driving the gana into the swamp, Kopporu had ensured that the Utuku would follow. Guo herself, on the front lines, had not seen the gana being driven away. But the Utuku scouts would not have missed it. The Beak of the Utuku would arrive at no other conclusion than that the right flank of the Kiktu—which had inflicted more casualties and humiliation upon her army than the rest of the Kiktu and their allies combined—had finally broken. Routed completely. The Beak would command a major and massive pursuit. She would want to slake her legendary vengefulness; and, besides, she would want the gana herself. And the meat of the Kiktu warriors.

A great wave of sadness threatened, momentarily, to wash over Guo. But she thrust it aside.

Kopporu's stratagem would not, she knew, win the battle. Even as inexperienced as she was, Guo had seen enough of the disaster on the Kiktu left and center to know that the tribe was doomed. The most that would be accomplished would be a complete mangling of the Utuku left, followed by a last futile charge out of the swamp in the attempt to rescue the center. Kopporu and her warriors would die in that charge, Guo knew.

But we will cost them very, very, very dearly. The Utuku will never forget the terrible Kopporu. And her warriors. And her battlemothers.

The utter ferocity which filled Guo in that moment caused her mantle to positively glow. For just a second, the green undercolor almost dominated. Her flankers saw, and were astonished; and made their own silent grim vows.

Suddenly, the forces of the Opoktu entered the clearing. Not warriors alone, either—Guo was puzzled, at first, to see the two Opoktu mothers and their consorts in the midst of the allied warriors. Then she realized their presence was inevitable. The Opoktu would not have agreed to Kopporu's plan if it meant sacrificing their mothers. Guo watched as the mothers filed slowly through the clearing and into the depths of the swamp beyond. They would not last much longer than the Opoktu warriors, of course. But Guo had come to admire the Opoktu, in the course of that day. The small tribe was usually spoken of slightingly by the Kiktu—although never, Guo had noticed, by Kopporu or Aktako or Gortoku. But Guo had seen their valor (and cunning) on the battlefield. None of the Opoktu mothers, she knew, would fall alive into the hands of the Utuku, to be made breeding slaves. At the end, the mothers would roll onto their sides, exposing their great underbellies to the mercy strokes of the warriors.

After the Opoktu warriors took their place, the clearing was suddenly filled by the other two battlemothers of the Kiktu right flank, and their flankers. Loapo, she saw with relief, still seemed relatively unhurt (her mantle, of course, carried many fresh flail marks—but those were a trifle, to the vast bulk of a battlemother). But then Oroku entered, and Guo could not prevent herself from hooting with dismay.

The third of the flank's battlemothers was moving slowly, and obviously in great pain. Her left ped was a maimed ruin—some squad of Utuku must have sacrificed themselves, in the singleminded effort to cripple the battlemother. They had come close to succeeding. And Oroku's visor was a tattered wreck.

Even by the standards of a battlemother, Oroku was slow and clumsy. Where Guo had managed to catch most of the darts piped at her on her shield, Oroku's visor had borne almost the entire brunt of the missiles. The tough wicker-like visor could only withstand so much punishment, even from light and flimsy blow-darts.

There are two darts sticking in her eye, realized Guo. *She must be totally blind, now, on her left side.*

Suddenly, she heard a great drumming from the plain. The Utuku, watching their enemy retreat into the swamp, had finally made their decision. Guo recognized the meaning of the drumroll. She had heard it three times earlier that day—*attack.*

The last of the Kiktu warriors were now filing through the clearing, moving past the creeping Oroku, toward their positions of ambush beyond. Not all of the warriors were being positioned on the edge of the clearing—where there would have been no room for them, in any event. Many warriors, in small squads, were being led to other places of ambush by swamp-dweller guides.

Guo suddenly realized that she had seen several eights of swamp-dwellers.

Kopporu has been preparing this trap for days, she realized. She was filled with admiration for her leader's cunning.

The last Kiktu to enter the clearing was Kopporu herself, along with Aktako and her personal guard. As soon as she saw the figure of Oroku—the battlemother was still only halfway through the clearing—Kopporu came to an abrupt halt.

There was no sign in Kopporu's mantle, but Guo knew the emotions that coursed through her leader's heart. Dismay; uncertainty; what to do?

Guo came to a sudden decision. She laid down her mace and shield and re-entered the clearing. Kopporu turned and stared, as she lumbered her way forward.

When Guo reached the center of the clearing, she said simply:

"She can no longer fight, Kopporu. I will take her to safety."

Guo did not even wait for Kopporu's agreement. She simply reached out her tentacles and picked up the huge form of Oroku.

"Leave your mace here," she commanded. Weakly, Oroku

obeyed. Guo turned and carried the wounded battlemother out of the clearing.

Even had Kopporu opposed her action—which she did not—she would have been unable to speak, so great was her astonishment. Not so much at the action itself, but at the very fact of it. She would never have believed any being could be strong enough even to pick up a battlemother, much less carry one.

Yet, when Guo returned to the clearing, after placing Oroku in the cycads beyond, she was not even breathing heavily. Upon reaching the center of the clearing, Guo picked up Oroku's mace. It was a common flint-bladed mace, she saw. But it would do.

"Leave it there," commanded Kopporu. "When the Utuku see it, they will be convinced we are routed."

For the first time in her life, Guo defied her battle leader.

"No, Kopporu. They will be convinced, anyway. And I will need the mace."

"Have you lost—" Kopporu stopped, realizing the truth. Guo would cast aside her shield, and wield a mace in both palps.

Guo turned, then stopped. A gukuy had suddenly entered the clearing. A Kiktu, not an enemy. The carvings on her cowl identified her as one of the Great Mother's attendants. The gukuy came to a halt before Guo, breathing heavily. Guo was astonished to see the tiny figures of several males. Two of the males were riding within the attendant's mantle cavity. The other four (one of them a eumale, as was Kiktu custom) were perched atop the attendant's cowl. Somehow, on that strangest day of her life, Guo was not surprised to see that they were bearing pipes and darts.

She recognized them, of course, although she did not know their names. They were the Great Mother's own childcluster—the young and still-infertile males, bonded together, who were destined to be the Great Mother's most precious bequest to her successor.

After catching her breath, the attendant extended her arms. Held in their grasp was a small bundle, wrapped in precious layers of oucloth. She proferred the bundle to Guo.

"The Great Mother bade me give this to you."

Guo had no need to open the bundle to see what was contained within. It was the Mothershell—the beautiful, jewel-encrusted, ceremonial shell of an orkusnail. Symbol of the Great Mother's guardianship of the tribe.

Stunned, she extended her arms and took the bundle. Dimly, she heard Kopporu whisper: "She *knew*." But the remark did not register on Guo's consciousness, at the time.

"And these also," said the attendant. Before Guo realized what was happening, the attendant reached up and grasped Guo's great cowl with her palps. Across the bridges of flesh thus made, the six males scampered. By the time Guo was able to gather her thoughts—and register a protest—the childcluster was perched atop her own mantle.

"Be silent!" said the attendant sharply. "The Great Mother bade me tell you this: *I bequeath to you the future of the tribe, daughter. Guard it better than I have done. Be ruthless toward all folly.*"

The attendant turned suddenly, back toward the plain beyond the cycads, and made to leave.

"Stop!" hooted Kopporu. "The Utuku are already entering the swamp—you can hear them! You cannot do anything now but join us."

The attendant looked back. Suddenly, to Guo's astonishment, blue rage and yellow contempt flooded the attendant's mantle.

She spoke, her voice filled with hate.

"The Great Mother saw, and made her decision. *But I do not forgive you.*"

A moment later she was gone, brandishing her flail as she re-entered the cycads.

"Why did she—" began Guo, but Kopporu interrupted her.

"Later, Guo! We have no time now!"

As if to punctuate the battle leader's point, Guo heard the sudden—very brief—sounds of combat in the cycads beyond the clearing. The attendant had encountered the advancing Utuku, and sold her life.

Kopporu was right. Hastily, Guo retreated to her place of ambush. By the time she got there, there was not a trace of Kiktu left in the clearing.

As soon as she had retrieved her own mace, she ordered the males atop her mantle to climb down and hide in the swamp.

Their reply, transmitted by the eumale, was short and to the point: *no.*

"I have no time for foolishness!" whispered Guo.

"It is our duty," replied the eumale. "Besides, with two

maces you will be shieldless. We will protect you from the
Utuku pipers."

Again, astonishment. It was Kiktu custom for a mother's
consorts to serve as her personal squad of pipers. But it was
an entirely ceremonial custom. Mothers did not fight in battles,
and, in any event, the weak siphons of males could not expel darts with any force and distance.

She was about to enforce her command physically (or try—
the agile males could have easily evaded her clumsy grabs)
when the Utuku vanguard began entering the clearing. All
thought fled in a rush of rage. Her every attention was focused
on her tympani, waiting for the signal to spring the ambush.

The fabled Utuku discipline, she saw, had already become
eroded by their short contact with the swamp. The Utuku
warriors lurched into the clearing in ragged files, swearing,
covered with mud and slime up to their underbellies. Their
heavy armor had, indeed, been a liability in the swamp. And
Guo saw that many had lost their shields. (Kiktu warriors, like
those of most tribes, did not use shields; preferring, instead,
the greater finesse of the fork.)

The clearing was soon packed with Utuku. Battle leaders
were attempting to bring order and discipline back to what
was now not much more than a mob—with only limited
success.

And then, before the Utuku leaders could overcome the
chaos and confusion, Kopporu issued the first of her battle
hoots. The Utuku were suddenly attacked—from the *other* side
of the clearing, the side nearest the plain.

It was a suicide mission, Guo realized. Only a handful of
Kiktu were conducting the attack—more could not have waited
in ambush while the Utuku passed by them.

They would not survive long, and Guo paid silent homage
to their honor. But they had succeeded in carrying out
Kopporu's stratagem. The Utuku warriors, hearing the sound
of unexpected combat to their rear, had all spun around and
were now facing south, away from the mass of the Kiktu forces
who were still lurking in ambush.

The Utuku battle leaders realized almost at once that they
had been duped. But it was too late—too late by far. Guo
almost whistled with glee, watching one of the Utuku drum-
mers pound on a mud-splattered drum. The soggy signal could

not even be heard above the hoots of the confused Utuku warriors.

Kopporu's next signal came. Guo almost lunged out into the clearing, before she realized that she had not heard the signal for the battlemothers to advance.

A mass of Kiktu and Opoktu warriors (and swamp-dwellers, Guo noted with surprise) flooded out of the cycads surrounding the clearing. From everywhere except the very northern edge of the clearing, where Guo and the other battlemother still lay in waiting.

Kopporu's plan was flawless, Guo saw. The Utuku had now lost every trace of rank, order and discipline. They were rapidly being crushed into the center of the clearing, into a struggling mass of flesh. And toward the north, toward an innocent looking patch of cycads where there seemed to be no Kiktu warriors.

They were being forced toward Guo and Loapo, after being compressed into a formation which was ideal for the simple tactics of battlemothers.

Crush. Crush. Crush. Crush. Crush.

The signal finally came, and Guo surged forward like a titan, two maces held high.

Chapter 16

Later, she herself remembered almost nothing of the battle that followed. Except, oddly, the role of her male companions. Perhaps it was because of the oddity of this new thing which had come into her life. Whatever the reason, there was some detached part of her mind which noted (with great surprise) that the childcluster was quite effective in protecting her from Utuku pipers.

True, the Utuku pipers were at a great disadvantage—squeezed, as they were, into a struggling mass of warriors. Still, there were many who managed to free themselves enough to raise blowpipe to siphon. But few of them were able to fire an effective shot, for they were almost instantly the target of a volley of small darts blown from the malebond riding high above the battle, atop Guo's cowl. It was the eumale, Guo noted, who always called the command for a target.

True, none of the darts carried the same force as a dart blown from a female piper. But her male preconsorts were amazingly accurate in their aim—and there were always six darts in that counter-volley. Guo saw more than one Utuku piper hoot with agony, its eyes a sudden ruin.

Nevertheless, she was struck by several darts. Two of them caused painful wounds within her mantle. But her eyes were never hit—and Guo, fighting without a shield, had fully expected to be blind within a few minutes. She had not cared, for she thought it was to be her death battle.

For one of the males atop her cowl, it was. She glimpsed an Utuku dart sailing above her cowl and heard a sudden hoot of pain. Thereafter, there were only five darts in the counter-volleys.

210

One of her unknown future husbands, she realized, was dead or badly injured.

Of the rest of that battle, Guo remembered nothing to the day of her death. She heard about it, of course, many times. Within not so many years, the Battle of the Clearing would become a stock in trade of chantresses across half a continent. They would tell, in traditional cadence and meter, of the day the horrible Utuku were hammered into a mass of slugflesh, until their bodies could not be distinguished from the muck of the swamp. The chantresses would even claim that, to this day, the blood of the Utuku still seeps from the soil of that clearing. Guo's Clearing, as they called it. Or, simply: the Crushing Place.

(It was not true, of course. The scavengers of the swamp are extraordinarily efficient. Within a few eightdays, there was little trace of the Utuku disaster in the clearing, beyond a few scraps of utterly inedible weapons and armor. But who would ever go into the swamp to see for themselves? The chantresses continued the tale, and were never challenged.)

When the signal came to disengage, Guo did not hear it. Only the insistent rapping on her cowl by her malecluster finally brought her back to consciousness from the mists of her battle fury.

"We have been ordered to withdraw," said the eumale.

Guo stared at the few Utuku survivors who were still in the clearing. All of them were maimed and crippled. She yearned to end their suffering, and then charge forth into the plain itself to continue the slaughter. But Kopporu's stern discipline restrained her. She turned and entered the cycads to the north.

Now that the battle was over, exhaustion threatened to overcome her. Exhaustion, and misery. After hours, the kuoptu which had flooded her mantle faded, replaced by brown grief. The same color, she noted dully, dappled the mantles of all the warriors within eyesight. The Kiktu had inflicted a terrible defeat upon the Utuku in the clearing. But they knew that, even at that moment, their tribe was being butchered and enslaved on the plain to the south.

Guo was so tired that she did not even wonder where she was going. At first, her vague supposition was that Kopporu was leading them to the east, to a part of the swamp from which they could issue forth in a hopeless attempt to rescue the tribe's mothers.

She held that thought for some time. It was difficult to determine direction in the gloom beneath the overhanging cycads. And there were more than enough dangers in the swamp to keep her mind concentrated on the few goa ahead of her. Patches of bottomless mud; clumps of dangerous-looking plants, their purple spines glistening with what might well be poison; predators—small predators, for the large ones had fled the sound of battle—but even the small predators of the swamp could be deadly: she saw the bodies of several gana, and one warrior, covered with venomous slugs and snails.

Eventually, it dawned on her that they were heading north, not east. North-*ward*, she thought—for the actual route they were following seemed to twist and turn in a bewildering manner. Had she and her flankers not been guided by a swamp-dweller, they would have soon become hopelessly lost. But, over time, even to her weary mind, it was clear that they were moving farther and farther away from the battlefield to the south.

Around her, unseen because of the constant screen of cycads, giant ferns, and other vegetation whose name she did not know, she could hear the movement of other files of warriors. Kopporu, she realized, had broken the flank into small groups which, guided by swamp dwellers, could make reasonably rapid progress through the narrow passageways in the swamp. Much more rapid, certainly, than the rigidly organized Utuku—who would not, in any event, soon enter the swamp. Not after the terrible slaughter which Kopporu had inflicted on their left flank.

Occasionally, on the path behind her, Guo saw swamp-dwellers dragging vegetation across the trail. Confusing their trail, so that by the time the Utuku did enter the swamp in pursuit, it would be difficult to determine the exact direction in which the Kiktu survivors—

—had fled.

She knew, then. Understanding came to her in a flash. Everything fell into place. Kopporu's strange maneuvers; the words and actions of the Great Mother's attendant; and of the Great Mother herself.

Kopporu has betrayed the tribe.

That thought had no sooner came to her, however, that the simultaneous memory of the Great Mother's actions drove it out of her mind.

One of my—husbands—is hurt. I forgot all about them. She stopped abruptly. A sharp pang of guilt.

"One of you is hurt. I'm sorry—I was so tired. I—forgot."

A soft voice came down from the cowl above. By its timbre, Guo recognized it as the voice of the eumale.

"No. None of us is hurt. Move on. We don't have time to stop now."

After a moment's hesitation, she stopped and laid down her maces. Then she reached up and grasped her cowl with her palps.

"There are dangerous things in this swamp. Many of them are poisonous, and even the smaller snails are almost as big as you. Come down, and—inside me."

A moment later, she felt the small bodies of the males rapidly moving down her tentacles. The last were the eumale and one of the truemales. Between them, they were bearing the body of another member of the bond.

"You said none of you were hurt!"

"He is not hurt," came the reply from the truemale. An exquisitely subtle weave of green love and brown misery rippled across his mantle. "Abka is dead. For long now—he was killed in the battle in the clearing."

"Move on," repeated the eumale. "There is nothing we can do for him now. And we cannot hold up the tribe."

Mention of the tribe brought the thought of Kopporu's treason back, in a rush. Guo set her huge body underway again, consumed with a kaleidoscopic welter of thoughts and emotions. Vaguely, she was aware of the fleeting ripples of color in her mantle. Every color: blue, red, ochre, yellow—yes, and green. She had no doubt as to Kopporu's motives. But treason was still treason. She was now—or would become, at the future ceremony—the Great Mother of what was left of the Kiktu. The tribe would want to hear her voice at Kopporu's—trial.

What would she say? What course of action propose?

Or even—the thought came to her unbidden—command?

She heard faint whispers among the males huddled within

her mantle cavity, but paid no attention. Until, moments later, she felt the stroking of a multitude of small arms along the great muscles of her rearhead.

The strokes brought sudden relaxation. And then, almost simultaneously, embarrassment and anxiety.

No male had ever entered her cavity before, much less *stroked* her. True, their arms were far away from the—*organs*— at the very rear of her cavity, but still—

"Stop that!"

The strokes ceased. Instantly, the eumale spoke sharply and the stroking resumed. A moment later, the small figure of the eumale and the truemale who had assisted him in carrying Abka's body appeared alongside her huge right eye. (Julius had noted, and been amazed by, the capacity of owoc and gukuy to focus their eyes at incredibly short ranges. Guo was staring at her preconsorts at a distance which a human would have measured in centimeters.)

"You are now the Great Mother of the tribe," said the eumale firmly. "And you are obviously confused and distraught. Over the state of the tribe, of course, but also over what to do about Kopporu. The tribe cannot afford your thoughts to be a mess. It will be part of our duty as your consorts to relieve your tension, so that you can think clearly. Don't be a silly spawn."

Guo couldn't prevent a hoot of surprise. At the impudence of the eumale, to some degree. But more at his uncanny perception of her thoughts.

"How did—"

The eumale whistled. "What else would you be confused about?"

Guo fell silent. The stroking continued, and, after a while, she admitted that it was quite relaxing. Very pleasureable, in fact. But from that train of thought her mind fled quickly.

The eumale and the other male did not leave their perch on her mantlerim. Guo kept her eyes on the path ahead, for the most part. But, now and then, her great right eye would swivel and examine her two new companions. They ignored these peeks, in the excessively dignified manner of youth. They were, Guo realized, no older than she. Still some time away from reaching sexual maturity.

(The thought was, simultaneously, the source of relief, anxiety, regret and vast curiosity.)

"What are your names?" she asked suddenly. "I am Guo, of the clan of—"

The eumale whistled. "We know who you are! Everyone does. I am Woddulakotat. This is Yurra. He is probably going to be our alpha." A quick, incredibly subtle network of green and brown. "Almost certainly. We hadn't decided yet, because Abka was also being considered. But now that Abka is dead—"

He fell silent. The green and brown shimmer on his mantle and Yurra's deepened and glowed. They were lost in grief for their bondmale.

Guo knew little of the complex workings of male society, beyond the simple basics which every gukuy in the tribe knew. Less, probably, than any infanta her age, for she had bent all her thoughts to the ways of the warriors. Males, she knew, bonded together in small groups when they were new-born spawn—the only way they could fend off the predatory attentions of the much larger female spawn.

Once made, those bonds were lifelong and deep. The males of a bond would marry a mother as a cluster. Males had few rights, in Kiktu society; but those which they had, they guarded jealously. The most precious of those rights was the cluster's control over which male would copulate at any given time with the mother. Mothers, it was said, usually had their preferences in sexual partners—but the mothers, normally dominant in their relationship with their husbands, had to accept whichever male had been selected for the moment by the bond. The alpha male would, as a rule, obtain more than his share of couplings—but not too much more, lest he be deposed by his co-husbands.

The malebond's rights in this matter were never challenged. The rights held true even when—as was the custom among the Kiktu and most of the tribes of the plains—visiting mothers exchanged a sexual partner with each other for a night. The choice of the partner to be sent into the mantle of the visiting mother was entirely the prerogative of the mothers' respective husband-clusters. From what Guo had heard (in whispers among infanta), it was a common punishment which males of a bond visited on those of its members who had fallen afoul of the bond's good will—to be dispatched into the mantle of an especially disliked visiting mother; there to labor through the night to satisfy an old, nasty, demanding mother.

Woddulakotat's strange name was normal for a eumale. The oddly truncated ending of the name signified his lack of sexual organs, his incompletion. (Normally, all Kiktu names—almost all words in their language, in fact—ended in vowels.) The length of the name, on the other hand, signified that the being's soul made up for his lack in other ways. The utter misery of a eumale's life, which was the norm in most gukuy societies, was not allowed among the Kiktu. True, the life of a eumale was sharply circumscribed by social custom—even more sharply than those of truemales. But within those limits, eumales were accorded a place of dignity and respect. More often than not, they assumed a position of leadership within the malebonds, along with the alpha husband.

Other peoples, Guo was dimly aware, derided the Kiktu for their coddling of eumales. The Kiktu ignored the derision, since it was (*very*) rarely expressed aloud; and because they considered the habits of other peoples little better than savagery.

Guo's thoughts began to turn again to the question of Kopporu's conduct, but she pushed it aside. She was much too tired to deal with that now. From what little she could see of the Mother-of-Pearl through the canopy of cycad branches, it was almost nightfall. Soon, she was certain, the leaders would order a rest for the night. On the morrow, when her brain was clear, she would ponder the problem of Kopporu. For now—she had new realities to deal with.

"You were very good in the battle," she said suddenly. The brown in the mantles of her two consorts faded slightly. "I didn't realize males could pipe so well."

The truemale—Yurra—whistled derisively. Delicate yellow traceries formed on Woddulakotat's mantle.

"They can't," announced the eumale. "The silly old farts wouldn't know what to do with their pipes if their lives depended on it."

Sudden brown flooded his little mantle.

"Which it did," he said sadly. "I shouldn't make fun of them. At the end, all the maleclusters took positions to defend their mates, pipes in arms. Not that it would do any good, of course, even if they knew how to use them. But not a one failed in his duty."

"We practiced," added Yurra. "For many, many eightdays.

It was Abka's idea. He said that if we became accurate enough, and all fired at once at the same target, that we could make up for our weak siphons."

"He was right," said Guo firmly. "I think you kept me from being blinded."

"You fought without a shield, with two maces," said Woddulakotat admiringly. "You were truly awesome." Yurra hooted vigorous agreement.

For a moment, the gigantic mother and her two consorts-to-be gazed at each other. Then, simultaneously, tinges of green began to flicker in their mantles.

Perhaps it will not be so bad, after all, being a mother.

The thought was still too new and unsettling. For the males as well, it seemed, judging from the speed with which those first, tentative flickers of green disappeared.

"If you intend to continue fighting in this crazy manner," said Yurra suddenly, "we should give some thought to making a kind of shield for your cowl. So that we can concentrate on piping, instead of dodging darts."

Guo was relieved, herself, at the change of subject.

"Good idea. I'll talk to my flankers about it."

The three of them began discussing the design and construction of the shield. Anchoring it, of course, was no problem—the thick, hard tissue of Guo's cowl made a perfect location for attaching a shield. The problem was in the design. More like a visor than a shield, it would have to be—so that the males atop her cowl, while protected, would still have gaps through which to pipe.

Shortly thereafter, the signal was passed down from somewhere ahead: *Make camp where you can for the night. We depart at first light tomorrow.*

Guo looked around. They were in a place where the path broadened slightly. To one side was a large mound of moss. One of Guo's flankers inspected the mound and announced that it was (relatively) free of pests. Guo and her flankers moved onto the mound. She noticed the apprehensive glances which her flankers cast about in the gloom. It was almost dark. The swamp was horrid enough in daylight. What monsters crept within it during the dark?

She commanded them to gather closely around her bulk—atop her mantle, even, as many as could fit. The flankers quickly agreed on a system of rotating guards. (So, Guo noticed with admiration, did the males of her cluster.) Then, feeling reassured by the proximity of Guo's great muscles, the flankers not on watch fell quickly asleep. No large predator would likely approach such a formidable creature as Guo, even in the dark. If they did, the watch would sound the alarm, and whatever predator might lurk in the swamp would soon learn the bitter lesson which Guo had taught, that very day, to the Utuku. Even in sleep, the great battlemother did not relinquish her grip on the maces.

Guo's last memory, before she fell asleep, was a faint whisper from Woddulakotat.

"Tomorrow, Guo, we will talk about Kopporu, and what you must do. But think on this, as you drift into sleep. I was there, at the end, with the Great Mother. My bondmates and I had taken position on her cowl, alongside her own cluster, for we knew that her husbands would be useless. We saw Kopporu's retreat, at the same time as the Great Mother.

"She did not hesitate, Guo. Not for a moment. She commanded an attendant, and gave her the shell; and ordered us onto the attendant. Then she gave the attendant the message for you, and bade her leave.

"I looked back, Guo, at the Great Mother. It was my last sight of her. Her mantle was glowing like the Mother-of-Pearl itself in midday. One color, Guo—one color alone. The deepest green I have ever seen."

Chapter 17

When Guo awoke the next day, the answer to her dilemma was clear. As she slept, her mind seemed to have reached a conclusion on its own. A problem, however, remained: How should she carry out her decision?

Here, she was treading on uncertain ground. By choice, she had spent as much of her short life as possible in the company of warriors. She knew little of the customs and traditions which prevailed within the yurts of the mothers and clan leaders, even though she herself was a high-ranked member of the tribe's prevalent clan.

She did not think in these terms, but the essence of her problem was that: *she needed a lawyer*.

Lawyers, of course, did not exist among the Kiktu. (They had only just begun emerging, as a distinct subset of the priestly caste, in the civilized realms of the south.) The Kiktu were barbarians. They had no written language beyond a crude system of notations which were even more limited than the runes of Earth's ancient barbarians. Like the tribes of northern Europe a millenia past, custom and law was maintained by oral tradition transmitted from one generation of clan leaders to the next.

Had Guo ever read the old Icelandic sagas, she would have found the scene toward the end of *The Saga of Burnt Njal* quite familiar. The tribe, gathered in full assembly, deliberating on a matter of law. Each old and wise being of the tribe advancing their arguments; only to be refuted when an older and wiser being remembered a different law which everyone else had forgotten.

Law and custom was the province of the old clan leaders. What was she to do? All the clan leaders were dead. There were not even very many old warriors left alive, Guo suspected. Other than Kopporu's personal guard, and the members of her own small clan, the vast majority of the warriors who had filled the ranks of the left flank had been the young and adventuresome warriors of the tribe who had flocked to Kopporu's standard.

The word of Kopporu's own clan members would inevitably be suspect in the tribal assembly which would judge Kopporu's conduct. The word of the old members of Kopporu's personal guard—Aktako and her close friends—would be even more suspect.

The young warriors who made up almost all that was left of the Kiktu would be torn and confused. On the one hand, their esteem for Kopporu's prowess in battle—once again dramatically confirmed—would draw them toward her. On the other hand, they would be horrified at Kopporu's actions.

Confusion and uncertainty would be the inevitable result. Chaos would develop, and grow. Different bands of warriors would advance alternate and conflicting proposals—with all the vigor and hot-headed impetuosity of youth. Who was to guide the deliberations, and maintain order? Kopporu? Impossible—she was the issue at hand. Gortoku? Or one of the other battle leaders? Possibly. But it was unlikely that members of other battle groups would accept the authority of any of the battle leaders. The battle leaders were all young themselves. Tried in battle, to be sure, but not in custom and law.

These were the thoughts that filled Guo's brain, as she made her way that morning along the path. The guide, she noted absently, was still leading them northward.

After a time, she became aware of Woddulakotat's presence. His little mantle, she saw with surprise, was suffused with azure irritation.

"Are you really so ignorant?" demanded the eumale.

"What do you mean?" She was too surprised by the question to be angered by its impudence. (She would learn, very quickly, that the subservient timidity of males was less fact than fiction; and, over time, would grow thankful for it.)

The azure was suddenly—for just a fleeting moment—replaced by green affection.

"Truly, you are a battlemother. Have you spent *any* time in the yurts of the mothers?"

"Very little. As little as possible, in fact. I was bored."

"You can no longer afford to be bored, Guo. The responsibility for the tribe is now in your arms."

Guo's own mantle flooded azure. "I know that! What do you think I've been thinking about, ever since we started off this morning?"

Woddulakotat made the gesture of reproof.

"Then why aren't you talking to us?" At that moment, Yurra appeared alongside him.

Guo was dumbfounded. "Why would I talk to you?"

Both males were now positively glowing azure—no, more! Bright blue.

"Idiot," said Yurra. "We are your closest advisers. You will have others, of course. But, always, a mother's closest advisers are her husbands."

Guo was too interested in the information to take offense at the truemale's outrageous conduct.

"*Really?*"

The two males stared at her in silence. Slowly, the blue faded from their mantles.

"As I said, truly a battlemother." Woddulakotat whistled humorously. "Guo, the one group of advisers you can *always* trust are your husbands. You do not need to take our advice, of course. Males are not always wise."

"Neither are females," interjected Yurra forcefully.

"But whether our advice is wise or not, you need never fear that it contains hidden motives. We are your husbands. Not yet, of course—but we will be."

"Did the Great Mother—"

"Always," replied Woddulakotat.

"Every night," added Yurra. Another whistle. "Well, not *every* night. Even in her old age, the Great Mother was a lusty—"

"Yurra!" Guo was shocked.

But, despite her prudish innocence, Guo was not really a timid youngster. She had been assured and assertive even before the battle. Now, with the battle behind her, she was rapidly growing in self-confidence. It was strange, to her, this idea that one would discuss important matters with—*males*. But...

And so, as the day wore on, she began slowly opening her thoughts to her preconsorts. Tentatively, at first; then with increasing frankness.

Not long after she began her discussion with them, Yurra and Woddulakotat brought another of their malebond forward. Iyopa, his name was. Guo discovered that every malebond had at least one member who specialized in learning the tribe's traditions and laws.

"The mother needs her own memory," explained Iyopa. The gesture of suspicion. "You can't always trust a clan leader's memory, no matter how old they are. *Especially* when the matter involves relations between the clans. It's amazing how every old clan leader suddenly remembers the law differently— always, of course, to the benefit of her own clan."

Iyopa was quite small, even for a male. But handsome, thought Guo. Very handsome, in fact.

Very handsome.

She forced her attention back to the problem at hand. Some part of her mind, throughout the ensuing day, never lost its awareness of Iyopa's good looks (and odd, new sensations began tingling in her body); but, for the most part, she was impressed with the young truemale's knowledge of Kiktu history. A bit vain, perhaps, and Guo thought that he was not really as smart as either Yurra or Woddulakotat. But Iyopa had a truly prodigious memory; and there was no question the truemale had applied himself to his task.

By midafternoon, Guo and her preconsorts had reached the stage of conclusions.

"You have to make sure of your flankers," said Yurra softly. "If they are not steady, all will be lost."

Guo considered, and agreed. Soon thereafter, upon entering a small clearing, she halted and gave the hoot which summoned her flankers. Moments later, the eight warriors stood before her. Their swamp-dweller guide arrived, as well, wondering at the delay. Firmly, but not disrespectfully, Guo asked her to leave for a moment, that she might discuss private matters with her flankers. The guide hesitated briefly; then moved out of hearing range.

Guo examined the flankers. All of them had survived the battle, relatively unharmed. A surprising fact in itself. The position of battlemother's flanker was prestigious among the

Kiktu—not least, because it was so dangerous. Unlike the mobile warriors, the flankers were fixed to their slow battlemother, and without the battlemother's bulk to protect them.

Flankers carried flails, but they did not normally use them in combat. A flanker's weapon was the greatfork. The greatfork was a two-tentacle weapon, a combination of a huge two-fork and axe. (A human specialist examining the weapon would have immediately recognized it, generically, as a halberd. In detail, of course, the weapon was different: two fork-prongs on one side, where a halberd has a single beak; and the axe-blade on the opposite was longer and shallower than the blade of a halberd. But the principle was the same.)

The greatfork was an ungainly weapon in combat, quite unlike the graceful flail-and-fork combination of the normal warrior. But grace was not its function. In battle, the task of the flankers was crude and simple: either by grasping with the fork, or by driving with the blade, to hold the enemy in position while the slow but irresistible power of a battlemother's mace was brought to bear.

Battlemothers always fought in the thick of the battle. The casualties around them were usually high—for flanker and foe alike.

Guo hesitated, ochre uncertainty rippling across her mantle. Once she spoke to her flankers, she was committed. But after a moment, the ochre faded. Her mantle was now gray, with a faint hint of black.

"Tomorrow—or soon, anyway—there will be a tribal assembly. Kopporu will have to answer for her actions."

The flankers said nothing. It was obvious from their stance and color, however, that they were not surprised by her statement. They, too, had drawn their own conclusions from observing the retreat into the swamp.

"At the assembly, I will enforce the traditions of the Kiktu. It is both my right and my duty—as the Great Mother of the tribe."

Yurra handed her the bundle, which the males had kept in safekeeping. Guo carefully unwrapped the bundle, and exposed the ceremonial shell within. The flankers gazed upon it. Their arms made the gesture of reverence. But Guo noted that there was no trace of orange surprise in their mantles.

They saw—and know. Good.

"Things will be—confused—at the assembly. We have lost all our clan leaders. I must—it will be necessary that I—"

Suddenly, one of her flankers raised her greatfork above her cowl, held crossways like a horizontal bar. It was the traditional salute of the flanker to her battlemother. Traditional, but hardly ever seen. The Kiktu were not, in truth, given to frequent displays of ceremony.

A moment later, the other seven flankers followed suit.

"We are yours to command, Great Mother," spoke the flanker who had first raised her fork. Her name was Kolkata, and she was the leader of the squad of flankers. A moment later, the others echoed her words.

The black tinge in Guo's mantle darkened.

"I may be forced to harshness."

This time, the words came as one, loudly:

"We are yours to command, Great Mother."

Guo stared at them. She was—surprised. She had thought it would be more difficult. (For all her unusual capacity for combat, Guo was not really a warrior, and did not fully understand the minds of warriors. On the day after the Battle of Lolopopo, Guo's flankers would have stood with her against the Kraken itself.)

The black in her mantle faded. For a moment, a green wave rippled across. Then Guo turned, and resumed the march.

Hours later, they entered a huge clearing in the swamp. Many other warriors were already in the clearing. Still more were trickling in from several directions—all in small groups, led by a swamp-dweller guide.

The word was passed along by couriers:

We rest here tonight. Tomorrow the tribe assembles.

Before they slept, Guo and her preconsorts dug a little grave, into which they lowered the body of Abka. It was strange, then, the anguish which she felt, for the loss of a husband she had never known.

Yet she grieved, and deeply; and found, in the pain, a well of courage and resolve.

The assembly began early in the day, and raggedly. There were no clan leaders to begin the deliberations with the customary religious rituals. Those rituals were brief and, in truth, not much more than perfunctory. But they had always served, in the past, to allow the assembly to come to order in a set and certain manner.

Guo saw that Kopporu was going to make no attempt to substitute herself as the leader of the rituals. The infanta thought Kopporu's decision was wise. Better to begin the assembly by bluntly demonstrating the truth to all.

Kopporu herself was standing toward the center of the clearing, on its northern side. She was weaponless, and her personal guard were not nearby. Guo was relieved. She had been concerned that Kopporu might attempt to intimidate the tribe. Such an attempt would not have worked; it would simply have inflamed the hotheads. Instead, by taking her stance, Kopporu was making clear to one and all that she accepted the authority of the tribe.

Still, Guo noted that Kopporu had subtly weighted the situation. Her personal guard was not standing nearby, true. But they were not all that far away, either.

Guo examined them. As hard-bitten a collection of old warriors as you could find anywhere on the Meat of the Clam. The scars crisscrossing their collective mantles were literally beyond counting. There could be no doubt in any gukuy's mind that Aktako and her group would deal ruthlessly with anyone who tried to take matters into their own palps. Not even the rashest young warrior would casually match flails with *them*.

But there was more. Guo saw that the Opoktu warriors were gathered not far from the center of the clearing, on the same side as Kopporu. The Opoktu were still outnumbered by the surviving Kiktu, by a factor of four to one. But the Opoktu had saved their entire tribe, except for those warriors who had fallen in combat. Their own two mothers, and four clan leaders, were standing prominently to the fore. In every nuance of the Opoktu stance, a subtle but clear set of messages was being conveyed to all who observed:

We are still a tribe with leaders, united.

We are so, because we chose the course of flight.

We stand with Kopporu.

Then, there were the swamp-dwellers. There were many eights of them, gathered together some little distance from Kopporu. Again, not near the battle leader. But near enough to come to Kopporu's aid, if necessary. And while the swamp-dwellers were not warriors, the still-healing scars on their own mantles demonstrated that they lacked neither courage nor willingness to fight. They were clanless outcasts, but their status had inevitably risen in the eyes of the Kiktu over the past days. Whatever their prejudices, the Kiktu were warriors—for whom courage counted much.

And, there was this: Any Kiktu had but to look about them, to see that they were in the middle of the Lolopopo Swamp. Lost, without their guides. And the guides were making clear, without effrontery, that they too would stand with Kopporu.

There was a last group, whom Guo had not expected. They would not be a direct factor in the assembly, but their presence was not insignificant. Scattered around the clearing, in small huddled groups, were refugees from every tribe which had fought the Utuku on the plain. The refugees had been found scattered through the swamp, and brought along with the retreat. Many were Kiktu; but the majority, thought Guo, were members of the five other tribes (besides the Opoktu) which had joined in alliance with the Kiktu. Whose clan leaders had also led them to disaster.

All of them were warriors, except for a single young Datga mother and her consorts. Most of them bore recent battle wounds. Each of them was silent, their pinkish-brown mantles giving testimony to their own fears and feelings of guilt. Each of them had chosen, as individuals, to take the same course that Kopporu had chosen for the left flank as a whole—salvation in the swamp. They, too, bore the burden of treason. Hence they would not speak at the assembly—even those of them who were Kiktu and had the right to speak. Their own conduct would be examined, and judgement passed.

Yet—their very presence was perhaps the strongest, if most indirect, reinforcement for Kopporu's position. For Kopporu alone was not on trial here. So were the ghosts of the clan leaders who had been responsible for the greatest single calamity in the history of the Kiktu and their allied tribes. The miserable, huddled shapes of the refugees was silent testimony to the ghastly scope of that disaster.

The assembly was slow in coming to order. Kopporu stood alone, making no attempt to impose her authority. She had apparently decided that it was best to allow the tribespeople to mill about for a time, pondering the situation.

Guo thought Kopporu's tactic was wise. And it gave her time to settle an important question. She looked for, and quickly found, the other two surviving Kiktu battlemothers. Loapo and Oroku were standing together nearby, with those few of Loapa's flankers who had survived. (Oroku's flankers, Guo would later learn, had all died in their frenzied efforts to save their badly wounded battlemother.)

Guo lumbered toward them. She was glad to see that Oroku was present. She had feared that the lamed infanta would not have been able to keep up with the tribe in its flight.

She was also relieved to see that Oroku's wounds were healing well enough, under the circumstances. There seemed to be no sign of the parasitic infections which so often accompanied bad wounds, especially eye-wounds.

The reason for the lack of infection was obvious, once Guo came near. The wounds—the entire left eye, in fact—had been savagely cauterized by fire. Guo was deeply impressed with Oroku's courage. The pain of that cauterization must have been incredible. But the treatment had killed any parasites—even though the infanta would be horribly disfigured for the rest of her life.

"You are well?" asked Guo.

Loapo made the gesture of affirmation. Oroku whistled amusement.

"As well as could be expected, under the circumstances."

"I had feared you would not manage the march through the swamp."

"I would not have," replied Oroku, "except for Loapo. And the warriors whom Kopporu sent to help me."

Mention of Kopporu brought back the necessities of the moment. Yurra, as prearranged, handed Guo the bundle containing the Mothershell. Guo showed it to the other two infanta, and recounted the attendant's words.

When she finished, she was relieved to see no trace of blue in their mantles. She had been especially concerned about Oroku's reaction. Loapa belonged to a relatively unimportant clan. There would have been no possibility of her becoming Great Mother, in any event. But Oroku, like Guo, was a member of the prevalent clan. Furthermore, she was older than Guo. Insofar as these things could be determined in the rather complex manner by which the Kiktu mothers chose the Great

Mother of the tribe, Oroku had been a more likely candidate than Guo. She had feared that Oroku might take offense at Guo's peremptory claim to the title.

Her fears proved groundless. Oroku simply examined the bundle and, within moments, made the gesture of consent. Loapo immediately followed suit.

"The Great Mother chose wisely," whispered Oroku. "I can think of no better person to become our Great Mother in this darkest of all nights." A faint, humorous whistle. "A *kuopto* Great Mother! I almost wish the clan leaders were still alive, so I could watch them tremble in fear. May they rot in the Meat for eternity."

A brown ripple washed across Oroku's mantle. "And besides, Guo, I will be spawnless. There are no males left to the tribe, except yours. Even if there were, what malebond would mate with a mother who looked like me?" She gestured at her horribly scarred face.

Long after, looking back, Guo would decide that her love for her husbands was born at that moment.

Yurra did not hesitate.

"I would be honored to serve you, Oroku." There was not a trace of ochre in his mantle—nothing but an exquisite tracery of every shade of green (with just a hint of white beneath). The little truemale made the gesture of obedience. "With my future mate's permission, of course."

"All of our bond will serve you, Oroku," added Woddulakotat. "I would myself, if I could, and willingly. Scars are a thing of the flesh. The tribe will need your soul." He also made the gesture of obedience. "With our future mate's permission, of course."

Guo was—amused, she thought at first. For all her preconsorts' formal submissiveness, she had come to know them well enough to be certain that, if she withheld her permission, the cluster would make her life utterly miserable.

She had no intention of withholding permission, of course, and immediately made that clear—to Loapo as well as Oroku. Jealousy was by no means an unknown emotion among the Kiktu (and all gukuy), but it was not closely tied to sexual congress. Not, at least, among mothers.

She realized, suddenly, that her own mantle was flooded with green. Love for her sisters, of course. But there was more;

much more. It had never occurred to her before that moment that greatness of spirit might dwell in the little bodies of males. She had a glimpse, then, of the future she would share with her husbands. Of a romance that would itself become a legend, recited by chantresses.

But it was a fleeting glimpse, for at that moment she felt a stirring in the air around her.

As she turned, she heard Oroku say: "We are as one, Guo. And remember the Great Mother's words: *Be ruthless toward all folly.*"

Silence was falling over the multitude in the clearing. And it *was* a multitude, Guo saw. There were far more survivors than she had at first realized. The huge clearing itself held over double-eight eighties of tribespeople—and she estimated that there were at least as many packed into the cycads surrounding the clearing.

Once the silence was complete, Kopporu began to speak. She spoke slowly, for she had to shout loudly enough to be heard by all. Nevertheless, it did not take her long to tell her tale.

The battle leader recounted, in a voice devoid of all emotion, her actions over the past few eightdays. She recounted all of the steps which she had taken, including the murders of Yaua and Doroto. She also explained, very briefly, the reasons for her actions. But she made no effort to justify them, or to advance any argument in her favor. She simply presented the facts, and a description of her motives.

When Kopporu finished, she allowed a moment's silence to pass before saying:

"Let the trial begin."

"Now," whispered Woddalukotat.

Guo moved forward into the clearing, her flankers on either side. The murmur which had begun to sweep the crowd after Kopporu's last words died away. Every eye was upon Guo.

When she reached the center of the clearing, Guo slowly turned and surveyed the entire crowd in the clearing. Once she was certain that all attention was riveted upon her, she said—in that incredibly loud voice of which only mothers are capable:

"*There will be no trial.*"

She waited for the surprised hoots to fade away.

"There *can* be no trial," she continued, "for there are no clan leaders here."

A voice spoke from the crowd: "The tribe may act as judge!"

"Who spoke?" demanded Guo.

Immediately a warrior advanced forward, her mantle suffused with blue—that particular shade of blue which, among gukuy, connoted not simply anger but the outrage of a superior offended by a subordinate. Guo recognized her at once. She was named Ruako, and she was a high-ranked member of Guo's own clan.

Good, she thought. *The other clans will not think I am playing favorites.*

"Do you know her?" asked Woddulakotat softly.

"Not well."

"I do, for she spent much time in the yurts of the mothers and clan leaders. Ruako is very full of herself. Ambitious and vain. Exactly what you need."

Guo spoke again, very loudly. "How can there be a trial, Ruako, when the accused are not here to answer the charges?"

The warrior's blue mantle rippled with orange. Confusion; astonishment.

"What do you mean, Guo? The accused is standing right there!" Ruako pointed with her palp at Kopporu.

"Kopporu?" demanded Guo. "Who has accused Kopporu of anything? I have heard no accusation."

Ruako emitted that peculiar spitting hoot which, had she been a human instead of a gukuy, would have been called "sputtering."

"What are you saying? Kopporu accused herself!"

"Ridiculous. Kopporu simply presented the tribe with a recitation of events. All of which lead to an accusation against the clan leaders. *Misconduct*." (The Kiktu term which she used carried much heavier connotations than the English word "misconduct"—gross dereliction of duty; criminal incompetence; reckless endangerment of the tribe.)

"Oh, that's good," whispered Yurra excitedly. "That's very good!"

Ruako's mantle was now positively glowing blue and orange. For a moment, the warrior was speechless. Guo took the opportunity to quickly scan the crowd. She was pleased to see the signs of relaxation everywhere her eyes looked. Like most cultures whose tradition is oral rather than written, the Kiktu took a great delight in debate and discussion. By immediately stepping forward, Guo had taken temporary command of the assembly. Then, by drawing out an opponent and focusing the tribe's attention, she had brought order and logic to what might have rapidly become a chaotic whirlwind of anger and action. Instead, the members of the tribe were settling back comfortably on their peds. More than one warrior, she noted, was showing faint tints of green in their mantles. Kopporu partisans, perhaps; or simply connoisseurs, enjoying Guo's display of skill.

"The clan leaders are not murderers!" squalled Ruako.

"How can you say that? That is precisely Kopporu's charge. Unfortunately, the clan leaders are not here to answer the charge. Hence, as I said, there can be no trial."

Again, the spitting hoot. "Ridiculous! Ridiculous! Who are the clan leaders accused of murdering?"

Guo paused, hoping another would answer. It was important that she maintain as much appearance of neutrality as possible.

To her relief, Gortoku stepped forward.

"They are accused of murdering—*those who are not here.*"

Gortoku spread her tentacles, in a gesture encompassing the entire crowd.

"*Where is the rest of our tribe?*"

Ruako started to speak, but Gortoku's loud voice overrode her words.

"I ask again: *where is the rest of our tribe?*"

The answer came at once, from many siphons:

"Dead on the plain!"

"In the bellies of the Utuku!"

"In the Utuku shackles!"

"*Just so!*" bellowed Gortoku. "And who is responsible for that—Kopporu? Or the clan leaders?"

Silence. Guo waited a moment, then spoke.

"I have *permitted* this discussion, in order that the tribe might see the truth for itself." She paused briefly, allowing everyone to take note of the word "permitted." Then, when she gauged the time right, she took the bundle handed her by Woddulakotat and opened it. She took the Mothershell in her palp and raised it high in the air, where all could see it.

"As we retreated into the swamp, the Great Mother sent this to me, along with her childcluster." Guo then repeated the Great Mother's last words.

"The mothers of the tribe"—she gestured to Loapo and Oroku— "have discussed this amongst ourselves, and have agreed to respect the Great Mother's wishes. I am now the Great Mother of the Kiktu."

Loapo and Oroku hooted their assent. *Very* loudly.

Ruako immediately began whistling derision, and uttering various words of scorn. The gist of which was: these are not mothers, they are mere infanta; they cannot make such a momentous decision; children should be seen and not heard; and so forth.

"What an idiot!" whispered Yurra.

"She's perfect," agreed Woddalukotat.

And, indeed, it was so. Many others in the crowd might have, privately, held similar views. But the manner in which Ruako had expressed them settled the issue. The authority of mothers in Kiktu society was more often honored in the breach, rather than in the observance. But it was *always* honored. The more so, in this instance, in that the infanta so ridiculed had played a glorious role in the battle just passed. Much more glorious—as more than one warrior noted, and loudly—than had Ruako. (And more than one warrior, as well, loudly contrasted the terrible wounds borne by Oroku to the scratches on Ruako's hide.)

Ruako was not so stupid as not to realize, quickly, that she had blundered badly. She attempted now to shift the question on to the general impropriety of the entire manner in which the assembly was being held. This was done through a hurried appeal to Kiktu prejudices.

"Outrage! Bad enough that Opoktu should be allowed at our tribal assembly! Even worse—clanless outcasts have been brought into our midst!"

For the first time since she finished her opening presentation, Kopporu spoke.

"It is not against custom for honored members of an allied tribe to be present at Kiktu assemblies." Then, very loudly: *"Or does Ruako now wish to slander the valiant Opoktu as well as our own battlemothers?"*

By this time, more and more members of the tribe were

enjoying the spectacle of Ruako's embarrassment. Like most arrogant people of high status, Ruako had made many enemies among the Kiktu. And even those who had nothing against her personally were becoming irritated at her conduct.

Again, loud voices were heard. Contrasting the glorious feats of many Opoktu in the recent battle to the modest role played by Ruako. Comparing, in puzzled tones, the great wounds which were clearly visible on many Opoktu to the— (Did she fall into a topobush, do you think? Is that where she got those two little scratches?)—almost unblemished mantle of Ruako.

Kopporu spoke again.

"As for the swamp dwellers, they are here on a matter which concerns my clan. And the tribe. I will explain when we have finished with the question before us."

She stepped back.

"Now," said Woddulakotat. "Yes," added Yurra.

For just a moment, Guo feared that ochre or pink might enter her mantle. Disaster. She brought the image of her slaughtered people to her mind.

Her mantle flooded black. She rose up slightly, and *bellowed*:

"I invoke the Motherlaw!"

Utter silence. Utter stillness.

In part, of course, the reaction of the tribe was due to simple, physical shock. The voice of a mother, unleashed in all its power, bears a close resemblance to thunder.

But, to a greater degree, the shock was mental. Motherlaw had not been invoked among the Kiktu in living memory. No, more—not for many, many generations. Guo could practically see the thoughts racing through the minds of every warrior in the clearing, as they searched back through the history of the tribe.

They found the answer almost at once, as Iyopa had predicted. It was, after all, one of the most famous episodes in Kiktu history. That time, long ago, when the Kiktu were still a small tribe. Reeling from defeat at the palps of the (now vanished) Laukta. Most of their clan leaders and mothers dead; half of the warriors wounded, dead, or dying; the ones who survived having done so only because of the incredible ferocity of the rear guard which had covered their retreat. At the center of that rear guard had stood a young infanta; who, after the battle, had declared herself the new Great Mother and had seized command of the tribe through invoking the ancient ritual of Motherlaw. She had maintained the Motherlaw for many, many, many eightweeks. Until the Kiktu recovered, and took their terrible revenge on the Laukta.

Her name had been Dodotpi. She was revered in the history of the Kiktu. Partly, of course, because she had saved the tribe. But partly, as well, because the Kiktu were warriors, and Dodotpi had been the greatest battlemother who ever walked the Meat of the Clam.

The entire multitude stared at Guo, and remembered the Battle of the Clearing; and wondered: *Or was she?*

Motherlaw. A custom whose origins vanished somewhere back in the mists of time. Almost never invoked. Great Mothers were deeply respected among the Kiktu, and even enjoyed a definite authority. (Quite unlike, in this respect, the semi-divine Paramount Mothers of the south, whose actual power was nil.) But it was still the clan leaders who ruled, except in battle, where the battle leaders came to the fore.

Motherlaw was not precisely "mother-rule." On the few occasions when Motherlaw had been invoked in the past, the Great Mothers had always appointed leaders from the ranks of the warriors to actually exercise the power. But their authority derived solely from the Great Mother, and could be withdrawn by her. And the Great Mother served as the final arbiter of law and custom. Judge; jury—and executioner.

Ruako broke the silence. She began squawling semi-coherent phrases, all of which indicated her vast displeasure and disagreement with Guo's person and behavior.

"Fork her," commanded Guo.

Immediately, her eight flankers charged across the clearing. As they approached, Ruako suddenly fell silent. Turned scarlet; and tried to flee. But the flankers were upon her. No less than four greatforks slammed into Ruako's mantle. It was the work of but moments to drag the whistling warrior back across the clearing. The work of but seconds to flip Ruako onto her back. (An unnecessary flourish, of course. The mace which now crushed the life out of Ruako's body would have done so regardless of which way the warrior was positioned. In truth, it would have splintered a boulder.)

Guo allowed the multitude to gaze upon Ruako's corpse for a brief moment, before speaking.

"Does the tribe remember our Great Mother's last words to me?"

Silence.

"*Answer me!*"

Several voices: "'Be ruthless toward all folly.'"

"*Louder.*"

"BE RUTHLESS TOWARD ALL FOLLY."

"*Just so.*"

Guo made the gesture of condemnation. Her mantle glowed blue.

"If the clan leaders had survived, their stinking corpses would now be lying next to Ruako's. They are condemned in the memory of the tribe."

She turned and faced Kopporu. "Kopporu!"

"Yes, Great Mother."

"You are now the battle leader of the Kiktu."

"Yes, Great Mother. Who do you appoint as the new clan leaders?"

"No one. We do not need clan leaders. We are still in battle—and will be, *until the Utuku are destroyed.*"

She paused, letting that thought penetrate the minds of her warriors. The formula was that proposed by Iyopa—the same, he said, as that adopted by Dodotpi so long ago.

"There will be no new clan leaders chosen until the Utuku are crushed and our tribe is avenged. Until that time, the Kiktu are an army. Each warrior will answer to her battle leader—and to her alone. *Regardless of clan.* The battle leaders will answer to Kopporu—and to her alone. *Regardless of clan.*"

She paused, allowing the tribe to digest the concept.

"*Do you understand?*"

There was no hesitation this time in the response, which came from many, many siphons.

Like myself, thought Guo, *the warriors have grown weary of clan leaders.*

Kopporu spoke.

"Great Mother, I have a difficulty."

"What is that?"

Kopporu gestured to the swamp dwellers. "The survival of

the tribe depends upon these—*brave people*. They have already aided us beyond measure, as all here know. Many of them have died in so doing. In return, they have asked for no reward except—adoption into my clan. I have promised to speak for them. But—"

Guo finished the thought. "But you cannot adopt them without the permission of the clan leader. Who does not exist. And will not, for—some time."

For ever, came the sudden, shocking thought. A tribe without clan leaders? Forever?

I must think upon that. Perhaps—back to the moment, fool! What am I to do?

"Put them in the battle groups," whispered Woddulakotat.

"Make one of them an adviser," said Yurra quietly. "And don't forget the Opoktu either."

"And the refugees," added Woddulakotat.

Guo pondered their advice for a moment, sorting it out. It made sense, she thought.

"Do the swamp dw—do these brave people have a leader?"

"Yes," replied Kopporu. She pointed to O-doddo-ua, and told Guo her name.

"Bring her forward."

When O-doddo-ua came up to her, Guo spoke quietly.

"I am sorry, O-doddo-ua, but I cannot allow you to be adopted into Kopporu's clan. Not now. Perhaps not—for a long time. By our customs, I would have to appoint new clan leaders. And—I cannot do that now. It is because—"

"I understand, Great Mother." The swamp dweller made a gesture which hinted at derision. Guo found herself warming to the gukuy.

"However, when the time comes you will be adopted. If not into Kopporu's clan, then into my own. I make that promise. In the meantime—"

She raised her head, and spoke to the multitude.

"All of the *brave people* who lived in the swamp will join our battle groups. They may either choose their own group, or, if they prefer, Kopporu will assign them to a group."

The black in her mantle returned in full force.

"All of the battle groups will welcome their new members. Do you understand?"

Her flankers, more or less casually, hefted their greatforks.

"Do you understand?"

"YES, GREAT MOTHER."

"Good." She made the gesture of contentment. "I am so glad. I detest folly."

The clearing was suddenly filled with humorous whistles. And a great green wave washed over the mantles, sweeping all ochre aside.

I have won. I have won. I have won.

"All of the refugees will do likewise. If they wish, they may form their own battle groups and choose leaders. But I would *prefer* that they join the battle groups which exist—either those of the Kiktu, or of the Opoktu. We do not need more confusion. Do you understand?"

There was no need, this time, to repeat the question.

She turned now and faced the Opoktu.

"You have, again, shown the honor of the Opoktu to the world. You have fulfilled your oath of alliance. You may now go your separate way, if that is your desire. I will provide you with guides to lead you through the swamp, wherever you wish to go."

The Opoktu mothers, clan leaders, and battle leaders exchanged opinions quietly, while Guo and her tribe waited. In much less time than she would have thought possible, they reached their conclusions. Lukpudo advanced to the center of the clearing, joining Guo and Kopporu. She spoke in a voice loud enough to be heard by all.

"We will remain with the Kiktu. Wherever the Kiktu go, we shall go also. In alliance!"

The clearing was filled with hoots of applause.

Lukpudo's next words were spoken softly.

"But just exactly where *are* we going?"

Guo looked at Kopporu. Kopporu whistled softly.

"To tell the truth, I never expected I would survive this day. So I didn't really give much thought to it. But—"

The Kiktu battle leader turned and looked to the northeast. Barely visible over the tops of the cycads surrounding the clearing was the Chiton. The great mountain was so far away it could hardly be discerned.

"Let us go to the mountain."

"To the *Chiton?*" A trace of orange rippled through Lukpudo's mantle. "It's—so far. All the way across the swamp."

"I know," replied Kopporu. "But O-doddo-ua says it can be done."

The swamp dweller spoke up. "Not easily, you understand. It will be a heroic trek, and we will suffer casualties. But, yes—it can be done."

Ochre tints appeared in Lukpudo's mantle. "But still—why?"

"Where else can we go?" asked Kopporu. "The plain will be covered with Utuku, hooting for our blood. They may even try to follow us through the swamp."

O-doddo-ua whistled derision.

"Perhaps the north?" asked Lukpudo uncertainly.

Kopporu made the gesture which was the gukuy equivalent of a shrug.

"To what purpose? How can our people survive in that wasteland? And I am certain that the Beak of the Utuku will have scouts watching the north as well as the plain. Once we emerged from the swamp, the Utuku would be upon us."

Lukpudo was not yet convinced. She now advanced her final argument.

"But—the Chiton is said to be a land of demons now."

Guo spoke.

"The whole world is a land of demons now, Lukpudo. What can demons on the mountain do to our people—that the demons on the plain have not already done?"

Lukpudo was silent.

Guo stared at the Chiton. So far away. A place of legends, and myths. And demons.

And pilgrims, she remembered. She turned to Kopporu.

"Have you spoken to the Pilgrims of the Way, Kopporu? The ones who go to the mountain?"

"Yes. Several times."

"What do they say?"

"They say there are demons on the mountain. Demons from beyond the Clam. Monsters, who move like the wind and slay like the lightning."

"Why then do they go there?"

Kopporu hesitated, searching for words. "They say—it is hard to understand. They say the demons are wise, as well as fierce. That they bring truth along with death. Justice itself, along with the flail of justice. They say that the battle leader of the demons is the most implacable punisher of evil which has ever lived in the world. A terrible creature, black as the night. But there is another demon, they say, who rules and commands."

"They go there to learn from this demon?"

Kopporu made the gesture of negation.

"No, Guo. They go there to plead with her. She is the wisest being in the world, they say, the one who knows the secrets of life, and truth, and justice. But she is silent, and will not speak. Not even to her children."

"Her *children?* She is—?"

"Yes, Guo. The Great Mother of demons."

Guo stared at the mountain. Moments later, when she spoke, her voice was like bronze.

"We will go to the mountain. I would see this Great Mother of demons for myself. If it is true that she knows these things, I will make her speak to me."

The battlemother gripped her mace.

"My people cry out for justice. If there is a secret of justice, I will have it from her. To hold such a thing secret would be evil beyond all evil."

...were buried in the world, A lamb to deserving, black as I... ...sight. And there remain, my friends, that you who shut and endureus.

They go thru. To be mindful this demand.

A support. Make the fortune of the sale.

No. Can I let the chance to give them her. She is the wisest being in the world. Now Sir, the one who knows the secrets of Imagination, substance... But that is what she will not speak, not ever, to... children.

Hear this and give...

So. Does The Great mother of mankind?

...you through the multitude... Minerva interposes when she comes home and was like a flower...

We will go as the mountains. I would see the Great Mother of...comes to myself if it's time that she sees their thing, will probably speak to me.

The knitter then gripped her time.

My heart certain to judge, if there is a spirit of justice, it will be...and not without nor without terror would be laid before us all.

PART IV:
The Loom

Chapter 18

"I've got a bad feeling about this," said Julius, watching the procession approach.

"Why?" asked Indira.

"Because I think we've become famous. And I think we'd have been better off if we'd just remained a small little bunch of happy-go-lucky, obscure, inconspicuous, fly-on-the-wall, nobody-type demons."

He chewed his lip. "Mark my words. I speak from experience. Somehow or other, we Jews got famous early on in the game. We should have listened to the Speckites."

"The *who?*"

"The Speckites. The Hebrews' next-door neighbors. You never heard of them?"

Indira frowned suspiciously. "No, I haven't."

"Imagine that! And you—an historian. Just goes to illustrate my point. The Hebrews went for the bright lights of Broadway and the Speckites stayed anonymous. Guess which one of us caught hell for the next few thousand years?"

Indira snorted. Privately, she thought Julius was probably right. But—

What's done is done.

She couldn't begin to estimate how many gukuy were in the column approaching them. Hundreds, she thought—possibly thousands. The head of the column was just entering the village; the tail of it was still not in sight. All down the valley, three or four abreast, marched the Pilgrims.

On either side of the column, scattered along its length, members of Takashi's platoon acted as an honor guard. The

243

platoon had been stationed in Fagoshau (as the gukuy called
their settlement in the big valley) when the huge column of
new Pilgrims arrived. After observing the progress of the
column up the eastern slope of the Chiton, Takashi had sent
a runner to the council requesting orders. The council, after
a quick deliberation, had passed on a formal invitation for the
newcomers to come and visit.

And they had—*all* of them.

At that moment, Takashi trotted up. When the young lieutenant drew up before her, Indira saw that he wasn't even
breathing hard—despite the fact that he had just finished
running up and down the entire column at her request. As
was so often the case now, she felt a contradictory mix of
emotions. Admiration for the young man's excellent physical
condition; uneasiness because she knew it was the result of
Joseph's relentless military training.

Still, she wished Joseph were there. The Captain had been
gone for days now, leading yet another punitive expedition
against a party of slavers which had been spotted the week
before on the southern plain near the Chiton.

"Punitive expedition," thought Indira. *There's a euphemism
for you. "Extermination squad" would be more accurate. Not
one of Joseph's expeditions—and there had been many, these
past two years—has failed to massacre every slaver they caught.*

Indira sighed. *And so what? Would you feel better if the
owoc were dragged into slavery?*

Takashi interrupted her musings.

"I count almost fifteen hundred of them, Indira. But that's
just the number in the column. There are more Pilgrims,
further back. Scattered groups of stragglers. All told, I'd guess
there's around two thousand new Pilgrims on the mountain."

"Holy shit," muttered Julius.

"Have they told you what they want?" asked Indira.

The gaze which Takashi leveled at her was hard as stone.

"Yes. They want to talk to the Mother of Demons. About
the secrets."

Indira uttered a silent curse. She had feared as much. Next
to her, out of the corner of her eye, she saw Julius' face twist
into a grimace.

Where did it get started? she wondered. *This myth of the
secrets—and the mother who holds them back from her children?*

When she first heard of it, from one of the gukuy Pilgrims, she had blamed Joseph. Had gone to him, in fact, and accused him hotly. Joseph had denied it, with equal heat. After a few minutes of argument, Indira had become convinced he was telling the truth.

She had never known Joseph to lie to her (or to anyone else, for that matter). Still, she had been confused and exasperated.

"How did this silly rumor get started, then?" she had demanded. "If you didn't start it?"

She would never forget the look on Joseph's face when he gave his answer. Like an ancient gold mask of Benin.

"It is not a rumor. It is the truth. Everyone knows it—gukuy and ummun alike."

It had not taken long to discover that Joseph was right. At the next council meeting, Indira had proposed that Anna Cheng replace her as the Admiral of the Ocean Sea. Anna had immediately refused, and was supported in her refusal by the entire council except Julius.

"Until you teach us the secrets, Indira," commented Ludmilla, "there is none who can take your place."

"There are no secrets!" she had protested angrily. The young members of the council had simply stared at her in silence. Even Julius had looked away.

The column was now close enough to examine the individual Pilgrims who were leading it. At the very front, in the center, marched a small and elderly gukuy. She was wearing none of the decorative strips of cloth with which southern gukuy generally adorned themselves. For that reason, Indira at first assumed she was from one of the barbarian tribes, who eschewed any clothing except armor. She was puzzled, however. There were a number of barbarian converts to the Way, many of whom had been trickling onto the Chiton for the past several months. But the religion had originated in Ansha and all of its leaders, so far as she knew, were from the civilized southern prevalates.

Then, when the column drew closer, she saw the elaborate carvings on the gukuy's cowl. The pigments which would normally have colored the carvings had been scoured clean. But she recognized the carvings themselves, from descriptions which she had been given by Anshac Pilgrims. They were the insignia of the prevalent clan of the Ansha.

Shocked understanding came to her.

"Is that—?"

Takashi nodded. "Yes, it is. Ushulubang herself."

"Holy shit," muttered Julius.

"Can't you say anything else?" snapped Indira.

Julius eyed her, then looked back at the column. A rueful grin twisted his face.

"I say it again: *holy shit.*"

The audience which followed, in Julius and Indira's hut, was one of the most disconcerting episodes in Indira's life. In Julius' life, as well, he told her later.

Extremely intelligent and well-educated people like Julius and Indira do not, really, believe there is such a thing as a "sage." Until they meet her.

That Ushulubang was extraordinarily intelligent became obvious immediately. The chief opoloshuku—a term which translates loosely as "disciple/teacher"—of the Pilgrims of the Way remained silent until she entered the hut. Then, she thanked Indira and Julius for their hospitality. In perfect English.

Indira was too surprised to respond with the customary phrases. Instead, she blurted out:

"You speak English!"

Ushulubang made the gesture of affirmation, with a subtly humorous twist.

"Certainly. How could I be certain the scribes have captured the true spirit of Goloku's teachings if I could not read the holy tongue myself?"

She reads English, too. And her accent's extraordinarily good—especially given that she must have learned from another Pilgrim.

Suddenly, Indira was filled with—not anger, exactly, but extreme exasperation. She had had more than enough of these bizarre new myths and legends which seemed to be springing up like weeds.

"English is not a holy tongue," she said harshly. "It is simply a language like any other. A ummun language, true. But the ummun have many languages."

The two other gukuy who had entered the hut with Ushulubang registered ochre/pink confusion/abashment. But Indira was surprised to see an emerald tint appear on Ushulubang's mantle. Green, Indira had learned, was a very complex color for the gukuy. The various shades carried subtle differences in meaning, which, though they all had love and tranquillity at their base, could express those fundamental emotions in a multitude of permutations.

Emerald is the color of contentment.

"As I surmised," said Ushulubang. The old gukuy made the gesture of profound respect. "I had hoped, but I could not be certain until I came here and spoke with you myself."

"Be certain of what?" demanded Indira.

The opoloshuku gestured to her two companions. "My *apashoc*"—the word meant "kin of the road"— "had told me that you were the guardian of the secrets. A jealous guardian, they said, who would not impart the secrets to the people."

Indira suppressed a sharp retort.

"But I did not believe them. I thought instead—"

Ushulubang paused for a moment.

"What have the apashoc told you of Goloku?"

Indira was taken aback by the question. She fumbled an answer: A holy person; a saint; a sage; possessor of all wisdom; embodiment of goodness; teacher of—

Ushulubang whistled derision.

"What nonsense! Goloku was a crude boor; a rascal; a drunk; a teller of lewd jokes; and most of all, she was a tyrant, hard as bronze."

Indira's eyes widened. The gukuy on either side of Ushulubang flashed bright ochre. Ushulubang glanced at them both, and again made the gesture of derision. (But the subtleties of the arm-curls contained also, in some manner Indira could not determine, the connotation of affection.)

"They did not know Goloku, as I did." For a moment, Ushulubang's mantle turned a deep, rich shade of brownish-green.

"I am the only one still alive," said Ushulubang sadly, "of Goloku's first apashoc. All that is left of that small band of sisters. There are not even many still alive of the later apashoc. Very few, of those who knew Goloku personally, survived Ilishito's persecution."

Indira knew the tale. She had heard it many times from the Pilgrims on the mountain. During Goloku's lifetime, her disciples had been few in number. After the founder of the Way died—of poison, it was said—the Paramount Mother of the time, Ilishito, had ordered the extermination of the sect. Guided, according to proclamations of the Anshac officials, by the divinations of the priests. From what she had been able to learn of Anshac society, Indira suspected that the decision had actually been made by the *awosha*—the ruling council of the Ansha females. Although, by all accounts, the Paramount Mother Ilishito had been more than cruel enough to have ordered the persecution herself.

Of the inner circle of disciples—those who had learned directly from Goloku herself—only Ushulubang had survived. Due, Indira thought, to the fact that Ushulubang was herself a very high-ranking member of the dominant clan. She had been officially expelled from the clan, and her clan markings scoured clean with caustic substances. But her life had been spared by the priests.

To their everlasting regret, I suspect.

Ushulubang's mantle returned to gray. "These young apashoc have never really understood Goloku. I do not criticize them, you understand." The pinkish tones in her two companions faded. "They have tried, and tried very hard. Under the most severe circumstances. But—they always lapse into the great error. The error which Goloku flailed us for committing, mercilessly, every day of her life."

"What error is that?"

Ushulubang's huge-eyed stare was piercing.

"The belief that Goloku brought us the Answer. When what she really brought us was a thing much greater. She brought us the Question."

Ushulubang rose. "And now, with your permission, I will leave you. Tomorrow, perhaps, we can speak again. But I fear I am old and weak, and it has been a long journey from Shakutulubac."

Indira nodded. That human expression was now familiar to the gukuy on the mountain. Ushulubang's reaction to it demonstrated, once again, that the old sage had prepared well for this meeting.

"I thank you." She turned to go.

"One moment, please," said Indira.

Ushulubang looked back.

"You did not answer my question. What did you mean—when you said that you were not certain until you met me?"

"When I heard that demons had come to us, and that there was one among them who knew the Answer, I had thought the tale must be wrong. But until today, I was not sure. Until you denied that Enagulishuc is the holy tongue, in words as sharp as stone."

"I do not understand."

"Just so did Goloku flail us, when we fell into error. When I heard your words, I understood why the Coil sent demons to the world, and my soul was filled with love. I had feared, in the depths of my heart, that we would lose the Way. Without a flail to lash the error of the Answer, it is so easy to fall aside."

"I do not understand."

Green ripples marched across Ushulubang's mantle.

"Just so. You have seen the statue of Goloku in the temple at Fagoshau?"

"Yes."

"It is no longer there. I smashed it with my flail when I saw it." A whistle of derision. "These *spawn*"—a gesture to her companions— "were shocked and aghast. That is because they had fallen into the error of the Answer."

A faint brownish ripple went across Ushulubang's mantle.

"Yet I should not be proud. I too had fallen aside, without realizing it. Until you flailed me, great mother of demons."

"I do not understand."

The gesture of profound respect. "Just so. Enagulishuc is indeed *not* the holy tongue. It is the tongue that will pave the road of holiness."

"I'm impressed," said Julius softly, after Ushulubang left. When she looked at him, Indira saw that there was no trace on his face of whimsy.

"So am I," she replied. "I always wondered what it would be like to meet the founder of Christianity."

Julius frowned. "What do you mean? Ushulubang's impressive, but she hardly seems divine."

Indira shook her head. "I wasn't talking about the Christ. Jesus inspired the religion that took his name. But Christianity was founded by St. Paul."

Julius stared out the doorway at Ushulubang's receding figure.

"You think so?"

Indira shrugged. "It's an analogy, and like any analogy it's suspect. For one thing, the Way of the Coil is a totally different doctrine than Christianity. Insofar as there's a parallel on Earth, it reminds me more of Taoism than anything else."

"You've always said Buddhism was the closest parallel."

"Yes, I have. But now that I've met Ushulubang, I will no longer say it."

Julius attempted to pursue the matter further, but Indira was clearly distracted. More than distracted, Julius eventually realized. She was completely lost in her own thoughts.

Indira met again with Ushulubang the following day. But the meeting was brief. Although Indira was burning with the desire to pursue what she had glimpsed of the sage's philosophy, practical matters had intervened—in their usual, overwhelming manner.

"How long will you stay?" she asked Ushulubang.

The sage made the gesture of completion. "I will die here, on the Chiton." A whistle. "Though not soon, I hope."

Indira shook her head. (Another human gesture which had become familiar to the gukuy.)

"I did not mean you personally. I meant—" She waved her hand, encompassing the huge throng outside the hut.

"We have come to stay," replied Ushulubang. The gesture of respectful inquiry. "With your permission, great mother of demons."

"Don't call me that!"

The gesture of obedience. "As you wish. May I ask why?"

"I am not the ruler of my people."

"So I was told. That is why I did not call you Paramount Mother."

Indira's irritation was replaced by curiosity.

"I do not understand the distinction."

Ushulubang whistled humorously. "There is, in some ways, no distinction. The Paramount Mothers of the *tashop arren* do not rule their peoples, in all truth, despite the hootings of the *awoloshu*."

Indira mentally translated Ushulubang's terms. The Anshaku

term *tashop arren* meant "the thickness of the meat." All of the gukuy religions which she had so far encountered, except that of the Pilgrims, based their cosmological concepts on the analogy between the world and a huge clam. In all the languages she knew, in fact, the term for "world" was actually "The-Clam-That-Is-The-World." The earth itself, rich and fecund, was "the Meat of the Clam." The pearly gray sky above was "the mother-of-pearl." The shell of the Clam protected the world from the unknown terrors which lurked in the Infinite Sea beyond. (When the gukuy had learned that the humans had come to Ishtar from somewhere in that Infinite Sea, their nature as "demons" had been confirmed. Who but demons could survive such a voyage?)

The religion of the Pilgrims did not seem to be much preoccupied with questions of cosmology and cosmogony. Like the ancient religions and philosophies of China, the Pilgrims were far more concerned with questions concerning social life and ethics. They accepted the basic cosmological concepts of their time—except for a slight twist. Goloku had said, once, that the world was not a clam but a snail. The distinction, to Indira, captured the essence of what made the religion of the Pilgrims such a new and revolutionary factor in gukuy history. Clams are passive. Filter feeders. Whereas snails—far more so on Ishtar than on Earth—were active animals who hunted for their food. To the traditionalists, the world simply *was*. To the Pilgrims, the world was *going* somewhere, in search of something.

Much like the ancient Chinese, the civilized realms of the south viewed themselves as the center of the world. The Chinese had called their land "the Middle Kingdom;" the southern gukuy called theirs "the thickness of the meat."

She had greater difficulty with *awoloshu*. The prefix "a" simply indicated the plural. "Wolosh" was the stem of the word. From the context, she assumed that Ushulubang was referring to the priests of the southern societies. But, in Anshaku, the term for priest was "wulush," not "wolosh."

She understood, suddenly. The word used by the sage was a pun. There was a type of snail on Ishtar, called *oloshap*. It was a scavenger and, as such, considered unclean by the gukuy. It also produced, when startled, a loud and ugly-sounding noise. (The Anshaku word for "fart," in fact, was a derivative—*shapu*.)

Chuckling, she shook her head. "I still do not understand why a paramount mother is different—"

"Are you familiar with the customs of the barbarians?"

Indira nodded. "To some degree. There are a number of former tribespeople among the Pilgrims."

Ushulubang made the gesture of agreement, which shifted to the gesture of regret.

"Not so many as I would prefer. The barbarians, despite their crudities, are a better-souled folk than the dwellers of the *tashop arren*. Especially the Kiktu. I raise this matter because the barbarians do not have the custom of Paramount Mothers."

Indira nodded again. "No, they call them the Great Mothers. They are not revered; but, I think, have more real say in the affairs of their people."

The gesture of respectful disagreement.

"To a degree, that is true. But the difference is much more profound. The Paramount Mothers of the *tashop arren* are the source of the people, the embodiment of the people's life. Among the barbarians, however, the Great Mothers are also the protectors of the people."

Indira frowned. "The protection of my people is in the hands of our Captain, Joseph Adekunle." (She pronounced it in the Anshac manner: Yoshefadekunula.)

"Just so. Yet . . . you are called the 'Admiral of the Ocean Sea.' The term may be translated, I believe, as the 'Leader of the Journey Through Infinity.'"

Indira gritted her teeth. *God damn Hector Quintero and Julius Cohen. Men and their stupid jokes.*

She attempted to explain the actual origin of the term in the colony's history, but Ushulubang interrupted her with a whistle.

"Males—and their stupid jokes. But Goloku taught us that humor is the palp of wisdom. A rough and heavy palp, at times. But such is often necessary, to open the valves of truth."

Once again, that piercing huge-eyed stare.

"The title is, I believe, most appropriate. Tell me, gre—Inudiratoledo: what is the principal means by which a being protects itself?"

Indira shrugged. "It depends on the being. Tentacles, for gukuy. Arms, for an ummun. And for both, the swiftness of their peds."

Ushulubang made the gesture of negation.

"No. The principal means by which a being protects itself is its *eyes*. For you must first see the danger, before you can deal with it."

Indira hesitated. "That is true. But—"

"What is the danger which always faces a people?"

"I—it depends."

"No. It does not 'depend.' It is *always* true—at all places; at all times."

She understood, suddenly. "The future."

"Just so—Admiral of the Ocean Sea Inudiratoledo."

Indira shook her head fiercely.

There is no time for this now.

"We must return to the original subject of our discussion."

"As you wish."

"How will your Pilgrims live on the Chiton? And where?"

"You have not yet given us permission to stay."

Indira frowned. "You do not need my permission. I do not own this mountain, nor do my people. If it belongs to anyone, it belongs to the owoc."

"You misunderstand. The Chiton is vast, with many valleys. There is more than enough room here for all of us—owoc, gukuy, and ummun alike." A humorous whistle. "The Pilgrims number among them both civilized and barbarian people. There is not a skill in the world which they do not know. Skills which, from what I have seen, you ummun often seem to lack."

Indira nodded. It could not be denied. In truth, over the past two years the humans had learned far more from the gukuy, in the way of practical skills, than the other way around.

"You, on the other hand, possess arts and skills which we lack. Most of those arts—sciences, you call them—are not yet of any use to my people. In truth, we do not even understand them. But I believe those arts will be necessary for us, in that dangerous place called the future."

The gesture of regretful affirmation. "And in the meantime, you possess a great knowledge of that skill which is most necessary of all. In this perilous place called the present."

"And what is that?" But she already knew the answer.

"The art of war."

❖   ❖   ❖

"Is *that* why they came here?" asked Julius later. "To learn how to fight their persecutors?"

"Partly. But it's more than that. Ishtarian society has reached the stage where the old ways are rupturing at the seams. In all societies—civilized and barbarian alike. The emergence of the Way is itself a symptom of that upheaval. So is the rise of this monstrous tribe from the far west."

"The Utuku?" He shook his head. "Well, let's root for the Kiktu."

Indira shook her head. Grimly: "It's too late for that, Julius. The Kiktu were utterly destroyed by the Utuku. Months ago, in a great battle on the other side of that huge jungle southwest of the Chiton. The Pilgrims learned about it from refugees fleeing the disaster. That's why they circled the mountain and came in from the east, in fact—to avoid the oncoming army of the Utuku. A number of the refugees are here with the Pilgrims. I was able to talk to one of them today myself."

Julius was pale. "The Kiktu were *destroyed*? Completely?"

Indira nodded. "Apparently so. Well, the refugee I spoke to said that some of the Kiktu fled into the swamp. But she seemed to view that as no more than a protracted death sentence. That aside, yes. And not just the Kiktu, but all of their tribal allies. They were surrounded and pinned against the swamp. Crushed. The tribes' mothers would have been crippled and enslaved. All others butchered for meat, except for young females conscripted into the Utuku army."

"Conscripted?"

"Yes. It's the Utuku custom to force young warriors and females to join their army."

Julius shook his head. "Sounds like a chancy proposition to me. What's to keep them loyal?"

"They are required to participate in a ceremony which guarantees they will not go back to their old tribe."

Julius turned even paler. "I don't think I want to hear this."

"Yes. They are forced to eat their tribespeople in the victory feast."

He looked away. "I knew I didn't want to hear it."

"You *must*, Julius. As Ushulubang said, there is the danger of the future—and the peril of the present. The entire Papti Plain is now open to the Utuku. They will be sweeping across it like army ants. With nothing between them and us but the slopes of the Chiton. And whatever army we can build to defend those slopes."

"Maybe they'll turn south."

"Toward the prevalates?" She shook her head. "I don't think so. Neither does Ushulubang. The Beak of the Utuku is reputed to be cold and calculating, as well as vicious. As powerful as the Utuku have become, they are still not ready to match flails with the Anshac. Not yet. They will need to consolidate their rule over the Papti first. And in order to do that, the Beak will see to the elimination of any possible threat in the vicinity. Such as demons living on the mountain that overlooks the plain."

She stared out the hut.

"Where are you, Joseph?" she whispered.

Chapter 19

To her relief, Joseph returned the next day. With, for the first time since he began the raids, a prisoner.

That is easily the biggest gukuy I have ever seen, except a mother, thought Indira, gazing at the figure on the litter. *Also, if I've learned to assess gukuy standards of beauty, the ugliest.*

Then she noticed the small figure of the male inside the warrior's mantle cavity.

That's strange. The males usually don't associate closely with warriors. I wonder what happened to his mate?

The female gukuy was unconscious, and horribly injured. Her left eye was a ruin, and there were two great puncture wounds on her mantle.

Spear wounds.

Nor was the gukuy the only injured member of the returning expedition. Jens Knudsen had been hurt as well. But it was merely a flesh wound, Indira was relieved to see.

"Merely," she thought ruefully. *God, how this life has changed us all.*

Maria De Los Reyes was examining the wounded gukuy, with a fierce frown on her face.

"Why didn't you just dismember her completely, while you were at it?" she demanded crossly.

"Can you save her life?" asked Jens.

Somewhat hesitantly, Maria nodded. "I think so. Her mantle cavity's obviously infected, but those poultices you put on the wounds have probably kept her from dying. It'll be touch and go, but—if this warrior's as tough as she looks, she'll survive."

Joseph smiled. "She's even tougher. Judging, at least, from the damage she caused—four wounded, two of them with broken bones."

Indira stared at the unconscious gukuy on the litter.

"*All* those injuries were caused by her? *Alone?*" She was genuinely shocked. Since the very first fight with slavers, none of Joseph's expeditions had suffered more than minor wounds to one or two warriors.

"All. The other slavers died like papakoy. This one—was terrible."

Jens winced and held up his right arm, which was heavily bandaged. "That's where I got this. She damn near tore my arm off. Her name's Nukurren, by the way, and—"

"Why did you let her live, then?" demanded Indira. "You've never done that before with any slavers you caught."

For a moment, the faces of the young human warriors assumed an expression which Indira had not seen on them for a long time. Uncertainty, hesitation; almost childlike confusion.

"I'm—not sure," replied Joseph. "Partly it was because one of the owoc slaves insisted."

"*What?*"

Ludmilla nodded vigorously. "It's true, Indira. We were astonished. Of course, the owoc are never—" She hesitated.

Bloodthirsty. Like we are.

"But still, I've never seen an owoc show any real concern for a slaver. As long as we bury the bodies. But the owoc was quite firm about it. She said this one was different."

Jens was frowning. "But that's not the only reason we let her live. It was also . . . I don't know. She was so incredibly *brave.*"

Indira sighed. She understood, even if Jens didn't. The culture of the human colony was rapidly being shaped by its necessities.

A warrior culture. One of whose inevitable features is deep respect for courage, even the courage of the enemy.

It was an aspect of warrior cultures which many people admired, even in the 22nd century—including professional historians. Romantically seductive, unless you understood the corollary.

When the Mongols took Kiev they spared the life of the

commander of the garrison, out of admiration for his courage. They did the same, later, at Aleppo.

Then they slaughtered everyone else.

Her musings were interrupted by the male in the wounded gukuy's mantle.

"Please. Do any of you—demons—speak my language?" The male was speaking Anshaku.

"Yes," replied Indira immediately. "I do."

Ochre and red rippled across the male's mantle, in the delicate, complex traceries of which only males were capable.

"Are you—are you the Mother of Demons?"

Indira sighed. It seemed she was doomed to that title.

"You may call me so, if you wish."

The male—a truemale, she now recognized—made the gesture of obedience. Then spoke again.

"Will Nukurren live?"

"She will live, according to our healer. Her recovery will be difficult, however. And—" A quick question to Maria. "—her eye cannot be saved."

"So long as she lives," said the truemale softly. To Indira's astonishment, the little male began stroking his companion's head. His mantle was flushed with that shade of green which, for gukuy, was the sign of romantic attachment.

Now this is something I've never seen. A romantic attachment between a female and a truemale?

She pondered the situation. Julius had long been puzzled by the active sex life enjoyed by the gukuy, the vast majority of whom were sterile females. Sex, he had explained to her, takes up a lot of biological energy, and he couldn't figure out why a species would evolve such an orientation when there was no possibility of reproduction between sterile females. Among the owoc, a cousin species, there was little sexual activity except between mothers and males. He had eventually developed an explanation which satisfied him. Though it was based on an elaborate (to Indira's mind, arcane) web of neurological reasoning and kin selection game theory, his hypothesis amounted to: "They're smart, sex is fun, and how are you gonna keep 'em down on the farm when they've been to gay Paree?"

Still, the sex life of gukuy followed definite rules. Sterile females coupled with other sterile females. Truemales with mothers. (Eumales with no one.) Indira had never observed a romantic relationship between a truemale and a sterile female. Even among the relatively tolerant barbarian tribes, such an attachment would be considered unnatural and perverted. And among the far less tolerant civilized cultures—such as the Ansha from which the truemale obviously came—such a coupling would be anathema, for which the priests would demand the death penalty.

There's a fascinating story here. I must learn it from him.

"What is your name?" she asked. To her surprise, the answer came from behind her. In the voice of Ushulubang.

"He is called Dhowifa."

She had not heard the sage coming. Ushulubang, she had already learned, was not given to ceremonious parades. At the moment, she was only accompanied by one of her pashoc—a young gukuy named Shurren, who, like Ushulubang, came from the Anshac capital of Shakutulubac.

Indira looked back at the truemale. Dhowifa had withdrawn further into the mantle cavity. Stripes of ochre and orange rippled along his mantle.

"Hello, great-nephew," said Ushulubang softly.

A moment later, the truemale replied: "Hello, great-aunt Ushulubang."

How many more surprises are there going to be today? wondered Indira. The two gukuy were not actually "nephew" and "aunt," of course—not, at least, in the precise sense of the English words. But those were the nearest equivalents for the Anshac terms. Closely related members of the same clan, separated by sex and two generations.

Indira saw that the mantle of Ushulubang's companion was dappled blue and yellow.

"What is the pervert Dhowifa doing here?" demanded Shurren. The tone of her voice was extremely hostile.

Ushulubang eyed her companion, then said mildly: "I should imagine he and his lover have come to live among the demons. Where their—arrangement—would seem natural."

Shurren's mantle turned ochre.

"Or have you forgotten, Shurren, that among the demons the males couple with the females?"

Shurren's mantle turned bright pink.

Indira felt a sudden surge of affection for the old sage. And the tiny hope which she had found the day before grew brighter.

Perhaps. Perhaps . . .

"That is not the same," protested Shurren. "The demons are—different from gukuy."

Ushulubang made the gesture of respectful submission— the traditional salutation of a student to the master.

"Ah. I am enlightened. Before this moment, I had always thought gukuy were different from each other as well. But I see now that it is not so. Truly, the pervert Dhowifa possesses a monstrous soul. Why else would he have chosen the organs of Ansha's greatest warrior to those of the Paramount Mother Ilishito?"

"Ilishito?" exclaimed Indira. "The same—"

"Just so. The same Ilishito who tortured the Pilgrims and slew all my apashoc."

Indira was confused. "But—this truemale does not seem old enough—"

Ushulubang made the gesture of negation. "Dhowifa was born long after the persecution. Ilishito lived to a great age, Indira. A cruel but vigorous mother. And much given to replacing old husbands with young malebonds."

Dhowifa spoke.

"Have you—what has happened with my bondbrothers?"

"After you fled with Nukurren, they were disgraced. Almost executed, in fact, but their lives were spared in the end. I do not know what happened to them after. I am not myself in the good graces of the clan, as you know."

The truemale's mantle turned deep brown.

Ushulubang made the gesture of acceptance. "What did you expect, nephew?"

"I don't know. I—could only leave."

Indira understood, then. Dhowifa had not simply violated accepted standards of sexual morality and abandoned his lawful mate. He had also abandoned his malebond.

The anguish must have been incredible. She stared at the huge, scarred body of Nukurren. *There must be something else inside that fearsome figure, to have won such love and devotion.*

"Take good care of her," she said to Maria suddenly. The doctor gave her an unfriendly sidelong glance. *As if I wouldn't?*

At Maria's order, four of the warriors picked up the litter and began carrying it toward her "hospital," a large hut which the colonists had recently built next to the long houses. As the litter began to move away, Ushulubang called out:

"Have you continued to practice your dukuna?"

The truemale's voice came back:

"Yes, great-aunt. It has been a comfort these past eightyweeks. I thank you for instructing me."

Shurren's mantle flashed orange.

"You instructed *him?*"

"Just so, Shurren. He was perhaps my best student. Of the clan, at least. He might well have become my best student of all, except that I was unable to visit him often. I was not welcome in the Divine Shell, you know. My visits were infrequent and surreptitious."

"But—*why?* Even though he is of your clan, I do not understand why—"

"Why I would waste my time instructing a foolish male?" Ushulubang made the gesture of abject apology.

"I have forgotten. Only females—and not even most of them; no, only those who follow the Way—feel sorrow at the evil of the world. The rest are dumb beasts."

Shurren's mantle rippled pinkish-brown. (A color frequently found upon Ushulubang's disciples, Indira noted—with great satisfaction.)

"I have offended you."

"Nonsense! To the contrary, Shurren, you have brought me sudden joy. Your words recall to my memory a long forgotten episode from the days I wandered the streets of Shakutulubac in the company of Goloku. Come, I will tell you about it."

Ushulubang and Shurren began moving away. Indira heard the sage's voice drifting back.

"It was a miserable night. The more so because Goloku had gotten drunk. Again." Indira smiled at the sound of Shurren's shocked hoot. "Oh, yes—it's quite true. Goloku was excessively fond of ashuweed. Often made a fool of herself. This night was no different. We encountered a small pack of eumales in one of the back alleys. Six or seven of the disgusting creatures. Beggars and thieves. Would you believe that drunken fool invited them to spend the night in her mantle?"

Shocked hoot.

"Oh, yes—it's quite true. I was appalled, of course—especially when it was discovered they couldn't all fit inside Goloku and she insisted that I accept half of them."

Shocked hoot.

"Oh, yes—it's quite true. Then, no sooner . . ."

The voices became indistinct. Indira was left alone with Joseph. Joseph was watching her, with the look he usually held in her presence. Reserve—no, deep anger, held in check.

Suddenly, as she had not done in a long time, Indira smiled at Joseph. Slowly, a hesitant smile came in return.

Maybe, thought Indira. *Maybe.*

It was still a faint hope, murky and uncertain. But for a woman who had felt no hope in years, it was as if a ray of sunshine had broken through the everlasting clouds of Ishtar.

Chapter 20

Nukurren regained consciousness the next day, and never lapsed back thereafter. Under the ministrations of the healer demon Mariyaduloshruyush and her assistants, the wounds began to heal quickly. Most of the assistants were demons, but two were gukuy Pilgrims from Anshac. One of them, a former helot named Ertatu, told Nukurren than she was healing much more quickly than the demon herself had expected.

"Mariya says you are the toughest gukuy she's ever seen," commented Ertatu, as she changed Nukurren's poultices.

"You can say that again."

Nukurren swiveled her good eye and saw the figure of Dzhenushkunutushen standing in the entrance to the hospital. The white demon advanced to Nukurren's side.

"How are you feeling?" he asked her. To Nukurren's surprise, he spoke in Anshaku. Very good Anshaku. During the long trek up the Chiton, Dzhenushkunutushen and the female demon Ludumila had spoken only Kiktu, and seemed not to comprehend Nukurren and Dhowifa when they spoke to each other in Anshaku.

Shrewd. The demons are cunning as well as ferocious.

Nukurren made the gesture of acceptance.

"I am alive and it seems I will remain so. That is unexpected."

"I am sorry about your eye," said the demon.

"It does not matter. It is a just punishment for my sins. It is only right that I should lose an eye, in payment for the Old Ones I helped enslave."

The demon opened his—*mouth*, Nukurren had learned, was

the name for demon beaks (except the demons claimed their real name was *ummun*)—and began to speak; then fell silent.

After a pause, he said: "I would like to talk to you, but I cannot. I must return to the training field."

"You are a trainer of warriors?"

"I am the—" Nukurren made him repeat the term until she could pronounce it. *Sharredzhenutumadzhoru.*

She understood the meaning of the title at once. *So I suspected. He is a centurion of the human legion. As was I, before I was sent to the Motherguard.*

(The actual term which Nukurren used, of course, was not "centurion." It was *gurren otoshoc*, which translates roughly as "chief troop leader." But the essence was the same as the ancient Roman term, which, over the centuries, was duplicated in different words in different human languages. Whatever the word, it referred to the sinew of all great armies—*top sergeant.*)

"You are preparing for war?" asked Nukurren. Interpreting the strange movement of the demon's face as hesitation, suspicion, she made the gesture of indifference. Then repeated it in words, realizing that the demon might not understand the curl of her arms.

"It does not matter to me, Dzhenushkunutushen. I am no longer a warrior, nor do I care what happens to any realm on the Meat of the Clam. It is true that you are demons, but—" The gesture of resignation. "You can be no crueler than any gukuy."

Dzhenushkunutushen stood. "There is no reason not to tell you. We will be fighting the Utuku soon. Very soon, I think, and we are not well prepared."

"The Kiktu have been defeated, then?"

"Destroyed completely, by all accounts."

Nukurren made the gesture of regret.

"I am grieved to hear it. Of all the peoples I encountered, the Kiktu were the best. Barbarous and crude, but rarely evil."

"So it is said. But they are gone now. Slain in battle, or food for the Utuku."

"Go then, Sharredzhenutumadzhoru." The gesture of amusement. "I would not wish to see you in the bellies of the Utuku."

Dzhenushkunutushen turned away, saying: "Any Utuku who bites me will die horribly."

Nukurren appreciated the humor of the remark. Then, after further thought, wondered if it was a joke.

Two days later, the white demon reappeared in the hospital. He was accompanied by the female demon who was skilled in the healing arts, Mariyaduloshruyush.

"Mariya tells me that you are now able to move about," said Dzhenushkunutushen.

"That is true. Not easily, and not very well. But I am able to walk."

"I would like to ask you—" The female demon began rapidly speaking in the human language. *Enagulishuc*, it was called. Nukurren thought she was displeased.

"She is angry with me," explained Dzhenushkunutushen.

"Why?"

"Because what I wish to ask of you will not be good for your health."

"Ask."

The female demon left abruptly, after making that odd motion of spreading her arms which Nukurren suspected was the demon equivalent of the gesture of disgruntled acceptance.

"I would like to ask you to come to the training field and observe."

"Why?"

"You are the best gukuy warrior we have ever encountered. I think you could teach us much. Yoshef—he is the" (Nukurren made him repeat the term until she grasped it) "*kapitanu* of our army—did not like the idea. He is suspicious of you. But I insisted."

"Why?"

The demon paused. Two small, bright blue demon eyes stared into one large, iron gray gukuy eye. Then:

"You know why—*Sharredzhenutumadzhoru*."

Three days later, feeling her health returning quickly, Nukurren went to the training field. She was accompanied by Ertatu, but Nukurren had no need of her guidance to find the way. The harsh sounds of demon voices were the only guide she needed. Much harsher sounding than usual. It was the demon battle language, she knew.

At the edge of the open field, Nukurren squatted and

observed the demons racing back and forth in complex maneuvers. It took her some time to separate the logic of the actions from the sheer dazzling display of speed. By now, of course, she had come to understand the demon way of moving, and so they no longer seemed to *flicker*. Still, they were so fast; so agile; so—*different*.

And then, as she watched, *not* so different. They were practicing tactical maneuvers, and once Nukurren became accustomed to the blinding speed of the demons, she was eventually able to discern the basic patterns of the exercises.

Nukurren's only previous experience with the demons in combat had been the attack on the slave caravan. That episode had been too chaotic for her to have made any assessment of the demons' tactical methods. Now, seeing those methods displayed in training exercises, Nukurren was puzzled by what she saw.

Eventually, the demons paused in their exercises and made that bizarre folding motion with their bodies which enabled them to rest on the ground. The word for that in Enagulishuc, Nukurren had learned, was *sitting*. She was fascinated to see water (at least, she thought it was water) dripping down the faces of the demons, and quickly deduced that such was the demon method of eliminating excess heat. It seemed bizarre to her, as well as messy and slightly disgusting. Gukuy expelled excess heat through increased evaporation in their breath.

Soon, Dzhenushkunutushen approached and sat down facing her.

"What do you think?" he asked.

Nukurren considered her reply. It would be unwise to offend the demon. He, and to some extent his lover Ludumila, had been the only demons to show some signs of friendship toward Nukurren and Dhowifa. On the other hand . . .

Nukurren decided. Whatever else, Dzhenushkunutushen was *gurren otoshoc*, and thus entitled to respect.

"A question. How many of you will mobilize for war with the Utuku?"

The demon hesitated. Then: "Triple-eighty."

"So few?"

Silence. The demon looked away for a time. It was, Nukurren realized, a critical moment.

Dzhenushkunutushen turned back. His bright blue eyes were unwavering.

"There are no more *ummun* than that on this world, Nukurren. Except a very few too old to fight."

Nukurren made the gesture which, in Anshaku, is called *unnudh wap kottu*. The gesture expresses a sentiment which is not readily translatable into English. A different human culture had an equivalent—that particular bow by which one *samurai* acknowledges another.

"I am honored by your trust," she said.

Suddenly, the demon rose partly erect. His stick-peds (*legs*, Nukurren had learned) were strangely bent, and he rested on the joints. He clasped together his forelimb extremities (*hands*) and nodded his head. Nukurren immediately understood that Dzhenushkunutushen was reciprocating the *unnudh wap kottu*. It did not seem a practiced gesture, and she thought that the demon had invented it on the spot.

Her surmises were confirmed.

They are terrible in war, yet they are not really warriors. They use the tactics of barbarians, yet they are more civilized than Anshac. Their arts and crafts are crude, judging from the poorly built hospital, yet their knowledge seems immense. They are a mystery beyond any I have ever encountered.

"Your tactics are crude and stupid. That would not matter, if your numbers were great. Against equal numbers of gukuy warriors, of any people, you will always win, because you are so much faster. After a time, however, when gukuy become accustomed to your skills, you will suffer losses which you cannot afford. Against Kiktu, you will always do well because the Kiktu fight much as you do. Stupidly. Against a good Anshac legion, you would be defeated by the third battle. Against an excellent legion, by the second. You have no chance against the Utuku. The Utuku tactics are crude, but they always send huge numbers into battle, and they are highly disciplined. You will break against them."

The white of Dzhenushkunutushen's mantle (*no, the demons call it "skin,"*) was flushed with pink.

He is embarrassed, interpreted Nukurren, *but this time, I think, he is not pleased.*

The demon took a deep breath.

"I guess I asked for that," he said softly, looking down at

the ground. He raised his eyes. As always, Nukurren was struck
by their dazzling color.

"Can our chances be improved?" he asked.

Nukurren made the gesture of uncertainty.

"The question has no simple answer. It depends on many
things. Some of these go far beyond battle methods. But—
insofar as your question involves tactics, the answer is: perhaps."

"Perhaps? Why—perhaps?"

"Because the true question you must ask of yourself. Are
demons willing to learn? Or are they as full of their pride as
most gukuy?"

Suddenly, Dzhenushkunutushen was laughing, and making
that side-to-side motion of his head which Nukurren had
learned was the demon gesture of negation.

"You still do not understand, Nukurren. We are not demons.
We are *ummun*, and barely beyond childhood. If there is one
thing we know how to do well, it is learn."

Nukurren was unconvinced. "Of you, that may be true. But
I do not think it is true of your *kapitanu*, Yoshefadenukunula."

Again, Dzhenushkunutushen made the gesture of negation.

"You do not understand him, Nukurren. It is his color which
confuses you. You think he is implacable. He is actually the
most uncertain of us all, but because we depend on him so,
can never show it."

Nukurren was silent, unconvinced.

"You will see," said Dzhenushkunutushen.

That night, in the hospital, Dhowifa prattled happily of the
events of the day. Again, as had been true since they arrived
among the ummun, Dhowifa had spent most of his time in
the company of Ushulubang. Only at night did he return to
the hospital.

Nukurren did not begrudge Dhowifa his absences. It had
been the worst of Dhowifa's pain when they fled Shakutulubac,
other than losing his malebond, to lose the company of
Ushulubang. And now he had found her again, and was able
to spend entire days in the sage's company, instead of a few
hours snatched from under the watchful eyes of the Ansha.

On this night, however, Nukurren would have preferred it
if Dhowifa had been silent. His incessant chatter was distracting

her from her own thoughts, which were focussed on the problem Dzhenushkunutushen had set before her.

By what tactics could a few demons defeat the Utuku hordes?

That night, Nukurren found no answer. But she did find many useful questions.

The next day, and for five days thereafter, she squatted silently by the training field, watching the demon exercises. She said nothing to Dzhenushkunutushen, and he, as if guided by some unspoken understanding, said nothing to her.

On the seventh day, Nukurren decided that her health was sufficiently restored. She told Dzhenushkunutushen to take her to the armory. Asking no questions, the ummun led her to a large wooden hut located some distance away. There, laboring with simple and primitive tools, Nukurren found several Pilgrims. Most of them were Anshac. To her surprise, she recognized the leader of the group. Her name was Utguko, and she had been, long before, the armorer for Nukurren's first legion.

Nukurren turned to Dzhenushkunutushen.

"I will need certain things to be made here." Dzhenushkunutushen made the gesture of assent and gave instructions to Utguko. Nukurren was interested to see that they conversed in Enagulishuc instead of Anshaku. They did so, she knew, not to keep secrets from her but because it was the wishes of the sage Ushulubang that Enagulishuc become the language of the Way.

"It will be done," said Dzhenushkunutushen to her, speaking now in Anshaku.

"Is good," she replied, in Enagulishuc. She interpreted Dzhenushkunutushen's stillness as surprise that Nukurren was learning Enagulishuc so quickly. Nukurren herself began to stiffen then, feeling the old hurt return, that she should be thought stupid simply because she was big and ugly. Then, after a moment, she relaxed. In truth, Nukurren *was* learning more quickly than would most gukuy.

"Tomorrow," she continued, still speaking Enagulishuc, "at training field. We see if demon can learn. If *will* learn."

After Dzhenushkunutushen left, Nukurren explained to Utguko her requirements. The old armorer was surprised, but she made no objections.

Early in the morning on the following day, when Nukurren returned, the materials she had requested were ready. Thoughtfully, Utguko had wrapped them in a reed-bundle, which made the bulky items easier to carry.

Hoisting the bundle onto her mantle, Nukurren made her way toward the training field. Her route took her through the demon village, past the longhouses of the warriors and the small huts of the older leaders. As she passed through the village, many demons emerged from the longhouses and began following her. To Nukurren's surprise, the Mother of Demons herself emerged from her hut and joined the crowd.

By the time she reached the training field, it seemed that every demon was present. On the field, in a small group, were those whom Nukurren had learned were their battle leaders. The *kapitanu*, Yoshefadekunula; the three *liyutenanatu*, Ludumilaroshokavashiki, Anadurumakfurrushen, Takashimitodzhugudzhi; and the Sharredzhenutumadzhoru, Dzhenushkunutushen.

Nukurren advanced to the middle of the field and stopped before the small group of demons. She unrolled the reed-bundle and selected, from the pile, a training fork and flail. The instruments were designed much like actual weapons, but were deliberately blunted and wrapped in resinous cloth to prevent serious injuries.

For a moment, Nukurren was tempted to speak in Enagulishuc. But she decided to use Anshaku instead. It was important there be no misunderstandings.

"First, you must learn you can be defeated. I do not believe you know this yet. Now you will learn. I do not know if you have such things as training spears. It would be better to use them. If you use real spears, I will be forced to move very quickly, and I may not be able to keep from harming you seriously."

The demons stared down at her. After a moment, the *kapitanu* called out a command. Soon thereafter, a male demon came onto the field, bearing spears which were simply blunted wood instead of metal-tipped.

The five battle leaders each took a spear.

"Your armor also," instructed Nukurren. Seeing the hesitation, she whistled derision.

"You are fools," she said.

The five demons donned their battle armor.

"Which of us do you wish to practice with?" asked Dzhenushkunutushen.

"All."

"*All?* That's ridiculous!"

"*Great fools.*" Nukurren fell upon them.

The combat which followed was savage and short. This time, Nukurren had the advantage of surprise, and she used it ruthlessly. Before the demons had even begun to react, Anadurumakfurrushen and Takashimitodzhugudzhi were sprawled half-senseless on the ground. Ludumilaroshokavashiki was able to avoid Nukurren's first flail-blow by virtue of her incredible speed, but, as Nukurren had foreseen, she was temporarily off-balance. Nukurren now pivoted against Dzhenushkunutushen, forcing him against Yoshefadekunula, and then hammered the white male mercilessly with both fork and flail. As she had suspected, Dzhenushkunutushen was very strong, but he was not as strong as Nukurren. He went down under the blows, entangling the demonlord in his fall.

That allowed Nukurren the time she needed to finish Ludumilaroshokavashiki. Again, she was impressed by the speed and dexterity of the female warrior; but it availed Ludumilaroshokavashiki nothing. She was overconfident, as Nukurren had known she would be. The demon lunged in with a headthrust of her spear. It was a clever feint, designed to draw forth a missed fork-stroke. But Nukurren's battle-experience was by far the greater. Instead of the fork-stroke she expected, Ludumilaroshokavashiki found her spear entrapped by Nukurren flair; and then, helpless, came the fork-stroke which spilled her to the ground, her armor splintering under the impact.

Nukurren spun about and, without even looking, rolled to the side. The demonlord's spearthrust missed her completely. She lashed with the flail and then, pleased beyond measure, saw that Yoshefadekunula had again avoided it by that impossible upward spring.

But I know it now, demonlord.

She could not deny the satisfaction it gave her to swat the demonlord in midair, with a stroke of the fork which was, perhaps, excessively harsh.

She spun about. Three of the demons were beginning to

rise, but Nukurren stilled them with quick touches of the flail.
These were not blows, simply touches. But they were enough
to drive home the lesson. All were now at her mercy, and there
would have been nothing, had they been using real weapons
in a real battle, to prevent her from slaying them.

She stepped back and set down her fork and flail.

"That is the first lesson. There will be no other today.
Tomorrow I will begin teaching you the Utuku way of war,
so that you may learn how to combat them. But today's lesson is the most important lesson of all, and you must think
upon it."

She rolled up her instruments in the reed-bundle and
carried them back to the hospital.

Late that night, Dzhenushkunutushen came to the hospital and sat by Nukurren's pallet. He said nothing for a time,
nor did Nukurren.

At length, Dhowifa spoke.

"Are you hurt?"

Dzhenushkunutushen's face *crunched*. The ummun crunched
their faces many different ways, but Nukurren thought this
was the gesture of ruefulness.

"I hurt all over."

"Good," said Nukurren. "It will prepare you for tomorrow.
Where you will hurt again, but will be wiser."

Again, the *crunch*. Slightly different.

"Some friend you are!"

Only her long years of *shoroku* kept Nukurren's mantle gray.
For some time, she did not trust herself to speak.
Dzhenushkunutushen rose and began to leave.

Softly, to his back, Nukurren said: "I have never had a
friend. Except Dhowifa."

The demon stopped in the doorway. He turned around and
came back to Nukurren's pallet. As always, she was struck by
the strangeness of his colors, the white passion of his skin and
the blue fury of his eyes.

"I have never known loneliness," he said. "I think you have
never known anything else."

"That is true. Except Dhowifa." She felt her lover's soft
touch.

Dzhenushkunutushen lay down on the floor next to the

pallet. "Tonight I will sleep here, Nukurren. There are lessons which you need to learn also."

Soon, Dzhenushkunutushen fell asleep, as, shortly thereafter, did Dhowifa. Nukurren remained awake long into the night. Never once did her *shoroku* waver. But the time came when one of the great palps which had brought terror and death to so many over the years reached out. Reached out, and gently touched the soft yellow hair of the demon lying next to her.

Chapter 21

In the days after the shocking defeat which the huge new gukuy had delivered to Joseph and his lieutenants, Indira found herself, much against her natural inclination, visiting the training field. She said nothing to anyone, simply watched as the new arrival—Nukurren—began showing the human warriors the Utuku methods of combat.

On the second day of the new training regimen, Ushulubang arrived. She was accompanied by Dhowifa, riding in her mantle cavity, and a large number of Pilgrims. Indira immediately knew, by some subtlety in their bearing, that these Pilgrims were former warriors. They were carrying reed-bundles laden with unusually designed weapons, including shields. From descriptions she had heard, Indira realized that these were replicas of Utuku weapons. After a brief consultation between Ushulubang and Nukurren, the Pilgrims donned the Utuku armament and began acting as the mock opponent for the human platoons.

Ushulubang then came to Indira's side. With Ushulubang was one of the Pilgrim warriors, older than the others. Although Indira could not interpret specifically the clan carvings on her cowl (which had all the arcane intricacies of medieval heraldry), Indira was sure that this new gukuy was of some high-ranked Ansha clan.

Ushulubang immediately confirmed her guess.

"Inudira, this is Ghodha. She is a new Pilgrim. Until our flight from Shakutulubac, she was a high commander in the Ansha legions. She is the most experienced war leader amongst the Pilgrims."

Ghodha made the gesture of respect. More properly, since the gesture of respect was generic, she made that specific version of the gesture of respect which signified respect by a high subordinate of one realm toward the august ruler of another.

In return, Indira bowed. Her bow contained none of the subtleties of Ghodha's gesture, however. Indira had realized that the humans would have to develop appropriate gestures with which to respond to gukuy, and so she had instituted the bow. The bow given to gukuy as a gesture of respect, however, was different from the one given to the owoc at the time of feeding. Much shallower—closer to an exaggerated nod than a deep bow. And she had insisted that there be no gradations in the bow.

But, as she had known would happen, the gradations were creeping in regardless. And she had immediately noted the different gesture which Jens Knudsen was using toward Nukurren, and which was almost immediately adopted by the other human warriors. The fact that the gesture resembled, in its outward appearance, the humble hand-clasping of a medieval monk toward an abbot did not fool her for a moment.

Within a generation, she thought wearily, *we'll be a proper bunch of samurai and mandarins.*

"You are distressed, Inudira," commented Ushulubang. "May I ask why?"

Indira stared. She had already come to recognize that Ushulubang was easily the most intelligent person—human or gukuy—that Indira had ever met in her life. But she was still astonished by the old sage's uncanny ability to interpret subtle nuances of human body language.

"I—it is difficult to explain."

Ushulubang gestured toward the training field.

"Would it ease your spirit if we desisted from this action?"

Indira immediately shook her head. "No, no. You will be a big help for my—children. I should have thought of it myself."

Then why didn't you? she asked herself. *The idea was obvious.*

But she knew the answer. *Because I cannot bear the future I can see—no matter where I look.*

"It is what will come of this that disturbs you," said Ushulubang.

Indira nodded.

"I believe I understand. Some day we must speak on this matter, Inudira."

Again, she nodded. But her nod contained, in some subtle way, the implication of hopeless resignation; and she knew the sage recognized it.

She tried to shake off the black mood.

"What is your opinion?" she asked the war leader Ghodha, pointing to the training field.

Ghodha hesitated.

"I would prefer to reserve my opinion, for the moment. I am not familiar with the tactical methods and abilities of dem—ummun."

Indira turned and gazed back onto the training field. By now, the human platoons were fully engaged in maneuvers with the Pilgrims. The Pilgrims were arrayed in a tightly knit formation. In essence, it was a phalanx. But Indira saw that the phalanx was much shallower in depth than the formations of the ancient Greeks and Macedonians. The difference, of course, was due to the weapons involved. The many-ranked phalanxes of Hellenic warriors had been designed to take advantage of the great reach of their long spears and pikes. The Utuku, using flails, were limited to a three-deep formation.

"Is that how the Utuku fight?" she asked Ghodha.

"Yes. It is very crude and primitive, and allows for no subtlety of maneuvers. But if the discipline is sufficient—and Utuku discipline is like bronze—then their—" Ghodha hesitated. "I do not know the Enagulishuc word. The Utuku call this formation a *kabu buxt*. We Ansha call it *arrut kudh pakta*."

Arrut kudh pakta. Indira made the translation. *Crest of the shell*, essentially.

"We call it a phalanx," she said.

"*Falanuksh*," repeated Ghodha. "With their great numbers, and discipline, the Utuku can be a terrible foe. Many armies have broken against them."

A long silence ensued. For the next four hours, Indira watched as the young human leaders, consulting frequently with Nukurren, began changing and adapting their tactics. They were fumbling, at first; grew more assured as time went by. But still, Indira knew, they were groping for answers.

The voice of Ghodha interrupted her thoughts.

"You are fortunate to have Nukurren. She was the greatest warrior of the Anshac legions."

Indira turned and looked at the Pilgrim war leader.

"I did not realize you knew her."

Ghodha made the gesture of negation.

"I did not really know her, Inudira." A faint ochre ripple, with a hint of brown. "The caste divisions in Ansha are rigid. I was high caste—not Ansha, like Ushulubang or Rottu, but very high. Nukurren belonged to no caste, not even a low one. She was born into a helot slave pool. Clanless and outcast." Another ripple, the brown now predominant. "As such, and despite her incredible prowess, she was despised by such as—myself. In my former time, as a high commander."

Ghodha paused, took a deep breath. (In this, humans and gukuy were quite alike—a thing difficult to say was usually prefaced by a full intake of oxygen.) The brown ripples spread and suffused her entire mantle. That shade of brown which signified remorse.

"All my life, before I decided to adopt the Way and follow Ushulubang, I have been trained in arrogance. It comes very easily to me. I have tried to combat it, but it is often difficult. I shall try harder in the future. I will not always succeed, I fear, but I will try."

Indira began to speak, but was interrupted by Dhowifa. The little male's voice was even softer than usual.

"Nukurren thought you were the best of the legions' high commanders," he said.

An orange ripple broke up the brown of Ghodha's mantle.

"It's true," added Dhowifa. "She told me several times." The quick, complex wash of ochre/pink/azure which suddenly colored the little male's mantle was exquisite in its subtlety. Indira was not certain, but she thought it was a brilliant emotional exhibition of diffident apology, leavened by humor (no, not humor—good feeling).

"Actually, she thought the best tactical commander was Ashurruk."

"Of course!" exclaimed Ghodha. "Ashurruk was superb on the battlefield."

"But she thought you were the best thinker. The best—I can't remember the word, I'm not a warrior—the best—"

"Strategist?" asked Ghodha.

A lightning-quick ripple of greenish color. "That's the word!" said Dhowifa.

Ghodha turned and gazed down at the training field.

"So." A whistle. "I must apologize to her."

"Oh, you needn't," said Dhowifa. "Nukurren was never offended by you."

"Perhaps not," replied Ghodha. The former Ansha commander's mantle was suddenly replaced by a dull, matte black. (Stolid determination, Indira knew, closely related to the ebony sheen of implacable purpose.) "I hope not. But my offense is much deeper. Until this very moment, I had never realized that common warriors thought about their commanders. Assessed them, even, much as commanders assess their troops." A short silence; then, a ripple of yellow contempt. "As if commanders are the only ones who think. As if warriors are but brainless beasts."

Indira felt a sudden wave of immense affection for Ghodha sweep over her. In that one moment, she felt a deep regret that she had no way of showing her feelings on her skin as could a gukuy.

She was born into an Anshac upper caste, and trained as a high commander of the legions. For such as she haughtiness and condescension and insult are as natural as breathing. Yet only such a one who also possessed a great soul would have left it all to follow a despised and outlawed sage, for no other reason than devotion to some higher purpose.

She turned away and gazed back onto the training field. The tactics which the young human leaders were developing, working with Nukurren, were beginning to crystallize. But it was also obvious to Indira that they were still hesitant, still uncertain, still unsure of themselves.

She watched as Jens Knudsen, passing by Nukurren during a pause in the action, casually stroked the huge warrior's scarred mantle. She watched as Ludmilla exchanged banter with the outcaste veteran. She watched as Joseph stood by the despised pervert, the former helot, the soulless monster whose mantle never showed any color; stood by her, deep in conversation, his brow furrowed with thought.

Young humans, barely beyond childhood, of every color; allied to a soulless monster whose mantle never showed any color; desperately seeking to forge an instrument which could stave off destruction.

And doing very well, thought Indira, *given their handicaps. They are almost there. They need only the finishing touch. And, most of all, the confidence that they are right. The confidence which the Mother of Demons could give them. The Mother of Demons, who knows the secrets.*

There are no secrets! she heard her own voice shrieking. But it was a lie.

This secret I do know. It was discovered long ago, in another time, on another planet.

A vivid image flashed through her mind, the superimposed vision of a dark forest in Poland, and the Utuku defeated. No, more than defeated. Shattered, slaughtered, butchered. Their blood soaking the needles of pine trees which never existed on Ishtar; their entrails strewn beneath the branches of an alien growth. Death and destruction in a demon forest.

At that moment, Indira almost spoke. Almost stepped forward and went onto the training field.

But other visions came, and paralyzed her. Vision after vision after vision.

Yes, I know the secret. And all the secrets which come with it.

She saw the horsetail standards of the Mongol tumens, shivering with triumph in the forest. And the pitiless faces of the horsemen and their generals. And the cities like hecatombs. And the peasant woman lying in the doorway of the wretched hovel in which she had toiled her life; her short life, now ending, as she lay there, naked, violated, bleeding to death; her last sight the disemboweled bodies of her children. Lives which had no meaning to the warriors who rode away, toward new triumphs, beyond the brief pleasure they had taken from ending them. But lives which had been as precious to their victims as the life of the Great Khan had been to him, in his grandeur at Qarakorum.

Indira turned and walked away. Her steps were quick, very quick, almost running; the pace of a mother abandoning her children. She was glad, then, that she had no way of showing her feelings as could a gukuy. For her skin would have fairly glowed with brown misery—that particular shade of brown which signified guilt.

❖   ❖   ❖

As soon as she left, Joseph and his lieutenants broke off the exercises and trotted over to Ushulubang. Jens Knudsen followed, after a brief exchange of words with Nukurren. Soon thereafter, all the human warriors and gukuy Pilgrims came as well, until the old sage was surrounded by a silent crowd. Only Nukurren remained behind, standing alone on the training field.

Ushulubang said nothing, until Joseph spoke in a voice filled with youthful anguish.

"Why will she not tell us?" he demanded.

"How to defeat the Utuku?" asked the sage mildly. Joseph nodded.

"Maybe she doesn't know," said Jens.

Ushulubang made the gesture of negation. "She knows. It is quite obvious."

Joseph's face was filled with fury. His body almost shook with rage.

"Then why will she not speak?"

Ushulubang's mantle flashed blue/black—the color of furious condemnation. The color of execution.

"Be silent, spawn!" bellowed the sage. The young humans stepped back, astonished. They had never seen Ushulubang in this state. The Pilgrims froze, their mantles flashing red fear. They, as well, had never see that terrible color on Ushulubang's mantle.

Ushulubang fixed her gaze on Joseph. And now the huge eyes of the sage had none of their usual gentleness and wisdom. Hers was the pitiless scrutiny of a prophet.

"Do not judge your mother, spawn. You do not have the right. You demand from her the Answer, when she is demanding from herself the Question. You do not understand how terrible that Question is. You do not even understand that there is a Question."

Ushulubang made the gesture of rejection. "Go, spawn. All of you. Return to your training."

Again, the color of execution. *"Go!"*

The crowd fled. Except—after a few steps, Jens Knudsen stopped. Stopped, hesitated, then turned. He made his uncertain way back to Ushulubang.

The sage, mistress of *shoroku*, had to fight hard to maintain control. Else her mantle would have been flooded with green.

I thought it would be this one. (A mental whistle of amusement.) *Whose soul bears, in truth, the passion of his color.*

Jens Knudsen began to speak, could not find the words. Ushulubang made the gesture of acceptance.

"Tonight," she said. "I will await you in my hut."

After Jens Knudsen left, and Ushulubang was certain he was beyond hearing, she made the whistle of amusement she had so long repressed.

"I thought that went quite well," she said to Dhowifa.

The little truemale's mantle rippled with ochre.

"You are so sure, Ushulubang? Things are—much as you predicted. But, still—it is so dangerous."

"Dangerous?" demanded the sage. "Of course it is dangerous! The Way is dangerous, Dhowifa. There is nothing so dangerous as the Question. The way of safety is the way of the Answer. Safety—and oblivion."

"I know, I know. At least, I think I know."

Dhowifa fell silent. Ushulubang completed the thought.

"But you think it is too perilous. To goad the Mother of Demons until her soul shatters?"

"Yes."

"There is no other way, Dhowifa. In this, I am right. She must be forced to tell the secrets."

"Are her secrets really so terrible?"

Ushulubang whistled derision. "Stupid spawn! Have you learned nothing? She has no secrets."

Dhowifa's mantle rippled orange surprise.

"But—"

"There *are* no secrets, Dhowifa. *That* is what she knows, and her children do not. How can the Question be secret? Only the Answer can be secret. And that is why she is so terrified, and cannot tell them what answers she does know. For fear of what questions those answers will bring."

"Then why did you say she must be forced to tell the secrets, if there are none?"

"It is the *telling* that is important, Dhowifa, not the thing told. The answer given is momentary, a vapor dispelled by the wind. But the *telling*—that is what lies at the center of the Coil."

"I do not understand why that is true."

"Because it is only in telling the answer that the Mother of Demons will finally accept the Question."

Dhowifa hesitated. "Is it so wise? To bring demons to the Way?" He gestured at Jens Knudsen. "That one, perhaps. He is young, and—very kind. He has meant much to Nukurren, these past days. But—the Mother of Demons? And the black demonlord? Can such fearsome beings really be—"

Ushulubang whistled derision.

"Be what, Dhowifa? 'Tamed'? Of course not. I do not wish to tame them. Quite the contrary. I wish to convert the demons in order to show the truth to the gukuy. Which is that we too are demons, and must be, and shall be. Because only demons have the courage to seek the Question."

Again, silence fell. After a moment, Ushulubang gestured at Nukurren.

"Soon, we must heal her."

Dhowifa's mantle rippled orange. "She is already healed, Ushulubang. Almost, at least. There will be scars, of course, and she will always be blind in one eye, but—"

"I was not speaking of those recent wounds to her body, Dhowifa. It is the great open wound in her soul which must be healed. The ancient wound which has bled all her life."

Dhowifa made the gesture of uncertainty. "She has seemed happy to me, these past few days. It has meant much to her, even though she will not speak of it, to find a friend in the demon Dzhenushkunutushen."

"You are wrong, Dhowifa. The friendship is a blessing, and a boon to her. As you have always been a boon to her. But there must be more. She must find the center of her Coil. She must find her life."

That night the demon Dzhenushkunutushen came to the hut of the sage Ushulubang, and spent many hours there, learning the Way of the Coil. The next night, he was accompanied by his lover, the demon Ludumilaroshokavashiki. Two nights thereafter, they were joined by Yoshefadekunula. The demonlord said nothing, but simply listened to the sage.

Night after night, Indira watched her children enter the hut. Night after night, she watched them leave. They did not speak to her, nor she to them.

And every night, after they were gone, Ushulubang

emerged. The sage and the Mother of Demons would stare at each other for long minutes, saying nothing. The one, filled with anguish, wishing she too could enter the hut; the other, filled with love, barring the way.

Soon, Mother of Demons, thought Ushulubang. *Soon. Soon you will find the courage to break your soul.*

Chapter 22

A scout arrived at the village, out of breath despite her excellent physical condition. She had run all the way from the big canyon with the news.

Two armies had been spotted approaching the Chiton. Each with thousands of warriors.

A few minutes later, "the Pentagon" was packed with all the members of the council, as well as the scout and Jens Knudsen. They were standing around the three-dimensional clay model of the Chiton which Julius had made.

"It's a good thing Joseph insisted on expanding this hut," muttered Julius. "We'd never have fit in the old one."

Indira forebore comment. She had opposed Joseph's plan to tear down the old hut and build a much bigger one in its place, around the clay model. It had been one of the many, minor clashes between she and Joseph over the past two years. And, as was usually the case, Joseph's will had prevailed.

And, as usual, thought Indira, *the boy was right.*

A rueful little smile came to her face.

Stop thinking of him as a "boy," Indira. Old fool. The youngsters have matured rapidly in this new world—just as they did in the ancient days on earth.

None more so than Joseph. How old was Alexander when he defeated the Persians at Issus?

She looked across the table at Joseph, who was staring down at the map. There was a frown on the Captain's face. Not a frown of worry, however. Simply the frown of calm, collected thought.

God, he's impressive. In my entire life, I've never met anyone who exudes so much—sureness.

Except Ushulubang.

The last thought brought a sudden decision.

"Someone go get Ushulubang," she said.

Joseph raised his eyes and stared at her. For a moment Indira thought there would be an argument. Joseph's thoughts were obvious: *Why Ushulubang? She's a sage, not a warrior.* But then, within seconds, Joseph looked at Jens and nodded. Jens raced out of the hut.

Joseph looked back at Indira.

"I just have a . . . feeling, Joseph," she replied to his unspoken question. "Founders of new religions have to be great politicians, in addition to everything else. And the Way is not a pacifist creed."

Sooner than she expected, Jens returned with Ushulubang. The former legion commander Ghodha was with her, as well as another Pilgrim whom Indira had never seen before. As soon as the sage entered the hut, Indira rapidly sketched the situation for her.

Ushulubang made the gesture of recognition (the one which indicated "recognition of current reality"; there was a different gesture for personal recognition).

"I suspected something of the sort was occurring, from the sudden activity."

Ushulubang gestured toward the gukuy at her side, the one Indira did not know.

"For that reason, I took the liberty of bringing Rottu with me, as well as Ghodha. She is—my other eyes." A humorous whistle. "Not, perhaps, the most subtle of philosophers. But very aware of the world, and uncommonly shrewd."

Indira stared at Rottu. The gukuy was slightly larger than average. And much older than most of the Pilgrims, although not as old as Ushulubang. Like Ushulubang, she bore the cowl-carvings of a high-ranked member of the Ansha. Rottu's carvings, however, had not been scoured clean. Other than the bright pigments in the carvings, there was not a trace of any color on her mantle.

Her shoroku is perfect, thought Indira. *Which is what you'd expect—of a spymaster. Spymistress, rather.*

Joseph looked at Rottu. "Can you tell us anything?"

"Describe the appearance of the armies." Indira was not surprised that Rottu's Enagulishuc, though heavily accented, was excellent.

The scout—Jauna Horenstein—quickly presented what details of the two armies had been observed.

Rottu extended her palp and pointed to the little wooden piece which represented the army approaching directly from the south.

"These are Utuku. From your estimate of their numbers, it is one of their *ogghoxt*. Such is the name of the major divisions of their army."

"You are certain?" asked Joseph.

"Absolutely. Only the Utuku, of all the peoples known to me in the world, equip and organize their armies in that manner. A few other peoples use shields instead of forks, but none of them could muster such a great force. And those peoples are far to the southeast, in any event. Beyond Ansha."

"How many warriors?"

"Approximately eighty-eighty triple-eight eighty. The number varies, from one *ogghoxt* to another, but not by much. The Utuku are highly organized, for barbarians."

Indira translated the numbers in her mind. The gukuy numerical system was based on the number eight, rather than ten. The term "eighty" meant the same thing as the human "hundred"—base multiplied by itself. Sixty-four. "Eighty-eighty" meant that multiplied again. Sixty-four times sixty-four. Plus "triple-eight eighty:" three times eight times sixty-four.

Five and half thousand warriors, she thought with a sinking feeling. *How can we possibly face so many? Even behind the protection of Adrian's Wall? And the fortifications are not finished in the other canyons, in any event. The Utuku would have only to choose a different route.*

Joseph spoke then, with not a trace of despair in his voice. "And the other army?"

Rottu made the gesture of ironic surprise.

"Now that is what is interesting." She looked at Jauna. "You are certain that they are *north* of the river?"

Jauna nodded vigorously.

Rottu stroked her arms together in that gesture which was the equivalent of a human scratching her chin. Her next question was addressed at Joseph.

"Do you maintain scouts on the western side of the Chiton?"

"Yes."

"And they saw nothing?"

"No."

"Thus this other army appeared out of nowhere. Already across the river. It can only have come from here."

She pointed to the pile of moss on the map which Julius had used to indicate the huge jungle that stretched southwest of the Chiton.

"From the Lolopopo Swamp."

Anna Cheng gasped. "But—the swamp's impenetrable!"

Rottu again made the gesture of ironic surprise.

"So it is always said. But I know that there have been some gukuy who have lived in the swamp. Escaped helots from the south. They must have provided guides for this other army to cross the swamp. After they were defeated by the Utuku many eightweeks ago."

She made the gesture of profound respect.

"It must have been a heroic trek."

Realization came simultaneously to everyone in the hut. Joseph vocalized it:

"The Kiktu."

"Yes. There is no other possibility. Logic tells us so—and then, there is your scout's description of the one who marches at the front of the army. That can only be a battlemother."

Joseph's face was impassive. "All accounts I have heard say the Kiktu were destroyed in the battle. Those few who survived were scattered refugees. Yet this is not a horde of refugees. It is a well-organized army, and big."

He looked at the scout. "How many again, Jauna?"

"More than two thousand. Probably three."

Joseph began to translate for Rottu, but the gukuy made the gesture of understanding.

"More than four eight-eighty," mused Rottu, "Probably six. Incredible."

She made the gesture of *profound* respect.

"I would not have thought it possible. Even for Kopporu."

"Explain," commanded Joseph.

"It is true that most of the refugees from the battle say the Kiktu were utterly destroyed. But I have heard a different rumor, from a few. They say that after the battle was lost, the leader of the right flank led a retreat of the entire flank into the swamp. An *organized* retreat, not a panicky rout. The leader's name was Kopporu, and she was reputed to be the greatest battle leader of the Kiktu."

Rottu's armstrokes were now rapid and vigorous.

"I discounted the rumor, at first. But recently I have spoken to a new refugee, who hid in a fuyu grove after the battle. By luck, she was not discovered, even when the Beak of the Utuku established her command yurt nearby. The refugee remained hidden in that grove for three days. And watched, while the Beak of the Utuku ordered the execution of more than double-eight of her battle leaders."

Rottu whistled with humor. "The death of Utuku battle leaders is naturally a blessing. But why? And why so many? True, the Beak is perhaps the cruelest ruler on the Meat of the Clam. Even so, her army had just won a great victory for her. One would have expected rewards, not executions."

Rottu stared at the map. "There must have been a great disaster in the middle of that battle. I wonder. Kopporu was, among other things, famous for her mastery of the art of ambush."

A moment's arm-stroking. Then, with the tone of assurance:

"It must be so. I can think of no other explanation. Several Kiktu refugees have told me that it was well known that Kopporu was opposed to the Kiktu clan leaders' plan of battle. She had predicted disaster beforehand, and then demanded the command of the right flank. She was admired for that nobility of spirit, it seems. But the truth was different. She hatched a plot, and carried it out. Led the retreat of her flank into the swamp. Set a terrible ambush for the Utuku who pursued. And then—led the remainder of her tribe across the Lolopopo Swamp. Seeking refuge, I expect, in the Chiton."

"Treason, you are saying?" asked Joseph.

The gesture of questioning.

"Treason, yes. Or—supreme loyalty."

Joseph took command of the meeting then.

"Our options are clear and simple. From what the scouts report, the two armies will contact each other at the base of the Chiton, before either can reach any of the canyons. A battle will inevitably ensue—in two days, at the earliest. Probably three."

He stared at the map.

"The Kiktu are outnumbered, but if we throw ourselves on their side, it may be enough to turn the tide."

"And the other option?" asked Takashi.

"We marshall our forces behind Adrian's Wall and wait—while the Utuku and the Kiktu fight it out. The Utuku will probably win, but the Kiktu will inflict massive casualties upon them. Very massive, I would think— if Rottu is right and they are still under the leadership of this Kopporu. Massive enough, probably, that the surviving Utuku will not be able to force their way up the canyon. They will retreat, and return to the main army for reinforcements. That will take some time, which we can use to prepare ourselves."

The other Lieutenant in the hut, Andrew MacPherson, spoke for the first time.

"So. If we join the Kiktu, we risk everything at once. If we wait on the sides, we give ourselves some breathing room. That, I think, sums it up."

Joseph nodded.

"Which do you prefer?" asked Takashi.

"It is not for me to decide. The decision is not simply a military one. It involves the fate of the entire colony—and everyone else on the Chiton, gukuy and owoc alike."

Indira took command.

"Joseph is right. The council must make the decision. And we should—"

"No!"

She was stunned into silence. Joseph's voice had been like a thunderclap.

She stared at him. "But, Joseph—the council is the only—"

"No."

"But—"

"No."

Silence filled the hut. Indira looked around. The faces of all the young members of the council mirrored Joseph's—even the face of Anna Cheng. She looked at Julius. After a second, he looked away.

Joseph's voice drew her back to him.

"This"—he said, pointing to the map, "is not a decision like any other. It is the decision that will change everything. It is the decision that will make the future. It is a decision which can only be made by that person who understands the future, and its perils."

His face was like stone.

"And its secrets."

Indira's mind was blank. Like a bird, paralyzed by the gaze of a cobra.

Black as night. Implacable.

Joseph's face softened, slightly.

"I'm sorry, Indira. I am not angry with you, as I was before. I have been listening to Ushulubang, these past nights, and—"

He took a deep breath. "I know that I terrify you. I even think that I understand why. Some part of it, at least. This decision—" He pointed to the map "—seems obvious to me. As simple and easy to make as—as whether to cherish the owoc. But you see deeper than I. Than any of us."

Joseph paused, groping for words. He glanced at Ushulubang. Then said:

"This decision is not simply an answer. It is a question. A great question. Maybe the greatest question of all. The answer may be obvious, but the question is not. Therefore, only you can make the decision."

She started to protest.

"It is true—*mother*."

Desperately she scanned the room. Every face was like stone—even, to her horror, that of Julius.

No, not every face.

"Leave," she commanded harshly. "All of you—except Ushulubang."

Without hesitation, the young humans filed from the hut, Joseph leading the way. As Rottu and Ghodha turned to leave, Ushulubang said to them softly:

"Gather the apashoc. Tell them the flails of the Pilgrims are now under the command of the Mother of Demons."

Julius hesitated at the doorway, and turned back.

"I'm staying," he announced firmly. Seeing Indira's hard gaze, he shrugged.

"Indira, Joseph's right. For years, we've been able to stay on the sidelines. A cozy little colony, in a cocoon. But all things come to an end. Whatever decision you make, we are going to plunge into the mainstream of history. To sink or swim. And if we sink, we'll pull others down with us."

"Don't you think I know that?" she demanded angrily. "But why do I have to be the one to make the decision?"

"Because you're the only one who can, love. Joseph's right about that, too."

"That's nonsense!" shouted Indira. "The decision is obvious. Tactically, strategically—even morally."

Julius shrugged. "Then make it."

Indira opened her mouth, then closed it. Desperately, she looked at Ushulubang.

"How may I be of service?" asked the sage.

Indira whispered, "Do you understand?"

Ushulubang's mantle flooded brown with grief.

"Yes, Inudira, I understand. You cannot bear taking responsibility for the future. You cannot bear being—the Mother of Demons."

Tears began pouring from her eyes. "Let me tell you the truth about the future, Ushulubang, and its secrets. And its agony."

She spoke for three hours, without interruption. Her words were disjointed, at times. She made no attempt to present her thoughts in an organized and scholarly manner. Had she done so, it would have made no difference, in any event. Much of what she spoke were names which were completely new and unfamiliar to the gukuy who listened.

So many names. So many, many, strange demon names. Names of places, for the most part.

Places of infinite slaughter:

Auschwitz. Dachau. Hiroshima. Tuol Sleng. Dresden. Nagasaki. Verdun. The Somme. Bokhara. Sammarkhand. Rwanda.

Places where the strong savaged the weak:

Rome, and its victims. Rome, sacked. Jerusalem, sacked, and sacked, and sacked. Magdeburg. The *Mfecane*. Amritsar. Wounded Knee. Nanking. Sharpeville. Vietnam.

Places where the rich battened fat on the misery of the poor:

The helotry of Egypt and Sumeria and Sparta. The slavery of Athens and Rome. The knout of the Tsars and the boyars. The Middle Passage. The plantations of the Caribbean and the South. The Belgian Congo. The sweatshops of the industrial revolution. The Irish potato famine. The coal mines of Appalachia. The German slave labor factories of World War II. The Gulag. The Great Leap Forward. The International Monetary Fund.

Names of cruelty:

Hitler. Stalin. Tamerlane. Ivan the Terrible. Pol Pot. Nazis. *Einsatzgruppen*. Ku Klux Klan. Inquisition.

Deeds of cruelty:

Kristallnacht. The pogroms of Russia. The lynchings of the American south. The Albigensian Crusade—and all the other crusades.

Name after name after name—in a babble, at the end, until she finally fell silent.

Throughout, Ushulubang had not even moved. Now, she stirred slightly.

"So. Truly, a terrible road. Worse than I had hoped. But not, perhaps, as much as I have sometimes feared, in the darkest nights of the soul. You are here, after all. On this world which we call Ishtar, because the name given to it by demons is one which we can all agree upon."

Indira snorted. "*Demons*. It's a good name for us. Who but demons could be so cruel?"

"Yes. And who but demons could be so courageous?"

The sage stared up at the ceiling of the hut. "It is such a wonder to me. To be so brave and powerful. To cross the Infinite Sea."

Indira shrugged. Ushulubang gazed at her for a moment, before speaking again.

"Tell me, Indira. Is it true, as I have been told, that you did not flee to our world? That you came here of your own will?"

"Yes."

"What was your purpose, then?"

She explained, as best she could. Of an Earth ravaged, but at peace. Of a humanity which was struggling to rebuild a planet. Of those few, among the many preoccupied with immediate necessities, who had yearned for the stars. Who had managed, after much labor and effort, to equip a single expedition to come to the one star in the vicinity of Sol which had been determined to possess a habitable planet.

"Just so. A terrible road—but a road of beauty, also."

"I suppose. Yes."

"Another question. Of the many names which you told me, there seemed to be one name which appeared more often than any other." The gesture of apology. "It is difficult for me to pronounce. The—Natushishu?"

"Nazis."

"Yes. Truly, a terrible tribe. Worse than the Utuku, even. Or, perhaps, simply more powerful. You said they swept across the land like a fire, leaving nothing but death and destruction behind."

"Yes."

"But you did not tell me what happened to them, in the end."

Indira stared out the doorway.

"They came to a place called Stalingrad."

"Another place of horror?"

Indira thought of the soldiers of the Wehrmacht Sixth Army, encircled by the Soviet counterattack. Over three hundred thousand of them, caught in a maelstrom they had never created. Years later, a few thousand would return to their families. The rest—part of the unknown multitude washed away into the ocean called History.

"No," she said. "It was a place of glory, and beauty."

"Did the glory last? And the beauty?"

She thought of Stalin's purges. Of the Gulag.

"No. But—"

"It was a place when the road forked. And the right fork was taken. Horrors along that road, as well. But not so many as along the other."

"Yes. Yes, but—"

Ushulubang made the gesture of understanding. "You are terrified, not by the agony alone, but by its inevitability. Not by the decision which fork of the road to take, but by knowledge that all roads must lead through horror. And that by choosing one fork it will be you yourself who creates the horror of that road."

She nodded.

"Just so. Do you remember when I smashed the idol at Fagoshau?"

Again, she nodded.

Ushulubang whistled derision. "Did you think I was so

foolish as to believe I could smash idolatry? Did you think I failed to understand that, after my death, new idols of Goloku would be erected?" Another whistle of derision. "And of me as well, I expect."

Indira stared at the sage. "I did not . . . I don't know."

"Just so. Many years ago, Inudira, I found myself at a fork in the road. Much like the one which you face here. I saw the fork coming, long before I reached it. In my confusion and fear, I went to Goloku.

"I told her that the day would come, after her death, when the apashoc would be savagely persecuted. I thought that because of my position in the Ansha that I might be able to survive. I alone, perhaps, among my sisters. If I debased myself, and groveled, and wriggled through the anger of the clan leaders like a slug.

"The idea was—loathsome. But, I thought, perhaps it would be my duty. So I went to Goloku."

"And what did she say?"

"She told me I had understood nothing of what she had ever said. She flailed me mercilessly, with words like stone."

Ushulubang's huge eyes were pitiless. Her mantle flashed black as night. Implacable.

"I shall now flail you with the same words. There is no Answer, *fool*. There is only the Question."

Suddenly, Julius spoke.

"Do you remember the first time we met?" he asked Indira. The question took her completely by surprise.

"What?"

"The first time we met. We had an argument. Do you remember what you said to me?"

Her mind was like a field of snow. Empty.

"I don't—remember. Why?"

His rubbery face twisted into a grin. "How strange. I have never forgotten it."

She shook her head, clearing away the confusion caused by Julius' odd question. Then, suddenly, remembered.

If there is one thing that historians know, it's that nothing great was ever achieved except by those who were filled with passion. Their passion may have been illogical, even bizarre to modern people. Their understanding of the world and what they were doing may have been false. It usually was.

But they were not afraid to act, guided by whatever ideas they had in their possession. Do not sneer at such people. You would not be here without them.

Moments later, Indira left the hut and walked into the center of the village. Joseph was waiting. He stood alone, apart from the others of the council. Whatever decision Indira had made would now fall upon his shoulders.

Before speaking, Indira looked around. The village was packed with people—gukuy and ummun alike. Even some of the owoc had come, understanding, somehow, that a great turn had come in the Coil of Beauty.

She looked up at the sky. The same sky, years before, had been colored with a huge red mark. All that was left of a man who had tried the impossible. Tried, and failed. But not before giving the future to his children.

She looked down at her boy, and spoke.

The story would be told for generations after, by chantresses across a continent. Of the day when the Mother of Demons matched flails with her soul.

> *So terrible was that soul!*
> *So great a struggle!*
> *Even the Mother of Demons*
> > *would not have conquered it*
> > > *Without the sage Ushulubang.*
> *So terrible was that soul!*
> *Its cry of defeat shook the world!*
> *You did not hear?*
> > *Listen.*
> > > *Listen.*
> > > > *It echoes still.*
> *The sound of that cry will never end.*

Chapter 23

Indira watched the battle from the southern slope, standing on a rocky outcropping which overlooked the plain. Four beings stood there with her: Julius, Andrew MacPherson, Rottu and Ghodha.

They were the nucleus of what Indira had told them was one of the secrets of war.

Create a general staff.

She would have preferred to have Joseph himself alongside her. But, reluctantly, she had agreed with Joseph's argument that his personal command was necessary in the colony's first full-scale battle. Of the three lieutenants, Andrew had been selected as the future Chief of Staff. It was a good choice, thought Indira. Andrew was a quiet and thoughtful young man. Not flamboyant, but very hard-working. And, while he had done the job capably, he did not have either Ludmilla or Takashi's flair as a platoon leader.

Indira watched Ludmilla's platoon racing in a loop around the right flank of the Utuku army. Ludmilla herself was leading the platoon, and setting a brutal pace. The ranks of the Utuku were already becoming ragged, as they tried to reform in the face of this new and utterly bizarre foe. Their attempts were hopeless, of course. Gukuy were faster than owoc, but they were still much slower afoot than humans. Any humans, much less the young warriors trained under Joseph's brutal regimen.

Not brutal enough.

"Andrew—make a note. We must emphasize long distance endurance as well as wind sprints. The Apaches could run a hundred miles a day. Faster, over long distances, than the cavalry of the US Army."

"Yes, Indira." He jotted in his notebook.

Still, there's a problem. Food. What good will it do for our warriors to be able to run a hundred miles a day—if they starve at the end of it? Our army cannot remain tied to the slow owoc.

"Julius—make a note. Resume the experiments with puke jerky."

"But—ah, yes, Indira." He jotted in his notebook. Muttering, under his breath. He was not altogether sure what to make of this new Indira. He had always adored her thin-featured face. Why did that face now remind him of a sword?

As Indira watched, Ludmilla's platoon suddenly wheeled and raced directly toward the Utuku right. Even from the distance, she could hear the drums, transmitting orders from the battle leaders. Raggedly, she thought. And it was obvious that the Utuku ranks were beginning to unravel.

Now.

But she had misjudged. Ludmilla had a better grasp of the immediate tactics. She held the charge for another few seconds, before she suddenly halted and cast her javelin. A split second later, the rest of the platoon followed.

The volley sailed over the front rank of the Utuku and fell among the battle leaders beyond. Like so many lightning bolts. Utuku shieldwork was designed to protect against looping flail-blows, not spears. And the wicker-like visors protecting the battle leaders' heads were like matchsticks when struck by heavy spears instead of blowpipe darts.

"Andrew—make a note for general consideration. Most of the great armies of human history placed a premium on low-echelon initiative and tactical flexibility."

"Yes, Indira."

Ludmilla's platoon was now racing away from the Utuku. Their assegais were strapped to their backs. In their hands they carried javelins. Each warrior in Ludmilla and Takashi's platoons had been given four at the beginning of the battle.

The javelins had been invented by Joseph, in the course of the new training which he had developed in consultation with Nukurren and Jens Knudsen. They were better designed for casting than the heavy-bladed assegai. And the blades were made of bronze obtained from the Pilgrims at Fagoshau. The irreplaceable steel-bladed assegai were saved for close-in work.

"Rottu—a question. How much bronze can we make every eightday?"

The gukuy hesitated before responding.

"I am not certain, Inudira. Not much, at Fagoshau. We can expand the bronze-works, of course. But there is no copper on the Chiton, and very little tin."

"Make a note, then. We must immediately establish reliable sources for the two metals. And expand the bronzeworks."

"Yes, Inudira."

Down on the plain, Ludmilla's sudden retreat had achieved its purpose. Large sections of the Utuku right were lumbering in pursuit. Very unevenly. Confusion and the sudden killing of many leaders were eroding the famed Utuku discipline.

And it is very hard to resist the temptation of chasing what appears to be a foe in flight.

She watched, gauging the moment.

Now.

But, once again, Ludmilla was right. The platoon leader did not order the counterattack for several more seconds, until the pursuing Utuku were strung out even further. Suddenly, her platoon divided and curved sharply right and left, racing back toward the Utuku. The bewildered barbarians were thrown into utter confusion.

Now.

Once again, Ludmilla was right. Two more seconds elapsed before she gave the command. The ensuing volley came at pointblank range, ripping through the Utuku like a scythe.

"Andrew—that last note?"

"Yes, Indira?"

"Emphasize it."

Racing off again, the platoon reformed in files and curved back around to the southeast. Discipline in the Utuku right flank was disintegrating. The warriors were little more than a mob now, all of them turning to face these terrible demons who were circling them. Within moments, they were faced completely away from the center of the battlefield.

Indira looked to the center. Takashi's platoon was drawn up there, holding the attention of the Utuku center while Ludmilla harrowed the right. They had no difficulty in doing so. Takashi's first volley had had a catastrophic impact on the battle leaders of the Utuku center. Since then, he had kept the attention of the warriors by trotting his platoon back and forth across their lines, feinting and lunging.

Her eyes moved to Joseph. The Captain was standing back, on a small knoll rising slightly above the plain, high enough to give him a view of the entire battlefield. Twenty young human warriors stood at his side, Jens Knudsen looming above the others.

Not far from them, off to the side, stood Nukurren. Gazing down at the huge, scarred figure, Indira felt a sudden sadness. They were deeply in debt to Nukurren, and had tried to express it. Ushulubang herself had offered Nukurren the command of the Pilgrim warriors who were even now approaching the battleground.

But Nukurren had refused. Had even refused to explain her refusal.

Yet, in the end, she had chosen to come to the battleground. The morning the little human army set off, Jens Knudsen had entered Nukurren's hut. In his arms he bore the great flail and twofork Nukurren had won years before in the Anshac legions, and her armor. He had saved them from the wreckage of the slaver caravan where he and Nukurren had first exchanged wounds, he explained, and now it was time to return them to her. Saying nothing else, he had left the hut.

Some minutes later the column of human warriors set off, followed by more than a thousand Pilgrims. All of the Pilgrims were armed with flail and fork; some with armor. Most were former warriors. Some were former helots, fumbling with the unfamiliar weapons in their palps, but determined to do their duty.

As the column passed Nukurren's hut, she had emerged. In armor, bearing her great flail and two-fork. To the humans, she had been awesome. To the gukuy . . . The Pilgrims had begun hooting then, in a fierce and wavering manner which Indira had never heard, but had no difficulty recognizing. So had the Bedouins ululated, saluting their champions.

But Nukurren had refused to acknowledge the salute. Had returned the admiration with bleak isolation. Had spoken to none. Had not taken a place in the column, neither with human nor gukuy. Throughout the long march which followed, she had remained to one side, parallel but alone.

As the march progressed, the Pilgrims lagged further and further behind, unable to match the speed of the human warriors. Of all the gukuy marching to battle, only Nukurren had been able to keep pace. But, always, she marched to the side. What role, if any, she intended to play in the coming battle, no one knew.

She least of all, thought Indira now, watching Nukurren standing alone on the slope.

Indira tore her eyes away, and looked back at Joseph. Stretching on either side of him were the remnants of Andrew MacPherson's platoon. Most of the warriors in Andrew's former platoon had been reassigned to the other two. But a small number had been organized into a new formation, led by Jens Knudsen. They were to serve as Joseph's reserve, for the critical moment of the battle.

Gazing down at Jens' new formation, Indira began to feel the old, paralyzing anguish. She fought it desperately. It had been she herself, after all, who had commanded its creation.

The warriors in the new formation were more heavily armored than the other humans. They carried no javelins, only the largest assegai. Theirs was not the role of Ludmilla and Takashi's platoons, the fluid ravaging of the opponent. Theirs was the role of shock troops. It was they who would be thrown into the *schwerpunkt*. Not for them the rapid maneuvers of the platoons; not for them, the tactical subtleties; for them—the shattering smash of the hoplite.

They had been selected, as individuals, for that purpose. The emphasis had been on sheer strength, rather than speed. Upper body strength, in particular. Only that kind of strength could sustain a warrior in the savage close-quarter combat for which that formation was designed.

They were all male. For the first time in the history of the human colony, the sexes had been segregated. Indira herself had commanded it. She had hated the truth, but would not shy from it. Only Ludmilla, among the human women, had the strength to serve in Jens' new formation. And Ludmilla was needed as a platoon commander.

She gazed down at Jens Knudsen. Even covered with heavy armor, his golden hair and milk-white skin was easy to spot.

Indira thought that of the younger generation of humans, Jens' was perhaps the gentlest and kindest spirit, for all his brutish size and musculature. Indira herself had named the new formation the "shock squad." Jens, with his usual self-deprecating humor, had called his squad the "meatheads."

"Too slow to run, and too dumb to figure out anything else," he had joked. But Indira could not mistake the pride in his stance, and that of his new squad, as they stood by Joseph's side.

Alexander's Companions.

They would suffer the highest casualties, and they knew it. But they were not afraid, because a new emotion was insinuating its way into their souls, like a serpent.

For the first time in the history of the human colony, an elite had been created. At Indira's own command. She began to look away, then forced herself to look back.

Not now, no. Not with Jens, never. But—Jens will die, and his children, and their children, and their children—and then, someday ... the Diadochi. And the Praetorian Guard, and the Janissaries, and the knights who savaged Jerusalem.

Nightmare visions flashed through her mind, ending with the *Waffen SS.* She felt her face grow stiff.

Julius gazed at her quizzically. Indira pointed to Jens.

"I was just thinking how the old Waffen SS would have drooled over him." A rueful grimace; trying to cast off despair with humor. "He could have served as the model for their recruitment posters."

Julius looked down.

"Oh, I don't know. He's much too ugly, with that great beak of a nose, and besides—" He looked back at Indira, his expression oddly cold. "Did I ever tell you my family's history?"

"Not really."

He shrugged. "Nothing spectacular. And most of it's long forgotten. But there's one episode, from two centuries ago, that was passed on from generation to generation. My family was in Denmark during the Second World War. They lived in Copenhagen, as a matter of fact, the same city where Jens was born."

Julius pointed down the slope to the young warrior.

"I stand here today because of his ancestors." His voice suddenly shook with anger. "Damn your fears, Indira! *Damn them all to hell!*"

His words were like a sudden, brilliant ray of sunlight, shattering all the darkness of the future. The nightmares fled from Indira's mind, gibbering in terror; and new visions came.

She remembered the small nation which, conquered and occupied, had still managed to save almost all its Jews from the Nazi butchers; had, through the unorganized and spontaneous actions of thousands of ordinary Danes, smuggled the Jews to safety. The blond-haired, blue-eyed people who had hurled defiance into the face of their racial brethren.

The kindness of that deed, toward a people of a different race, had come from the common pool of human decency. But the courage had come from their own history, and their own legends, and their own heritage.

They too had remembered Barbarossa. And if the Germans had chosen to remember the sword of the conqueror—had even named their brutal invasion of Russia after him—the Danes had chosen to remember the shield of the lawgiver.

The Nazi vision, she knew, had been closer to the truth of the past; but the Danish vision had been true to the future. If, in reality, kings had been unjust tyrants, yet, still, it had been within the shell of kingship that nations forged their justice. The kings were gone, long gone; but justice remained. And if the kings had been hard as iron, the justice was harder still. For justice had been long in the making, and it was not a feeble reed. It was the gleaming steel sword Excalibur, born of ancient dreams, shaped by myths and legends, forged by human struggle, and tempered in the blood of centuries.

As Indira watched the battle unfold below her, she felt as if her mind were split in two. One half observed the present carnage—attentively, coldly, objectively. The other half ranged across the breadth of human history, like a shaman taking the form of an eagle, spotting all the possibilities of the future. And, finally, leaving all fear behind, filled with the joy of flight and the glory of distant vision.

Joseph's powerful baritone suddenly rang above the din of battle. Refocusing her attention, Indira saw that Joseph had sent Takashi's platoon plunging into the fray. The Pilgrims had finally arrived, and were taking their place before the Utuku center. Takashi's platoon made a sudden lunge. The Utuku drew back, clustering their shield wall. The feint had succeeded, and

Takashi's platoon was now racing across the enemy's front, toward the east.

As planned, the warriors of the Utuku center were paralyzed. The Pilgrims surged forward, to keep them immobile. The Utuku center would be completely out of the action when Takashi fell—

Indira looked back to the southeast.

—on the rear of the Utuku right. Whose attention was completely fixed on Ludmilla's confusing maneuvers.

Takashi was setting an even more brutal pace than Ludmilla. He and his warriors seemed to fly across the ground, as if possessed by a determination to match the exploits of Ludmilla's platoon.

"Andrew, take a note. We must give each platoon a name, or a number. Some title by which they can be remembered, and to which their soldiers can identify. In human history, that was called the regimental tradition. It will help develop the morale of the army."

"Yes, Indira."

A minute later, the slaughter began. Watching the ferocity with which Takashi's platoon ripped into the Utuku, Indira felt a moment's fear that they had forgotten what she had told them.

But, again, the commander on the spot had simply gauged the timing better. When they broke off and raced away, not one of the human warriors was more than slightly scratched. But they left a mound of bodies behind them.

"Andrew—that note. The one concerning low-echelon tactical control."

"Yes, Indira."

"Carve it in stone. Better yet, cast it in bronze."

Ludmilla's platoon now copied Takashi's maneuver, from the other side. Lunge in, at a speed which was almost incomprehensible to the gukuy, and butcher the front ranks. Race away before the ranks behind could overwhelm you with their numbers.

Working from two sides, Ludmilla and Takashi's platoons were ravaging the Utuku right. Their javelins were now used up; they were wielding the assegai. Fifteen hundred gukuy warriors were now nothing more than a hooting mob, milling about in confusion, their mantles rippling red and ochre, while less than two hundred and fifty human warriors continued their systematic slaughter. Only three human casualties had been suffered so far—and Indira had been relieved to see one of them hobbling off the field under her own power. Winny Mbateng, she thought it was.

Thank God. Even if your daughter's crippled from the injury, Janet, there will be a place for her. Adrian has been howling for help.

Indira saw an Utuku piper take aim at one of the human warriors. She caught her breath—then released it a moment later, when the piper's aim was thrown off by the press of the mob around her.

It's ironic. The gukuy consider pipers nothing more than auxiliaries. But they're what I fear most. Those darts have a range of thirty yards, blown by a gukuy with a powerful siphon. And they're quite accurate within half that distance. Light, of course. Even against a thin-skinned human they can't do much damage unless they strike the eyes or the throat. The light armor which our warriors wear is probably enough to turn most darts, as well as absorbing some of the shock of a flail-blow.

But if they ever learn how utterly vulnerable we are to animal product—

"Ghodha—and Rottu. Do any gukuy armies use poisoned darts?"

Rottu's mantle remained gray, but Ghodha's rippled orange.

"No, Inudira," replied Rottu. "There are a few small clans of savages in a swamp far to the southeast who are reputed to use poisoned darts. But no civilized people does so. Not even the barbarians. Not even the Utuku. It is a foul abomination in the eyes of Uftu and Kaklo alike. And the war goddess of the Utuku as well."

Indira was simultaneously relieved—and intrigued. Goloku, in her teachings, had not attempted to deny or undermine the existence of the old religious pantheons. She had simply absorbed them within a new and profoundly more philosophical approach to reality.

Like Vedanta Hinduism. Sort of. Oh, stop trying to find an exact analogy, Indira. There is none. The Way is unique to itself—and better, I think, that any of the great religions of Earth. I can think of no Terran religion, at least, which

*from the outset based itself on the principles of dialectics rather
than formalism.*

She remembered the schismatic Patriarchs of the later
Roman empire. The persecution of the Arian heretics, and the
Nestorians, and the Monophysites. And the rigid Aristotelean
logic of the medieval churchmen. And the Inquisition; and
Bruno burning at the stake. And Galileo's trial.

*Perhaps that much we can avoid. Ushulubang and I,
together, can sow much salt in the ground of future dogma.*

Then she remembered the statue at Fagoshau which
Ushulubang had shattered with her flail.

*But neither she nor I will live forever. And it is indeed true,
as Goloku said, that beings will always lapse into the error
of the Answer.*

She straightened her slender shoulders.

*But we can try. And, in failing, shorten the road to the
future. And its pain.*

*And stop day-dreaming about the future! There's enough
agony on today's road.*

She forced her eyes back to the plain. The human platoons
were continuing their butchery, like a well-oiled machine of
destruction.

*God, these kids are good. It's amazing how well they're
carrying out my proposal—which they only heard two days
ago.*

The night she made her decision to throw their strength
to the aid of the Kiktu, Indira had spoken to the little army
of human warriors. She had told them the story of the battle
of Liegnitz, in a place called Poland. There, Subedei's Mongols
had met the forces of European chivalry under the command
of Duke Henry of Silesia. Those forces included knights from
all the major militant orders as well as Henry's own troops—
Knights Templar, Teutonic Knights, Knights Hospitaler.

She had described the European knights. Heavily armored,
dangerous at close quarters. And—very slow; easily confused
by any tactics beyond a simple, direct charge.

She had described Subedei's Mongols. Lightly armored;
extremely fast; extremely disciplined; shrewd and cunning; well
coordinated in battle.

Then she described the battle itself. And told them how
the Mongols had cut to pieces the flower of chivalry.

Joseph and his lieutenants had taken over from there. The new tactics which they had been developing recently, with Nukurren's advice, fit perfectly into the plan which they developed for the coming battle. The plan which they were now implementing on the plain below—with, it was obvious to Indira as she watched, the same result that had ensued centuries before, on a planet light years away.

After another minute, Indira looked away. Even from the distance, it was impossible not to hear the hoots and whistles of the Utuku being butchered.

Not a trace of what she was feeling showed on her face.

And what am I feeling, anyway? Joseph and his lieutenants would have arrived at the same plan on their own. With Nukurren's help, they were already almost there. My lecture on Mongol cavalry tactics only added some polish.

No, that's a lie. Don't hide from it, woman. They're not superhuman. Only the Mother of Demons could have given them the confidence they needed, in their first real battle.

She took a deep breath.

So be it. There will also be hospitals. And medical academies. And trade. And religious toleration, enforced by the demons. All that the Mongols gave—and more. We are not, after all, Neolithic barbarians. Whose cruelty derived, in part, from their naive understanding of the world.

When she now spoke her voice, for the first time that day, had a trace of its usual softness.

"Julius—make a note. We must found a university. At once—regardless of other things."

He smiled. "Yes, Indira. Does that mean I get to go back to research?"

Indira looked at him; and reached out and stroked his cheek. But she did not smile in return.

"Yes, love. But the first thing you must study is the problem of making puke jerky."

She looked away. "And the problem of poison darts. Abomination or not, they will be used soon enough. We must try to find an antidote, if possible. If not—"

Her voice was like iron.

"—we will develop our own poisons. Remember the gukuy who killed Adams—and then died herself? As you said at the time: *it cuts both ways, asshole.*"

She heard Julius sigh, and mutter something. She was not sure, but she thought she heard the words correctly. She suppressed a laugh.

"Like Damascus steel," he had mumbled. "No, worse—like a damned blade of Toledo."

Indira turned her eyes to the west. That part of the battle which the humans were waging was progressing well. She now had time to study the methods of their new—allies? She was not sure of their status, for there had been no opportunity to establish communication with the Kiktu. By the time the human platoons had reached the plain, the battle had already started.

Crude and primitive, was her first thought. The battle on the Utuku left seemed nothing but a swirl of confusion, so unlike the precision she had watched on the human side.

Her eyes were almost immediately drawn to the huge figure at the center of the Kiktu lines.

"Ghodha—a question." Indira pointed. "Is that a battlemother?"

"Yes, Inudira. There is another, as well. Further along the Utuku lines."

Indira followed Ghodha's gesture.

"Yes, I see her now." A moment later: "But—she seems different from the other one. The one in the center."

Ghodha's whistle combined, somehow, humor and awe.

"All battlemothers in the world are different from the one in the center, Inudira. The one in the center is a—what is the word, Rottu? The one the Kiktu use?"

"*Kuoptu.*"

Indira was not familiar with the term. Rottu explained.

She looked back. And felt a certain awe herself. She had seen gukuy mothers before. There were several of them among the Pilgrims. Huge beings, as big as elephants. Immensely strong, she imagined. But extremely slow-moving and awkward.

The battlemother on the plain below bore a certain generic resemblance. Huge—bigger than any gukuy mother Indira had yet seen. Almost as big as an owoc mother. And, compared to the warriors around her, slow and awkward.

There the comparison ended. If a normal mother could be likened to a gigantic St. Bernard, the battlemother on the plain below was like the Fenris wolf of Nordic mythology. Indira winced, watching an Utuku warrior smashed into jelly beneath the battlemother's club. And another. And another.

"She fights with two clubs, I notice. But the other battlemother only with one."

"Yes, Inudira. The other battlemother is fighting in the usual manner, with mace and shield. Battlemothers need shields to protect them from darts. They are always the main target of pipers. The one in the center is taking a great risk. She seems to be relying on her visor alone—and that odd shield on her cowl."

Indira looked for the Utuku pipers. She spotted one almost immediately. Sure enough, the piper was taking aim at the battlemother. Indira held her breath. Suddenly, however, the piper reared back, clawing at her eyes.

At her side, Indira heard Ghodha's hoot of surprise.

"Look! I did not see them earlier! There are males on the battlemother's cowl—with pipes! Behind that strange shield. They are protecting her from the pipers."

Indira looked back. A moment later she saw another Utuku piper reel back.

"Is that common?"

"It is unheard of! True, the Kiktu have the custom that a mother's consorts are her personal guard of pipers. But it is not taken seriously, even by the Kiktu. Not even the barbarians, for all their loose habits regarding males, allow the silly things to participate in battle. Males are too emotional for battle. They would lose their heads."

Indira watched another piper blinded. When she spoke, her voice was harsh.

"Welcome to the new world, Ghodha. Where Answers are falling, and Questions are being asked."

From the corner of her eye, Indira saw Ghodha's mantle ripple ochre and pink.

Between Ushulubang and myself, she thought fiercely, *I intend to see a lot of those colors in the future.*

A moment later, she relented.

Ghodha is not, after all, one of Ushulubang's close apashoc. A new Pilgrim, hoping that there may be an end to evil, somewhere. Selected for her new post not for her profound grasp of the Way, but simply because she is the most experienced war leader among the Pilgrims.

Do not sneer at such people, Professor Toledo. However often they fumble the task, they are the creators of the future.

"Explain to me what you are seeing, Ghodha. You are more experienced in such things than I."

The warrior's scarred mantle became tinged with faint green. She began pointing with her palps.

"The Kiktu are fighting better than I have ever seen barbarians fight before. Not as well as the Anshac legions, of course. But better."

The gesture of grudging admission.

"Much better, in fact. You see how they are not simply swarming mindlessly, as usual?"

Indira looked again. After a moment, she saw what Ghodha was pointing to. Order began to appear out of chaos.

"They are fighting in organized groups. I can see it now. Sloppy, I think, but—organized."

"Yes. They are very sloppy." A whistle of derision. "You should see the Anshac legions!"

Again, pink and ochre rippled.

"What am I saying? Even the Anshac are nothing, compared to your own ummun apalatunush."

Ghodha turned and looked to the south. Indira's eyes followed. Ludmilla and Takashi's warriors were racing back and forth, slicing the Utuku flank to ribbons. The platoons had broken into squads, now, each of which operated independently—but still within the organized control of their leaders.

Indira turned and pointed back to the west.

"Explain further."

Ghodha looked away, slowly. Indira was amused at the veteran warrior's obvious reluctance to forego the pleasure of watching master craftsmanship in her trade.

A moment later, Ghodha continued.

"The Kiktu possess three strengths in the art of battle. As individuals, their warriors are excellent. It cannot be denied. There are none on the Meat of the Clam who surpass them in the use of fork-and-flail, and few who can claim to be their equal. Look there! You will see what I mean."

Indira followed Ghodha's pointing palp. She saw, at the edge of the battle, that a Kiktu had somehow managed to lure a single Utuku away from the lines. The single combat which followed was horrifyingly brutal, but illuminating. The Kiktu warrior picked apart the Utuku's clumsy defenses. Within seconds, the Utuku shield was stripped away by a flail-blow that was almost too fast for Indira to follow. Seconds later, the Utuku's right ped was a bloody mass of shredded flesh, and the Utuku slumped. A split-second later, the Kiktu's fork slammed into the left side of her opponent's mantle. The Kiktu threw herself to the side, levering the Utuku onto her back. The four flail-strokes which followed completely disembow-eled the doomed warrior.

More than disemboweled, thought Indira, repressing a sudden taste of vomit. *All the vital organs of a gukuy, except the brain, are located right under the belly, with no cartilage or shell or thick integument to protect them. That's not just guts being strewn all over the plain. That's her heart, her liver, her inner lungs—everything.*

Somewhat shakily, she asked Julius: "This is what you were telling me, isn't it?"

Julius' face was pale, but his gaze was steady.

"Yes, love. Although—I won't be so smug about it, anymore. Not after seeing that."

He took a deep breath.

"The gukuy pay a price for the way their bodies evolved. In their manipulatory limbs as well as their peds. For reasons I can only guess at, gukuy evolution put almost all their fine control into their arms. Wonderfully precise and delicate organs, those are. Maria told me she's planning to train gukuy sur-geons. She thinks they'll make better surgeons than humans, once they learn the skill.

"But their tentacles lost something in the bargain. They're very strong, and fast. But they don't begin to have the fine coordination of human arms and hands. That's why the gukuy can't really use weapons like spears. Or swords. With spears, they'd miss their targets. And with swords, they'd be more likely to hit with the flat of the blade rather than the edge. What results is—"

He pointed to the battlefield. Then, suddenly, turned away. Indira could see him struggling with his own stomach.

When Julius turned back, his face was even paler.

"But, like I said, I won't be so smug about it any more. Never having seen a gukuy battle, I expected something much more clumsy. I never dreamed that you could do so much damage with a flail."

Indira turned back to Ghodha.

"Continue, please."

"Their second strength is their speed."

Somehow, watching the battle, Indira no longer found the term "gukuy speed" an oxymoron.

"The Kiktu are very swift and agile. Nothing, of course, compared to"—a quick, admiring glance to the south— "ummun, but for gukuy—very fast. Very fast. You see how they lure Utuku after them into little traps?"

Indira watched for a minute or so, and nodded.

Ghodha made the gesture of admiration.

"The Kiktu excel in the art of ambush. Many foolish and arrogant Anshac legion commanders have led their warriors to disaster, from underestimating the cleverness of the barbarians."

Ghodha now pointed to the center of the Kiktu lines.

"Finally, they have the battlemothers." Faint ripples of blue and yellow appeared on the warrior's mantle.

"It is a barbarous custom. But—"

The blue and yellow vanished.

"—I admit, it is terrible to face a Kiktu battlemother in battle. Especially one with good flankers."

Ghodha paused, examining the battle.

"The flankers of this battlemother are excellent. You see how they force the enemy to face their battlemother's maces? Leaving them nowhere to dodge aside?"

Indira nodded.

"Nothing can withstand the strength of a battlemother. The strongest armor is like paper beneath the blows of her mace."

Indira winced. Just that moment, an Utuku warrior *burst*— like a ripe tomato—under the mace of the battlemother.

"Faced with a battlemother, a warrior can only rely on speed and agility. That is the purpose of the flankers—to nullify the enemy's maneuvering room."

The sound of Joseph's bellow drew her eyes back to the center. He had decided, Indira saw, that the climatic moment of the battle was upon them. Quickly scanning the field, Indira thought his judgement was correct. The Utuku right had been shredded by the platoons; the left, forced to fight the Kiktu alone, were on the verge of collapse; there remained only the huddled center to be—smashed.

Joseph was already racing off the knoll, straight toward the Utuku center. Jens and his squad kept pace with him. A moment later the human warriors drew even with the Pilgrim line. The Pilgrims immediately followed the charge.

The drums of the Utuku center began beating frantically.

Ordering what, I wonder? What orders do you give your butchers—when the demons come?

Of the human warriors plunging toward the Utuku center, only Joseph held a javelin. At the last moment before reaching the enemy line, he cast his weapon.

Indira watched—first with surprise, and then with awe— as Joseph's javelin rose higher and higher into the sky. Higher and higher. Beyond its flight, far back, stood the figure of the *ogghoxt* commander.

I don't believe it.

"I don't believe it," whispered Julius. "That's a gold medal in the Olympics."

The javelin reached the top of its arc and began sailing down.

"No, Julius," she said.

Straight toward the *ogghoxt* commander.

I don't think she even sees it coming.

The javelin struck right between the commander's eyes, and sank at least two feet into her head. She fell like a stone.

"That spear cast belongs to an earlier time. Only Homer could have done it justice."

Joseph and Jens, side by side, smashed into the Utuku. The other members of the shock squad formed a wedge behind them. As the ferocity of their attack split open the Utuku center, the Pilgrims poured in behind, widening the breach.

On the left, Ludmilla and Takashi now ordered a change in tactics. The platoons abandoned all subtlety and fell onto the Utuku, assegais flashing. The Utuku right flank, already demoralized, began to give way completely.

On the right, Indira heard a sudden burst of gukuy voices, speaking in a tongue she did not know.

Kiktu battle language, she realized. Far back, perched upon a battlemother who had remained out of the fray, she spotted the figure of a gukuy. The new commands were issuing from her, and being passed forward. Suddenly, the Kiktu warriors abandoned their fluid maneuvers and smashed directly into the Utuku.

That must be Kopporu. She, too, realizes that the decisive moment is here.

The Utuku left began to collapse.

"Oh, shit," she heard Julius whisper.

She looked to the center, and held her breath. Joseph, Jens, and their small squad of shock troops had become isolated. Inexperienced in a large battle, using combined forces, they had overestimated the ability of the Pilgrims to keep pace with them. They were surrounded now by Utuku warriors. Here, in the relatively unblooded center, the Utuku battle commanders had been able to maintain a semblance of discipline and control. Now, seeing the demons finally immobilized, the Utuku took courage and began a frenzied assault.

The Mother of Demons watched her children begin to die. The combat was furious, the carnage incredible; and for every human boy who fell, a dozen Utuku were slain. Some strange, new, cold part of her mind took satisfaction in the fact. But—

Indira watched the blood gush from Harry Jackson's neck, half severed by a flail blow, and knew he would be dead within seconds; and remembered the time she had held him in her arms, trying to console a sobbing eight-year-old boy desolated by the death of the little owoc spawn he had tried to shelter. She watched an Utuku warrior, with her dying effort, wrestle Esteban Sanchez to the ground. Watched as the flails of other Utuku rained down upon him. Watched Jens try to save him, be driven back, then rally. Watched the methodical fury with which he butchered the Utuku assailing his comrade. Watched his heroic effort fail of its purpose. For even at that distance Indira could read the lifelessness in Esteban's body, when Jens finally reached him. Watched a cluster of Utuku surge over Ahmed Khoury and Ed Kincaid, stripping flesh from bones. And saw them recoil, their murderous work done, from Joseph's terrible vengeance.

The Pilgrims pushed forward, trying to break through to the isolated humans. The shield wall held them back. The Utuku warriors in the center were regaining courage, seeing the demons finally die. The Utuku flanks were now caving in completely, and Indira thought the battle would be won. But not in time to save the handful of boys trapped in the center pocket.

And now we're learning the oldest secret of war, she thought bitterly. *No battle plan survives contact with the enemy.*

Were it not for Joseph and Jens, she knew, the little pocket of human warriors would have been overrun by now. But those were the two strongest of the human warriors, the greatest, and they were now in the fullness of their rage, and their power, and their glory. And while a part of Indira's mind wept for her dying children, and another part quailed at the fearsome slaughter Joseph and Jens were wreaking in their downfall—

Some other part, some ancient part, some grim and savage part she had never known existed, tracing its long and twisted lineage back to the Incas and the *Mahabharata,* howled its banshee triumph and shrieked fierce exultation.

Die, cannibals, die. You face the true demons now. The great ones! The old ones born anew! The ones from the deepest pits of damnation. You do not know their names? I will name them for you, cannibals. Tremble! Wail! The one, you may call Shaka Zulu. The other, Ragnar Lothbrook.

It was only that part of Indira which kept her gaze steady, and her eyes dry. The Mother of Demons had sent her children into battle, and she would not flinch at their death.

A sudden movement to the side caught her eye. A figure was racing down the slope. Was already at the bottom. Was already crossing the plain. Was already approaching the battle zone.

"No gukuy can move that fast!" protested Julius.

"Watch, ummun," commanded Ghodha. "We too have legends."

To Indira, what followed seemed a slow-moving dream. Her mind felt suspended.

To the Pilgrims, Nukurren passed through their lines like a wraith, sweeping them behind her in sudden hope, hooting renewed confidence and determination. The Pilgrims poured into the great gaping hole Nukurren was tearing in the Utuku center, ululating, their mantles blue and black. Hesitation was cast aside, uncertainty scorned, all fear abandoned. Of high caste or helot birth, it mattered not at all. They were the Warriors of the Coil, now, the Flails of the Way, and there were none who could withstand them, led by their champion.

To Julius Cohen, biologist, Nukurren struck the shield wall like a charging grizzly bear, scattering warriors like so many leaves. During the carnage which followed, as Nukurren ripped through the Utuku ranks with mind-boggling ferocity, Julius found it impossible to think of her as a gukuy warrior armed with weapons. All his learned theories vanished. All his professorial estimates of the limitations of the molluscan Bauplan seemed a mirage. Watching Nukurren now, he could think of nothing, at first, but some great predator from the Terran past, a tyrannosaur stalking the earth of an alien planet. Until a different image came, of that *dragon* which lives only in the dark imagination of mankind.

To the Utuku also she was a monster beyond belief, whose fork struck like a flail and whose flail struck like the very lightning. Under Nukurren's blows, their shields shattered, their armor splintered, their tough mantles shredded like jelly, their blood gushed forth like fountains and their entrails shrouded the earth. Every blow of her flail, every stroke of her twofork, was *kutuku*. They could no more withstand her than they could have withstood the Great Kraken itself, and, in the mounting terror of her passage, their courage fled with the wind. Scarlet-mantled, half-paralyzed, they fell like gana beneath the flails of the Pilgrims who followed.

To Joseph Adekunle, and Jens Knudsen, and the other young men in the center who still survived, Nukurren came like something out of their distant past. An alien creature, bringing to life the history which they had learned, but not really understood; had heard, but not truly grasped. A misshapen, tentacled, colorless form, who brought them all the rainbow hues of their ancestry.

Separated from their origins by light-years and centuries, orphaned, cast adrift save for a handful of adults, the human youth finally came into their inheritance. All of it. The truths, the myths, the legends; and, foundation of them all, that bleak, unyielding, boundless courage which made all myths, all legends, and all truths possible.

They knew, now, the Spartans at Thermopylae; and the sunken road at Shiloh; and the *impis* at Isandhlwana; and Chuikov's 62nd Army in the shattered factories on the Volga.

Despair and exhaustion vanished. Bleeding, bruised, maimed, they hurled themselves upon the shield wall which surrounded them. And broke it; and then slew, and slew, and slew, and slew.

The young men, fiery savage children of a gentle civilized mother, slew with neither ruth nor pity. Because they knew, now, in the freshness of their youth, what their mother was only beginning to accept, in the fullness of her wisdom.

Watching Nukurren come, they knew Horatius at the bridge, and heard Roland's horn at Roncevalles. They hailed Musashi's honor, saluted Pendragon on his throne; and knelt to Saladin's mercy. And felt, beneath their feet, shaking the very mountain, the giant Barbarossa, waking from his sleep.

But all Indira saw, or ever remembered, was floating beauty on a plain of death. The strange grace of an huge and ugly gukuy, scattering destruction like seeds of grain. The utter silence of a warrior, in the bedlam of a battlefield.

Above all, throughout the years to come, she remembered the *shoroku* of a helot born to hopelessness. That royal, imperial *shoroku*. The color of that scarred mantle, bearing the burden of a new world's hope as if it were but a feather. That gray, that beautiful gray, that glorious gray, that impossible gray. That gray which never wavered.

Indira scanned the battlefield. A vast scarlet wave swept across the mantles of the entire Utuku army, a tsunami of terror. The same color was everywhere, within seconds. And followed, moments later, by a cacophony of hoots and whistles. The Utuku ranks dissolved completely before her eyes. Most of the enemy warriors were still alive, but they were nothing but a panicky mob. Even as she watched, she saw an Utuku battle leader trampled underfoot by a mass of warriors seeking nothing now but their own lives.

Dimly, she heard Ghodha say, with a tone of great satisfaction: "The battle is won. And wonderfully! The Utuku have been defeated before, on occasion. But there is no record of them being routed. Today, we have done it!"

Wonderful, yes. New legends were forged this day, and will be chanted, again and again. And will give courage in the future. Courage we will need.

Courage I need now.

The next voice was the one she dreaded—that of Andrew

MacPherson. Born in Scotland, not twenty years ago. Hardly more than a boy. The Chief of Staff of the Mother of Demons, and her army:

"What are your commands?"

She postponed the moment.

"Rottu—a question. I have asked it before, but . . . I will ask again. The Utuku warriors who have been recruited from other tribes. They can—"

Rottu immediately understood the question.

"Yes, Inudira. Their old clan markings will have been carved off their mantles. They can be easily recognized by those scars."

Rottu answered her next question before she even asked.

"And, yes, it is easy to determine which are recent recruits. And which have been long accustomed to the Utuku savagery."

The moment could be delayed no longer.

"Any of the recent recruits who surrender will be taken alive."

"And the others, Indira?" asked Andrew.

She thought of the Sixth Army, dying in the Russian winter. Nazis, some. Most—ordinary workers and farmers, many of them barely beyond childhood. Each of them a unique universe, never seen before, never to exist again; in all the eons of the galaxies. Her voice froze in her throat; until, far below, she saw Nukurren standing over her bleeding children, guarding them from the swirling chaos; and found the color gray.

"Kill them," she said, in a voice that never wavered. "Kill them all. Make certain they are all dead. Spear the wounded. Spear the mortally injured. Spear any of which there is any doubt at all. There must be no survivors from this battle, except the captive new recruits. Perhaps those can be salvaged. If not, we will kill them later."

The eyes which she turned on Andrew were like ice.

"Do you understand, Andrew? *Not one survivor.* No Utuku who can bring the tale of this battle back to the Beak. That monster must be kept in darkness, for as long as possible. We need as much time as we can create for ourselves, to prepare for the future battles. And—if this army simply disappears, even the most hardened Utuku warriors will be filled with terror. We will need that terror."

"I understand." A moment later, he was racing down the slope.

Indira turned away and began walking up the slope. After taking a few steps, she stopped. Julius enfolded her in his arms, and she began sobbing like a child.

Behind her, Rottu watched. Very carefully. She had never witnessed it before personally, but she had listened to reports from the Pilgrims who had spent time among the ummun. She knew she was seeing the ummun equivalent of brown grief. Dark brown, she judged. Very dark brown.

Satisfied, Rottu turned away. She had learned much, this day. Her report to Ushulubang would be long and full. And even the old sage would admit that some questions have answers. Answers, at least, which are good enough for the perils of the present.

The answer to one question was obvious. The Mother of Demons was, indeed, as Ushulubang had suspected, the mistress of the art of war. Rottu had thought the sage was probably correct, in this as in most things. But she had not been certain—until she watched triple-eighty ummun warriors destroy half an Utuku army.

But that was a small question. Now, she would be able to answer Ushulubang's big question as well.

She gazed down at the plain. Below her, the massacre was already underway. The Kiktu and the Pilgrims were methodically butchering the mass of the enemy, milling in stunned confusion, while the fleet warriors of the ummun apalatunush relentlessly brought down those Utuku who tried to flee.

She looked away—not from horror, but from the indifference of long experience. She was an old gukuy. Not as old as Ushulubang, but old enough. Old enough to have seen more cruelty and brutality than she could remember. The world had always been so. She had thought it always would, until she met Ushulubang.

I have your answer, Ushulubang. A good enough answer, at least, to lead us forward to the questions of the future. And the Way is no longer a narrow path. It has suddenly broadened into a wide road. Full of pain, as ever. But also, I think, a glory beyond description.

She looked up at the gray canopy of the sky, trying to imagine the things which the demons said lay beyond. Trying to imagine the splendor of that Great Coil of Beauty.

❖   ❖   ❖

Indira might have found some small comfort, then, in that terrible moment, had she turned back. For she would have seen Rottu, for the first time in years, relax her *shoroku*. And allow rich shades of green—in all of that color's many hues— to wash across her mantle, like great waves in the sea.

Chapter 24

When it became obvious that they were nearing their
destination, Kopporu approached Guo.

"I believe we are almost there now, Guo. The place where
the Mother of Demons waits for us."

"I hope so," replied the infanta. She was breathing heavily.
For any gukuy, much less a mother, the long climb up the
canyon to the top of the Chiton was tiring. Since they reached
the plateau above, the way had become easier. But it was still
an arduous march, even for an army hardened by many
eightweeks in the Swamp.

At least we are done with that, thought Kopporu.

Yet, in some strange way, she felt a regret.

The swamp had been horrible, even beyond her worst
dreams. They had lost many warriors there. Lost in mudholes;
lost to predators, big and small; lost to hideous parasitic infections; and some, lost in ways they would never know.
Warriors who simply—disappeared.

The worst time had come crossing the river. Gukuy generally avoided large bodies of fresh water—and almost never
ventured upon the ocean. Terrible predators lurked in water.
Small predators in any body of water beyond the size of a
stream or little pool. In larger bodies—certainly in big rivers—
the predators were huge and fierce.

They had lost almost double-eight warriors crossing the river.
Most of them to poisonous water-slugs.

We would have lost many more, had it not been for Guo.

Of the many legends which would emerge from that incredible trek across the swamp, Kopporu knew, none would

be chanted so often as the day the battlemother Guo slew the great kraken of the river. Kopporu herself had been paralyzed with fear, for a moment, when she first saw the monstrous form of the kraken plowing up the river toward the Kiktu army. Twice the size of the biggest mother who ever lived—the biggest *owoc* mother who ever lived—with palps as big as a gana and a beak like a cave.

But Guo had not hesitated. She had lunged down the river and battled with the monster, after ordering her flankers away. For once, Guo fought something bigger and slower than she, and the young battlemother had used the advantage shrewdly. Eluding the kraken's palps, luring it back downstream, she had given the army the time it needed to finish the crossing.

Kopporu looked up at the five little males who were proudly riding atop Guo's cowl, behind their shield of battle. Pipes in arms, as always.

Guo's preconsorts had secured their own place in legend, that day. The Kiktu had had to make another shield afterward. The kraken had made splinters of the one that had been there before. But Guo's malebond had remained at their posts. And had managed, finally, to blind the kraken in one eye.

From that moment, Guo had pressed the fight. In the end, while the entire army watched from the safety of the riverbank, the kraken had tried to flee. To no avail. Guo was in full *kuoptu*, and had pursued, hammering the monster with her maces, until the great beast was nothing but a mass of bloody flesh drifting with the current.

No, thought Kopporu, *the Swamp was not simply a place of horror. It was also the place where the people recovered their soul.*

She looked back at the long column behind them. Looking, partly, to reassure herself by its great length that she had saved many people for whatever lay in their future. But also, and more, looking for the signs of that new people's strength.

For it *was* a new people. Kiktu, still, somewhere at its heart. But Kopporu saw the files of the Opoktu, marching with a dignity they had never possessed, in the days when they had been merely the smallest tribe on the Papti Plains. The Opoktu were small in no one's eyes, now.

She saw also many swamp-dwellers—*former* swamp-dwellers—scattered here and there, a part of many different

battle groups. A cherished part, not a despised one. The
southern ex-helots might still—so much could not be denied—
remain less adept at battle than Kiktu or Opoktu. But their
courage was doubted by none. The tribespeople would have
perished, many times over, had it not been for their guides.

Scattered through the battle groups, as well, Kopporu saw
many former members of other tribes. Refugees, once; no
longer. Honored and respected members of—

*—of what? Kopporu asked herself. What are we now? The
tribe called Kiktu? No, no longer. We are not even a tribe,
in any proper sense. No clan leaders, outside the Opoktu. Even
the clans themselves have gotten vague at their edges, with
so many new adopted members.*

*How many eightdays has it been since I heard a warrior
even use the name "Kiktu"? The Opoktu still, on occasion, call
themselves by their own name. But, even among them, I have
noticed that it is only their clan leaders and old warriors who
do so. The rest of the Opoktu simply use the phrases which
have become common to the army as a whole.*

*Kopporu's army. And, more and more often, the Guoktu.
Guo's people.*

Ranging further down the column, Kopporu's eyes fell on
still another group of gukuy. The sight of them removed all
fond memories, and brought the harsh realities of the present
back to her mind.

The Utuku captives. And Guo's temper.

If that young fool cannot restrain herself, we will all die.

Guo was not only young, and still given—on occasion—to
childish tantrums. But what was worse, knew Kopporu, was
that she had not witnessed the demons in battle. Guo herself had been preoccupied throughout the battle, too busy
smashing the Utuku before her to pay much attention to
anything else.

But Kopporu had seen. Kopporu had commanded the entire
battle from the rear, instead of the front lines. It was an
unheard of practice among the tribes, but it was one of the
Anshac methods which Kopporu had finally been able to
implement. And there had been no demurral; not even any
whispered private remarks. Aktako would have heard, and told
Kopporu, if there had been. The warriors knew that Kopporu's
courage had been proven many times before, on many

battlefields. And the disaster on the plain had—*finally*—taught even the proud Kiktu that courage alone was not enough.

So Kopporu had watched—from atop the mantle of the crippled battlemother Oroku. That had been Oroku's own proposal. In such a manner, she had explained to Kopporu, she would still gain honor from the battle, which her maimed and useless ped prevented her from joining directly.

It had proven to be an excellent idea. From that high perch, Kopporu had been able to follow the entire course of the battle. She had been able to send commands to the battle groups, taking advantage of every opening she saw in the Utuku formations.

And she had also been able to watch the *other* half of the battle. She had been able to see everything. From the moment the first demons began flickering down the slopes of the Chiton and hurled themselves onto the right flank of the Utuku.

It was—like nothing Kopporu had ever seen. Utuku warriors had begun falling dead, eights at a time. By magic, Kopporu thought at first. Until she finally realized what the demons were doing with those strange, huge—darts?

Within moments after the demons appeared, the Utuku right flank had been driven back—the Utuku battle line broken in half. From then on, Kopporu had only to face the Utuku left flank. Even the Utuku center had remained out of action, paralyzed by a small number of flickering demons.

At first, Kopporu had been vastly relieved. It had been such a horrible shock, to come out of the Swamp and run into an Utuku army at the foot of the Chiton, blocking their access to the mountain's hoped-for sanctuary. The despair which had swept over Kopporu in that moment had been the worst she had ever felt in her life. The Utuku army was almost twice the size of her own, and the terrain favored them. The battle would take place in the narrow stretch of land between the slope of the mountain and the river. No way, even, to retreat this time. A river crossing would take far too long, even if another kraken was not encountered.

Seeing no choice, she had ordered the battle groups into line. And prepared to sell their lives dearly.

Until the demons arrived.

Great relief, and gratitude—at first. And still, Kopporu admitted to herself, to this moment.

The demons saved us. Never doubt it.

But, as she watched the demons in battle, another emotion had come to take its place beside the relief and the gratitude.

A great, growing, terrible fear.

I must make Guo understand! She is still so full of pride, because we defeated half of an Utuku army. Routed them. Destroyed them.

But we could not have done it without the demons. And what is more, she must understand that the demons destroyed the other half. A small battle group of demons turned double-eight their number of Utuku into so much scavenger-meat.

And suffered only a few casualties in so doing! Most of them in the center, at the fiercest point of the struggle.

Whereas we—lost many warriors.

Kopporu's greatest moment of fear had come when she saw the killing of the Utuku commander. She had seen a new demon appear, racing down the mountain like the wind. Black as night. Implacable. Racing toward the Utuku center. Other demons had surrounded it and followed. Then had come the—dart.

The black demon had—hurled?—its dart high into the air. So very high. So very far.

At first, Kopporu thought the demon had simply missed its mark—and missed it badly. Until, watching the dart begin its downward course, she realized the truth.

It is not possible, she remembered thinking, as she watched. *It is not possible.*

But it had been so. The Utuku commander was slain. Struck by lightning from the sky. Dead, Kopporu knew, without ever realizing what caused her doom.

She had known, then, that these were truly demons.

Already, Guo's temper had almost caused disaster. After the Utuku were routed, Kopporu's army had begun slaughtering the survivors. There would be no mercy for any Utuku—*especially* not for any Utuku with fresh cowl scars. Recent recruits, those were—some of them even former Kiktu, who had eaten their own people to save their worthless lives.

Kopporu's warriors had been particularly vigilant in their search for any such. Vigilant, and vengeful.

Until a demon had arrived before Kopporu, where she stood with Guo, overseeing the massacre. Not the implacable demon, but one which seemed overcome by misery.

In tribal trade-argot, the demon had ordered Kopporu to halt the killing of the new Utuku recruits.

"Others must be kill," the monster had said. "Not new Utuku. New Utuku take alive. Our mother say so."

Guo's mantle had turned bright blue, then. The battlemother had bellowed with rage, and raised her maces.

No one—no demon—no one—will stop my people from avenging themselves upon those who ate the flesh of their own tribe!"

In a movement too fast for Kopporu to follow, the demon had flickered back, out of range of Guo's maces. But it had not fled. Nor could Kopporu see the slightest tinge of pink in the brown misery of its hide.

Guo's words of rage could have been heard all over the battlefield. Kopporu's eyes scanned the field. And, within a heartbeat, saw the sight she feared most.

A file of demons was racing toward them. At their head sped the one who had slain the Utuku commander. The implacable one—black as ever.

Sooner than Kopporu would have thought possible, the demons stood before them. Ranging themselves in a half-circle, their darts held ready.

The implacable demon stepped forward. Its way of walking was still strange to Kopporu, although she was beginning to see how the demons moved. But, strange or not, Kopporu could not miss the poise and sureness of the monster's stance.

The demon spoke—in Kiktu, to Kopporu's relief. Trade-argot was a crude language.

Much too crude for negotiations. And if there was ever a time to negotiate, Guo—you young idiot!—it is now.

"Why have you threatened my battle leader?" demanded the black demon.

Before Guo could erupt again, Kopporu explained the situation quickly. From the corner of her eye, Kopporu saw that Woddulakotat was whispering rapidly and urgently into his future-mate's tympanus. She felt some relief, then. The eightweeks in the swamp had taught Kopporu much. Not least of those lessons had been to remove her prejudices concerning the wisdom of males. Especially the eumale Woddulakotat, who, young as he was, had proven to be a shrewd and quick-witted adviser.

The demon pondered Kopporu's words for a moment, and then spoke softly.

"I can understand your emotions. But—are you the battle leader Kopporu?"

Kopporu made the gesture of affirmation.

"We had thought it must be so. Let me take the moment to extend my admiration to you, battle leader Kopporu. And that of my mother, and all my people. The exploit which you and your people have accomplished in crossing the Lolopopo will live for ever. And you have proven your worth—again—on this field of battle."

Kopporu relaxed slightly. She recognized diplomatic flattery when she heard it, of course. But that was all to the good. A demon which was willing to extend some flattery was not, hopefully, given to the same temper tantrums as *the fool* Guo.

But flattery, as always, served only to sweeten the sour food which followed.

"But I must still insist that you stop the killing of the new Utuku."

Kopporu could not restrain Guo in time.

"Why?" roared the battlemother. *"And who is this mother—who can give commands to my people?"*

Kopporu emitted the soft whistle which serves gukuy as a sigh of exasperation.

Who do you think—idiot?

The answer came as no surprise.

"Her name is Inudiratoledo. She is my mother—and the mother of us all."

The Mother of Demons. Whose children are like bolts of lightning.

The demon's—head?—turned away. Kopporu saw its little eyes scanning the field of battle.

"As to your first question—why? I do not know the answer. Although," the demon added slowly, "I am beginning to understand. This—and many things about my mother which were not so clear to me before."

Strangely, its eyes began to shine. As if there were a sudden film of water upon them.

But the moment passed, almost before it began. With a quick gesture, the demon wiped its eyes. Then it stepped forward, and there was no mistaking the meaning of that motion.

The Law will now be spoken.

"What is your name, battlemother?"

It was not a question, really. It was a command. Spoken in such a tone that even *the fool* Guo answered without hesitation.

"Then, listen to me, Guo. Listen carefully, and never doubt what I say. This—"

A quick gesture encompassed the battlefield.

"—is how it is for one reason. And one reason only. It is not so because of the flails of your warriors, nor the power of your own mace. You fought well. Very well. But you would now be nothing but meat in the bellies of the Utuku—"

Guo began to protest, but the demon's voice overrode even hers.

"*Except for one thing, battlemother!* Except that our mother told us a secret. A terrible secret. A secret which destroyed an army."

The blue in Guo's mantle faded, replaced by dappled ochre, pink and orange.

"It is true, then?" the battlemother asked uncertainly. "She is the one we have heard of? The one who knows the secrets?"

The demon hesitated. Kopporu saw something change in the monster's shape. She was not sure what it was. Something in the way its—tentacles?—attached to its upper body. The attachments seemed to move downward somehow, and the demon suddenly looked smaller.

"Yes," it said softly. "She is the one. The one who knows the secrets—and what comes with them."

It pointed again to the battlefield.

"This resulted from one of her secrets. But there was another result as well. *This*—also caused my mother a great and terrible anguish. I know it is so. I have been told by those of my warriors who saw her leave."

All softness vanished. The demon's next words could have forged the bronze blades of a flail.

"I will not visit further grief upon my mother, nor allow others to do so. *Do you understand, battlemother?* I hope so.

I have heard much said of the Kiktu, and all of it good. I would welcome you as friends—and perhaps more. And so—I know this to be true—would my mother. But that is for the possible future. For the present, the matter is simple. If you do not stop the killing—"

The last words struck like the flail itself.

"—then the *only* gukuy who will survive this field of battle will be the Pilgrims and the new Utuku. You, and all your people, will join the other corpses."

Kopporu had turned on Guo, then. She herself knew the tones of authority, and she explained to Guo in the simplest of terms that, Great Mother or no, Guo was still nothing more than a warrior under her command. *Did she understand?*

Even Guo, even the *young fool* Guo, who had forced the black demon to declare his authority over them, had finally understood. The battlemother had remained silent, while Aktako and the rest of Kopporu's guard carried the word to the warriors.

The warriors had obeyed. Reluctantly, true. But Aktako and her cohorts knew how to enforce commands, and the slaughter of the new Utuku stopped. Or, at least, the slaughter of those Utuku whose cowl-scars were *very* fresh. "New" Utuku, after all, is a term which can be interpreted in different ways; and the warriors were in no mood for any but the most literal interpretation.

Kopporu suspected that the young demonlord knew how often the Kiktu warriors were violating the spirit of the command, but the monster said nothing. After a time, Kopporu decided that the demon was not, in truth, seeking a confrontation. Simply a lessened pain in his mother's heart.

Do demons have hearts, I wonder?

The Mother of Demons would never know how many Utuku could have been spared. But she would see captives—several eighties of them, in the end—and would perhaps be satisfied.

I hope so. I hope so.

And now the moment had come. At the head of her army, Kopporu entered a clearing in the center of a small—village, she thought. On three sides of the clearing stood oddly-built, square yurts. On the fourth side was a grove of those plants which the Old Ones called "oruc."

And in the grove itself, to Kopporu's amazement, were several owoc. Feeding on the leaves. Their mantles rippling with green.

The tension in her body eased, slightly.

The Mother of Demons cannot be a cruel monster, then. No owoc would remain in the vicinity of such. Certainly not with that color on their mantles.

Then Kopporu saw the Mother of Demons herself, and was unable to prevent orange from glowing in her mantle.

She is so small! Smaller than any of them!

She had been expecting an enormous creature. As big as—as what? How big would a Mother of Demons be? Like a kraken, Kopporu had thought.

Kopporu did not doubt for a moment what she was seeing, however. There was no mistaking the stance of the demons in the clearing. The small one was clearly the center of authority and respect.

There were many demons in the clearing, she saw. Most of them with darts in their palps, but not all. She saw a number of very small demons, clutching the peds of the big ones, peeking around at the new arrivals.

Children. Like new-spoken spawn. Shy, but filled with curiosity.

The tension eased further.

Surely not even the Mother of Demons would order a massacre in front of such.

There were gukuy in the clearing as well. A good number of them. Several were standing near to the Mother of Demons, one of them—an old gukuy—at her very side. Clearly, these gukuy also occupied positions of respect and authority.

Kopporu was not certain, but she thought most of the gukuy were Pilgrims of the Way. Perhaps all of them. She had no doubt that the old gukuy standing next to the Mother was a Pilgrim. It was somehow obvious.

Her tension eased still further. The Kiktu had always approved of the new religion, since they first became aware of it. Even the old clan leaders. The ideas of the Pilgrims were strange, of course. Difficult to grasp. But one thing had always been clear about them. Unlike all other southerners, the Pilgrims venerated the Old Ones. Not, Kopporu thought, for the same reasons as the Kiktu. But the veneration itself was enough. The Kiktu had granted permission for the Pilgrims to pass through their territory, which many of them had. Seeking refuge, they said, in the Chiton.

I had not realized there were so many of them.

Over time, a number of the Kiktu themselves had adopted the Way. Young warriors seemed especially attracted to the new creed. Kopporu knew that, during the trek through the Swamp, many more had become converted by their sisters. There were no clan leaders to give them stern lectures about hallowed tribal ancestors.

Kopporu knew little, herself, of the beliefs of the Pilgrims. She had been curious, and had felt the desire to investigate. But the necessities of command had driven all other thought aside.

One thing she did know, however. The Pilgrims would defend themselves, flails in palps, against attack. But they were not given to violence. Indeed, they were known to speak against it. Kopporu looked again at the old gukuy.

A Pilgrim sage. I am certain of it.

Surely the Mother of Demons would not order a massacre in front of such.

Kopporu and Guo were now alone at the head of the column, except for Guo's preconsorts. Kopporu could see Woddalukotat and Yurra, peering out from under Guo's cowl.

Advise her, young males. Advise her.

When she was still a few goa from the Mother of Demons, Kopporu halted. Guo drew to a halt beside her.

The Mother of Demons advanced. Alone, Kopporu saw with surprise. Closer and closer, until she was standing at tentacle's length away, directly in front of Kopporu.

"You are Kopporu, the battle leader of your army."

Her voice was odd, and her accent harsh, but her command of Kiktu was excellent.

Kopporu made the gesture of affirmation.

"I am Inudiratoledo. The being who is sometimes called the Mother of Demons. You and I will speak at length, battle leader, and soon. But first, I must speak to another."

Suddenly, in the quick and flickering manner of demons, she was standing in front of Guo. Very closely, looking up at the huge head of the battlemother looming above her.

Kopporu felt a moment's fear. Guo's maces were in their

halters, of course—not even the *young fool* was so stupid as to have marched into the lair of the Mother of Demons with her maces in her palps. But she would not need maces. Whatever terrible power the Mother of Demons wielded, it was obviously not a power of the body. The Mother of Demons would be like a tiny slug in Guo's great palps, her life crushed out of her body in a moment. With her arms alone, Kopporu thought, Guo could kill the Mother of Demons.

Then, to both Guo and Kopporu's astonishment, the Mother of Demons reached up her—palps?—and stroked Guo's arms. Guo began to flinch, then—at a sharp whisper from Woddulakotat—froze.

"And you are the Great Mother Guo. So young. I had not realized how young. My warriors did not tell me."

The demon continued stroking Guo's arms. After a moment, the arms began to relax.

"So very young, to have taken such a burden on yourself. So much courage that must have taken. And much wisdom."

Kopporu repressed a whistle of derision.

Courage—yes. Too much, even. But wisdom?

Kopporu began thinking many unkind thoughts concerning Guo's "wisdom." Until she remembered the day, eightweeks before, in the big clearing of the Swamp. When the *young fool* Guo had shown more wisdom than the rest of the people combined. Guo alone—and, Kopporu knew, her young preconsorts.

As long as she keeps her temper. And listens to Woddulakotat, and Yurra.

The Mother of Demons made a strange gesture with her head. Pointing, Kopporu realized, with that oddly flat, armless face.

"And who are these two? Introduce me, if you please."

Guo's mantle was rippling with many colors, now. Orange and ochre predominated. Blue—Kopporu saw with relief—was completely absent.

Guo's voice was hesitant.

"They are named Woddulakotat—he is the eumale—and Yurra. They are my preconsorts. And my close advisers."

Petulantly, then: "My closest advisers, and the dearest to my heart. Even if some of my people don't approve."

Kopporu repressed a whistle. One of the old warriors had

made the mistake of lecturing Guo, a few days earlier, on the impropriety of allowing her preconsorts to remain in her mantle once they were out of the Swamp. The necessity of protecting the little males could override custom in the swamp, she had allowed, ponderously, but once they were out of it—well. It just wasn't done. They were not, after all, properly wedded.

Guo's answer had been short, to the point, and very rude.

It really isn't proper, thought Kopporu wrily. *But I'm afraid it's too late, anyway, to save Guo's morals. I've heard the noises she's starting to make at night. With her preconsorts nowhere in sight. Not even mature—neither she nor they! She'd deny it, of course, but I know the truth. They're starting to—practice.*

A strange noise was coming from the Mother of Demons. Her face was twisted into a bizarre shape.

Humor. That must be the way the demons whistle amusement.

"People are often foolish, Guo. My own husband"—the demon gestured toward a large, roundish-shaped demon nearby— "is my closest adviser also. And, always, the dearest to my heart."

Guo's mantle was suddenly tinged with green. Slowly, her own arms began to return the caress of the Mother of Demons.

Kopporu knew, then, that her people would live. And forgave Guo all of her many, many, many sins.

Chapter 25

By the end of the first eightweek, Indira knew that the critical moment had passed. There was still much to be settled, and much, *much* more to be done. Her life seemed to have become nothing but an endless round of meetings and discussions, and she knew that there was no end yet in sight.

But the details—*details!* she thought—were not important, now that the central concept for which she had battled had been accepted by all parties.

They would become a single people. United, as one flesh, within the shell of this strange new idea the Mother of Demons had brought to the world, from beyond the sky. The—*nashiyonu*, she called it.

Already, Indira knew, in all the valleys of the Chiton, the strange new word was being spoken, from the siphons of gukuy from many different tribes and peoples. Many of whom—most of whom—had barely begun to learn the Enagulishuc from which the word derived.

A strange demon word, belonging to a strange demon language. What other word could describe such a strange idea? A people which is not a people. A tribe which is not a tribe. A prevalate in which no clan prevails. (Even, it was whispered, in which the clan themselves barely exist.)

Who, then, is a part of this—*nashiyonu?* Anyone who chooses to belong. Yes, *chooses*. It has nothing to do with clan status or birth.

Anyone. Even *owoc.*

Indira repressed a grin. The gukuy who were squatting in the command circle were all very intelligent beings. Even the recently arrived tribespeople were rapidly learning to interpret human facial expressions and body language. Ushulubang and Rottu, she knew, were already mistresses of the art.

When it came to diplomacy, humans had the great advantage of being naturally adept at *shoroku*. Indira had no intention of losing that advantage, so she allowed no signs of her feelings to show. But it was difficult not to grin, thinking of the owoc.

In truth, the owoc had not really chosen to become citizens of the new Nation. The concepts would have meant absolutely nothing to them. Indira had simply *decreed* that all owoc were nashiyonuc by nature. *All* owoc, everywhere in the World-That-Is-A-Clam, not simply the owoc on the Chiton.

She had expected some resistance to the idea, especially from the Kiktu. The tribespeople venerated the owoc, true. But, as Indira had suspected, the veneration stemmed from ancient totemic concepts. It had nothing to do with any notion that owoc were *equal* to gukuy.

But Ushulubang, as she so often did, had immediately supported Indira's proposal. Very vigorously. The Kiktu had been uncertain, but they had acceded to the wishes of the old sage and the Mother of Demons.

For a moment, Indira's eyes met those of Ushulubang. The sage was, as always, squatting across from her in the command circle. The two of them were careful not to give the impression that they were acting in collusion. Which, in the narrow sense of the term, they were not. Indira met privately with Ushulubang, but no more often or for longer stretches of time than she did with Kopporu, or Guo, or the Opoktu clan leaders.

The fact remained that they were conspirators. The vision toward which they were each groping was different—or, perhaps more accurately, seen from different angles. But their goals, in some fundamental sense, were identical.

The question of the owoc illustrated that unity of purpose perfectly. Goloku, in her teachings, had often spoken of the need to cherish the owoc, and to oppose their oppression. In this, as in so many things, most Pilgrims interpreted her words simplistically. As a statement of ethical principle.

As such, of course, it was an excellent principle—one of which Indira heartily approved. But Goloku's teachings also carried a more subtle and sophisticated thought, under the simple morality of the precept.

If you allow the weakest to be oppressed, you open the valves to your own oppression. If you flail one who is weaker than you, you will be flailed yourself, by one who is stronger. Do not complain then, fool. Was it not you who blessed the flail in the first place?

Indira had, finally, accepted the awful responsibility which had fallen on her shoulders. But she took this much grim satisfaction in the taking—whatever else, she would ensure the survival of the owoc. It might well be true, as Julius often said, that all species were doomed to extinction. So be it. But the owoc would be granted their rightful time in the universe, to live out their gentle lives in peace, free of fear.

Indira knew what forces she was unleashing on this planet. Those forces would do much that was good. But they would also wreak havoc and destruction. Often, she would wake in the night, trembling. Julius would hold her in his arms, until she finally fell back asleep. Always, then, one thought would enable her to face the nightmares.

Soon enough, the word would spread to all the peoples of all the lands of the world. Abuse the owoc, and you will incur the terrible wrath of the Nation. For all owoc, it is said, belong to the Nation.

Watching Indira and Ushulubang, Julius made no attempt to restrain his own grin.

Look at the two schemers. Butter wouldn't melt in their mouths, no sirree. Ha! Machiavelli's Daughter Meets Cardinal Richelieu. Love at first sight.

Feeling eyes upon him, Julius turned his head and met the calm gaze of Rottu.

Oh, yes. Let's not forget "Tentacles" Borgia.

But, the moment the quip came to him, he dismissed it. Not without a certain feeling of shame. He had come to know Rottu rather well, over the past two months. To know her, and to grow to like her. And, as he learned her history, be somewhat awed by her.

Hard as steel, yes. But never evil. Would you have survived her life, Julius Cohen? With your soul intact—as she did?

He looked away. After the meeting, he would spend the

rest of the day in the company of Rottu. He saw more of Rottu than he did of Indira, now. Somehow—Julius never did understand how Indira had maneuvered him into it—Julius had become Rottu's partner in crime.

"Research," Indira had called it. "You and Rottu will jointly organize a research team."

Yeah, right. "Research team." Such a nice phrase. It brings to mind starry-eyed visions of Julius Cohen, paleontologist, plumbing the secrets of the unknown.

Treacherous, sneaky, conniving she-devil. An historian, to boot, who knows perfectly well what the phrase really means— and could have said so in plain language.

Manhattan Project Marries Peenemunde. Absent-Minded Professor of Death and Destruction, Meet Your New Associate—Her Squidness, the Spy.

Julius grinned again, very widely. Unlike Indira, he had no fear of having his emotions easily understood by the gukuy. For two reasons. First, he didn't give a damn. Second, he had a secret weapon whenever needed. The gukuy possessed, as a rule, very good senses of humor. But Jewish jokes baffled them completely.

Except, possibly, Rottu. Julius glanced at his partner again.

When I told her I was making her an honorary Jew, she immediately replied that she was too old to convert and besides, she didn't want to be circumcised. Now, where the hell did she learn about that? I think she's getting coached by Indira on the side.

Treacherous, sneaky, conniving she-devils—the lot of them.

Rottu met his glance. A second later, the Pilgrim spymistress looked away, conveying in some subtle manner the message: *Stop daydreaming, Julius. The meeting is about to come to the key point.*

Julius snorted. He wasn't in the slightest concerned about *that*. He should worry? When Indira, Mistress of the Dark Secrets, was running the show?

Paying little attention to the meeting, Julius began pondering the *real* problem he had on his plate. Wasn't there anything on this miserable soft-wooded planet that would make a decent bow?

He mimicked Indira in his mind. "The Mongols made composite bows." *That's great, sweetheart. How? I'm a 22nd century paleontologist, not a 13th century nomadic bowyer.*

He dismissed the problem from his mind. Rottu had heard vague rumors of some kind of sea-monsters whose weird innards might make suitable material for a bow. She said she would look into it, but it would be a long time before she discovered anything. Very few gukuy peoples had anything to do with the ocean, because of its dangers. And those were far away, and little known.

So forget bows, for the moment. We don't have enough time for long-range planning. The main armies of the Utuku will be here within a few months, by Rottu's estimate.

Chemical warfare, by God. There's the thing.

He began chewing his upper lip. By now, he had completely blanked the proceedings of the session out of his mind.

Greek fire. Or its Ishtarian equivalent. Rottu's already sent an expedition back into the Swamp. O-doddo-ua says there's a kind of oily quasi-vine there which burns like nobody's business. She promised to bring back a pile of the stuff. If we can concentrate whatever the active substance is, we've got the makings of a nice firebomb. By then, Adrian should have finished building the catapults—no, what's the right word? Trebuchet, I think. I'll ask Indira. She ought to know. The Wicked Witch of the Sky designed the damned thing, after all. Like a magician pulling rabbits from a hat, the way she hauls things out of that chamber of horrors called History.

Feeling a sudden tension in the air, Julius focused his attention back on the meeting.

He stared at Indira. He could tell, by subtleties in her posture he could not begin to analyze consciously, that she was poised to strike.

I love you, she-devil.

"Pay attention, Guo!" whispered Woddulakotat fiercely. "Stop daydreaming. They're getting around to the meat of the question."

Guo repressed a whistle of derision. She adored her preconsorts—especially Woddulakotat—and would under no circumstances reprove them publicly. The fact remained that they were still, in some ways—especially Woddulakotat—a bunch of silly males. Fretting over foolishness.

For an eightday, now, since the discussion had finally turned to the problem of building a new army, her preconsorts had

been agitated over the issue of the army's commander. A wrong
decision here, they insisted, would be disastrous.

Guo must see to it that the right decision is made!

*Silly males. The right decision will be made. As always. And
I won't have to do anything.*

The Goddess will not fail us.

Her preconsorts, she knew, were much taken by Ushulubang
and the teachings of the Way. Most males were, especially
eumales. Had not Goloku taught that all gukuy are equal within
the Coil? Did not Ushulubang flail his Pilgrims with that
precept, every day? In the most outrageous manner possible?
Imagine! Allowing that *pervert* Dhowifa to ride about in her
mantle, and proclaiming him the best of the new apashoc.

Guo did not object, actually. She rather liked Dhowifa. The
pervert had begun to spend much time with Guo's preconsorts.
He missed, Guo knew, the company of his own long-lost
malebond. After an initial hesitation, her preconsorts had
allowed Dhowifa to become a bondfriend. True, Dhowifa was
an unnatural gukuy. But—after the Swamp, and everything else,
it no longer seemed of much importance. And he was close
to Ushulubang, and wise in the Way himself.

Guo did not object to the Way, either. She knew that the
new religion was sweeping through the ranks of the Kiktu,
pushing aside the old tribal beliefs. But she didn't care. She
was inclined to the opinion that beings should believe in
whatever they wished. And, even if that had not been her own
inclination, she would not have objected. For the Goddess
herself had decreed that all must respect the beliefs of others, and their right to advocate that belief.

Guo herself, however, was not moved by the Way. She found
its logical intricacies boring. Her husbands-to-be could chatter all they wanted about the subtleties of the Question; she
would have none of it. Even if Guo had lost her respect for
the clan leaders, she had lost none of her respect for the old
beliefs of the Kiktu.

The truth was simple and straightforward. The Goddess Uk
had created the world, and rained life upon the Meat. She
had given all to the gukuy, and told them to enjoy the bounties
of the world. But the gukuy had fallen into sin, and displeased
Uk. So the Goddess had returned to the world, to set the
gukuy back on the road of righteousness.

It was well known, of course, that no gukuy could gaze upon the sight of the Goddess and live. So the Goddess, in her mercy, had assumed a different form. She had returned in the guise of a demon. A Mother of Demons. With her children, and their glistening spears, to enforce her will.

Let foolish males and others believe in the tales of the demons. The demons were full of tall tales—especially the old fat one, the Mother's mate. Tales of great coils in the sky, beyond the Mother-of-Pearl. Tales of a double coil within every living thing, which created it and shaped it as it grew. Tales and tales and tales.

All nonsense. Guo knew the truth. The Mother of Demons had come to the world to explain the secrets to the people. The greatest secrets of all—the secrets of the future. She said it was not so, of course. The Mother of Demons said she had no magic power over the future. Only the knowledge of the past, of a different world, which enabled her to see the forks in the road ahead. But Guo knew she was lying. The Goddess would blind the gukuy if she told them the secrets all at once, as they really were. So, in her mercy, the Goddess lied, and told only some of the secrets. And only part of those secrets.

It was enough. Once, Guo had meant to force the truth from the Mother of Demons. Remembering that time, she almost flushed red. She would have been destroyed. But the Goddess Uk had loved Guo, and spared her.

"Stop daydreaming!" hissed Woddulakotat.

Guo brought her mind back to the present. The Pilgrim Ghodha was speaking.

"There remains the question of who will command the new army. I believe it can only be"—she pointed to the implacable demon sitting next to his mother—"Yoshef. My reasons are as—"

"No," said the Mother of Demons. "It must be Kopporu."

"You see?" whispered Guo. "Did I not tell you?"

Foolish males. As if the Goddess would fail.

There had been no sign in Kopporu's mantle of her tension. Thus, when the tension suddenly vanished, there was no sign of her relief.

But Ghodha had little of Kopporu's mastery of *shoroku*. The

Pilgrim warrior's own mantle rippled with colors. Predominantly ochre.

"I—do not agree, Inudira. At least I must be convinced."

Ghodha turned toward Kopporu and made the gesture of respect.

"I have the greatest admiration for Kopporu's capabilities as a warrior, and a battle leader. But I watched the battle with the Utuku. It is a simple fact that Yoshef and his apalatunush caused as much destruction as Kopporu's warriors, despite their much smaller numbers. And suffered few casualties in so doing—whereas the Kiktu suffered many. For a barba—for a gukuy, Kopporu is an excellent battle leader. Even a great one. But Yoshef is beyond comparison."

Indira leaned forward.

"I will try to convince you, Ghodha. But it would be better, I think, if Kopporu could convince you herself. Kopporu has said nothing, so far, in this discussion. Out of—not modesty, perhaps, but a desire not to seem self-serving."

She looked at Kopporu. "But this is no time for such pretense, Kopporu. I know full well that you agree with me on this matter. Explain why."

Kopporu hesitated for a moment. What she was about to say would, she suspected, inflame some mantles. But Indira's will was like bronze, as she had demonstrated many times over the past eightweek.

"I also watched the battle, Ghodha. And I do not disagree with your assessment of the relative roles played in it by Yoshef's people and my own. But the question before us regards the future, not the past. We must be guided by different considerations."

Ghodha interrupted. "If by that you are referring to the sensitivities of your tribe, I think—"

Kopporu whistled derision. She respected the Pilgrim warleader's talent, but she was becoming more than a little irritated by her superciliousness toward "barbarians."

"My *people*, Ghodha—who include far more than Kiktu—would have no difficulty accepting Yoshef as a commander. They would accept it in the same way that they have accepted Enagulishuc as our common language—and for the same reasons. No, more than accept it. They would feel a great sense of confidence, knowing they were led by the demon who slew the Utuku commander with a single cast of his spear."

Kopporu drew a deep breath. *Here it is.*

"But it would be a false confidence. The army would not be stronger with Yoshef as its commander rather than me. It would be weaker."

Another deep breath.

"*Much* weaker."

A small uproar followed. Quickly quelled, however, by Indira's firmness.

"Explain, Kopporu," she commanded.

Kopporu held up an arm.

"One. The incredible success of Yoshef's apalatunush in the recent battle was due primarily to surprise. The Utuku had never seen dem—ummun before. Suddenly, monsters were upon them, fighting in a manner which they had never experienced. The ummun had won half the battle before it even started. But this element of surprise will not last forever. We will enjoy it in the next battle, because no Utuku survived this one. Over time, however, the gukuy of all lands will become familiar with ummun and their battle tactics."

She held up a second arm.

"Two. The ummun are by no means invincible, or indestructible. You, Ghodha, are impressed by the fact that the ummun suffered few casualties in the battle. I was impressed by that also. But, since I have spent some time now with the ummun, I have been impressed by another fact.

"There are very few ummun. Not more than triple-eighty warriors. It is true, the young ummun will eventually be able to take their place in the apalatunush. And, over time, their numbers will grow. But there will always be far more—*far* more—gukuy than ummun. Once that fact becomes known— which it will, there is no way to keep it a secret forever— our opponents will understand that they need only kill a few ummun to cripple the apalatunush."

A third arm. And a fourth.

"Three. And, closely armed, four. Our opponents are powerful in numbers. Does anyone doubt that the Beak of the Utuku would sacrifice eighty—or more—warriors in order to kill a single ummun? Or any of the awosha of the south? And that is my fifth reason. The Utuku are our immediate enemy.

Soon enough, the Beak will seek to avenge her humiliations upon us. But the Utuku are, in many ways, the most poorly equipped to fight ummun. Given their numbers, their tactics have worked well against the tribes of the plain. But they are very badly designed against the ummun methods."

A little diplomacy, here. Kopporu made the gesture of respect.

"You yourself, Ghodha, are a former battle leader of the Anshac legions. Would the legions have fared so badly against Yoshef's apalatunush?"

Ochre. Then, the gesture of grudging admission.

"Probably not. *Certainly* not—in a second battle. Where they understood what they were facing."

"Exactly. The Anshac discipline is, in all essential regards, as good as that of the Utuku. But the Anshac are far more flexible and clever."

One of the Opoktu clan leaders spoke.

"But we are not at war with the Ansha," she protested.

"Not yet," replied Kopporu. "But we will be."

Another uproar, quieted by Indira.

"Explain," she commanded.

Kopporu held up a sixth arm.

"The reason loops back to the question. I have listened carefully to everything Inudira has said, over the past many days. Most of it has been strange to me, and new, and difficult to comprehend. But one thing has become clear. I understand it, because I myself spent a lifetime as a warrior trying to change my tribe's methods of war. Tried and, for the most part, failed. Why? Because—as Inudira has explained—the way in which a people makes war is ultimately an extension of the way they live. Tribes will fight like tribes. Prevalates like prevalates. Savages like savages."

Kopporu groped for words.

"I cannot explain this well. Inudira could explain it much better. This much I know. The whole world is changing—and was, even before the ummun came. You all know this is so. You especially, Ghodha. Nowhere is change coming faster than in the south. Why are there so many former helots among my people? Because the lot of the helots is growing worse in the south. More and more helots are becoming outright slaves. The prevalates are going to war with each other more and more often.

More and more, they are encroaching on the plains. And now, a great new cloth is being woven. We are weaving it here, on the Chiton. The cloth we call the nashiyonu. The new army we are building is only a single thread in that cloth—and not the most important one. Think of all the other threads we have decided upon. The new yurts for teaching new skills. The new trade routes we will seek to uncover. The new arts and crafts we will create. All of these things, sooner or later, will bring us into battle with the Ansha—and all the southern prevalates."

She fell silent. After a moment, all eyes turned to Indira.

"Is this so, Inudira?" asked Ghodha.

"Yes. Everything Kopporu has said, and more. I will elaborate on her words, at a later time. But Kopporu has stripped the meat from the shell."

She looked at Kopporu.

"Your conclusions, battle leader?"

"The army of the nashiyonu must be a gukuy army, in its essence. It must be built and led according to the best principles that we know, along with the new things which Inudira will teach us. But those must be principles which *gukuy* can use. Principles of the flail, not the spear. The ummun apalatunush will have a place in that army, for there are special things which they can do which we cannot. But they will not be at the center, when the clash of armies comes.

"The army should therefore be commanded by a gukuy. Whether that gukuy should be myself, or another, is a different question. But it must be a gukuy. We can, and will, learn much of the art of war from the ummun. And there will always be ummun in positions of command and advice. But no ummun could ever understand a gukuy army as well as a gukuy.

"And, it would be a waste. There are so few ummun, and they know so much. Even the young ones, who remember little of any world than our own, know far more than any gukuy. I would not see them wasted on a battlefield, any more than necessary."

She made the gesture of profound respect to Joseph.

"I, too, was awed by Yoshef's cast of the spear. But I would rather see him cast his thoughts into the sky."

In her mind, Ushulubang also made a gesture of profound respect. Not toward Joseph, but toward Indira.

Shrewdly done, Mother of Demons. As always. There will be no hesitation, now, at selecting Kopporu.

With quite a different mental gesture, Ushulubang considered Ghodha.

I believe I shall make a point of talking more often with that one. Rather too full of the Answer, she is. Answers which would have killed her, and them, had it been she who tried to lead an entire people through the Swamp. Even now, she cannot see past Kopporu's crude armor. It has not yet occurred to her to wonder: how is it that a "barbarian" could see things which I could not?

Because the barbarian, whether she knows it or not, follows the Way of the Question.

But that is for the future. For the moment, there is still a matter to be resolved. There is, after all, a core of meat at the center of Ghodha's prejudices.

For the first time since the council began that day, Ushulubang spoke.

"I fully support the proposal to make Kopporu the commander of the army. But a problem remains, which is the nature of the army itself."

She waited, allowing the council to digest her words.

"Is it to be a Kiktu army? No, clearly not. Kopporu has told us herself that she seeks to adopt Anshac methods—and even more. The methods which Inudira has begun to explain. But that will require the tribespeople to learn a whole new way of war. A difficult thing to ask, especially of warriors who are rightfully proud of their accomplishments in battle."

Another pause.

"Then, there is the problem of the Pilgrims. Many of them will want to join the army. Some were warriors themselves, in times past. From Ansha, and other prevalates. But most are helots, with little skill or training in the craft of war."

Another pause.

"And finally, there is the problem of the former Utuku. Warriors all, and brave ones. Do not deny it, simply because of your distaste for their *former* habits. They have renounced those habits, and they too must somehow be incorporated into the new army."

A long pause.

"You see the problem? It is not enough to have a

commander. She must be able to command an army—an *army*, a whole and well-knit cloth. But we do not have such a cloth, today. Nor do we have much time in which to weave one."

Ushulubang looked at Rottu. "You estimate that the Beak and the main army of the Utuku will arrive at the Chiton in three eightweeks, am I not correct?"

The spymistress made the gesture of tentative affirmation.

"Approximately. The former Utuku whom I interviewed all agreed that the Beak took the main army south after the battle of the Lolopopo. Leaving only two *ogghoxt* to watch the Swamp in case Kopporu emerged. One *ogghoxt* we destroyed. The other will remain in its assigned position south and west of the Swamp. In the meantime, the Beak is preoccupied with completing the conquest of the Papti Plain. Not all of the tribes joined with the Kiktu. Several retreated south, and are still opposing the Utuku."

She made the gesture of certainty.

"They will not succeed in that opposition. But they will keep the Beak occupied for some time. Enough time—barely—for us to weave a new army. And there is an added benefit. Refugees from broken tribes are trickling north. Some have already reached the Chiton. At my suggestion, Kopporu has already dispatched small battle groups into the plain to seek for such refugees. We can add their threads to the cloth."

Rottu fell silent. Seamlessly, Ushulubang continued.

"We have everything we need to weave our army. We have the nashiyonu, which is our loom. And we have the warp and the weft—the ummun, the tribespeople, the Pilgrims, the former Utuku, the new refugees. But—"

"We need a shuttle," said Kopporu. "Someone—it will have to be gukuy—who knows the Anshac methods of war. And the ways of the tribespeople."

"Just so."

Kopporu's mantle turned black.

"And someone who will be able to instill discipline of bronze. A warrior so feared and respected that none will dare challenge her."

"Just so."

After a moment, one by one, all who were present began staring at Dhowifa.

PART V:
The Shuttle

Chapter 26

Dhowifa himself brought the summons. As she watched her little lover approach their yurt, Nukurren found it hard not to whistle derision.

He's getting fat, the lazy little creature. Look at him waddle along! Even slower than usual. He's gotten used to riding in Ushulubang, and working no other muscles than those of his siphon. Which he works constantly.

But, as always, Nukurren did not begrudge Dhowifa the new life he had found on the mountain. She did not begrudge him the comfort of his new friendship with Guo's malebond, nor the joy he found in Ushulubang's company.

No, not at all. After eightyweeks of misery as an outcast, Dhowifa had found acceptance. More than that, he had found hope and purpose. He was well into the Coil, now, learning the Way of the Pilgrim, and learning it very well. Still shy at times, uncertain, diffident. But Nukurren knew that if Ushulubang had, at first, called Dhowifa the best of the new apashoc out of her desire to shake the error of the Answer, she did so now because it was the simple truth. And many apashoc, especially the younger ones, were learning to shed their bigotry and seek discourse with the unnatural truemale whose understanding of the Question was subtle, supple, and uncanny.

Dhowifa's happiness stemmed from other things he had found on the mountain, as well. He had spent hours in the company of the Mother of Demons, during meetings of the council. Returning each time with new awe and wonder at what he had heard. And a growing adoration for Inudiratoledo herself, and the new world she was making.

No, Nukurren loved Dhowifa, and was glad for him, and listened, patiently if not attentively, to everything which Dhowifa told her. But she herself said nothing. It was not that she disbelieved. Simply that—she didn't care.

She didn't seem to care about anything, anymore. It was as if she had lost her soul along with her eye. Her heart kept beating, her lungs kept breathing. Beyond that—nothing. She had no need of *shoroku* to keep her mantle gray. Her soul itself was gray. All around her, day after day, she watched a new world being created. A strange new tapestry, woven of mysterious alien threads, colored in dazzling hues.

With, as always, no place in it for her.

It was not that she was outcast. Not at all. Oh, no, not at all.

She was admired, now. Respected, praised, even adulated. New chants were being chanted, throughout the Chiton, of the battle which was called Shatalunungurdu. (Ushulubang had decreed that strange name, for reasons known to none, save, perhaps, the Mother of Demons.)

Glorious, triumphant chants. (Longwinded ones, too, but none complained.) Chants which told of the exploits of heroes and champions. Of the sagacity of Kopporu, and the battlecraft of her warriors, and the might of Guo, and the honor of her malebond (and none objected to the presence of males in a battlechant, unheard-of though it was), and the valor of the Pilgrims against the shield wall, and the ferocity of Ludumilaroshokavashiki and Takashimidudzhugodzhi, and the fleetness of their apalatunush, and the spearcast of Yoshefadekunula, and the courage of his Companions (for so, in fact, they were called in the chants), especially the great warrior Dzhenushkunutushen.

And, most of all, of Nukurren the Valiant. Many new chants had been composed, over the past eightweeks, by chantresses of all peoples. Pilgrim chants and Kiktu chants, and Opoktu chants, and chants by former swamp-dwellers, and even, in a strange unrhythmic meter, a short chant by a young demon named Anagushohara. Each chant was somewhat different. A Kiktu chantress might dwell on the details of the battle on the Utuku left flank; a Pilgrim chantress, on the fury at the shield wall. But in one respect, all chants agreed:

The height of the battle, the decisive moment, the turning

point, the pivot of history, the opening of the Way and the salvation of the peoples, had been the Charge of Nukurren. The *Kutaku* of the Coil, as many chants called it.

> *Oh, glory and grandeur and triumph and hope!*
> *Oh, valor and courage and heroism and nobility!*
> *Nukurren the Mighty! Nukurren the Bold!*
> *Nukurren the Champion!*

Nukurren had heard the chants. Had been unable not to hear them, for all that the chants grated on her soul. During the long days after the battle, she had remained in the hospital at Dzhenushkunutushen's bedside. Nukurren herself had suffered only minor mantle-wounds during her charge, quickly healed. But Dzhenushkunutushen had lain near death. He had not suffered any single great wound. But he had nearly bled to death, for it seemed as if his entire body had been flailed.

As, indeed, it had been. Most of his wounds had been received at the very end of the battle, in the last moments before Nukurren reached the little band of human warriors in the center. For, at the end, Yoshefadekunula had fallen, knocked down in the press of the fray by the staggering body of another demon, mortally injured. Unhurt, but helpless, the demonlord had been the target of all the remaining Utuku. At last, the cannibals had seen their chance to destroy the implacable demon who had been the most terrible of them all, and they had fallen upon him.

Or, had tried. But the cannibals never reached the black monster. Their flails never touched him. The assault of the Utuku broke against the demonlord's companion, who stood over his prostrate form, unmoving, unyielding, accepting each blow of the flail and returning it with a stroke of the spear. And if Utuku flails tore the demonlord champion's flesh, his spear split Utuku brains; if their flails spilled his blood, his spear spilled their lives; and if they gave him pain, he gave them oblivion.

Then did the cannibals falter, for the spear-strokes were unstoppable. If the white passion of the demonlord's companion seemed mysterious to them, they had not the time to wonder at it. For the blue rage of their mantles was the palest of shades, compared to the color in the monster's eyes. The demon's white passion quickly vanished, covered with red blood.

But the blue never faded from his glare, and it seemed, to the Utuku who faced him, to be the color of Fury Itself.

They faltered. And then gray death arrived, for Nukurren was there. The demonlord's companion finally collapsed. But the demonlord himself had regained his feet, and took up his spear, and fell upon them. Black as night, implacable. Endless night, then, to the Utuku who had flailed his companion.

For days Dzhenushkunutushen lay near death. Indeed, would almost certainly *have* died, were it not for the strength of his body. Other demons in the hospital, weaker than he, did die in those days. Three of them. Two had been among the human warriors in the center, and they had died soon after arriving in the hospital, from terrible wounds.

The third was a female demon. Though many of the apalatunush warriors who had ravaged the Utuku right would bear scars, only two had been slain. Of those two, only one had survived the battle itself, to be brought to the hospital.

The female demon lingered for days before she died. Her name, Nukurren learned, had been Shofiyaburrunushtayn. She learned the name from the many demons who came to the hospital. All of the demons came, Nukurren thought, to sit by the side of their wounded and dying. Nukurren found the demon way of expressing grief, like so much else about them, to be messy, unsightly and grotesque. But she did not doubt for a moment that the water which leaked from their eyes, transparent though it was, bore the essence of brown misery.

The Mother of Demons herself came, many times, to sit with Shofiyaburrunushtayn and Dzhenushkunutushen. Nukurren was mildly interested to note that the Mother of Demons, alone among them, never *wept* (such, she learned, was the Enagulishuc word for that strange means of showing grief). She merely sat there, silent, still; her flat, armless face as rigid as bronze.

In her visits to the hospital, the Mother of Demons spoke rarely, and never to Nukurren. At first, Nukurren wondered (not caring, simply curious) if the Mother of Demons was angry at her for some unknown reason. All the other demons who came to the hospital spoke to Nukurren. Spoke to her often, in fact, and sometimes at tedious length; expressing their gratitude and their affection.

Eventually, Nukurren thought she understood. The Mother

of Demons never showed her grief because it was so great
that the showing of it would break her completely. And if she
never spoke to Nukurren, it was not out of anger. It was
because to speak to the gukuy warrior who had saved so many
of her children (perhaps, in the end, all of them—for battles
are fickle things) would be to acknowledge her own responsibility for sending them into their death. A responsibility which
the Mother of Demons had taken, and had accepted; but could
not yet, thought Nukurren, call by its own name.

The day came, after Shofiyaburrunushtayn finally died, when
the healer demon Mariyaduloshruyush pronounced Dzhenushkunutushen safe from danger. Shortly thereafter, the Mother
of Demons arrived at the hospital. The young male demon was
conscious now, if still very weak, and he and his mother exchanged a few words before he fell asleep. For long, then, did
the Mother of Demons remain, holding the huge, deadly hand
of her child in her own tiny and much deadlier one.

The Mother of Demons sat on one side of Dzhenushkunutushen's pallet. Nukurren, as she had done for many days,
squatted on the other. As always, the Mother of Demons said
nothing to Nukurren; did not even look at her.

Much later, the Mother of Demons arose and made to leave.
But at the doorway, she stopped, motionless for a time, and
then turned back. She came to stand before Nukurren and
then, still silent, bowed to the warrior.

Nukurren recognized the bow. Nukurren was very obser-
vant, and had already learned many of the subtle methods by
which the demons expressed their sentiments. But no subtlety
was needed here. The bow which the Mother of Demons gave
to Nukurren was not the bow which ummun gave to gukuy.
This was the great bow, the special bow. The bow which had
no name in Enagulishuc, but which the Kiktu called the *gukku
tak tu rottonutu*, the "homage to the Old Ones"; and the Pilgrims, in Anshac, the *purren owoc*.

Truly, the Mother of Demons, thought Nukurren, after
Inudiratoledo left the hospital.

She, alone, almost understands.

There was no place for Nukurren in this new world being born, for the chants were absurd. Grandiose, preposterous, ridiculous—*lies*. That the chantresses themselves, and those

who listened to the chants, thought them the truth mattered not at all. Lies, believed, are still lies. And untruth was made even the worse, by the fact it was thought to be true.

For there *was* no Nukurren the Valiant. That creature did not exist, had never existed, could never exist. There had been no glory in her charge. Neither glory, nor grandeur, nor courage, nor valor, nor justice, nor hope for the future, nor even the thought of triumph.

There had been nothing in it. *Nothing.*

It had been that *nothing* which had made her charge truly irresistible. Nukurren knew, had long known, that she was a great warrior. But not the greatest warrior in the world could have carried through that charge. Her charge had been irresistible *because* it was not a warrior's charge.

To be sure, she had used all her warrior's skill—and immense skills they were. But the soul of that charge had been the shriek of a newborn spawn, realizing, from the first moment of consciousness, that the universe was a cannibal. Knowing, always, that there was *nothing* in the world; nothing but pain and solitude, which endured, and endured, simply because the universe was a torturer enjoying its sport. A cannibal, lingering over the feast.

Nukurren had gone to the battle, but she had not intended to participate. She had come, simply because—she did not know, exactly. A professional interest, partly, to see how well the demons had learned the lessons she had taught them. But, mostly, she had gone because Dzhenushkunutushen had given back her weapons and her armor, and she had never realized he possessed them. She had been moved, then. She had been moved, not by the still-new and uncertain friendship embodied in Dzhenushkunutushen's return of her belongings. No, she had been moved by her astonishment that a monster could exist in the world who would salvage the possessions of a creature who, at the time, had done nothing to him but harm. She had come to the battle, in the end, wondering if such a capacity for friendship was possible.

Then, at the battle itself, she saw Dzhenushkunutushen die. (He did not die, as it happened. But Nukurren had been certain he would, and had been utterly astonished to find him still alive when she broke through). She watched Dzhenushkunutushen die, and the demonlord he cherished, and the other

demons for whom he was their champion and protector, and
knew they were dying because they were young. The universe
had not given them time. The universe had given them, demons that they were, all the colors of creation. It had given
them all the things which Nukurren had never had, and never
would. It had even given the demons the power to extend
friendship to one whom all others had cast out since birth.
And then, had denied them the time to learn from the friendship. Had cast them, in the fearlessness of their youth, into
a battlefield that needed the cunning of experience to survive.

The universe, which had tortured Nukurren all her life,
would extract this final, gleeful moment of agony.

Though it never showed on her mantle, Nukurren's *shoroku*
had broken then. Had shattered into pieces. The one tie which
might have held her back, her love for Dhowifa and concern
over his wellbeing, had snapped like the slenderest thread.
Dhowifa was safe, now, with Ushulubang and the demons, as
safe as he could ever be.

Nothing, now, held Nukurren from her revenge.

The Utuku cannibals who died under her flail and fork that
day, died horribly by eights and eights, had simply the mis-
fortune of being the manifestation, to Nukurren, of that ulti-
mate cannibal. They could not stand against her any more than
they could have withstood Death itself, Despair itself, *Nothing* itself.

Nukurren had wreaked her terrible rage on the universe,
and had taken from it the last, full, bitter measure. Her spirit
had blazed the blinding blue of pure fury, and her soul had
been filled with the purest black of the most pitiless executioner. But never, not once, had she allowed the universe to
see the colors of her vengeance.

No, she would repay the universe in the same bleak hue
with which it had always tormented her. She had not expected
to survive the charge, but she had intended, on that last day
of her life, to have the grim satisfaction of casting her death
into the beak of creation in the same color it had first spewed
her forth. *Nothing*.

In the event, to her surprise, she had survived. Had survived, she realized later, only because she had not expected
to, and had not cared if she did.

She still did not care. She was glad that Dzhenushkunutushen and most of the other young demons had survived.
She was especially glad that the demon Ludumilaroshokavashiki had survived, to bring comfort and joy to
Dzhenushkunutushen during the many hours she spent in the
hospital with him. (Even, toward the end of Dzhenushkunutushen's convalescence, making love to her mate; and
if the demon way of lovemaking was, like so much else,
messy and wet and grotesque, Nukurren had not minded.)
Nukurren was glad, even, that the demonlord had survived.
She did not much care for Yoshefadekunula, but she knew
how much he meant to Dzhenushkunutushen, and Ludumilaroshokavashiki, and all the demons.

But Nukurren's own survival meant nothing to her. She had survived, but so had the universe. Cannibals had died, but the cannibal remained. So it had always been. So it would always be.

When she heard what Dhowifa had to say, she felt a slight
curiosity. Nothing more. Later, in the command circle, after
Kopporu explained the proposal to her, Nukurren felt, if anything, even less.

So. Once again, I am to be a mercenary.

Then, harshly:

*Be thankful, fool. Not many people would hire a one-eyed,
perverted mercenary. And you have no other skills. And
nowhere else to go.*

"I accept," she said, and turned away.

"*Stop.*"

The voice belonged to the Mother of Demons.

Nukurren turned back.

"Yes, Mother of De—"

"Call me Inudira."

Nukurren made the gesture of obedience.

"Tell me how you understand our proposal, Nukurren."

"You want to hire my services as a trainer of warriors. It
is a common job for mercenaries. The pay is not as good as
battle pay, but—" she gestured to her eye "—I am satisfied.
I do not ask as to the pay itself. So long as Dhowifa and I
have food and shelter, I will not complain."

Inudiratoledo made the demon gesture of negation, a
peculiar sideways shaking of the head.

"That is what I thought. You are wrong, Nukurren. We have no use for a mercenary."

"Those are my only skills."

Again, that odd gesture.

"That is not my point. The skills of a warrior are not the same as the nature of a mercenary. Your skills we need, and badly. But not if they come with the soul of a mercenary."

"I do not understand."

"I will try to explain. Has Dhowifa told you what we are hoping to do here? The—*nashiyonu*—we wish to weave?"

"Yes."

"Do you believe it can be done?"

Nukurren hesitated.

"Speak honestly."

There could be no defying that voice.

"No. I do not believe it can be done."

"Why?"

Nukurren made the gesture of resignation.

"The world is a place of evil. It has always been so. Evil cannot be destroyed."

"On the world from which I came, Nukurren, there was also much evil. Much evil, and much as you have seen it on this world. There is still some to this day. But not so much as in the past."

"The demons have conquered evil?"

"You cannot conquer evil, Nukurren. Evil is not a thing from beyond, a foe to be vanquished. It is a thing which emerges from within the life of a people. It can only be changed, by changing that life. That is what we seek to do."

Nukurren considered her words. She had never thought of it in that manner.

Perhaps I should start paying more attention to what Dhowifa is saying.

"How long will it take, this change?"

"A very long time, Nukurren. It will not happen in your lifetime, or in mine. Not for many generations to come. We can only begin the change. And even in that beginning, we will create new evils alongside the ones we lessen. But we will be on the right road."

"You are certain—that it is the right road?"

"Yes, Nukurren. I have spent my life studying that road.

The one we travel will be different, in many ways. No two roads are ever the same. But—there are always certain forks, where certain choices are made. We are at such a fork to-day.

"Long ago, in my world, such a fork was reached, and a people made a decision. They made the right decision. In so doing, they did not eliminate all evil. By no means. They brought much evil with them, and created still more. Great wars had to be fought, to change those evils. But those wars, and those changes, would not have been possible had they not made the right choice at an earlier fork."

She hesitated.

"I do not have the time now to explain all this. Soon we will be creating a new kind of school, where I will explain this—and much more—at great length. I would be glad if you chose to become a student. But for the moment—

"When that people came to that fork, Nukurren, and made their choice of road, there were many other peoples who were angry at the choice. It was a new choice, and one not to their liking. The new people—the new *nashiyonu*—were a small people, surrounded by powerful enemies. They had to fight for their existence, knowing little of the art of war. They eventually won their battle, but it was very difficult.

"It would have been even more difficult had they not had the help of a warrior. A veteran from one of the old and powerful prevalates. A master of the skills of battle. That veteran came and showed them the ways of war. He was not a mercenary, Nukurren. He did not come because he had been paid, he came because he wanted to help create a new road. That is what we need."

Nukurren was silent, for over a minute. Then, she said: "I must think."

The Mother of Demons nodded. "Yes. You must. It is not easy to accept hope. Hope is the most terrible emotion of all, Nukurren, for it has no color. It is color itself, and thus we fear it more than any color."

Nukurren pondered these words. She remembered the face of the Mother of Demons, days past, as she sat in the hospital where her children lay dying. Unyielding, like bronze, where that of all other demons had been twisted and contorted; waterless, where all others had been wet. And Nukurren understood, then, that the words the Mother of Demons had just spoken were words she had torn from her own soul's despairing grasp.

"I will return," she said. "First, I must think."

Once outside the command circle, Nukurren found a number of gukuy waiting. For her, she realized. And one demon.

Most of the gukuy present were barbarian tribespeople, but there were three Pilgrims, as well, and one she thought was a swamp-dweller. She recognized one of the Pilgrims, although she did not know her name. Long ago, the Pilgrim had been a warrior in the Anshac legions, and Nukurren remembered seeing her from time to time in the Warrior's Square.

She made the gesture of recognition, and apologized for not remembering the Pilgrim's name.

"I am Rurroc, Nukurren."

"When did you leave the legions?"

"Not until we sought refuge in the Chiton. But I had long been a follower of Ushulubang. Since shortly after you and Dhowifa fled Shakutulubac."

"Why did you become a Pilgrim?"

"Because of you."

For a moment, Nukurren's *shoroku* almost wavered.

"Because of *me?*"

The gesture of assent. "Yes, Nukurren. Many warriors joined the Pilgrims after you fled. At least double-eight that I know of." Sensing Nukurren's puzzlement, Rurroc continued: "It was because we thought it was very unjust."

"Why? I was a deserter. And I stole one of the Paramount Mother's husbands."

The gesture of dismissal. "Not that. Everything that went before."

Nukurren was silent for a moment. Finally, she said, "I had not realized anyone cared."

"Many cared, Nukurren. But it was impossible to tell you, then. You were not easy to approach."

Nukurren thought back to the past, and, grudgingly, admitted to herself that Rurroc was possibly right. She had, perhaps—

One of the Kiktu whistled amusement. Nukurren stared at her. She had recognized the warrior at once, of course.

"What do you find so humorous, Kokokda?" she demanded, speaking in Kiktu.

"You! There you are, pondering Rurroc's words. 'Perhaps I was a mite touchy.' 'Possibly I was, just a tiny bit'—what is a good Enagulishuc word, Dzhenushkunutushen?"

The demon laughed. "How about 'prickly'?" The demon explained the term, while all the warriors practiced pronouncing it. Their efforts were made difficult by the fact that most of them were whistling gleefully.

Throughout, of course, Nukurren maintained her *shoroku*. But, at the end, she too joined in the humor.

"I suppose I have been, perhaps, just a trace—*purrikkulai*." She made the gesture of welcome to Kokokda.

"I am pleased to see that you have survived."

"I owe it to you, Nukurren," replied Kokokda. There was no trace of humor in her tone now. "Had it not been for the lesson you gave me long ago, I would also have become as foolish as the clan leaders. It was a hard lesson, but well worth it."

"Hard?" demanded Nukurren. "Foolish sp—what is the Enagulishuc word for 'spawn'?"

"Child," replied Dzhenushkunutushen. "The plural is children. Boy, if male. Girl, if female."

"Foolish *dzhiludh*. Very stupid *gurrul*. That lesson was not hard. The beaks of Utuku at the victory feast are hard. The flail tips of Anshac legions are hard. Helotry is hard. Slavery is hard. Life is hard. The universe is hard."

Again, the group of warriors whistled. When the humor died down, Nukurren scrutinized them carefully. Nukurren knew one of the other Kiktu personally. She had spent a pleasant afternoon in Ipapo's company, long ago, during the time when she and Dhowifa lived in exile among the Kiktu. She made the gesture of recognition, which Ipapo returned.

Nukurren now examined Aktako. She had seen the Kiktu warrior, but had never spoken to her. Dhowifa said she was Kopporu's lover as well as the chief of her personal guard. Aktako was the oldest gukuy present, and not particularly large. But Nukurren sensed instantly that she was a deadly warrior. Aktako stared back at her, and the two veterans exchanged an unspoken, ungestured, recognition.

Whether she knew them personally or not, they all had one thing in common, which was immediately obvious to Nukurren's experienced eye. They were the toughest veterans at Kopporu's disposal.

Tough enough, I think. Aktako certainly. And, of course, Ipapo. And Kokokda as well, if she has truly learned her lesson. Which she must have, or she would not be here. The others? Yes, I believe so.

She was silent, thinking. Those thoughts, at first, moved far away from the gukuy before her. But, after a time, her thoughts returned and settled upon them. Throughout her long silence, they had squatted patiently. Now, returning her gaze, they remained still and motionless.

Nukurren understood, and appreciated, and then accepted, their own acceptance of her. And she thought that perhaps the Mother of Demons was right, after all. She was still skeptical, but—the eyes were there, after all, staring back at her unflinchingly. The eyes of outcasts, refugees, exiles, with nothing in their gaze but confidence and trust.

"Do you think it can be done?" Nukurren asked. She was looking at Aktako, but it was Kokokda who answered.

"Train a new army? Yes, Nukurren, it can—"

"That is not the question," interrupted Aktako. "She knows the answer to that question."

Aktako made the gesture of bemused uncertainty.

"Who knows, Nukurren? I did not think we could cross the swamp. But I was determined not to give that muck the satisfaction of my defeat. And, after a time, we were through the swamp. Then, we met the Utuku *ogghoxt*. I did not think we would survive the battle. But I was determined not to give the cannibals the satisfaction of a meal. Then the demons came, and destroyed the Utuku. And perhaps that is what you need to ask yourself."

Aktako gestured toward the young demon.

"I think there is more to this world than we know, Nukurren. So I think we should not assume the world will always defeat us. Did not this same world allow demons to exist? And who knows what can happen to a world which has demons in it?"

Nukurren looked away from Aktako's hard stare, and examined the gaze of a much smaller pair of eyes. Eyes of fury.

"And why are you here?" Nukurren asked.

The demon made that strange facial gesture which served them as a whistle of amusement.

"You are my friend, Nukurren, and I thought you could use some moral support. Besides, my wounds are almost healed, and it's my job. I'm the Sharredzhenutumadzhoru of the apalatunush. We ummun and the gukuy warriors will need to learn to coordinate our efforts." The armless, flat-faced gesture of ruefulness. "We didn't do so well in the last battle."

"Not true. The Pilgrims did extremely well," said Nukurren forcefully. "The demons were stupid. Especially the big male demons who led them, thinking they were invincible. Mindless sp—*dzhiludhurren*. Very stupid *buyush*. I shall tell Ludumilaroshokavashiki to seek another mate. Why waste love on one who is determined to die?"

Nukurren could not misunderstand the meaning of the gesture which the young demon now made, alien though it was. The slight bow, the clasping hands.

We were invincible, Nukurren. We had you. And still do. Teacher.

Suddenly, she was filled with love for the young demon. As always, her mantle remained gray. But she made the gesture of fondness to the boy. With some difficulty, for it was a gesture she knew but had never made herself before. Then, to the assembled warriors, she made the gesture of respect. And finally, to Aktako, she made the *unnudh wap kottu*.

"I think you are right, Aktako," Nukurren said. "And, even if you are not, we should not give the world the satisfaction of our surrender."

"Wait here," she commanded them, and went back into the command circle.

"You spoke of an ancient warrior, who taught a new people the craft of war," she said to the Mother of Demons. "What was her—his—name?"

"Steuben. Baron Friedrich von Steuben."

Nukurren made the gesture of negation.

"That is too long."

She turned to leave. "I accept, Mother of Demons. I will be your *shutuppen*."

The ranks of the future army of the nashiyonu were drawn up in the center of the valley. In ragged files.

Very ragged, thought Nukurren. *But the immediate prob-*

lem is that they are still separated. Tribespeople here; Pilgrims there; and the former Utuku clustered away from everyone else. Avoided by everyone else. We must put a stop to that. At once.

She was not concerned. She had served as a trainer for the Anshac legions, whose warriors came from everywhere.

For a moment, she pondered her course of action. In general, she had no intention of taking charge of the daily training of the warriors. Her assistants, she thought, were quite capable of that task. Nukurren's principal responsibility lay elsewhere. It would be she who would shape and develop the structure and methods of the new army, particularly its tactics.

To be sure, the new battle leaders would be filled with grand schemes and ambitious projections. And, in truth, many of these would be worthwhile and potentially valuable. Nukurren was well aware of Ghodha's capabilities, and all she had heard regarding Kopporu led her to believe that she would make an excellent commander for the army.

Still—officers were by nature a fanciful folk, much given to impracticalities and vaporous theory. Nukurren eyed Aktako and the other members of her cadre.

No, no. Here lies the heart of the new army. They will make excellent trainers, as well as troop leaders. After today, I will not have to concern myself much with that task. But today—is the first day. So—

She spoke to Aktako. "I believe it would be wise if I personally led the training today."

Aktako made the gesture of assent. "I agree, Nukurren. It is essential that the warriors see us as a united group. Since you are the leader, the—we do not have a title yet—"

"*Shutuppen.*"

Aktako groped for a moment with the unfamiliar word.

"—the *dzhu*—*shutuppen*, then, I think it would be best if the warriors take your measure immediately."

Nukurren eyed the other cadre. It was obvious by their stance that they were in agreement. And, she was pleased to note, it was equally obvious that Aktako was already accepted as Nukurren's second-in-command.

Yes. They will be excellent. Better than any I have ever worked alongside.

"Do you have practice flails and forks?" she asked. Aktako made the gesture of affirmation.

"Good. I will need them. Bring several sets. At least four."

A slight tinge of orange entered Rurroc's mantle.

"You are going to start by teaching them weaponry?"

Kokokda whistled. Dzhenushkunutushen laughed.

"No, Rurroc," said Kokokda. "She is going to start by teaching them the most important lesson of all. I remember that lesson well."

"So do I," said the demon. "And I'm glad, this time, to be on the other side of it."

The Kiktu veteran and the young demon exchanged, each in their alien way, the gestures of amusement.

"Trust us, Rurroc," said Dzhenushkunutushen. "It is a lesson much better behind you than before you."

"Much better," agreed Kokokda.

The lesson began very quickly. Immediately following Nukurren's first command, which was that all the battle groups would accept several Utuku members.

The command stirred up great outrage. All praise of the much-chanted Nukurren the Valiant vanished. And, though it did not vanish, the knowledge of Nukurren's prowess was drowned under a wave of indignation. These were warriors, after all, who loved their chants but did not, at bottom, take them too seriously.

Three Kiktu warriors were especially vociferous in their displeasure; exchanging loud quips on the subject of pitiful, decrepit, tired, over-large, old, ugly, beaten-down, one-eyed sexual deviates. At Nukurren's command, Aktako gave them practice weapons. The warriors advanced boldly upon Nukurren, expressing great contempt at the use of toys.

Very soon thereafter, two of them limped painfully back to their battle groups. The other did not recover consciousness for some time. Whereupon she too rejoined her battle group, and took her place alongside a former Utuku. Maintaining silence throughout.

Soon, Nukurren was comfortably into the routine. It had been many eightyweeks since she had trained recruits, but it was something one did not forget.

YOU ARE GARBAGE BENEATH MY PEDS. YOU ARE LOWER THAN WORMS. YOU ARE SHIT. YOU SMELL LIKE SHIT. YOU LOOK LIKE SHIT.

As the ranks began to take ragged form, Nukurren considered the formations she would shape them into.

NO, THAT'S A LIE! YOU SMELL WORSE THAN MY SHIT. YOU LOOK WORSE THAN MY SHIT. AND MY SHIT IS THE SMELLIEST, UGLIEST SHIT IN THE WORLD. DO YOU KNOW WHY? DO YOU KNOW WHY?

She decided she would start with the basic structure of an Anshac legion, the division of the army into cohorts of triple-eight warriors.

BECAUSE I AM NOT NUKURREN THE VALIANT. I DO NOT KNOW THAT NUKURREN. THAT IS SOME OTHER NUKURREN, THE NUKURREN OF YOUR FANTASIES.

Each cohort would be led by a . . .

I AM THE REAL NUKURREN.

No. We must use an Enagulishuc term.

I AM NUKURREN THE CRUEL. NUKURREN THE MERCILESS.

She motioned toward Dzhenushkunutushen. The young demon trotted toward her.

NUKURREN THE VILE.

"What is the Enagulishuc term for cohort leader?"

The demon's face crunched. "I don't know, Nukurren."

I AM THE SHITTIEST GUKUY WHO EVER WALKED THE MEAT OF THE CLAM.

"Find out. Discuss it with Yosephadekunula. And with Inudiratoledo, if necessary. We must have clear ranks and structure."

"Yes, Nuk—*shutuppen.*"

YOU WILL LEARN. OH, YES—YOU WILL LEARN.

As Dzhenushkunutushen moved away, Nukurren eyed him fondly.

YOU WILL LEARN TO HATE ME. AND THAT IS GOOD.

He has been a good friend.

BUT YOU WILL LEARN SOMETHING WHICH IS MUCH, MUCH, MUCH MORE IMPORTANT.

And he will become a truly great warrior, if I can beat some sense into him.

YOU WILL LEARN TO FEAR ME.

Out of the corner of her eye, she caught sight of Aktako.

The Kiktu veteran looked at her, and made a small gesture of amusement.

YOU WILL TREMBLE WHEN I FART.

Aktako will be a great help. And, I think, also a friend.

YOU WILL TURN SCARLET WHEN I COME NEAR.

For a moment, Nukurren pondered this strange new thing which had come into her life, this friendship. This wonderful new thing. But her attention was almost immediately diverted.

YOU—I MEAN YOU, SNAIL! WHAT IS YOUR NAME?

Although the Pilgrims, as a rule, were showing themselves more willing to accept Nukurren's commands than the tribespeople, still there were some—it was important to treat all gukuy equally, after all.

WHAT IS YOUR NAME? YOU ARE OFFENDED? YOU DARE TO TURN BLUE? AKTAKO—THE FLAILS!

She concentrated a bit on the task while she thrashed the unlucky Pilgrim, but not much.

ARE THERE ANY MORE WORMS WHO DREAM OF BEING SNAILS?

Comfortably back and forth, only half her mind on what she was doing. Routine requires little concentration.

ANY?

To her mild surprise, there was one. A young Opoktu. Quite good, too, Nukurren thought. After the Opoktu dragged herself back into the ranks, Nukurren told Aktako to find out her name. In a few eightdays, if she proved to be as intelligent as she was skillful, they would promote her.

ANY MORE?

She resumed her consideration of the army's structure. It was Anshac practice to divide the cohorts into eight groups of eighty warriors, but Nukurren had long thought such groups were awkward. Too large to be flexible; too small to have much impact.

ANY TWO? ANY THREE?

She decided she would adopt the ummun apalatunush as the first sub-division of the cohort. She had been impressed by their performance in the battle.

ANY FOUR? ANY FIVE?

The formations had been large enough to operate independently, yet Ludumilaroshokavashiki and Takashimidudzhugodzhi had been able to control their maneuvers with no difficulty.

ANY SIX?

The apalatunush numbered eighty and six-eight, approximately—

NO? NO? SUCH A PITY.

What is the ummun way of counting that?

I WAS ENJOYING THE EXERCISE.

A "unnunduredh," I think.

PERHAPS AT A LATER TIME. WHEN YOU HAVE LEARNED TO CRAWL.

I will have to speak to Ushulubang about this. We must decide if we will adopt the ummun way of numbering as well as their language.

NOW. LET ME EXPLAIN THE TRUTH—NAKED; STRIPPED OF ITS SHELL.

Her thoughts hesitated, stumbling for a moment.

YOU ARE NO LONGER KIKTU OR PILGRIM OR OPOKTU OR UTUKU.

Yes, and I must listen to what she has to say about the Way. And Dhowifa. I must listen to him more carefully, from now on.

YOU ARE SIMPLY NUKURREN'S SHIT.

I must put all bitterness behind me. I am no longer Nukurren the mercenary. I can no longer think like Nukurren the outcast. I am the—

YOU WILL DO WHAT I SAY, WHEN I SAY, WHERE I SAY IT, HOW I SAY IT. AT ONCE. NO—SOONER THAN THAT!

Shutuppen. Nukurren rolled the name in her mind's arms, examining it from every side.

Do you understand?

It is a good name, she decided.

DO YOU UNDERSTAND?

For the first time in eightyweeks, she felt life return to her soul, in all its myriad colors.

But to the scarlet-hued warriors who watched her, pacing back and forth like a nightmare, there was nothing in her mantle.

Nothing but cold, pitiless, gray.

DAVID WEBER

Honor Harrington (cont.):

Field of Dishonor

Honor goes home to Manticore—and fights for her life on a battlefield she never trained for, in a private war that offers just two choices: death—or a "victory" that can end only in dishonor and the loss of all she loves....

Other novels by DAVID WEBER:

Mutineers' Moon

"...a good story...reminds me of 1950s Heinlein..."
—*BMP Bulletin*

The Armageddon Inheritance

Sequel to *Mutineers' Moon*.

Path of the Fury

"Excellent...a thinking person's Terminator."
—*Kliatt*

Oath of Swords

An epic fantasy.

with STEVE WHITE:

Insurrection
Crusade

Novels set in the world of the Starfire ™ game system.

And don't miss Steve White's solo novels,
***The Disinherited** and **Legacy**!*

continued ☞

HARRY TURTLEDOVE: A MIND FOR ALL SEASONS

EPIC FANTASY

Werenight (72209-3 ◆ $4.99) ☐
Prince of the North (87606-6 ◆ $5.99) ☐

In the Northlands rules Gerin the Fox. Quaintly, he intends to rule for the welfare and betterment of his people——but first he must defeat the gathering forces of chaos, which conspire to tumble his work into a very dark age indeed....

ALTERNATE FANTASY

The Case of the Toxic Spell Dump (72196-8 ◆ $5.99) ☐

Inspector Fisher's world is just a *little* bit different from ours...Stopping an ancient deity from reinstating human sacrifice in L.A. and destroying Western Civilization is all in a day's work for David Fisher of the Environmental *Perfection* Agency.

ALTERNATE HISTORY

Agent of Byzantium (87593-0 ◆ $4.99) ☐

In an alternate universe where the Byzantine Empire never fell, Basil Agyros, the 007 of his spacetime, has his hands full thwarting un-Byzantine plots and making the world safe for Byzantium. "Engrossing, entertaining and very cleverly rendered...I recommend it without reservation."   **—Roger Zelazny**

A Different Flesh (87622-8 ◆ $4.99) ☐

An extraordinary novel of an alternate America. "When Columbus came to the New World, he found, not Indians, but primitive ape-men.... Unable to learn human speech...[the ape-men] could still be trained to do reliable work. Could still, in other words, be made slaves.... After 50 years of science fiction, Harry Turtledove proves you can come up with something fresh and original."   **—Orson Scott Card**